YOUR FAULT

MERCEDES RON

Bloom books

Originally published as *Culpables: Culpa tuya*, © Mercedes Ron,
2017. Translated from Spanish by Adrian Nathan West.

Published by Bloom Books, an imprint of Sourcebooks
P.O. Box 4410, Naperville, Illinois 60567-4410
(630) 961-3900
sourcebooks.com

Originally published as *Culpables: Culpa Tuya* in 2017 in Spain by Montena,
an imprint of Penguin Random House Grupo Editorial S. A. U.

Cataloging-in-Publication data is on file with the Library of Congress.

Printed and bound in the United States of America.
VP 10 9 8 7 6 5 4 3 2 1

To my sister, Ro,
thanks for being my playmate,
for listening to me, for laughing with me and at me,
and for always being there when I need you.

PROLOGUE

THE RAIN FELL, SOAKING US, FREEZING US, BUT IT DIDN'T MATTER; nothing did, not anymore. I knew everything was about to change. I knew my world was about to crumble apart.

"There's no turning back now. I can't even look you in the eye." Desolate tears ran down his face.

How could I have done this to him? His words sank into my soul like knives tearing me open from the inside.

"I don't even know what to say," I said, trying to control the panic that threatened to shatter me. He couldn't leave me. He couldn't, could he?

He looked full of hatred, contempt… It was a look I never thought I'd see from him.

"We're done," he whispered, his voice cracking but firm.

And with those two words, my world sank into darkness, shadows, solitude…a prison designed expressly for me. But I deserved it. This time, I deserved it.

1

Noah

I WAS FINALLY EIGHTEEN YEARS OLD.

I still remembered eleven months before that, when I started counting the days until I'd be an adult, able to make my own decisions, able to leave. Obviously, things had changed in those past eleven months. So much so that I could hardly believe it. Not only had I gotten used to living here, but I even struggled to imagine living anywhere else. I'd found a niche at school and in the family I'd ended up with.

All the obstacles I'd needed to get through—not just over those months, but ever since I was born—had made me stronger, or so I thought. Much had happened, not all of it good, but the best thing I'd managed to hold on to was Nicholas. Who'd have ever thought I'd wind up in love with him? And yet I was so madly in love that it made my heart ache. We'd had to get to know each other, to learn to make it as a couple, and that wasn't easy; it was something we had to work on every single day. Our personalities often clashed. Nick wasn't easy to put up with, but I was crazy about him.

That's why I was sad about my upcoming birthday party.

2 | MERCEDES RON

Nick wasn't going to be there. I hadn't seen him in two weeks. He'd been spending a lot of time in San Francisco those past few months. He had a year left before he finished his degree and was taking advantage of all the doors his father had opened for him. The Nick who got into trouble was far away now. He was different: he'd matured, improved, even if I was afraid his old self might reemerge when I least expected it.

I glanced at myself in the mirror. I'd pulled my hair back over the crown of my head. It looked nice, perfect for the white dress my mother and Will had given me as a birthday present. My mother had gone overboard organizing the party. She said this would be her last chance to play the mommy role because in a week I'd be graduating from high school, and soon afterward, I'd be headed to college. I'd sent out tons of applications, but in the end, I'd opted for UCLA. I'd had enough of moving around and changes; I didn't want to go to another city, and I certainly didn't want to leave Nick. He was at the same school, and even if he would probably wind up moving to San Francisco to work at his father's new firm, I couldn't worry about that just then. There was still lots of time, and I didn't want to get depressed.

I stood from the makeup table, and before I put on my dress, I looked down at the scar on my stomach. I stroked that place where I would be marked, forever damaged, and I shivered. The sound of the shot that ended my father's life echoed through my head, and I had to take a deep breath to keep from losing my composure. I hadn't told anyone about my nightmares or how scared I was every time I thought about what had happened, how my heart started galloping whenever I heard loud sounds too close by. I didn't want to admit that my father had traumatized me again or that I couldn't stop thinking about him right beside me, dead, or the way his blood had splashed on my face. I kept all that to myself. I didn't want anyone to know I was even more damaged

YOUR FAULT | 3

than before, on the edge of insanity, prey to the fears that man had awakened. My mother, on the other hand, was more relaxed than she'd ever been because the fear she'd kept hidden had disappeared. She was happy with her husband: she was free. But I still had a long road to travel.

"You're not dressed yet?" It was that voice, the one that made me crack up almost every single day.

I turned toward Jenna, and a smile spread across my face. My best friend was stunning, as always. She had recently cut her long hair to shoulder-length. She tried to get me to do the same, but I knew Nick loved my hair long, so I'd left it untouched. It reached nearly to my waist by now, but I still liked it.

"Have I told you already how much I admire that pert butt of yours?" she asked, slapping my ass for good measure.

"You're nuts," I said, grabbing my dress and throwing it over my head. Jenna walked over to the safe, just under a shelf of shoes. I didn't have the combination, I'd never used it, but once Jenna learned about it, she started using it herself, hiding all sorts of stuff inside.

I giggled when she brought out a bottle of champagne and two glasses.

"A toast, to our newly crowned adult," she said, filling the glasses and handing me one. I grinned. If Mom saw me, she'd kill me, but what the hell? It was my birthday; I deserved to celebrate, right?

"To us," I added.

We clinked our glasses and brought them to our lips. It was delicious; it had better be—that bottle of Cristal had cost more than three hundred dollars. But that was just how Jenna was. She did everything big, she was accustomed to luxury, and she'd never had to ask for anything.

"That dress is amazing," she said, gawking.

I smiled and took another look. It really was nice: white, tight-fitting, with delicate lace sleeves descending to my wrists, letting my skin show through its geometric openings. My shoes were fantastic, too, with heels so high, I was almost as tall as Jenna, who had donned a flounced burgundy dress for the occasion.

"There's a ton of people downstairs," she said, setting her glass next to mine. I guess she wasn't in a rush. I needed a drink, though, so I picked mine back up and downed it in one sip, feeling the bubbles pop in my throat.

"You don't say!" I exclaimed, to conceal my nerves. Suddenly, it felt hard to breathe. That dress was too tight; my lungs couldn't expand.

Jenna looked at me and smirked.

"What's so funny?" I asked, envious of her. What I'd have given not to be the center of attention.

"Nothing, I just know how you hate stuff like this. Take it easy, though. I'm here, and I'll make sure we do it right."

She kissed me on the cheek, and I smiled at her, thankful. Maybe my boyfriend *was* missing my birthday, but at least I'd have my best friend by my side.

"Shall we?" she asked, smoothing down her dress.

"I guess we've got no choice!"

The yard was completely transformed. Mom had gone all out, renting a white tent full of round pink tables and flashy chairs and balloons. The servers were wearing suit jackets and bow ties. On the far end was a bar and several long tables with trays of every food you could imagine. All this luxury wasn't like me, but I knew my mother had always wanted to throw me this kind of party. She'd joked about me turning eighteen and going off to college, and we'd talked about what we'd have at the party if we ever won the lottery...and we'd done it! And she had gone totally overboard.

When I went outside, everyone shouted "happy birthday" in unison. I guess they were trying to surprise me. My mother came over and gave me a big hug.

"Happy birthday, Noah," she said, and as I pulled her close, I was surprised to see so many people lined up behind her. Not only were all my friends from school there, and all the parents Mom had made friends with, but even neighbors and friends of William's. Uncomfortable, I unconsciously began to scan the garden, looking for Nicholas, the one person who might have calmed me down. But there wasn't a trace of him... I knew it: of course, he wasn't going to come—he was in a whole different city, and it would be a week till I saw him again, at graduation—and yet...a small part of me still hoped I might find him bustling through the crowd.

It took more than an hour to greet everyone, and afterward, Jenna came over and dragged me to the bar—to the special section cordoned off for those not yet twenty-one.

"There's a fancy cocktail just for you," she said, bursting out laughing.

"My mother is off her rocker," I said while the bartender served me. He smiled. It was obvious he could barely suppress his laughter. Great. He probably thought I was your typical rich girl.

I was taken aback when I saw the drink. It was served in a martini glass and was hot pink with a rainbow sugar rim and a strawberry garnish on either side. A ribbon was tied around the stem with an *18* embroidered in tiny white pearls.

"It still needs a little something," Jenna said, bringing out a flask and pouring its contents into our glasses. I'd have to watch out if I didn't want to be stumbling drunk by midnight.

The DJ was good, the music was varied, and my friends were

dancing like they were possessed. The party was a success, no doubt about it.

Jenna hauled me off to dance with her, and we started jumping all over like idiots. The heat was killing me: summer was just around the corner, and you could tell.

From the edge of the dance floor, Lion was watching us, leaning on a pillar and observing as Jenna shook her ass in a frenzy. I laughed and left her with the others. I was exhausted.

"You bored, Lion?" I asked him.

He smiled, but he seemed a little worried and didn't look over at me.

"Yeah, happy birthday," he said, as though he hadn't heard. It was strange, seeing him there without Nick. Lion wasn't friends with many people in my grade: he and Nick were five years older than Jenna and me, and the age difference was evident. The kids in my class weren't particularly mature, and our boyfriends never liked hanging out with them.

"Thanks," I said. "You heard from Nick?" I felt a pang in my stomach. He still hadn't called or texted.

"He told me yesterday he was up to his neck in work. At the office, they barely even give him time to eat lunch. He did manage to find the time to tell me to keep my eye on you."

"Seems like you're keeping it on someone else," I said, noticing he was still staring at Jenna. She turned and smiled at us both, looking completely, genuinely happy. She loved Lion, was in love with him, couldn't stop talking about him on the nights when she'd stay over: about how lucky we were, being with two guys who were such close friends. I knew Jenna was incapable of falling for anybody else, and I was glad to know Lion felt the same about her. I couldn't get enough of Jenna; she was a true best friend, and I loved her. She had always been there when I'd needed her and had helped me understand what a real friend was. She wasn't jealous, manipulative, or resentful like Beth back in Canada, and she was incapable of hurting me, at least on purpose.

She came over and kissed Lion with a loud pop. He lifted her, and I turned away, dispirited. I missed Nick; I wanted him there; I needed him. I looked back at my phone. Nothing. No missed calls, no texts, no emails. That was starting to piss me off. All he needed were a few seconds to write. What the hell was going on with him?

I walked over to the bar for the twenty-one-and-overs. The crowd there had thinned out, and the guy who'd served me my birthday drink was working with the help of a young woman. I sat down and tried to figure out my approach, hoping I could flirt with him and get an actual drink.

"Any chance you could make me something not pink, but with a bit of kick to it?" I asked, thinking he'd tell me to piss off. But to my surprise, he glanced around, and when he saw no one was looking, he filled a shot glass with clear liquid.

"Tequila?" I asked.

"If anyone asks you, it wasn't me," he said, glancing away.

I laughed and drank it down. It burned my throat, but it was good.

When I turned, I saw Jenna dragging Lion off to a dark corner. It depressed me, seeing all my friends hugging and kissing.

Damn you, Nicholas Leister, why can't I get you out of my head for at least one second a day?

"Another?" the bartender asked. I knew I was overdoing it, but it was my party. I could have what I wanted, right?

Just as I was about to knock it back, a hand appeared out of nowhere to snatch it from me.

"I think you've had enough."

That voice.

I looked up, and there he was: Nick. Nick in a button-down

and slacks, his dark hair starting to fall out of place, beaming with suppressed excitement, joyful.

"Oh my God!" I shouted, bringing my hands to my mouth. A smile appeared on his face. *My smile*, the one he reserved just for me. I jumped into his arms.

"You came!" I shouted, pressing my cheek into his, squeezing him, smelling him, feeling once again whole. He squeezed me back. At last, I could breathe. He was there. Thank God! He was there with me.

"I missed you, Freckles," he whispered in my ear before pulling my head back and kissing me on the lips.

I felt my nerve endings awaken. It had been fourteen days since I'd felt his lips on mine, his hands on my body.

He pushed me back and looked me up and down.

"You're gorgeous," he said hoarsely, grabbing my waist and pulling me close.

"What are you doing here?" I asked, trying to keep myself from kissing him again. I knew we needed to restrain ourselves: there were people everywhere, our parents were there, and their presence unnerved me.

"I wasn't about to miss your birthday," he said. I could feel the electricity between us. We'd never been apart for so long, at least not since we'd started going out, and I was used to having him all to myself every day.

"How'd you get away?" I asked, not wanting to let him go.

"Don't ask," he said, kissing the top of my head. I closed my eyes in ecstasy, smelling his cologne.

"Lovely party." He laughed.

I scowled at him. "It wasn't my idea."

"I know," he assured me.

I felt my heart swell with happiness and relief. How I'd missed his smile.

"You want to try the Noah special?" I asked, winking to the bartender, who got straight to work.

"You've got your own cocktail, Freckles?" he asked, raising an eyebrow when he saw the pink liquid with its strawberry garnish. His expression was hilarious. "I guess I have to try it…"

The poor thing drank the whole glass without complaining, even though it tasted like melted gumdrops.

I grinned from ear to ear, and he couldn't resist doing the same. His hand reached out and pulled me in, and he brought his lips to my ear, just brushing the sensitive skin there, and that scant contact was enough to make me feel like I was about to die.

"I need to be inside you," he said.

My legs trembled. "We can't. Not here," I whispered, trying to control my nerves.

"Do you trust me?" he asked.

What kind of stupid question was that? There was no one I trusted more.

He could read my response in my eyes, and he smiled in turn.

"Wait for me behind the pool house," he said, with one last peck on the lips. I grabbed his arm as he turned.

"You're not coming?" I asked.

"The idea is supposed to be that no one figures out what we're doing, babe," he said, turning around to greet the guests, exuding confidence. I watched him for a few seconds, feeling the butterflies shift in my stomach. I didn't want to admit that I was scared to go off by myself, away from all the people, in the dark.

I grabbed a shot that was sitting on the bar and drank it, trying to control my breathing. That was enough to calm me for a few seconds. I took a deep breath and walked to the pool, past the tent where everyone was dancing and having fun. I walked along the edge of the water, trying not to fall in, and finally reached the small cabin behind it. On the other side of it were trees, and farther off, you could hear the sea, its waves crashing against the cliff. I leaned against one of the walls, trying to maintain my composure as I heard the guests chattering.

I closed my eyes just before I heard him arrive. His lips covered mine so quickly, I couldn't say anything. I opened my eyes. There he was, staring at me. His eyes said it all.

"You have no idea how much I've missed doing this," he said, grabbing my neck and kissing me softly.

I melted in his arms.

"I've been dying just to touch you," he continued, holding my waist, burying his nose slowly in my neck. I wrapped my fingers behind his head and brought him back to my lips. We kissed desperately, warming each other like fire, our tongues twisting together and his body pressing into mine. I wanted to touch him, wanted to feel his skin beneath my fingers.

"Did you miss me, Freckles?" he asked, caressing my cheek and looking at me as if I were his gift and not the other way around.

I tried to say yes, but I was breathing so fast that nothing escaped me but a sigh that grew more intense when he planted his lips on my neck.

"I'm not going to leave you again," he said.

I laughed joylessly. "That doesn't depend on you."

"I'll take you with me, wherever I have to go..."

"That sounds romantic," I said, kissing him on the jawline.

He cupped my face in his hands. "I'm serious. I'm hooked on you."

I tried to laugh again, but he silenced me with a kiss full of restrained passion.

"I want to get you out of that damned dress." He grunted, rolling it up over my waist. As he looked at my tanned skin, I saw desire in his eyes, long buried, fed by the distance and time that had kept us apart.

"I'd make love to you all night long," he said, his hands sliding under the elastic of my waistband and making me shiver.

"Or do you want to wait?" he asked. "I'd take you to the apartment, but I guess people would notice your absence."

"You guessed right..." I said, biting my lip. I'd never done it with him in this kind of situation, but I also didn't want to wait. Nick pushed me into the wall and ground his body against mine ardently.

"We'll make it a quickie. No one will notice," he whispered in my ear.

I nodded, and he tugged at my panties until they slipped to the ground.

I brought my fingers up to his tie and tugged until it came loose.

"I want to see you," I said.

He smiled and kissed the tip of my nose, grabbing my hands and lifting them over his head.

I stood still, watching him as he unbuttoned his pants. A second later, he had pinned me against the wall. His expression was gentle, his pupils dilated, transmitting me a million different messages as he prepared me to feel him inside me. Then he entered me. I'd started taking the pill a few months back, and I was grateful that I could actually feel him without any kind of barrier between us. I moaned, and he clapped a hand over my mouth.

"Don't make a sound," he warned me.

I nodded, my nerves taut as a bowstring. He moved slowly at first but then sped up. With every thrust, the pleasure inside me grew. He took his hand from my mouth and touched me where I needed him most.

"Nick..."

"Wait..." he said, grabbing my thighs and lifting me. I closed my eyes, trying to hold it all in. "Let's come together..." he whispered in my ear.

He bit down on my lower lip, and a wave of ecstasy crested. I couldn't take it anymore. I moaned, he covered my mouth with his, and I felt him tense and grunt, accompanying me on my journey to infinite pleasure.

I leaned back, trying to control my breathing. Nick was still holding me up.

"I love you, Nick," I said when his eyes met mine.

"You and I aren't made to be apart," he responded.

2

Nick

JESUS, I'D MISSED HER! THE DAYS HAD BEEN ENDLESS. AND DON'T get me started on the weeks. I'd had to work twice as many hours so I could go home early, but for this alone, it had been worth it.

"You all right?" I asked, my breathing still agitated. We'd never done it like that before. I tried to control myself with Noah, to treat her the way she deserved, but this time, I'd been unable to wait. As soon as I'd seen her, I'd wanted to make her mine.

She smiled and said, "That was…" but I kissed her before she could say more. I was afraid of what she'd say, and my desire was too strong to talk just then. She was gorgeous that night, especially in that virginal white dress, and I could barely contain myself.

"I love you like crazy, you know that, right?" I said.

"I love you more," she responded, and as she did, I noticed there was a little blood on her lips.

"I bit you too hard," I said, running my thumb across her lower lip and wiping away the tiny dot of blood. Fuck. I was an asshole. "Sorry about that, Freckles."

She licked her lip, distracted.

"That was different," she said. It sure was.

I stepped back and buttoned my pants. I felt guilty: Noah deserved to do it in a bed, not against a wall and on the fly.

"What's up with you?" she asked, worry in her eyes.

"Nothing. Sorry." I kissed her again, pulling her dress back over her legs and suppressing the temptation to start right back up where we'd stopped. "Happy birthday, by the way." I took a small white box from my pocket.

"You got me a present?" she asked, excited. She was so sweet, so perfect... Just seeing her put me in a good mood. Just touching her turned me on in a way I'd never known.

"I don't know if you'll like it..." I said, suddenly nervous.

Her eyes opened wide with surprise as she looked at it.

"Cartier?" she said. "Are you crazy?"

I shook my head and waited for her to open it, revealing a tiny silver heart on a chain that glimmered in the darkness. She smiled, and I sighed with relief.

"It's beautiful," she said, rubbing it with one finger.

"This way, wherever you go, you'll always have my heart with you," I said, kissing her on the cheek. It was the cheesiest thing I'd ever said, but that was what she'd done to me. I was now an idiot in love.

I could see her eyes were watering.

"I love it. I just love it!" she said, then kissed me on the lips.

I smiled and told her to turn around so I could put it on her. Her dress had a generous neckline, and I couldn't help but kiss her while I was back there. She shivered, and I restrained my urge to be inside her once more. When the clasp was closed, I turned her around and looked at her. She was radiant.

"How do I look?" she asked.

"Perfect, as always," I replied.

I knew we had to go back, even if it was the last thing I felt like doing just then. I wanted to be alone with her—I mean, I always wanted time alone with her, but especially then, after so long without seeing each other.

"Am I presentable?" she said innocently.

I smiled. "Of course you are," I said, buttoning my shirt and picking my tie up off the floor.

"Let me," she said, and I laughed.

"Since when do you know how to tie a tie?" I asked, remembering that I'd always been the one to tie hers when I still lived there.

"I have to learn because my hot-ass boyfriend abandoned me for his bachelor pad," she replied, tightening the knot.

"Hot, huh?"

She rolled her eyes. "Let's go back before everyone figures out what we're up to."

I'd have preferred everyone did know what we'd been up to. That would keep all the little boys away from my girlfriend. But even after all we'd been through, most people still thought we were just stepbrother and stepsister.

I let her go first and lit a cigarette while I waited. I knew Noah didn't like me smoking, but if I didn't, I'd lose my mind. Before I walked back, I noticed something. Her underwear was under my feet.

Had she left without anything under her dress?

———

Back at the party, I saw her talking with a group of friends: two guys, one of them with his arm resting around her back. I took a breath to calm down and walked over. When Noah saw me, she gave me a hug and leaned her head against my chest.

That was enough to calm me down.

"Have you seen Lion?" I asked her, looking around. I was a little worried about him. He had called me when I was in San

Francisco to tell me his brother, Luca, was getting out of jail soon. He'd been in for four years; he'd gotten caught selling drugs, and there had been nothing they could do to keep him from going behind bars. I wasn't too happy about him coming home. I guessed I was glad for my friend, since he was on his own and his brother was the only family he had left, but I knew what the brother in question was capable of, and I wasn't sure having an ex-con around was what Lion needed at that point in his life.

"Not for a while, actually," Noah said. "Anyway, it's probably a good time for you to go see our parents."

Hearing that made me tense. Since Noah had been kidnapped, there was no more hiding that we were serious about each other, and our parents didn't like it one bit. And they tried to make that clear to us every time we saw each other. I knew my father wouldn't let something so scandalous get out: after all, we were a family in the public eye, and to the outside world, we would go on being stepsiblings and nothing more, he insisted. What surprised me was that Raffaella refused to take our side, after what she'd told me the day the police came to our house. In fact, her attitude had become increasingly suspicious.

"Well, well, well, my son's returned," Dad said with a false smile.

"Hey, Dad," I greeted him. "Hey, Ella." I tried to muster a friendly tone. To my surprise, she smiled at me and gave me a hug.

"I'm happy you made it," she told me. "Noah was forlorn till you showed up."

I looked over at her. She was blushing. I winked.

"How are things at the firm?" my father asked.

The bastard had put me under Jenkins, a bossy asshole who would run the firm until I had enough experience to take the reins. Everyone knew I was perfectly qualified, but my father still didn't trust me.

"Exhausting," I said, trying not to scowl at him.

"That's life," he said. Now I was getting in a bad mood. I was tired of hearing that shit. I'd matured a great deal in the past few months, was playing the part that was expected of me, and was busy every hour of the day. Not only was I working for my father, but I was still in my last year of law school and had my finals and the bar exam to think about. Most of my classmates knew nothing about the ins and outs of running a firm, and I already had more experience than most attorneys. But there I was, with my father still not trusting me.

"Can I have this dance?" Noah interrupted me, trying to keep me from talking back to him.

"Sure."

I walked with her out onto the dance floor. They'd put on a slow song, and I pulled her in tight, trying to keep my anger and frustration from affecting the only person at that party who mattered to me.

"Don't get angry," she said, stroking my neck. I closed my eyes, letting her touch relax me.

My hand slid down her waist and stroked her lower back.

"I can't feel mad around you knowing you've got nothing on under your dress."

"I didn't even realize it," she said, grabbing my biceps to stop me from caressing her.

She was gorgeous. I leaned my forehead into hers.

"Sorry," I said, disappearing into the beauty of her eyes.

"Are you spending the night?" she asked with a grin.

Dammit! Always the same argument. There was no way I was staying there. I'd moved out months ago, and I hated having my dad around keeping an eye on me. I couldn't wait for Noah to move into town. Everything would be better when she was with me.

"You know I'm not," I said, looking over at the crowd. Occasionally, some bystander glanced back over. I didn't suppose brothers and sisters were supposed to dance like that, but I didn't give a fuck, either.

"I haven't seen you for two weeks. You could make the effort to stay over," she said, her tone changing. I knew that if this kept up, we'd be arguing, and I didn't want that.

"So we can sleep apart? No thanks."

She looked down in silence.

"Come on, Freckles, don't be like that... You know I hate staying here, I hate not being able to touch you, and I hate all the stupid shit my father feels compelled to say to me."

"Well, I don't know when we're going to be able to see each other, then, because I can't go into town this week. I've got finals and graduation, I'm up to my ears in obligations."

Damn it.

"I'll come pick you up so we can hang out," I said, trying not to raise my voice.

She sighed and looked away.

"Don't make me feel guilty, please," I asked her. "You know I can't stay here."

I grabbed her face, forcing her to stare into my eyes.

"You used to," she said.

"Back then, we weren't together."

We kept dancing, the argument apparently over. Raffaella kept her eyes on us the whole time.

3

Noah

ALMOST ALL THE GUESTS WERE GONE. JENNA WAS SAYING HI TO MY
mom, and Nick was in the back smoking a cigarette with Lion. I
looked around at the disorder left behind after the party and was
thankful for the first time that we had someone who came every
day to clean our house.

After so long socializing, I was happy for that moment alone
to appreciate the good fortune I had. The party had been incredible: all my friends had been there and had bought me amazing
gifts that were now piled on a table in the dining room. I was
about to take them to my room when I felt arms wrap around
my waist.

"You got a ton of presents," Nick whispered in my ear.

"Yeah, but none of them can compare with yours," I said,
turning around to look at him. "It's the prettiest gift I've ever
gotten, and it means so much, coming from you."

"Will you always wear it?" he asked me. A part of me realized
that was important to him: he'd put his heart into that necklace. A
warmth radiated from the middle of my chest.

"Always."

He smiled and pulled me close. His lips grazed mine sweetly, almost too sweetly. I tried to step forward and kiss him more deeply, but he stopped me in my tracks.

"Want more?" he asked. Why wouldn't he kiss me for real? I opened my eyes and saw those bright blue irises that gave me shivers.

"You know I do," I responded, breathing fast, my nerves on edge.

"Then come with me tonight."

I sighed. I wanted to go, but I couldn't. To start with, my mother didn't care at all for me going to stay with Nick. When I did it, I usually pretended I was spending the night with Jenna. Beyond that, I had to study. I had four finals coming up, and if I failed them, I'd be putting too much at risk.

"I can't," I said.

He stroked my back softly, so softly that it made my hair stand on end.

"You can, and if you do, we'll pick up where we left off outside." He brought his lips close to my ear.

I felt butterflies in my stomach and desire growing inside me. His tongue slid across my left earlobe, and then his teeth sank into it... I wanted to go... But I couldn't. I had missed the way he looked at me, that body of his that intimidated me while at the same time offering me a limitless feeling of safety.

"I'll see you, Nick," I said, taking a step back.

Irritated but amused, he asked, "You know if you don't come, you won't get laid again until after you graduate, right?"

That was a low blow, but it was true. I barely had any time, definitely not enough to go into town and see him, and if he wouldn't come here either, because he was worried about running into his dad...

"We could go to the movies," I stammered.

Nick cracked up. "Sure, just as you say, Freckles," he agreed, pressing his lips chastely to my forehead. I could sense the irony in it. "I'll see you in two days. To go to the movies. And whatever comes afterward."

I wanted to grab him, to beg him to stay with me, to tell him I needed him because only with him would my nightmares go away, but I knew there was nothing I could say that would make him spend another second between those walls.

I watched him go downstairs with a casual attitude, get into his Range Rover, and drive off without a second thought.

The next two days, I barely even went out for fresh air. I had to cram so much information into my head that I thought my brain would explode. Jenna kept calling me to complain about our teachers, her boyfriend, and life in general. She always freaked out when exams were coming up, and to make things worse, she was in charge of the graduation party, and I knew it was making her crazy that she couldn't devote all the time she wanted to it.

That night, I was supposed to see Nick to go to the movies, but I was terrified of my Friday exam, the last one I had. I wanted to see him more than anything in the world, but I knew he'd throw off my concentration. Just having him around made me flustered, and if we did hang out, there was no way I would manage to study afterward. I needed to call and tell him, even if he might get mad. We hadn't seen each other since my birthday, and even when we spoke on the phone, I was pretty out of it.

I decided to text him. I didn't want his voice to distract me, I didn't want an argument, so I just hit *send*, put my phone on silent, and tried to forget him for twenty-four hours. When exams were over, I'd do whatever he wanted, but right now, everything was on the line, and I was determined to get the best grade possible.

Two hours later, I was still in my room looking like a

madwoman, my hair undone, on the verge of tears or maybe murder. Just then my door opened almost soundlessly.

Shit! He'd gotten dressed up to take me out. I smiled awkwardly and put on my most innocent face possible. "You look handsome."

Nick raised an eyebrow in a way that made it impossible for me to guess what was going through his head as he came over to my bed.

"You stood me up," he said calmly, and I didn't know if he was reproaching me or still trying to figure out what was up.

"Nick…" I said, feeling guilty and afraid of how he would react.

"Come here," he said gently. His expression was strange, as if he were thinking about something. I was surprised he hadn't just laid into me.

I wanted to kiss him. I always wanted to kiss him. If I had it my way, I'd spend every minute of every day in his arms. I got up on my knees and crawled to the edge of the bed, where he was waiting for me.

"I think that's the first time in my life a girl's stood me up, Freckles." He wrapped his hands around my waist. "I'm not sure what to make of it."

"I'm sorry," I stammered. "I'm losing it, Nick. I'm worried I'm gonna fail. I don't know anything, and if I don't pass, I won't graduate, they'll revoke my college admission, and I won't get the job I want. I'll end up just being some idiot living with my mom."

His lips hushed me with a quick kiss. "You're the hardest worker I know. You're not going to fail."

"I am, though, Nick. I'm being serious. I think I might even get a zero. A zero, can you imagine? Mr. Lam won't have mercy on me, and I used to be his favorite. I had the best grades in the whole class…"

From his face, I could tell he thought I was starting to go off the deep end. Okay, maybe so, but still... He grinned.

"You want help relaxing?"

Please, God, don't look at me like that...not now, when you're so handsome in that shirt and I look like a wreck.

"I am relaxed," I lied.

"You want me to help you study, then?" His hand pushed aside a lock of hair from my face, and I sighed at the tenderness of that gesture.

Nicholas helping me study? There was no way that would end well.

"No need," I murmured. I was scared that if he stayed there, we'd do everything but look over my notes for chapter eight from history class. Nick was hot, but I couldn't risk an F.

He smirked in that seductive way of his and took a step back, rolling up his sleeves, taking off his shoes, and walking around the bed to sit down as he picked up my book.

I felt tingly as I imagined us in that same bed, doing all sorts of things that weren't studying. Nick started turning the pages until he reached the section I had marked a few minutes before.

I forgot everything, my tests, college, all of it. I just wanted to sit on his lap and run the tip of my tongue across his jawline.

I edged over, and he looked up, shaking his head.

"Be still," he joked. "We're going to study, Freckles, and when you've got it all down pat, maybe I'll give you a kiss."

"Just one?"

He laughed and looked at my notes. "Let's get started, and if we make it to the end, I promise I'll make sure all that stress goes away."

He said that as cool as a cucumber, but I was as anxious as I could be.

———————

Two and a half hours later, I knew the material forward and backward. Nick was a good teacher... To my surprise, he was patient, and he told everything in story form. More than once, I found myself eagerly listening to him, actually attentive and interested in the Civil War. He told me things that hadn't even come up in class or in my text.

When he closed the book, he asked me to recite it all back to him, and when I managed to, chapter and verse, he smiled with pride and with a spark of desire in his blue eyes. "I'd give you an A."

I smiled from ear to ear and pounced on him. He squeezed me tight. We spun around in the bed, and he kissed me thirstily. I slid my tongue in his mouth, and he toyed with it, nibbled my lip, sucked it.

I moaned as his hand traveled down my hip, lifted my leg, and flung it around his waist. I felt a gentle pressure that sent me off to heaven...

"I wasn't too happy when I read your message," he said, rolling up my shirt and kissing my stomach.

I closed my eyes and leaned my head back. "I'll bet," I said.

"But I had a good time studying with you, Freckles," he said, aroused and amused. "It reminded me of all the things I still have to teach you."

When he said that, he pulled down my pants, and there I was in my underwear with him on top of me, his mouth too close to a certain part of my body for me to keep my thoughts in order. I tried to wriggle away a little, but a hand on my abdomen held me still.

"I did promise you a kiss, didn't I?"

I could have melted. I tensed when I realized what he was referring to.

"Nick..." I didn't know if I was ready for it. We'd never done that before, and I suddenly wanted to get up and run away.

Nicholas climbed back up, propped his elbows on either side of my face, and looked at me calmly.

"Just relax," he said, burying his nose next to my neck, smelling me and kissing me softly.

I closed my eyes and writhed beneath him.

"You're so good..." he said, going down, his lips brushing against my stomach, making me quiver.

When he reached his destination, he stopped for a few moments. It was incredibly erotic, seeing him there between my legs, with an expression of pure desire on his face, desire for me and no one else.

He pulled down my panties delicately, and I was so embarrassed, I looked away, going along with it without knowing whether I would even like it, just trying not to think.

He began kissing my thighs, first one, then the other. He opened my legs gently. I was already in tremors. And I had no idea what was about to come.

"Oh God!" I said, squirming.

He grabbed me around the waist, and I felt his mouth moving in circles down there where I was most sensitive... I let myself vanish into that perfect moment. When it got too intense, I brought a hand down to beg him for a break.

"It's even better than I imagined," he said, stopping a moment before going back for more. He looked up to ask if I wanted him to continue.

Jesus...

"Yes, please..." I groaned. And once again I let myself go until the feeling was so intense, I found myself clutching the sheets and shouting, "God...!"

It was the most erotic experience of my life.

When I recovered, Nicholas was resting his chin on my stomach and looking at me as if I were a treasure he'd found at the bottom of the ocean. I blushed, and he laughed, coming up beside me and pulling me into his arms.

"Shit, Noah...remind me why I never did that to you before."

I turned around and pressed my face into his chest. He was still dressed, but it wasn't hard to see the erection outlined in his pants.

Did he expect me to do the same?

I was almost paralyzed by anxiety as Nick kissed my head, turned around, and got out of the bed.

"Where are you going?" I asked as he headed toward the door.

"If I don't leave now, I'll stay here all night," he said, and I noticed something hurried in his tone.

I grabbed my pants, which were next to me on the cushion where we'd left them, and slipped them back on, getting out of bed and walking toward him.

"I'm done Friday, Nick, and then we'll have the whole summer to ourselves."

I hugged him. He hugged me back and sighed with resignation.

"If you don't get an A, you're going to hear it from me."

I laughed and pulled away to look at him.

"Thanks...for everything," I said, feeling myself blush again.

He reached out and caressed my cheek. "You're the most beautiful thing that's ever happened to me, Freckles, so don't ever worry about thanking me."

I felt my heart swell with joy and grief when he kissed the crown of my head and left me there alone.

———

I aced the exam. When I ran into Jenna in the hall five minutes after turning it in, we both looked each other in the eye and started jumping up and down like fools. People were staring at us, some of them laughed, some looked irritated, but I didn't care... My time there was over: I was never going to have to wear a uniform again, no one would be able to treat me like a girl, I would never have to show my report card to my mom or have her sign it—all that was over. I was free, we were free, and I couldn't have been happier.

"I can't believe it!" Jenna shouted, squeezing me tight, the day we got our grades. We went to the cafeteria, and as soon as we walked in, we heard all our classmates wreaking havoc, shouting, laughing, applauding. It was a regular bash. The underclassmen looked at us like we were idiots, some envious, some depressed at the long years that remained until they finally got out of there.

"We're thinking of having a bonfire on the beach and burning our uniforms," one guy told me with a radiant smile. "Are y'all in?"

"Hell yeah!" Jenna and I both shouted at once. As we giggled hysterically, we must have looked drunk—drunk on happiness.

An hour later, after celebrating with our class, running through the halls, and killing time acting like clowns, I left that school, which I had to admit had brought me more good things than bad. I remembered how I'd hated it at first, but if I hadn't gone there, there was no way I'd have gotten into UCLA to study English, and that had always been my dream.

I hurried outside when I got a message from Nick saying he was waiting for me in the parking lot. He was standing by his car and smiled wide when he saw how happy I was. Unable to control myself, I ran over and jumped into his arms. He grabbed me in midair, held me up, and gave me the kind of kiss you usually only see in romance movies.

I'd made it through school, my grades were perfect, I was on my way to a college I couldn't have dreamed of before, I had the best boyfriend in the world—a boyfriend I adored—and in two months, I'd be living on my own on campus with a bright future in front of me.

Nothing could be better.

4

Nick

MY GIRL HAD GRADUATED. I WAS THE PROUDEST GUY IN THE world. I couldn't help it: not only was she gorgeous, but she was smart as a whip. She'd come out near the top of her class, she'd had all kinds of schools begging her to attend, but she'd chosen to stay in Los Angeles with me. I don't know what I'd have done if she'd decided to go back to Canada the way she'd been planning at first.

I couldn't wait for her to move into my apartment. I hadn't told her, but I wanted her to live with me. I was tired of dealing with all the bullshit restrictions our parents had imposed on us as soon as we'd started going out. Since Noah had been kidnapped, her mother had turned super-paranoid, and both my father and Raffaella had made it known they didn't like us being in a relationship. I'd thought everything would go back to normal once I moved out, but actually, the opposite had occurred. They hardly ever let Noah come see me, let alone stay the night. We had to make up all kinds of dumb excuses and stories to be able to spend time together. I really didn't care what my father or his wife thought; I was twenty-two years old, almost twenty-three, and I would do whatever the hell I wanted. But it was different for Noah. I always knew the five-year age difference would cause us problems at some point, but I never could have imagined all these headaches.

Still, now wasn't the time to think about all that. Now was the moment for celebration. I'd agreed to take Noah to the stupid bonfire on the beach her classmates had organized. I wasn't particularly into the idea, but at least it meant we'd be together. The next day, Noah would be busy with graduation, and her mother wanted to take her out to dinner afterward, so either we went out today, or I would have to go back to sharing her with everyone. I knew it was selfish, but those past few months, between her school obligations, my travels to San Francisco, and the roadblocks our parents were throwing up, I hadn't seen her even half as much as I'd wanted to. So I was going to make sure tonight counted.

The ride to the beach was pleasant. Noah was so happy about graduating, she couldn't stop talking the whole twenty minutes it took us to arrive. I liked the way she moved her hands around when she was excited about something. Just then, they seemed to have a life of their own.

I parked as close as I could to the masses of people gathered there. It wasn't just Noah's classmates on the beach. It looked like every graduating class in Southern California had shown up.

"I thought there were just going to be a few of us," Noah said, no less perplexed than I was.

"Yeah, just a few million, maybe..."

Noah smiled, tried to ignore my response, and turned to look at Jenna, who appeared just then in a bikini top and skintight shorts and shouted, "Let's start drinking!"

A group of guys who had been trailing her cheered, raising their glasses in the air.

After getting out, Noah hugged her and cracked up laughing.

Then I walked up. Towering over Jenna, I leaned down, snatched her drink away, and poured it out in the sand.

"Hey!" she protested, indignant.

"Where's Lion? He should be here," I said, not concealing my amusement at her irritated expression.

"Idiot!" she growled, turning around and ignoring me.

Noah shook her head, wrapped her arms around my neck, and stood on her tiptoes to address me.

"Are you sure you don't mind being here?" she asked, tickling my neck with her long fingers.

"Go have fun, Freckles. Don't worry about me," I answered, bending down to press my lips into hers. They were so full, so soft that I thought I'd lose my mind. "I'm going to go find Lion. When you miss me, you can come looking for me."

"I miss you already," she responded. Just then, Jenna pulled her away from me and dragged her off to do God knows what kind of stupid shit.

I scowled at her and let her leave with Noah to where their friends were getting ready to burn their uniforms. It was a tradition… I could still remember the day I had burned my own.

I walked over to a smaller fire with just a few people standing around it and looked at the flames, my hands tucked into my pockets, thinking, fantasizing about all the things I wanted to do with Noah that summer, all the possibilities that would open up for us in the months to come.

Then I saw Lion standing beside another fire as far as possible from the crowd. He had a beer in his hands and was staring into the flames just like me, but he didn't look like he was dreaming or making plans. He looked worried, even depressed. I walked over to talk to him.

"What's up, man?" I asked, clapping him on the back and bending over to retrieve a bottle from the six-pack at his feet.

"Just trying to make this dumbass party pass as quickly as possible," he replied, then took a long drink of his beer.

"By getting drunk? Jenna's already tanked, and one of you will need to drive, so if I were you, I'd slow down," I warned him, but he ignored me and brought the bottle straight back to his lips.

"I didn't even want to come here, but Jenna wouldn't shut up about it," he told me, looking straight ahead.

"She just graduated, dude. You can't blame her for not knowing what the fuck's going on with you. I don't even know myself."

He exhaled for a long time and tossed the bottle into the fire, where it shattered into tiny pieces.

"Things at the garage aren't going well, and the last thing I want is for my brother to get out of prison and see me unable to keep the family business afloat..."

"If you need cash..."

"No, Nicholas, I don't want your money. We've already had this talk a million times. I can work it out. It's just, things aren't going the way I'd like, that's all."

By his expression, I could see he wasn't telling me the whole story.

"Lion, before you get into some kind of trouble..."

He turned to me, and I shut my mouth.

"You used to have no problem with getting into trouble. What the fuck's happened to you, Nicholas?"

I stared at him without blinking. "Someone kidnapped my girlfriend, that's what happened."

Seeming to regret his remark, Lion looked past me and took a cigarette from the back pocket of his jeans.

"Speak of the devil...here she comes now," he said. I turned around to see Noah approaching with a huge smile on her lips and her hair blowing in the breeze.

I forced a smile and opened my arms to hug her as she reached me. She kissed me on the chest and then turned to Lion.

"Jenna's looking for you," she informed him.

"Great," he replied curtly. Noah's expression changed, and I suddenly wanted to beat that shitty mood out of him.

Noah glanced over at me as he walked off toward the mass of people. "Is something up with him?"

I shook my head. "He's having a bad day. Ignore him," I told her, kissing her cheek, which was warm from the fire, and then her neck. For days now, my lips had been longing for her flesh, and the last thing I wanted now was to see something as stupid as Lion's mood sour her evening. "I love you," I said, moving down to her throat, tasting her skin, enjoying the effect my caresses had on her.

"Nick," she said a minute later, when I'd reached the curve between her breasts.

I separated from her for a second, bewitched but also aware that more than a few people were looking at us, anticipating a show. I cursed, grabbing her hand and leading her away.

"Let's take a walk," I said, steering her away from the bonfires and toward the dark night and the harmonious breaking of the waves. There was no better place in the world, and I liked experiencing it calmly, without all the racket from that stupid party.

Noah was strangely quiet, lost in thought, and I didn't want to bother her. Eventually, she turned toward me.

"Can I ask you a question?" she said, with a trace of anxiousness in her voice.

"Sure, Freckles," I responded, stopping by a tree that had sunk its roots in the sand and spread out powerfully above us. I sat down and pulled Noah between my legs so I could look her more easily in the eyes. "What's up?"

She shook her head. "Nothing, it was a stupid question," she replied evasively. She was blushing, and that piqued my curiosity in ways I hadn't thought possible.

"There's no such thing. What is it?" I pressed her.

"Seriously, don't worry about it. It's dumb."

"You're red as a tomato, and that's just making me that much more interested. Spit it out."

I hated her doing this to me. I wanted to know everything she was thinking or feeling, I didn't want her ever to feel ashamed of anything. Plus, I was so intrigued that I couldn't let her off the hook without telling me what was going on in her mind.

Her eyes met mine briefly, and she started playing with a lock of her own hair.

"I was just thinking...you know, about what happened the other night, when you..." By now she was red as a beet.

I tried not to smile. We'd never done anything like that. I'd wanted to take it slow with Noah, introduce her to sex a little at a time, always being sure she was ready.

"When I went down on you for the first time and it blew your mind?" I asked, looking forward to her reaction.

"Nicholas!" she exclaimed, looking around, as if it were possible for anyone to hear us. "Jesus, forget about it. I can't even imagine why I thought it was a good idea to talk about this."

I pulled her in close and forced her to look at me.

"You're my girlfriend. You can talk to me about anything you want...so the other day, what about it?" I tried to calm her down. These subjects always made her shrink with embarrassment; I knew that from the many times I'd made crude comments in her presence. "Didn't you like it?"

Hell yes, she had liked it. I'd had to put my hand over her mouth so no one would hear her shouting with pleasure. But did we have to talk about this right now? The memory of it was getting me hot, and this was neither the time nor the place.

"Of course I liked it. That's not what I wanted to talk about."
She looked away. "I was just wondering if...like...if you wanted
me to do the same thing to you."

I almost choked on my own saliva. There was timidity in her eyes
but also desire—yes, desire in those honey-colored irises. Dammit! I
would have to make a new rule: no more conversations with Noah
about sex in public places. I already felt myself getting impatient...

"Christ, Noah, are you trying to give me a heart attack?"

She smirked. "So you have thought about it," she replied.

"I don't think any guy with a pair of eyes who's had you in
front of him could fail to think about that, my love. Of course, I've
thought about it, but we don't need to do it unless you want to."

Noah bit her lip. "It's not that. It's more...like it's not fair. I
mean, you had to do it with me and I..."

I burst out laughing. "Had to do it? You say that like it was
torture. Noah, I did that because I wanted to. I enjoyed it, a lot,
and I plan on doing it again whenever I get the chance."

She opened her eyes wide, surprised but also excited. Sometimes
I forgot how innocent she was.

"Then I'm gonna do it, too," she affirmed, with some hesitation in her voice.

"No," I said. "That's not how it works. The things I do to you
and the things you do to me are independent. This isn't tit for tat.
When you feel like it, just do it, and if that moment never comes,
don't worry...I'll find someone who's more willing."

Hearing my joke, she slapped me on the shoulder. "I'm being
serious!"

"I know," I said earnestly, "but I don't want you doing things
you don't want to do, okay?" I kissed her on the nose. She blinked
a few times, then continued:

"So you don't mind? I'm not saying I don't want to. It's just
maybe...I don't know if I'm ready yet."

And that was why I had fallen in love with her. Any other girl without a backbone would have just given in to keep me happy. Noah wasn't like that; if she wasn't sure of something, it didn't matter what you did to try and convince her—she was going to go on being true to herself.

"Come here," I said, pulling her close and kissing her as if I would never kiss her again. "Having you by my side is enough, babe."

Noah smiled, and a few seconds later, we were in the middle of an epic make-out session.

5

Noah

I WAS GRADUATING. I DON'T KNOW IF YOU'VE EVER BEEN THROUGH something like that, but it's amazing. I knew the hard stuff was still ahead of me—I still had to go to college, not to mention any number of other, worse things—but still, you just can't compare graduating from high school to anything else. It's a step toward maturity, a step toward independence, a feeling so gratifying that I could barely contain myself as I waited in line next to my classmates and listened to our names being called.

We walked out in alphabetical order, which meant Jenna was several places in line behind me. The ceremony was organized to a T, very fancy, out in the school's gardens, with huge panels reading CLASS OF 2016. I still remembered the celebrations at my old school, in the gym, with a balloon or two and not much more. Here they had even decorated the trees on the edge of the green. The chairs where friends and family sat were lined with costly green and white fabrics—the school colors—and our gowns were green, too, and were the work of a famous designer. It was an insane waste of money, but by now nothing scandalized me anymore. I was surrounded by multimillionaires, and this was just how they lived.

"Noah Morgan!" was the next name uttered into the microphone. I jolted, climbed the stairs nervously to collect my diploma, and looked with a huge smile on my face at the rows of families. I saw Nick and my mother standing and clapping, and they were as excited as I was. My mother was even jumping up and down. I shook the principal's hand and joined the rest of the graduates.

The valedictorian—her GPA was .2 points higher than mine—mounted the stage once everyone had received their diplomas to give her graduation speech. It was sweet, funny, entertaining, and tender, and I doubt anyone could have done better. A few tears slid down Jenna's face, and I laughed to keep from doing the same. I'd only been there a year, but it had been one of the best in my life. Once I'd put my prejudices aside, I'd not only prepared myself for college magnificently, I'd also made a lot of good friends.

"Congratulations, class of 2016. We're free!" she shouted into the microphone, elated.

We threw our mortarboards into the air. Jenna hugged me so tight, I could barely breathe.

"And now it's party time!" she shouted, applauding and jumping all around. I giggled, and all at once, we found ourselves surrounded by hundreds of people trying to reach their children to congratulate them. We said a quick goodbye to one another and went off to look for our parents.

A pair of strong arms wrapped around me from behind and picked me up off the ground.

"Good job, brainiac!" Nick said, setting me down and kissing me loudly on the cheek. I turned around and hugged him.

"Thanks! I still can't believe it!"

I wanted to kiss him, but my mother appeared, pushed him aside, and embraced me.

"Noah, you graduated!" she shouted like another one of the schoolgirls. Her enthusiasm was contagious. I shrieked and laughed and watched Nick shake his head, amused at my mother and me. William walked up beside her and gave me a hug of his own once my mother had let me go.

"We've got a surprise for you," he announced.

I looked at the three of them with suspicion.

"What have you done?" I asked.

Nick grabbed my hand and pulled me along with him, saying, "Come on," and the four of us walked across the garden. With all the people there, it took us ages to reach the parking deck.

No matter where I looked, there were huge cars everywhere, some of them with giant colorful bows, others with balloons tied to the mirror. Who could be crazy enough to buy one of those cars for an eighteen-year-old kid?

Nick covered my eyes with one of his big hands and started guiding me across the lot.

"What are you going?" I asked, tripping over my own feet. I was starting to feel nervous but also excited.

No way...

"Over here, Nick," my mother said, more animated than I'd ever heard her in my life. Nick turned me around, then stopped. A second later, his hand moved away, and my mouth fell open, literally.

"Tell me that red convertible isn't for me," I whispered incredulously.

"Congratulations," my mother and William said, both of them beaming.

Nick dangled a ring of keys in front of my nose.

"No more excuses not to come visit me," he said.

"You all are crazy!" I shouted hysterically when I was able to react.

They'd bought me a goddamned Audi...

"Oh my God! Oh my God!" I started squealing.

"You like it?" William asked.

"Are you kidding?" I replied. I was so overwhelmed, I had no idea what to do or say.

I ran over to Mom and William and hugged them as tight as I could. I'd been dropping comments about saving up to buy another car. Mine had broken down five times in the past few months, and I was spending so much money at the shop that it would have been cheaper to buy me a new one, but...an Audi! I never guessed they'd give me something like that!

"Honestly, I can't believe it," I said, getting inside. The car was precious, bright, gleaming red. There wasn't a single corner of it that didn't seem to be sparkling.

I heard shouts of joy all around me. I wasn't the only one who'd gotten a car, obviously. All those giant ribbons made the lot look like a gift shop.

"It's an A5 Cabrio," Nick told me, getting into the passenger seat.

Still in shock, I started shaking my head.

"This is incredible," I said, hitting the button and listening to the motor's soft roar.

"You're incredible," he corrected me, and I felt a warmth spread through my interior. I was in heaven. I looked at him and, for a brief moment, was lost. My mother had to call out to me twice to get me to react, and when I did, flummoxed, Nick chuckled.

"Shall we see each other at the restaurant?" William asked, resting his hands on my mother's shoulders.

Mom had made a reservation at one of the best restaurants in the city. Afterward, my graduation party would be at the Four Seasons in Beverly Hills. They'd pulled out all the stops on the catering and gotten a hall that accommodated five hundred, apart from renting out two floors of the hotel so no one would have to worry about going home till the next day. I had complained at first—it was excessive, and the students had paid for all of it, even if we did get a discount, since the father of one of our classmates was an investor in the hotel.

"When I graduated, we had the party on a cruise ship and didn't come back for five days," Nick had said when I'd told him how shocked I was at what my class was planning. When I'd heard that, I'd decided to keep my opinions to myself.

I nodded, dying to take off in my new car. The seats were beige leather. It had that new car look and that new car smell…a smell I was encountering, just then, for the first time in my life.

I put it in gear and pulled out of the lot, leaving that school behind…forever.

———

"Noah, slow down, you're overdoing it," Nick said from the passenger's seat. The wind was blowing in our faces, pushing back our hair, while I hooted and laughed like a banshee.

The sun was setting, and the views just then were dazzling. Cars were driving past me, the starless sky was painted a thousand colors ranging from pink to orange, and the stars were just starting to twinkle. It was a perfect summer night, and all I could do was smile as I thought of the month and a half I had to spend with Nick, together, no more exams. And then I'd move to the city. I couldn't imagine a more perfect future.

"They shouldn't have bought you this damn car," he complained between clenched teeth. I rolled my eyes and slowed down.

"You happy now, Grandma?"

"You're still over the speed limit," he said earnestly.

I ignored him. No way I was slowing down to seventy. Seventy-five was fine. Anyway, everyone in that city drove like a maniac.

"This isn't NASCAR… You want to chill?" he said. He was joking, but the remark made my smile freeze, then slowly fade away.

I had tried as hard as I could not to think about my father, and I definitely didn't want to remember him just then. But something brought him insistently into my thoughts. Maybe it was seeing all my friends with their dads on that special occasion. I kept asking myself what it would have felt like if he'd been there, if he hadn't been crazy...or dead. In that alternate universe, Nick wouldn't be the one beside me just then, and he sure as hell wouldn't be telling me to slow down.

But what kind of stupid thought was that? My father was a drunk, a criminal with a killer's instincts, he had tried to murder me... What the hell was going on with me? How could I be missing him? How could I be sitting there imagining a life that never had existed and never would?

"Noah?" Nick called to me. Without realizing it, I'd slowed down to forty-five, and cars were honking and passing me. I shook my head. I'd gotten lost in myself again.

"I'm okay," I said, trying to get back to that state of euphoria I'd been in just a few minutes before. I stomped on the accelerator and ignored the nagging feeling in my heart.

———

Soon we were at the restaurant. It was gorgeous inside. I'd never been there, and I was excited to try the food. I'd told my mother I didn't care where we went, as long as they had the best chocolate cake. That was my one request.

Mom and Will must have been right behind us. I got out of the car, and Nick did, too, walking around to see me. He looked fantastic in those dark pants, with a white shirt and gray tie. I fell in love with him all over again every time I saw him in businessman mode, as I called it. He smiled the way he only did with me and smirked as I looked down and realized I still hadn't stripped off my gown. I pulled it off, giving him a view of the pink dress I was wearing, with the patterned lace back. It fit me like a glove.

"You look incredible," he said, pulling me close. Even in my heels, I felt minuscule next to him. My eyes were level with his lips, which were tempting, the way every inch of him was.

"You, too," I said, tickled because I knew how much he hated compliments. I didn't know why, but he always got really uncomfortable whenever I called him handsome. It wasn't a secret—we'd only been parked there three minutes, and five women had already turned their heads to give him a slow, shameless once-over.

He kissed me before I could say anything else, and after a moment, I pushed him away.

"Easy, we've got the whole night ahead of us," I said.

"I'm on the verge of taking you to my apartment and forcing you to live there all summer," he blurted out.

That idea, the two of us living there with no parents to bother us, made my heart swell... but obviously it couldn't happen.

"I wouldn't say no," I told him.

"Really?" he said, pushing me into the car. I wrapped my arms around him and tried to give him a kiss, but he jerked back, clearly expecting an answer. That allured me, and I wanted to keep playing.

"Yeah, I wouldn't mind spending the night with you, naked, in your bed..." I admitted, digging my fingers into his hair.

In his eyes, there was hunger. I was seducing him. I'd figured out I had a talent for it.

"Don't start what you can't finish," he warned me, now ready to kiss. But this time, I was the one who turned away. I was toying with him, but his expression promised passion and danger. I'd realized by then that the slightest contact with my lips was enough to completely disarm him.

I knew I couldn't take it too far. We were in the middle of a parking lot, and our parents were about to arrive. But I wanted him so bad...

"Tonight," I said, kissing his chin, his throat, his neck. "Make me yours, Nick."

He held my waist with one hand, while the other forced my head back.

"I don't need to make you mine—you are mine," he replied before kissing me the way he'd been wanting to do since before we arrived. His tongue pushed into my mouth immodestly, wrapped around mine, tasted me, maybe punished me—I wasn't yet sure.

Just being with him, just touching him, was enough to make me lose control. It didn't matter how much time passed; it didn't matter that we'd spent the whole previous day together. I never got tired of him, never lost that painful attraction that brought us together like two magnets.

But before my body could melt in his arms, or else undergo spontaneous combustion, a horn honked, startling us and making us step back from each other.

"Your mother," he said with a frown.

"Your father," I counterattacked.

They glowered at both of us.

"Could you all keep it under control? We're in a public place," Mom reprimanded us, with an accusing look at Nick. She'd been doing that kind of thing a lot lately... And I didn't like it one bit. We'd need to have a talk about that. William appeared a moment later, glaring alarmingly at his son.

When we went inside, I realized we weren't the only ones who had chosen that place for our graduation dinner. Several class-mates waved to me as we passed. I smiled at each and every one of them. The maître d' led us to the terrace. We were seated next to a swimming pool. Lit candles stood in the center of all the tables. It was a cozy place with relaxing piano music in the background—a live musician, as I would realize some time later.

Nicholas sat down next to me, and our parents sat across from us. For some reason, I felt suddenly uncomfortable. One thing was the four of us eating a pizza in the kitchen, another was having dinner in a place like that, especially since Nick hadn't eaten with the family for months, and the tension in the air was palpable.

Everything was fine at first. My mother couldn't keep her mouth closed—nothing new there. We talked about my new car, college, Nick, his job, William's new firm, which I knew Nick was anxious to lead someday... I started to feel more comfortable. My mom ignored the fact we were a couple. In some sense, that was irritating, but it also smoothed things over.

It wasn't until the end of dessert, when I'd swallowed the last bit of my chocolate cake, that my mother decided to blurt out something she must have been keeping under wraps for weeks:

"I have another surprise for you," she announced when we were all sitting there stuffed. I brought my glass to my lips, so happy, I didn't see coming the bomb she let off a second later: "You and I are going to Europe for a girls' trip for four weeks!"

Wait...what?

6

Nick

No fucking way.

The look I gave that woman was enough to knock my father off guard. Noah glanced at me for a few seconds, unable to speak.

"Mom, have you lost your mind?" she finally managed to whisper.

Why is she being like that? Why the hell isn't she telling her that not in her wildest dreams would she go to the other end of the world and spend the whole summer without me?

"You're growing up. Soon you'll be off to college…" Raffaella said, carefully avoiding me. Good for her. I'll bet one look at me would have made her freeze from terror. "I think it's the last chance we'll have to do something like this together, and maybe you're not as excited about it as I am, b-but…" Then she burst into tears.

I took a sip of wine, trying to control my rage. I was squeezing Noah's hand so tight, it must have cut off her circulation, but it was either that or lose my shit and start blurting out all the curse words I was struggling to keep down.

My father looked askance at me for a moment and brought

his glass to his lips. Had this been his idea? Had he been the one to put that ridiculous notion into his wife's head?

Why the hell was I even asking? Of course it had been him; he was the one paying for the damn trip.

Just then, my last hope faded away.

"Of course I want to go, Mom," Noah said, and her words were like a slap to the face.

Did I not have any say in that decision? Why the hell was I even sitting there?

I let go of her hand. I was getting more and more pissed off. I had to go, or else I was going to let everything fly. But going wouldn't solve a thing, I realized, nor would starting a scene; not if I wanted to be taken seriously, anyway... What I needed to do was stay there and make my opinion known, tell them they weren't just going to up and steal a month from my girlfriend and me.

Noah turned to face me. I could see she was as tormented by the news as I was... that, at least, was something.

Before Raffaella could say another word, I interrupted her.

"You don't think you should have checked with us before booking the trip?"

It had taken all the willpower I had to formulate that question in the calm tone of voice I'd used.

Raffaella looked at me, and when I saw her eyes, it was evident that any hope I'd had that Noah's mother would accept me as her boyfriend had vanished. She didn't want me to have Noah. There was no more doubting that.

"Nicholas, she's my daughter and she's just turned eighteen. She's still just a girl, and I want to take a vacation with her. Is that so hard to understand?"

Before I could reply, Noah jumped to my defense:

"Mom, I'm not a girl anymore, okay?" She flicked her hair back and continued. "And you shouldn't talk to Nick that way.

He's my boyfriend, and he has every right in the world not to be happy about the trip."

To say I wasn't happy was the understatement of the year, but I let her go on talking.

Raffaella's eyes were damp. Her face made me sick to my stomach.

"I'll go with you, Mom."

What?

"But next time, either we all go, or none of us do," Noah added, unaware of how those words were echoing in my brain or how all at once, I'd started to see red.

Her mother smiled, but I felt feverish and had to stand. Despite my father's look of admonishment, I announced that I was leaving. I tried to control my voice, but my hands were clenched into fists, and what I wanted most was to hit someone. I didn't even know if I wanted Noah to leave with me. I was every bit as pissed at her as I was at her mother.

"Nicholas, sit down," my father ordered, not wanting to draw attention to us. Always worried about appearances, always with that disappointed expression. I took off toward the door, not even stopping to wait for Noah. I needed to get outside and take a breath of fresh air.

I headed for the car, but I realized I didn't have the keys—why in the hell hadn't I taken my own car? I turned around and leaned on the driver's side door and saw Noah walking toward me. She couldn't keep up with me in high heels. I took out a cigarette and lit it. She'd probably bitch about it. I didn't care.

When she reached me, her cheeks red, trying to meet my eyes, I looked away toward the people entering and exiting the restaurant.

"Nicholas..."

I didn't answer. I just listened to her breathing, and after a moment, I looked down.

"What did you want me to do?" she asked.

I grunted. A month, a whole month without Noah: all my plans, all the stuff I'd wanted to do with her, all that was in the trash can. I was going to take a trip with her; we were going to see the sights; I'd thought I'd make love with her every single day that summer, enjoy her company, but no, she hadn't even hesitated to accept her mother's gift. It hurt because I thought I would come first for her, and I'd been wrong.

"Give me the keys. I'll take you to your party."

I knew she wanted to talk, but the thought of her being gone, the thought of her being taken from me, even if it was just a month, was eating away at me, and of course, there was nothing I could do about it.

After standing there in silence, she reached into her purse, handed me the keys, and walked around to the passenger side.

It was for the best. If she'd decided to argue with me, I wasn't going to be responsible for what I said.

1

Noah

THE TENSION IN THE CAR WAS UNBEARABLE. HE WAS ENRAGED. I could tell. I could see it in his eyes.

I understood why he didn't like the idea of me leaving for a month, but what was I supposed to do? My mother had organized the trip, she'd even paid for it, and I couldn't turn her down. She was my mother, after all. We'd always talked about me graduating, about college, about how we'd go shopping together for furniture for my dorm room. We'd even joked about going backpacking through Europe to share a last summer together while I was still her little girl, as she liked to say. A part of me wanted to take that trip; I didn't want to lose the chance to be alone with the woman who had given me life along with everything I had... I couldn't just reject her outright.

But my body also ached when I thought about how I wouldn't see Nicholas for four whole weeks. I had plans with him; I, too, had wanted to spend every second of every day in his apartment, even more now that I knew his work was piling up and that his trips to San Francisco would last longer than the two weeks the last one had.

I looked over at him. His eyes were fixed on the road, his hands clutching the steering wheel with fury. I was scared of whatever might be happening in his head, but I didn't know what to do or say to keep him from getting angry with me.

"Are you not even going to talk to me?" I asked, gathering my courage. In lieu of looking at me, he ground his teeth, and the veins tensed in his neck.

"I'm trying not to ruin your night, Noah," he said a second later.

Trying?

"Nicholas, you can't blame me for all this. You can't make me not go. This is my mother we're talking about!"

"And I'm your boyfriend!" he screamed. There it was—we were going to end up arguing, and that was the very last thing I'd wanted that night. As my nerves frayed further, I wondered what more there was he wanted to say.

"Don't do this to me. Don't make me choose between my mother and you," I begged him, trying not to whine or shout.

Nicholas sped up so fast, I had to grip the door handle. I caught a glimpse of the Four Seasons. A long line of cars waited in front of the valet stand, and lots of people I knew were there with their boyfriends and girlfriends. I envied the smiles on their faces. Mine was gone, for a change.

Nick stopped behind a Mercedes and looked over at me.

"If I were given a choice, I would always choose you," he said so coldly, it chilled my blood. I looked at him incredulously. His tone hurt, and I felt guilty because of what he was suggesting. I shouldn't have to choose between the two people I loved most in the world, especially because I loved them in two totally different ways: I loved my mother above all else, but the love I felt for Nicholas was impossible to explain; it was a love that hurt. I adored him, but his intensity frightened me. I got out, turning back around when I realized he was still in the driver's seat.

"You're n-not going to stay?" I asked, voice trembling. Shit! There I was again, feeling abandonment, dependency... I didn't want him to leave me; I needed him next to me; I needed to share that night with him, a night when my boyfriend was *supposed* to be with me.

He looked away toward the people climbing the steep stairs toward reception.

"I don't know. I need to be by myself," he hissed in that tone I hated, the one that reminded me of the old Nicholas.

I could feel the rage overtaking me. It wasn't fair. It wasn't fair for him to take this out on me when I'd had nothing to do with it.

"Fuck you, Nicholas! We were supposed to spend the night together for the first time in weeks, and you're ready to waste the opportunity." My anger reaching a fever pitch, I shouted, "Just go! I'll have way more fun without you!"

The jerk didn't even wait to see me go inside. Making the tires squeal—making *my* tires squeal, because it was *my* car—he sped up and disappeared down a side street, leaving me with no options for getting away if I got tired of the stupid party.

I walked over to the steps, where my classmates were chatting excitedly. I could have joined any number of groups there, but I wasn't in the mood to pretend I was all happy. I wasn't: I was wounded. Wounded and pissed.

"Hey, Morgan!"

I turned around and saw Lion's smiling face. My eyes lit up. The last time I'd seen him, he'd been distant and cold. I was happy to see him so happy. Just as Jenna had become my best friend and confidante, so I'd grown to really care about Lion: he was great, caring, kind, and never intimidated me. I'd thought he would at first, especially because he was Nicholas's friend, but nothing could be further from reality. Lion was a sweetie. He walked over, and I hugged him.

"Congratulations!" he said.

"Thanks!" I replied.

"Where's Nick?" he asked, looking around, and my smile immediately disappeared.

"He left. We had a fight," I said, and to my surprise, Lion laughed, provoking a bitter stare from me.

"I'll give him half an hour, and he'll come crawling back, and you won't get him off of you... That's the longest he could stand to be away from you," he said, ignoring my irritation and taking out his cell phone.

"Good for him. I'd just as soon he stayed gone."

Lion rolled his eyes with his attention on his screen. "Jenna will be here in ten. You want to go on in with me?" he asked.

I nodded. It should have been Nicholas there celebrating with me, but screw him, he'd missed his chance. I'd gotten dressed up especially for him, I'd even bought underwear at this mega-expensive shop Jenna had told me about, and now he would never see it. I was so bitter and disappointed that I had smoke coming out of my ears.

The vestibule was impressive. The people were packed in like sardines, and lots of parents were there, too, having drinks. A few guys in uniform showed us where to go, and Lion followed their directions with me behind him. Everyone was laughing and talking, and then we reached the terrace.

It was spectacular! This must have been the greatest graduation party in history! Under the open sky, there were tall tables with green satin tablecloths surrounding a dance floor. The floral arrangements were exquisite: white peonies, if I wasn't mistaken. The waiters in their elegant uniforms came and went with trays of canapés and glasses of something or other—I didn't know what, but it couldn't be alcohol.

Lion was as fascinated and intimidated as I was. Neither of us had grown up surrounded by such luxuries, and I'm sure we both felt out of place among all those rich, distinguished people.

"They sure know how to throw a party," he said.

"You're telling me," I agreed, bowled over by the beauty of that spectacle. Pale white lights lit up the terrace, and the aroma of the flowers was bewitching. The party music hadn't started yet, and I could still hear the captivating sounds of the violin and cello players softly welcoming us.

"There you guys are!" a familiar voice said behind us. We turned to find Jenna with a huge smile on her face. "Can you believe how many people are here? What do you think? Did I overdo it? Or were you expecting more? Don't tell me you don't like it!"

Jenna had been one of the people responsible for organizing the party. She'd spent the better part of the year on it, and I had to say, she'd outdone herself. She was crazy if she thought we didn't like it.

"What are you saying?" I asked. "It's incredible!"

I hugged her, admiring her beauty. It was in her genes, of course. Her mother, Caroline Tavish, had been Miss California in her younger days. That title had opened doors for her, all right, since it made one of the richest men in America want to marry her. Jenna's father was a millionaire, with oil rigs all over the world, and he was hardly home more than two days a month, but according to Jenna, that didn't mean he didn't love her mother like crazy... And why wouldn't he? She was the kind of woman who would leave any man breathless. Jenna had inherited her body and her height, but her face was warmer, sweeter, more childlike than her mother's, her beauty less stern and imposing.

"I can't believe we've graduated!" she said, leaping into Lion's arms and leaving a luscious kiss on his lips. He wrapped an arm around her waist and pulled her in close. They said something, I don't know what, and Jenna turned to face me with a furrowed brow.

"Where's your Nicholas?"

I don't know why she was so fixated on calling him that. Nicholas wasn't mine, was he? Honestly, at that moment, I had no idea.

"I don't know and I don't care," I responded. But of course I did.

I didn't understand why, but Jenna always defended him whenever we had a fight or argument. Maybe she'd known him all her life, but she was *my* friend—she should be taking *my* side and defending *me*.

"You outdid yourself, Jenna," I said.

The night started with a bang. Someone—or more than just someone—had brought along alcohol, and in less than an hour, all those present were drunk and stumbling over the dance floor. The lights started blinking, and I found myself surrounded by people. Siblings, cousins, friends of the graduates were in attendance. It started to weird me out when I felt a bunch of guys I didn't know rubbing up on me and trying to get me to dance. I pushed them away and walked off the dance floor. I was sweating, and I stood to one side, where a bartender was serving shots to the older people. I'd already had a few drinks. I wasn't drunk, but I was buzzing.

"You want one?" a girl asked me when the bartender walked away for more ice. On the table were crystal glasses with a thick pale liquid in them over ice.

"What are those?" I asked suspiciously.

"White Russians."

If she'd said Red Frenchmen, it wouldn't have mattered. I had no idea what that meant.

"It's vodka, Kahlúa, and cream. Delicious. They say it's an aphrodisiac." She batted her eyes. Was she flirting with me?

Just what I needed, a girl hitting on me! But the thought of coffee was enough for me to forget her sexual orientation and grab one of the drinks off the table. I put the straw in my mouth and tried it.

"Oh my God, it's delicious!" I shouted. The girl laughed.

The vodka was hardly noticeable. It didn't burn at all; it tasted like a coffee-flavored milkshake.

I looked closer at the girl. She wasn't familiar at all. She must have been a friend or relative of one of the graduates. Her black hair was pulled back in a ponytail on the top of her head.

I went on drinking my new favorite cocktail. Jenna was dancing with Lion on the dance floor. Without realizing it, I drank two more and fell into conversation with the girl, whose name was Dana. She was nice, and either I was just drunk, or she was incredibly funny. One of her jokes made me laugh so hard that I was unable to react when she grabbed the back of my neck and planted a kiss on my lips. It was so quick and so unexpected that I needed a second to push her away.

"What are you doing?" I asked, feeling woozy.

She just laughed. "I wanted to taste the vodka on your lips," she said.

The situation was so surreal that I didn't know what to say.

"I've got a boyfriend," I told her a few seconds later, or maybe it was minutes—I don't know. The alcohol was coursing through my brain. Had I just kissed a girl?

"It was only a peck. Relax," she replied, her eyes turning quickly to something or someone behind me.

I shivered.

I could feel him even before I turned to see if it was him. There Nicholas was, his bright eyes seeing straight through me even from far away. He hurried over.

"You should go," I told Dana hurriedly. I was afraid for her life.

She chuckled, grabbed her White Russian, and walked onto the dance floor, disappearing just as Nick came around in front of me.

"So you like girls now?" he said, looking like he was trying to remain calm.

I didn't let him intimidate me.

"Maybe?" I told him, irritated. I was furious with him. He'd left me hanging on the day of my graduation, surrounded by people I didn't want to see, feeling alone, and to top it off, someone had kissed me without my permission.

"What are you drinking?" he asked, taking the glass out of my hands.

I thought he was going to set it down, but instead, he drank it. I should have been angrier, but already my only thought was to savor that liquid on his lips, just as the girl had done with me. A White Russian on those lips...delicious...

"You know how much alcohol this has in it?" he said after draining the glass and setting it down behind me. I wanted to feel him out; I wasn't sure what kind of mood he was in... I mean, I knew he was angry, but his eyes harbored something else.

"I guess a lot, because if I were sober, I'd have already told you to go to hell."

He leaned his head to one side, observing me, and brought his body close. Without touching me, he placed his palms on the table behind me, imprisoning me between his arms.

I couldn't breathe. His sky-blue eyes were seeking out mine.

"There's no reason for you to be mad, Noah," he said, now serious. "I'm the one getting hurt here. You're going off to Europe on vacation."

"I repeat: it wasn't my idea."

Nick took a deep breath and stepped back, giving me space.

"So we're at a dead end," he said with a poker face.

Part of me knew he wasn't entirely wrong to be upset, but I wasn't ready to admit that. I didn't want to calm down. I didn't want to be understanding... I wasn't happy with the situation either. Going to Europe with my mother wasn't in my plans, and it made me angry and sad that I couldn't spend that month with Nick. My mother was the one I was really mad at, but Nick was there, and I had to get my anger out on someone.

"Maybe you shouldn't have come back. You said you didn't want to ruin my night, but now you're doing it."

Brow furrowed, Nick asked, "You want me to go?"

Was there a touch of disappointment in those eyes?

"What's for sure is I don't want to stand here arguing with you."

Looking me over, he responded, "I think you've had a bit too much to drink, smarty-pants."

Feeling full of myself, I glared at him, reached across the table, filled a glass from the punch bowl, and downed it. It had been spiked so much that the liquor in it burned my eyes, but it was worth it to see Nick's furious face.

"You're acting like an idiot," he said, "and the person who's going to have to deal with it later is me."

I shrugged and walked off toward my friends on the dance floor, joining them without looking back. At some point, I dropped my glass, and it spilled on someone's feet, but I didn't care. Jenna came over to dance with me. After twisting and shouting until my stomach was upset, I stopped, looking around.

I knew Nick hadn't left. He'd been staring at me the whole time. I hadn't expected that. Certainly not when we were arguing.

At some point, I stumbled, and an arm grabbed me around the waist. A strong, muscular, attractive one...Nick's.

I turned around and clung to him. "I see you're still here," I said.

"And I see you can barely stand. If your goal for tonight was to get under my skin, congratulations, you did it."

"I don't know about getting under your skin, but I'd be more than happy to get under those clothes you're wearing or between some sheets…"

Nick didn't laugh. He seemed to be trying to figure out what to do with me.

I tried to caress his neck and hair the way I knew he liked, but he grabbed my wrists and stopped me.

"Let me take you upstairs, Noah," he said. Looking around, I saw other couples had had the same idea.

"Okay. Sounds fun…" I said with a grin.

Nick exhaled a breath and led me out.

"Fun's the last thing it's going to be," he said to himself, but I heard him perfectly.

Had he been trying to play it cool because other people were around?

Dammit!

8

Nick

WE LEFT THE PATIO AND WALKED STRAIGHT TO OUR ROOM—I'D already gotten my key earlier. When we went in, we stood there staring at each other, and neither of us knew what to do or say. Should I stay mad at her? Should I kiss her all over? Noah seemed to be asking herself the same thing.

"So we're about to have fun, huh?" she asked, skillfully pulling down her zipper and letting her dress fall to the floor.

I'd never seen that underwear and bra and those sexy heels... She left me breathless.

She started to trip, and I quickly bridged the two feet between us, grabbing her around the waist, carrying her into the bathroom, and setting her down on the sink.

"Noah, you're drunk."

She shrugged. "Not so drunk that I don't realize you brought me in here to punish me for going to Europe."

I frowned. "I'm the one who's getting punished tonight, Freckles, not you."

"Well, I can think of a lot of other things we could do besides punish each other."

I couldn't resist smiling. There she was, half naked, her cheeks red from alcohol or embarrassment at the situation or who knew what. Unable to take it anymore, I cupped her face in my hands and pressed my lips to hers, not using my tongue, just playing a bit, because I had to, otherwise I thought I might lose my mind.

She started unbuttoning my shirt, and I stepped away.

"I think you should maybe take a cold shower first..."

Noah shook her head. "No, no cold, I'm good," she said, pulling me back in.

When we kissed that time, it was more intense, and my hands climbed her back, unclasping her bra. She looked incredible, with those freckles all over her breasts and shoulders. I kissed them and moved up to her earlobe, catching it between my teeth, sucking on it like a piece of candy, making her quiver.

"I don't want you to go," I confessed, picking her up and carrying her out of the bathroom while she squeezed her legs around me, forcing me to tense my muscles.

Instead of answering, she kept kissing me as I laid her on the bed, holding back a bit to keep from crushing her, moving my lips down to the hollow between her neck and collarbone.

She shifted beneath me, trying to rub me closer. I lay down next to her and stared at her, entranced. Her breasts were rising and falling with her labored breathing.

"I could spend the whole night just watching you," I said, propping myself up on my right arm while my other hand stroked her ribs, passed over her flat stomach, and trapped her left breast between my fingers.

"Nick, get on top of me," she said, her eyes closed, wriggling beneath my hand.

"I want to watch your whole body flush as I touch you, Noah."

Her honey-colored eyes opened and stared straight into mine. "But..."

I hushed her with a kiss while my hand crept into the elastic of her waistband. "I don't want you to go to Europe," I repeated, serious now, reaching inside.

She twisted and closed her eyes again.

I started fingering her, and the sight of her face made me nearly gasp. There was nothing I would have wanted more than to be there, watching her react to my caresses, seeing her bite her lip, listening to the soft sighs of pleasure she let escape from her lips.

I couldn't go a month without her. I couldn't stand it. I loved seeing her happy. Doing this just one time since I'd returned from San Francisco wasn't enough for either of us, and the thought of her being gone a whole month made me want to show her just how bad I was going to miss her.

"Are you going to go?" I asked her, rubbing her harder.

"Yes…" she said, and once more, I was angry.

"Are you sure?" I hissed as my hand moved faster.

I knew she was about to finish, but I stopped at the moment of maximum intensity.

Her eyes opened wide as if she couldn't understand what was going on. Her pupils were dilated from desire, and her mouth was hanging open, about to free a cry of pleasure that now wouldn't come.

I couldn't look at her. I closed my eyes and lay on my back. My whole body hurt. This was punishment for me, too, but the rage was too much for me. I couldn't even explain how it was consuming me.

"Why'd you stop?" she asked.

How could I tell her how lost I felt just then? How could I make her see that leaving me was going to mean I'd be living in hell?

I said nothing, and Noah crept close and rested her head on my shoulder, stroking my chest over my shirt.

"I don't want this stupid trip to cause problems for you and me, Nick."

I ran a hand over my face and looked over at her.

"If it's that important to you, I'll talk to my mom, and we could..."

"No." I cut her off. "Just give me time to get used to the idea... I want you with me all the time. I know it's impossible, but that doesn't make it any easier... It just pisses me off, that's all."

She looked pensive, and I could tell she was unhappy with the situation, too. She bent over and kissed me on the cheek.

"I love you, Nick. Do you love me?"

"I love you more than I love myself," I responded, stroking her bare back.

"That must be difficult," she said, smiling like a little girl.

"Very funny," I said, rolling on top of her and trapping her in my arms.

My lips hovered slowly over hers as she sank her fingers into my hair.

"Are you tired?" I asked, pressing my mouth into her neck.

"Finish what you were doing before," she whispered.

I needed her. I had needed her since we'd fought in the car. I needed her to make me feel like I was the only one, the only one she wanted, the only one she lusted for.

"You want me to make love to you, Freckles?"

Blushing, she took off my shirt. I could see the desire reflected in her eyes. She licked the center of my chest, my neck, my chin, and my body stiffened as I pinned her hands over her head, feeling her teeth sink into my ear.

She stretched up, and I let her kiss my lips, darting my tongue in and out of her mouth softly as I pressed my hips into hers.

"I love you, Nick," she said, arching her back as my hand had its way with her again.

"I love you, too."

And that was how we finished the night: doing the one thing that didn't cause us any trouble.

9

Noah

THE INTENSE MORNING LIGHT WOKE ME. WE'D LEFT THE THICK curtains open and were enjoying the panoramic view of the elegant houses in Beverly Hills as well as, farther off, the taller buildings downtown and everything in between.

Nicholas was pulling me into his chest, and his legs were intertwined with mine. I could hardly breathe, but I loved it—I loved sleeping with him. There was no better way to spend a night. For weeks, I hadn't been able to sleep straight through like that, without waking up, without nightmares.

I turned gently until I was face-to-face with him. He was adorable when he slept, with those serene features, those big eyelids resting closed... He looked so young like that, resting there next to me. I would have liked to know what was going through his mind. What might he be dreaming of just then? I lifted a hand carefully and stroked his left eyebrow without waking him. He was so tired, he didn't budge. Then I reached his cheek, his chin. How could one person be that handsome?

At that moment, an unexpected thought popped into my head: What would our children look like?

I knew I was losing it; I still had years before I even needed to think about starting a family, but the image of a little black-haired boy appeared in my mind nonetheless. Our son would be handsome, with Nick's genes, there was no getting around it...but how would he act with a baby? The only child he could stand to be around was his little sister. I'd even had to chew him out for being nasty around kids at the beach or at restaurants. Anyway, I wouldn't have to worry about it for a long time, plus there was that little detail, the fact I might not even be able to have kids because of the glass that had stabbed me that awful night. Thinking about it made me sad, and I was happy when Nick opened a drowsy eye and looked at me.

I smiled. "Hey, handsome," I greeted him, watching him furrow his brow as he tried to get the lead out. Without a furrowed brow, Nick wasn't Nick.

He reached out an arm and pulled me close. "What were you doing, Freckles?" he asked, and his breath tickled my cheek.

"Admiring how extraordinarily pretty you are."

He grunted. "For God's sake, don't call me *pretty*. Anything but that," he begged, lifting his head.

I laughed, seeing him with mussed hair and that crabby face that was just like a whiny little boy's.

"Are you laughing at me?" He distracted me with his eyes, then grabbed me and started tickling me.

"No, no, no!" I shouted, trying to wriggle away. "Nicholas!"

Soon I attacked back, jabbing his washboard stomach with one finger so hard, he leapt up and fell out of the bed.

"Jesus!" I cackled. I was crying; my stomach hurt from giggling so hard.

He got up, pulled on one of my feet, and jerked me to the edge of the mattress. Before I could fall, he threw me over his shoulder like a sack of flour and walked toward the bathroom.

"Now you're going to get it," he warned me, turning on the shower.

"I'm sorry, I'm sorry!" I begged, still cracking up.

He didn't care, and he stuck me under the cold water, where my T-shirt clung to me like a second skin.

"It's freezing!" I shouted, pulling aside and shaking. "Nicholas!"

At my protests, he pushed his way in and turned the knob, and hot water began to cascade over us.

"Silence. You've had your fun. Now it's my turn," I said, pulling my T-shirt over my head and standing before him naked.

His eyes traced out every curve of my body.

"I doubt there's a better way to wake up in the morning," he said, bending over to taste my lips.

A half hour later, I was wrapped in a towel, my hair dripping, sitting on the balcony while Nicholas ordered room service. It was strange not to hear people shouting in the halls. I had assumed all those drunk students would make it impossible to sleep, but I was wrong. Maybe the walls in the hotel were soundproof.

I turned to look at Nick as he hung up. His hair was wet, same as mine; he was shirtless, and his sweatpants were hanging off his hips, revealing the dark hair that started at his belly button and went down from there. My God, what a body! His abs were rock-hard, his obliques perfectly worked. How the hell did he do it? I knew he went to the gym and surfed, but that body was a masterpiece, something not of this world.

"You looking at me?" he asked, sitting down next to me at the table.

I felt the blood rush into my cheeks. "You got a problem with that?" I asked, ignoring the way the sunlight reflected in his blue eyes at just that moment.

With a wry grimace, he continued. "Come here."

He pulled me over onto his lap. I was naked under my towel, which slipped up over my thighs when I sat on top of him.

"You don't have anything on underneath there?" he asked in a tone that sounded surprised, then disapproving just one second later.

I rolled my eyes. "There's no one here, Nick."

He looked around. We were totally alone, our only company those spectacular views of the city.

"There could be a pervert with binoculars watching us right now from one of those buildings over there," he said, holding up my towel.

"Your loss. I'm getting dressed," I said, getting up and going inside.

Looking at myself in the mirror, I wondered how it was possible that the sad girl from yesterday could have turned into the one staring back at me. I guessed that was love, a roller coaster of crisscrossing emotions and feelings. One minute, you're up, and the next, you're on the ground, and you don't even know how you got there.

I bent over our suitcase. It was silly, but it made me feel special to see my clothing there next to his Marc Jacobs shirt.

The dress I put on was simple, sea blue with yellow flowers. My mom had bought it for me. It probably cost a fortune.

When I started putting my makeup on, my eyes settled on my neck, and I grunted, pulling my hair back to reveal two hickeys. I ran out of the bathroom, furious.

"Nicholas!" I shouted. He was talking on his cell phone. Breakfast had arrived, and he was eating on the balcony, chitchatting away like nothing mattered.

"Hold on," he said to whoever was on the other line.

I pointed to my neck and clavicle. And the dickhead smiled! I was so pissed, I picked up a pillow and threw it at him.

He raised a hand to protect himself and cursed.

"I'll call you back," he said, hanging up. "What the hell's gotten into you?"

I hated someone leaving a mark on me. I couldn't stand anyone leaving marks on my skin. It brought back bad memories, and I didn't have to explain it.

"You know I hate getting hickeys, Nicholas Leister," I said, trying to control my voice.

He walked over, reached out to pull my hair back, and looked closer. "I'm sorry, I didn't realize," he said.

"Sure," I said, pushing him away just as he started to stroke me. "I've already told you, Nicholas, I'm not a cow—I don't want anyone branding me."

He laughed so hard, I wanted to hit him.

"Come on, Freckles, we fought enough yesterday. Let's relax in peace." He pulled me into a hug. I was stiff as a board, but he soon grabbed my hair and pulled my head back, forcing me to look at him.

"Forgive me, and I'll do whatever you want," he said.

"What?" I responded.

His eyes clouded over. "Anything you want. I'm serious. If it comes out of those lips, I'll do it. I'm yours."

I knew what that perverted mind of his was thinking. I smiled, enjoying the situation, feeling powerful.

"Fine," I said, wrapping my hands around his neck. "There is something I want you to do."

10

Nick

"No fucking way," I said.

We were parking in front of an animal shelter.

"You said anything," my insane girlfriend responded, getting out of the car, excited as a five-year-old.

"I was talking about sex."

Noah laughed. "I know. But since this is about me, not you, you're going to buy me a little kitty."

Again with the fucking cat! I hated cats—they were stupid; you couldn't even train them. Plus, they were so needy. They crawled all over you constantly. I preferred a dog. I preferred *my* dog, dammit! The dog I'd had to leave at my dad's house because my apartment building didn't allow them.

"I've told you a million times, there's no way I'm keeping a cat in my apartment."

Noah glared at me and shook her head. Before she could start back up with her nonsense, I pulled her into my chest and covered her mouth with one hand.

"I'm not buying you a cat. Period."

Her tongue started licking at my hand so I'd let her go. I

squeezed her ribs, and it reminded me of the way she'd poked me that morning. We were both ungodly ticklish.

I let her go before I lost my nerve.

"Nicholas!" she shrieked.

"You slobbered all over me," I said, wiping my hand on my pants.

She ignored me. "Okay, fine. If you won't buy me a cat, I'll buy it myself." She turned on her heels and walked into what must have been any man's hell. I followed her, exasperated, smelling animal fur, piss, and shit, hearing hamsters running back and forth and cats meowing, all of it so loud, I had to struggle not to drag Noah out.

With an Olympic effort at pretending I wasn't there, she turned to the employee behind the counter, a young guy, her age, probably. His eyes lit up when he saw her.

"How can I help you?"

She looked over, and when she saw I wasn't going to do anything, she turned indifferently to the guy and said, "I want to adopt a cat."

Coming out from behind the counter with a huge smile on his face, happy to help her any way he could, the attendant headed down a hallway, and I followed behind Noah.

"This way. Just yesterday, we picked up some kittens from a parking deck. Someone had abandoned them there, and they can't be more than six weeks old."

Noah said a long and aggrieved "oh." I rolled my eyes while the jerkoff took us back to a room with a bunch of cages full of cats of all shapes and colors. Some were sleeping, some mewing, some just being a pain in the ass.

"Here they are," he said, showing us a cage at the end of a row. Noah walked over as if it concealed a magic treasure.

"They're so tiny!" she said in that voice girls have when they talk to kittens or babies.

I came up behind her and looked at the mangy beasts lying on a blanket. Three were gray with white spots on their paws and head. One was black all over. Right away, they gave me a weird feeling.

"Look how they're playing," the guy said in a little-bitch voice. I scowled at him and edged over to Noah.

"Can I pick one up?" she asked, using all her feminine charms.

"Yeah, whichever one you want."

Of course. So which did Noah pick?

The black one, obviously.

"He's the calmest one. I haven't seen him playing since they got here."

The other three were anything but—they were jumping all over and slapping each other with their paws. They'd probably given the poor runt one hell of a time.

Noah brought the kitten close to her chest and caressed it like a mother holding her baby. The damned thing started meowing, and at that point, I knew it was game over.

I sighed.

"Look, Nick," she said, her eyes tender.

The cat was ugly as hell, black, its hair standing on end, but I knew Noah wasn't the type to pick the cutest or the most playful one. She would go for the outcast, the one that had been ignored, the one nobody loved... That reminded me of myself.

"Fine, shit, you can keep the fucking cat," I conceded.

A huge smile crossed her face.

The employee led us to the counter where I had to sign a ton of papers promising to take care of the cat and get it vaccinated and a bunch of other nonsense. Noah started picking through a small selection of supplies for sale, and when she came back, she had a ton of stupid toys for this animal that didn't even have a name.

"You gonna pay for that?" I said, needling her. I didn't give a shit about the money; I just wanted to let a little air out of her balloon.

"You said whatever I wanted," she reminded me, grabbing a collar, some food bowls, and a soft blue bed, and laying them on the counter.

The damned cat was in a little cage, which they handed over to us to take him away.

"I hope he adapts well and that you all enjoy him," the cashier said, eyes on Noah. "Don't forget to take him to the vet in a couple of weeks to get him fixed and take care of his vaccines."

Fixed... Well, now I felt bad for the poor guy.

Ten minutes later, we were on our way to my apartment. Finally, I would be able to be with her and do what I'd been thinking about for months.

I turned to look at her, and an involuntary smile crossed my face. She looked just like my little sister did when she got a new toy.

"What are you going to name him?" I asked, pulling off the freeway and heading into my neighborhood.

"Huh. I don't know yet..." she said, carefully petting the Nameless One.

"Don't call him something stupid like Nala or Simba, please," I asked, parking in my spot. I got out and opened her door. Seeing Noah almost intoxicated, I glared at that animal that was trying to take my spotlight.

"I think I'll call him N," she said as we walked toward the elevator.

"N?" I repeated, doubtful. Had she lost her damned mind?

Offended, she replied, "Yeah, N. For you and me, for Nick and Noah."

I laughed. "I think you had too much caffeine this morning."

She ignored me as we walked into my apartment.

"You're going to have to take care of him when I'm not around," she said, letting him out in the middle of the room and watching him investigate his surroundings.

"In your dreams. Your cat, your responsibility," I said, dropping all its accessories on the floor.

She gave me a salty look, and I pulled her close before we could start arguing again.

"You're the one person in the world who can make me give in at times like this," I said, leaning over to kiss her neck. Noah closed in to give me better access. Her skin was soft and smelled so good... I saw the hickey I'd left on her... I liked it; it drove me wild to see the marks my kisses had left on her, but I'd never say that aloud, knowing how much it would piss her off.

"What if I told you that I love the idea of sharing a pet with you?" she said suddenly. Seeing my confusion, she shrugged, as if she felt guilty. "It's going to be ours. Our cat, both of ours, like we're its parents."

That made me take a deep breath. I knew that phrase had something much deeper hidden behind it, something that would never let her go, and that made my blood boil. I kissed her gently on the lips.

"It's fine. I'll take care of K," I said, stroking her hair, hoping to make light of the situation.

She smacked me jokingly. "His name's N!"

I laughed, picked her up, and sat her on the kitchen counter. "There's something I wanted to talk to you about," I said, feeling unnerved, with no idea how she was going to react. "I want you to come live with me when you start school."

11

Noah

"ARE YOU SERIOUS?"

Go live with him? I'd need to think about that calmly because I could tell from looking at him that he was serious.

"Please," he said, putting his hands on my cheeks. "Please say yes."

That was too much. I couldn't be in that situation just then. I got down from the counter and walked toward the bedroom.

"Nicholas, I'm eighteen years old," I said. "Eighteen." I repeated it in case he didn't get it. As anxiety took hold of my insides, the thought that we weren't at the same stage, that he needed more than I could give, scared me in a way it never had before.

"You're way more mature than any girl my age. You don't even seem like an eighteen-year-old. You know that, Noah. If you lived here, we could see each other every single day, every night." He leaned against the counter and crossed his arms. "Do you not want to live with me? Is it that?"

Ugh. How could I explain to him that it had nothing to do with wanting or not wanting? How could I tell him I was just too young to take that step without getting scared? Or that what actually worried me was that we *would* live together and he'd realize how fucked up I still was because of all the things that had happened to me in the past, that he'd end up getting tired of me or, worse, dropping me?

"Of course I want to," I said, approaching him cautiously. He looked at me, not moving a muscle. "What I'm afraid of is we'll go too fast and end up ruining what we have."

He shook his head. "That's ridiculous, Noah. You and I can't go too fast; we're already moving at the speed of light. That's just how things are with you and me. You know me—you're perfectly aware I would never have even considered taking this step with anyone but you. And if I'm doing it, it's because I know it's right for us, it's what we need, because I can't be far from you...and you can't be far from me either."

Calm down, I told myself, *calm down...* Living with Nicholas... it would be like a dream, it really would, seeing him every day, loving him every day, always feeling safe with him...

"I'm scared I won't be what you expect," I admitted, my voice quavering.

His body slackened, he stretched out, and his finger traced a line across my cheek. As his eyes roved my face slowly, I felt he was savoring every one of my features.

"I want to see that face of yours when I wake up," he confessed, and now his finger stopped on my lower lip. "I want to kiss your lips before I go to sleep," he continued in a hoarse voice. "I want to feel you every time I go to bed. To dream with you in my arms. To watch you while you sleep. To take care of you every second of the day."

I looked up and saw in his eyes that each of those words was coming directly from his heart. He was serious. He loved me. He wanted me with him. I felt my heart speed up; something inside me swelled with happiness. I was melting—how could I love him so much? How could I give him so much of myself, and why did it feel so natural?

"I'll do it. I'll come live with you," I said, not even believing my own words.

A radiant smile spread across his face. "Say it again," he asked me.

"I'll come live with you. We'll live together."

No more nightmares, no more fears. With him next to me, I would slowly recover. With him, I could get over anything. He touched my face, pulled me close, covered my lips with his. I felt his smile. I made him happy, it was true, I could see it, and I loved it.

"God, I love you so much!" he shouted, squeezing me around the waist. I hugged him and laughed as I looked over his shoulder and saw N staring at us from the end of the hallway, small, black, with glowing eyes. The three of us would live together. Nick, N, and me.

———————

Unfortunately, the next few days flew by. My mother had no idea I'd be going to live with Nick as soon as our trip was over, and I wasn't planning on telling her until I absolutely had to. He had been in a good mood, but it got worse and worse as the date of my departure came closer and the idea of me being gone for a month became more palpable. He was taking my going to live with him seriously: he had emptied half his closet and his dresser so I would have space for my clothes, which I took over on the sly when I visited him. The apartment, which had been a little too macho for my taste, was now turning into something more welcoming: we'd gone together to buy colorful cushions, and I'd made him change out the dark sheets in his room for some white ones that made the place look homier. Nick was happy. For all he cared, I could paint the place pink. As long as I was there, it didn't matter to him. I had taken some of my favorite books, and my mother seemed not to have noticed.

The city was already getting hot. Gone were the days when you needed a sweater or long pants. Nick had taken me to the beach almost every day. We had swum, and I had tried unsuccessfully to learn how to surf...but still, the day came when Mom and I had to go, and we wouldn't be back till mid-August.

My God, I was so excited, but I didn't know what I'd do being separated from Nick for so long!

We were in my room, with a suitcase open on my bed. Nick was sitting at my desk, playing with N and deliberately ignoring me. He'd been crabby for two days. He didn't want to hear a word about my trip, he certainly didn't want to talk about it, but there I was, ready to leave in a couple of hours, and he'd need to get used to the idea. He had taken things out of my backpack and put them away five times without me realizing it. He'd even hidden my passport, which I found three days later among his work papers. He had threatened to tie me to the bed if I didn't stay. I had tried my best to ignore his attempts to sabotage the trip because I knew he was upset about it, as much as or maybe more than I was.

"I'm warning you, the heat in Spain is awful, and you don't like shellfish, so you're going to hate it. Plus, the Eiffel Tower's overrated... You get to the top, and you're like, is that it? Don't expect much out of England either. It's not special, the weather's garbage, and the people are stiff and boring..."

"Are you going to keep being a pain in the ass?" I cut him off, losing my cool. I walked over and took N out of his hands. He'd bought him a stupid toy that he was crazy about. Nick's arms were covered in scratches.

I tried to turn back around, but he pulled me and N into his lap. The cat was almost squashed between us.

Seemingly unsure of whether he should say what was on his mind, Nick finally asked me not to go. I rolled my eyes. Not again.

"Go, N, sic him!" I said to the cat, lifting him and placing him in front of Nick's face. "Or no, better behave, actually. You don't want this psycho throwing you down a drainpipe." I cuddled him and kissed him on his fuzzy dark head.

Tense, Nicholas said, "So now you're ignoring me?"

"Once I've answered the same question ten thousand times, yeah, I think I'll move on to ignoring you," I replied. But I couldn't be offended at that grimace: I would miss those eyes, those hands, that body, all of it...! "I don't like to repeat myself."

My words had gotten to him, obviously.

"Put that fucking cat down and look at me," he grumbled, taking N out of my hands and placing him on the floor. I met his eyes, ready for a fight.

"I don't want you doing anything stupid or dangerous," he warned me, holding on to my hips, almost as if he thought he could keep me there that way. "Don't drink, and don't start conversations with strangers."

"Are you listening to yourself?" I jerked away. Why did he have to be so jealous and controlling? I couldn't stand it. Did he not trust me, dammit?

I started stuffing things into my suitcase without looking at him, then tugged on the zipper, and...dammit! It wouldn't close!

He pushed past me and tugged it until it unsnagged.

With resignation, he admitted, "I'm going to miss you." He looked crestfallen. He continued: "What am I going to do without you?"

I tried to keep calm as I stood on tiptoe to get a better view of him.

"Before you know it, I'll be back, and you'll have me all to yourself. And once I'm back, I'll move in," I promised him, hoping that would fix his mood.

He rubbed my arms up and down their length. How could his attitude change so quickly?

"I love you, Freckles. I don't want anything bad to happen to you. It makes me sick to think I won't be there to take care of you while you're away."

I felt something warm inside me. I was going to miss him, all right. Terribly.

I kissed him tenderly on the lips. "I love you, too. I'm going to be fine…"

In his eyes, I could see those words weren't enough, and I realized this trip would be a major test of our relationship. I had no idea how we were going to deal with so much time apart.

12

Nick

I TOOK THEM TO THE AIRPORT. MY FATHER SAID HIS GOODBYES AT the house because he had work to take care of. I wasn't at all amused to have to spend my last hour with Noah with her mother in the back seat of the car, but once again, I just had to deal with it. The whole trip pissed me off, I'd made that evident, but there was nothing I could do.

I glanced at Noah, who was sitting there quiet and pensive. She had insisted on bringing the stupid cat along and was petting him as she stared absently out the window. I reached out, grabbed her hand, and guided it back over toward the gearshift. I felt a hole in my chest. I hated it! For Christ's sake, it was just a month—it wasn't that big a deal! Since when had I turned so fucking dependent?

I had to get a grip. I couldn't be going crazy like this just because I couldn't see her for a month. I needed to clear my head. That separation would be a test to see how we could deal with being apart. When she saw I was staring at her, she smiled, but I could see the sorrow in her eyes.

Her mother, on the other hand, had a huge grin on her face. Sher couldn't have been more pleased. Why did she not mind being away from her husband for a month? I didn't get it, and unconsciously I found myself squeezing Noah's hand even tighter.

When we reached LAX, I parked and got the suitcases out while Raffaella went for a cart. Noah edged over and kissed me on the lips.

"What are you doing?" I asked, trying to sound amused, even if I wasn't.

"Just getting a kiss in before Mom comes back." Did that mean she wouldn't kiss me in front of her mom when we were inside?

I didn't know, but I kept the thought to myself, knowing that for my part, I would kiss her wherever and whenever I wanted.

A half hour later, we'd checked their bags, and Raffaella was agitating to get to their gate. It was still an hour till boarding. Honestly, she was exasperating.

"Mom, you go ahead. I need to be alone with Nicholas for a little bit before I leave," Noah said. Her mother's only answer was a furrowed brow. She looked at me, at Noah, and at the cat. Her way of doing it made me feel suddenly protective. After all, that was our cat.

At last, she said goodbye to me and walked off, leaving us alone.

I wrapped an arm around Noah's shoulder and pulled her close, kissing the top of her head while we walked at a snail's pace toward security.

"I shouldn't feel so sad, Nick," she confessed.

It was true, dammit! We shouldn't be so depressed. It was a month... There were couples that didn't see each other for a whole year. I didn't want Noah to leave feeling sad. I didn't want her to suffer, especially not over something that was supposed to make her happy. I reproached myself for trying so hard to get her to stay. If I'd been supportive of that trip from the beginning, maybe she wouldn't be so down right now and wouldn't have that sorrow in her eyes.

"Don't be, Freckles," I said, pulling her into my chest. N meowed. He wasn't enjoying being squeezed between the two of us. "What I meant to say was that Spain is nice and warm, and the Eiffel Tower's beautiful. You'll love it." She smiled when I said this. "I'll see you when you get back. I'll be waiting for you with this little creature." I nodded toward N.

"Nicholas, please take care of him, don't even joke about forgetting to feed him, and don't give him alcohol, please," she said.

"I just did that once. It was wine, and anyway, the cat loved it," I replied.

She hugged him close to her once more, then passed him to me, saying, "Here, take him." I held him up with one hand, while the other cupped Noah's chin as I kissed her.

"I love you," I said, savoring her lips for the last time in a month.

"I love you more," she said.

I watched her leave, and my stomach was in knots. Her long hair in that ponytail hanging down from the top of her head, her legs in those tight shorts...she was going to catch the eye of every guy she came across. I tried to put the thought out of my mind. Now it was just N and me.

As soon as I got back home, I felt down. I dropped the cat; he could go entertain himself while I looked through the apartment with longing. I had no idea what I was going to do for those four weeks without her. I knew my life had changed in a way I could never imagine. I couldn't even remember what it felt like to be single, without anyone at my side. It was like I could only see my past through a blurry lens, as if Noah had marked a definitive break.

The apartment was impeccable. Noah was no neat freak, but the day before she left, she got a little hysterical and had to make sure every single thing was where it was supposed to be. That wasn't like her; she only did it when she was really stressed. That was something I had figured out in recent months.

It made me nervous knowing she was a thousand miles away, flying across the country to New York, where she had a layover before continuing to Italy. I'd never had a fear of flying, and I'd caught more planes than I could even count, but now that Noah was up there...I was surprised how horrible images of disasters flooded my mind. I saw the plane malfunctioning, plunging into the water, getting highjacked... The possibilities were infinite, and there was nothing I could do to calm that anxiety in the middle of my chest.

Five hours later, my phone rang, waking me. I hadn't even realized I'd fallen asleep. I woke up disoriented and unsettled.

"Nick?" she said on the other line.

"Are you there?" I asked, trying to focus.

"Yeah, we're at JFK. It's huge. I'm so sad we can't stop here and go into the city. It must be incredible." Noah sounded happy, and that helped my mood a bit, even if I did miss her.

"I'm calling dibs on New York," I said, and she chuckled.

"What?" I could hear a racket around her. I could imagine men in suits with rolling bags heading into the city that never sleeps, mothers with irritating snot-nosed kids, the woman coming over the speakers calling out to people about to miss their flights...

"I'm saying I want to be the one who shows you New York. That's what I meant." I got up off the sofa and walked to the kitchen sink.

"Promise me we'll come here together, Nick. In wintertime, when there's snow," she exclaimed. The idea must have excited her.

I smiled like a dummy imagining me and Noah together in New York, walking the streets, stopping at the cafés... We'd have hot chocolate, and I'd take her to the Empire State

Building, and when we got to the top, I'd kiss her until we were both out of breath.

"I promise, babe," I whispered.

I heard someone calling Noah from far away. It had to be her mom.

"Nick, I gotta go," she said hurriedly. "I'll call you once we're in Italy. I love you!"

Before I could respond, she hung up.

———————

Noah reached Italy safe and sound and called only briefly. According to her, any more would have cost a fortune. I wanted to tell her not to worry about the phone bill, but she insisted we wait and speak over Skype when she could use the Wi-Fi at the hotel. The problem was the time difference was huge, and she would be out when I was sleeping and vice versa.

The days passed, and the Skype calls were brief summaries of what she'd been doing during the day. Whenever she called me, she was exhausted, and we never talked for more than five minutes. I hated that. I hated being so far away from her, not getting to talk to her for hours, not touching her, but I'd promised myself I wouldn't sour her trip. So, whenever we did connect, I put on my best face, even if inside I was cursing the day she left.

I devoted most of my time to going to the gym and surfing, and on the weekends, I visited Madison. The Saturday after Noah left, I hopped in the car and headed straight for Las Vegas. Lion wanted to come along. I was glad, since I hadn't seen him all week. Maddie already knew him, and they got along great.

"I'm curious to see how you'll deal with three more weeks without Noah," Lion said as we hurtled down the interstate. It would be nighttime when we got to Vegas, so we wouldn't see my sister till the next day. We'd reserved a room at Caesar's. It was true that we were there for family reasons, but that didn't mean we wouldn't indulge in a couple of drinks or hit the blackjack tables... When all was said and done, Vegas was still Vegas.

"I mean, I don't blame you," he went on, raising his voice helplessly. "Jenna just left with her parents for that stupid cruise two days ago, and I'm already climbing the walls. And I'm luckier than you: she's coming back in five days."

That was the first time Jenna had gone on vacation and left Lion behind. The year before, they'd come to the Bahamas with Noah and me, and apart from that, she'd only left for a weekend with her parents in the Hamptons. I guess all the parents had gotten together that year and decided to fuck us over, dragging our girlfriends off to the ends of the earth.

"I can't wait to have her living with me. When she moves in, all the bullshit will be over, and her mother will have to take our relationship seriously," I said. It was three in the afternoon, so that meant Noah would already be in bed. If only I could be in bed with her at that moment!

Lion didn't respond. It was weird for him to clam up like that, and I stared at him for a second before asking him what was up. His mood seemed to have gone south. I guess neither of us was especially good company just then.

Looking out the window, he replied, "I just wish I had a place I could take Jenna to, somewhere we could live together, somewhere up to her standards. Not my shit apartment."

I was surprised to hear him say that. Ever since I'd met him, more than five years ago now, I'd never known him to complain about money, not once. We were from totally different worlds: I had a trust fund, and at the firm, I was making a cushy salary. I'd never had to worry about material matters, they were always taken care of when I grew up, but still, I knew how hard it was to try to make it when you didn't have a millionaire father watching over you. The year I lived with Lion, I learned money doesn't grow on trees, that there were people out there who had it hard, who struggled to make enough just to eat. He couldn't count on his older brother, who was about to get out of the pen for the third time—worse, he had to foot the bill for him, his apartment, the garage.

I'd raced and fought and all that not just because I liked it but because it was a way to help Lion out. We were brothers, even if we came from different places, even if there were times—like now—when the monumental differences between us became clear.

"You know Jenna doesn't care where you live, Lion," I said, feeling bad as I did. Lion shouldn't have to go through this; he shouldn't have to be thinking about such things. There was nobody who deserved to live a calm, happy life more than him. Jenna would never be a burden for him—she was like me; she probably had a trust fund waiting for her when she turned twenty-one that would take care of all her problems. I mean, her father was an oil magnate!

"I do care, though. You think I don't know who she is, what she's used to?" There was resentment in his tone. "I'll never be able to give her even half of what she needs."

"Not everything in life is money."

Lion laughed. "That's exactly what a rich kid would say."

Okay, that was going too far, and on any other occasion, I would have told him to go fuck himself, but I knew there was something sincere and deep behind those words, something that really was getting at him.

I didn't respond, and he didn't say anything else. We just turned up the music, and we didn't even stop for lunch.

When we arrived, our mood improved: it was impossible not to be affected by the atmosphere of Las Vegas, the people, the attractions, the lights, not to mention the hotel... Caesar's was something else. It was practically a city of its own, with boutiques featuring all the finest brands... The girls would have gone crazy there. Maybe it wasn't Italy, but the place was top-notch; there was no denying it. Our room was on the west side of the hotel, which was huge, and we had to walk forever to reach it.

"What do you want to do?" Lion asked, going out on the balcony to light up a cigarette.

"Have a couple of drinks," I said. I didn't want to tell him this, but every time I went to see Madison, I got a little depressed. I hated knowing my mother was so close; I just couldn't take it.

We went back downstairs to one of the many bars in the hotel, one that was right alongside the casino. Lion was a card shark, and I imagined he'd play a game or two before we went back to our room. It was late, and I was tired after the drive, but I enjoyed myself, drinking a few glasses of aged rum to calm my anxiety and lift my spirits.

"You in the mood for some gambling?" Lion asked thirty minutes later, once we had a decent buzz going on.

"You go. I'd rather stay here," I said, taking out my phone to check my messages in case Noah had written.

I'd sent her a text not long before, half joking, half-serious, asking if she needed me to send her something so she'd remember me. We hadn't talked for two days, and I was pretty sure she must have just arrived in London.

She had responded:

Having something to remember you by would mean it was possible to forget you.

Sarcastically, I replied:

What is that, Shakespeare?

A second later, I could see she was texting me back, and I felt a warmth inside myself I only ever felt when I thought about her.

> I've just been here two hours and I guess all the literature written here is soaking into me. Anyway, if you don't like romantic messages, don't send them, idiot.

Along with that came a long row of frowny-face emojis. I grinned.

> I'm going to give you something more than just romantic messages when you come back from that dumb trip. We don't need a bunch of old dead writers. You and I are poetry, my love.

I had no idea how I was going to make it through those next two and a half weeks.

———

The next morning, I got up early and jumped in the shower, trying to put on a good face before I saw my sister. I was planning on picking her up, then meeting Lion. After that, we'd decide what to do.

I drove out of the touristy area in that insane city and soon reached the ritzy development where my sister lived. I got out and put on my sunglasses, regretting how much I'd drunk the night before. In the best of cases, my mood those past few days had been pretty bad, and I didn't feel like having to deal with any nonsense or unpleasant surprises. And so, when I saw the woman holding hands with my sister and walking toward me, I had to take a few deep breaths and remind myself that there was a six-year-old girl in front of me. Otherwise, I would have gotten in the car and peeled out without looking back.

The tall blond woman walking toward me was the last person in the world I wanted to see.

"Nick!" my sister shouted, jerking away from my mother and running toward me. Ignoring the jabbing pain in my temples provoked by that high-pitched shriek only Madison was capable of, I picked her up off the ground as soon as she reached me.

"Hey, Princess!" I greeted her, hugging her and ignoring my mother, who walked up to us.

"Hello, Nicholas," she said timidly, standing stiffly the way she always did. She hadn't changed much since the last time I'd seen her, some eight months ago, when she and her stupid husband had neglected my sister and she'd ended up in the hospital with diabetic ketoacidosis.

"What are you doing here?" I hissed, setting Maddie down close to me. She stood there between us, grabbed my hand, and reached up for her mother's as well.

"Finally, the three of us are together!" Madison shouted joyfully. I don't know how many times she'd asked me to come visit her at home, to play with her in her room, to come to her birthday party. All those requests conveyed a single intention: getting my mother and me together in the same room.

"I want to talk to you," she said, tense but trying not to show it. She was impeccably dressed, her short blond hair pulled back with a ridiculous headband. She was just like the women who lived in my neighborhood, like all the women I hated for being so dumb, so frivolous. But her looks meant she'd always been treated like a queen bee by every man she ever met. They all idolized her, and they all wanted to have sex with her.

"I'm not interested in anything you have to say to me," I replied, trying to keep my tone of voice from showing the effect she had on me—how little I could stand her presence.

Memories from my childhood began to crowd my mind: my

mother putting me down at bedtime, my mother defending me from my father, my mother waiting for me on Sunday with pancakes... But after those memories came others...others I didn't want to relive.

"Please, Nick—"

"Nick!" Madison interrupted her. "Mommy wants to come with us. She told me so."

I scowled at my mother, and the fury in my eyes must have been intimidating because she rushed to reply.

"Madison, it'll be better if you two go alone. I need to get my hair cut, darling. We'll see each other tonight." She bent over and kissed the top of Maddie's head. It was weird to see that gesture of affection. I guess a part of me thought she'd be cold with her or indifferent—anything but sweet. My mother could be sweet, of course, but she could be a bitch, too.

Maddie just looked up at us. I wanted to get out of there, now. It took all the self-control I could muster to remain cool when my mother stepped forward and kissed me on the cheek. What the fuck was that about? What was she thinking?

"Take care, Nicholas," she said, then went back inside.

I didn't devote even another second of attention to her, turning instead to my sister and smiling as best I could.

"What kind of torments do you have cooked up for me today?" I asked her, picking her up and sitting her on my shoulder. She started laughing, and I knew that whatever sorrow she'd felt before was now gone. With me, she was never going to be sad. I'd promised myself that years ago, the very first time I met her.

———————

Lion was waiting for us at the door to the hotel. I could see in his face that he was as hungover as I was, and I couldn't help but laugh when Maddie took off running to hug him, shouting in that hellish screech.

Lion picked her up by one leg and dangled her. I laughed as she shrieked like a banshee. Only a crazy person would feel safe leaving a little girl like my sister with two wildcats like Lion and me.

"Where to, missus?" my friend asked that little monster with her big blue eyes and golden blond hair.

Maddie looked all around, unable to decide. The possibilities were endless. We were in the fun capital of the world.

"Can we go see the sharks?" she asked, jumping up and down.

I rolled my eyes.

"Again?" We had gone to the aquarium a million times, but my sister, unlike most girls her age, loved to stand in front of the glass wall and provoke the killer sharks.

So we went there after lunch. My sister was happy and kept running back and forth. Lion watched her, and they acted like idiots in front of the sand tiger shark, which honestly was scary as hell. In the meantime, I took my phone out to see if Noah had been in touch, but there was nothing from her. I decided to use some stronger medicine.

"Hey, midget, come here!"

Maddie stared daggers at me. "I'm not a midget!" she protested.

Whatever you say, I thought.

"Come here, let's send Noah a photo."

Her eyes lit up when I mentioned Noah's name. I imagined that was the same way my face must look whenever I talked to her or spent time with her.

I held my phone up for a selfie and pulled Maddie in tight.

"Stick your tongue out, Nick, like this!" she said, and her own little pink tongue poked out between her lips. I laughed, did the same, and snapped the photo, sending it with the message:

I miss you, Freckles, and this little monster with me does, too. I love you.

13

Noah

WHEN I WOKE UP THAT MORNING, THE FIRST THING I DID WAS turn on my phone. The night before I had fallen asleep before I could respond to Nick's last message.

He had sent another four since then. I smiled like an idiot when I saw the photo he had sent of him and Maddie sticking their tongues out and smiling. He was so handsome, with that black hair all mussed up...and that little girl who looked so much like him and at the same time so different... I knew that when he went to see Maddie, it was hard for him to stay in a good mood, and I worried about him during those hours of sorrow.

I missed him. I wanted so badly to hear his voice, to have him beside me.

Luckily my mother had her own room, so I was alone when I dialed his number. I waited anxiously for him to respond. It was late in the US, so he was probably still sleeping, but I didn't mind waking him, I was so impatient to talk to him.

"Noah?" He picked up on the fifth ring.

"I miss you," I said simply.

I heard him sitting up and imagined him turning on the lamp

on the nightstand and running his hand over his face, waking up for me.

"Don't wake me up just to tell me that, Freckles," he said with a grunt. "Tell me you're having a blast, that you're not even thinking about me, because otherwise, that stupid trip doesn't make any sense."

I smiled, sad, and rested my head on my pillow.

"I am having fun, you know that, but it's not the same without you," I said, knowing that despite what he said, he was happy to hear I missed him. "How was it with Maddie?" I asked, wishing I could have been with him. I loved going with him to see his sister: it showed me a Nick who was completely different, one who was sweet, patient, fun, protective.

After a pause, he said, "Mom brought her." His tone was one I knew very well. "If only you could have seen her...looking all stiff like a forty-year-old Barbie doll, forcing me to treat her in a way she definitely doesn't deserve just because Maddie was in front of us."

Shit. His mother. I still remembered how upset he'd been after seeing her in the hospital when Maddie got sick. The desperation in his voice, his eyes damp after seeing her for the first time in years.

"She shouldn't force the situation like that," I complained. I understood that Nick's mother might want to have contact with him again—after all, he was her son—but that wasn't the way to do it, putting him on the spot.

"I don't know what the hell she wants, but I don't want to see her again. I don't give a shit about her or her life." His tone was furious, but there was sorrow in it, too, even if he was good at covering it up. I knew him, though, and I knew there was a part of him that was hungry to find out what his mother had to say to him.

"Nicholas, don't you think that..." I started, but he cut me off straightaway.

"Don't go down that road, Noah. Forget it, don't even try. There's no way I'm talking with that woman or even being in the same room with her again." His tone was frightening. That was only the second time I'd even considered suggesting he see his mother again. The first time, he'd lost his mind. There was something he wasn't telling me. It was impossible that he hated her so much just because she'd abandoned him when he was a boy. That was horrible, sure, but I knew there was something else, something he wasn't telling me.

"Sure, sorry," I said, trying to calm things down.

I could hear him almost panting on the other line.

"What I'd like right now is to be inside you, forget all this bullshit, and just make love to you for hours and hours. I curse the second you left."

I could feel butterflies in my stomach when I heard him say that. He was mad, but it didn't keep me from warming up inside. I wanted to be in his arms, too, wanted him to kiss me all over, hold me down with his big hands, push me into the mattress, so hard but so tender and careful at the same time...

"I'm sorry this trip has been so terrible for you, I really am. I'd like to be with you right now, too." I tried to make my words reach him, but I knew Nicholas was someone who needed contact to feel good, to feel loved... I wasn't sure if my words would suffice to make him understand how much I loved him and how bad I felt when I thought about him suffering because of the thing with his mother and with no one able to help him but me because it was something he never talked about with anyone else, not even with Lion.

"Don't worry about me, Noah, I'm fine," he said a second later.

A part of me wanted him to wish me a pleasant trip, but the other undoubtedly wanted to upbraid me for ever leaving.

I heard my mother waking up in the next room over. We had slept late, and if we wanted to do all the things we had planned that day, we needed to get started.

"I have to go," I told him, wishing I could talk to him for hours. He was silent on the other end of the line.

"Be careful. I love you," he finally said and hung up.

The trip was amazing. It was true that I missed Nick, but I couldn't believe I was lucky enough to be in all those amazing places. Italy I'd loved: we had seen the Colosseum, had walked through the narrow streets, had eaten tortellini and the best raspberry gelato I'd ever had. Now we'd been in London for two days, and I couldn't feel more in love with the city. Everything about it seemed straight from a Dickens novel, and all the books I had read across the years were set in that city, all those romantic period tales of women walking or riding in a horse-drawn carriage through Hyde Park, with their chaperones... The buildings were elegant, old but beautiful and classy. Piccadilly was full of people: executives in suit jackets with briefcases, hippies in colored hats, tourists like myself, milling in crowds and admiring the lights of that street. Harrods fascinated me, even if the prices were mind-blowing, but I guess for people like the Leisters, it was no big deal to pay ten pounds for a chocolate bonbon.

My mother was as crazy about it all as I was, but she was more used to it because she and William had traveled all over. They'd gone to London for their honeymoon and then spent two weeks in Dubai. My mother was clearly on a different level from me: I could tell from how she reacted to everything we saw. I was constantly freaking out; even the dumbest sights left me slack-jawed. My mother laughed, but at the same time, I knew, however many places she'd visited, she felt incredibly fortunate.

The days passed, and soon we'd been away for almost two weeks. We still had France and Spain left, and I still had yet to share a room with my mother. It had been three days since I'd talked to Nick, and I'd always been able to do so from my private bedroom in our suite. But in France, they mixed up the reservation, and we wound up sharing not only a room but a bed as well.

"Do you like Paris?" my mother asked as she took off her earrings. She was already in her pajamas, while I was wrapped in a towel, my hair still dripping, after just coming out of the shower.

"The city's gorgeous," I responded, putting on my underwear. I turned to the mirror where my mother was brushing her hair, and I could see her eyes linger for a second on the scar on my stomach.

I shouldn't have stood there without anything on in front of her. I knew she got sad every time she laid eyes on the evidence of the time I'd almost been killed. Bad memories were surging up in her, I could tell, and I wanted her to be happy again, to think about something nice before she started blaming herself for something that wasn't her fault.

"Have you talked to Nicholas?" she asked a minute later, when I had gotten into bed in my pajamas and was waiting for her to finish putting on all the lotions and face creams she'd brought.

"Yeah, he said to tell you hi," I lied, hoping she wouldn't notice. Mom and Nicholas were in a bad phase, so I tried never to mention them to each other when we talked.

She nodded, pensive.

"Are you happy with him, Noah?" she asked abruptly.

I didn't expect that question, and I waited a few seconds before responding. The answer was easy: of course, I was happy with him, happier than I'd ever been with anybody. I remembered then when we were in the Bahamas and we still weren't technically going out yet, and Nick had asked me the same thing. Was I happy? I told him that with him, I was. And what about when we weren't together? Was I completely happy in that hotel room, miles and miles away, even knowing that he loved me and that we'd be together again soon?

"Your silence is worrying me."

I looked up and realized she had misinterpreted my hesitancy.

"No. Of course. Of course I'm happy with him, Mom. I love him," I explained.

Her brow furrowed as she observed me. "You don't look especially convinced." Despite those words, she did seem somewhat relieved.

"The problem is, I love him too much," I said. "Without him, my life wouldn't have any meaning, and that worries me."

My mother closed her eyes for a moment. When she opened them again, she said, "That doesn't make a bit of sense."

Of course it did, and I was completely serious. With Nick I was safe. He protected me from my nightmares, gave me the security I had been missing my entire life. He was the only person I could tell my problems to. When we weren't together, I felt I was losing control of myself; thoughts that shouldn't exist and feelings I shouldn't feel bombarded me.

"It makes perfect sense, Mom, and I'd have thought you of all people would understand, seeing how in love you are with William."

She shook her head. "You're wrong there. No man should be the reason for your existence, understand me?" The color had drained from her face, and there was something unsettling in her expression. "My life revolved around a man for a long time, a man who didn't even deserve a minute of my time. When I was with your father, I thought he was the only person who'd ever put up with me. I came to believe that no one else would love me, that I'd be totally alone if I didn't have him by my side."

My heart started pounding. My mom almost never talked about my father.

"The pain he inflicted on me was nothing compared to the fear I felt of not being with him... Men like your father get inside your head, and then they do what they want with you. Never let a man take control of your soul because you never know what he'll do with it: hold it and venerate it, or let it crumble to pieces in his hands."

"Nicholas isn't like that," I shouted, feeling every nerve in my body on edge. I didn't want to hear those words coming from my mother. I didn't want her to tell me how possible it was that my heart could get shattered again. Nicholas loved me; he would never leave me. He wasn't like my father—he couldn't be.

"I'm just saying that you come first and everyone else after... You need to always prioritize yourself, and if your happiness depends on a boy, you should reexamine things. Men come and go, but happiness is something you alone can cultivate."

I tried to keep her words from affecting me, from getting inside me, but they did, and powerfully. That night was a clear example of how much so.

My hands were tied; there was a blindfold over my eyes, not a bit of light could get in. My heart was beating at a thousand miles an hour, cold sweat covered my body, and fear had made my breathing speed up. I knew a panic attack was coming.

I was alone. There was no one there. Infinite darkness surrounded me, and that was what made me so afraid. Then someone took off the blindfold, my hands were no longer tied, and an intense light came through the window. I took off running down a long hallway with a voice inside me telling me I should stop because there was nothing good waiting for me on the other side.

But still, I went on, and when I ran through the door, I found an army of Ronnies aiming their pistols at me. I stopped, scared, shaking, feeling sweat soaking into my shirt.

"You know what you've got to do..." they all told me in unison.

I turned to find a pistol in a broken wooden box on the ground. Hands trembling, I grabbed it, and after a few seconds' indecision, I turned off the safety like a professional, got up, and turned to face the person in front of me.

"Don't, please..." my father begged, kneeling on the ground with a terrified look on his face.

My hand was shaking, but there was no turning back.

"Sorry, Papa..."

The sound of the shot made me open my eyes, but I didn't really wake up until I saw my mother there shaking me, frightened.

"My God, Noah!" she said as I sat up, disoriented. I was sweating and shaking like a leaf. I was bundled in blankets as though someone had tried to pin me down, and I'd been crying, as I realized when I brought my hands to my face.

"I...I had a nightmare," I confessed.

I saw the fear in my mother's blue eyes as she looked at me.

"Since when have you had those kinds of nightmares?" she asked, as if this confession changed how she thought of me. Her eyes were the furthest thing from placid. What I saw in them, once again, was...*that* look.

I wasn't about to tell her nightmares were a normal thing for me, something I only ever escaped from when I was with Nicholas. I didn't want her to worry, and I didn't want to admit that I had dreams of killing my father, that I was the one pulling the trigger, the one who spilled his blood on the ground.

I got up and went toward the bathroom, but my mom grabbed my arm to stop me.

"How long has this been going on, Noah?"

I needed distance from her. I needed that look of worry out of my mind. I didn't want her to feel bad again. I didn't want anyone to know what was going on inside me.

"Just this once, Mom. It's probably because we're in a strange room. You know new places make me nervous."

She didn't seem convinced, but she also didn't stop me when I pulled away, went to the bathroom, and locked the door.

I wanted to call Nicholas. He was the only one who could calm me down. But I didn't want to have to tell him what had happened—not like this, with this distance separating us. Not when he didn't have any idea about my nightmares either.

I splashed water on my face and tried to look relaxed. When I went back out, I ignored my mother and lay back down over the sheets.

Noah, please, don't...

My father's words went on echoing in my head until finally, somehow, I managed to go to sleep.

There were five days left until we went home. I was exhausted, not just physically but mentally. I desperately needed to sleep for twenty-four hours straight, and I would only be able to do it with Nick holding me in his arms. Luckily, I hadn't had to share another room with my mother, but the bags under my eyes were the perfect reminder of what had happened, and she wouldn't forget it.

Then again, there was the slight problem that I hadn't told her I wanted to move in with Nick. I knew she would lose it, but I had made my decision, and there was nothing she could do to make me change my mind.

My mother was more suspicious than usual, as if she could tell something she didn't like was going on, that something wasn't right. I tried to bring her nosy questions back to neutral territory, but I knew once we got back to California, there'd be hell to pay. That's why I was counting the days till I saw Nick again. With him, I'd have the strength to face her.

After all those years, with my father dead, my mother still couldn't protect me, because it was all in my mind, inside me... and even I had no idea what to do about it.

14

Nick

In just two days, Noah would be back. I don't think I'd ever been so anxious to see anyone in my entire life. I was torn between wanting to kiss her all over and wanting to choke her for leaving me here, and I didn't know which urge was stronger.

She had been weird the last few times we'd talked. She told me she was tired and was dying to see me, and I was counting the hours until it happened. I had fixed up the apartment—it was trashed before—had bought food, had even wiped the cat down with moist towelettes, for which he'd scratched me all over, and I'd had to count to a hundred not to throw the fur ball off the balcony.

I wanted us to have the best night of our lives when she returned. I wanted her to realize all she'd missed out on when she'd left me back here. I wanted her life to depend on me the way mine depended on her.

I'd spent basically the whole month at home or at work, trying to get ahead. I wanted to be done with school as soon as possible. If I kept my head down, I could graduate early, and as long as my grades were good, I could get my father to finally take me seriously.

The next night, as I was getting out of the shower wrapped in a towel, trying not to get water all over the apartment, someone rang the doorbell.

I cursed softly and went to answer: it was Lion.

"I need your help," he said.

As he walked in, I turned around and kicked the door closed with my heel. I hadn't seen him for a week, and the person standing before me bore only the slightest resemblance to my old friend.

"What the hell happened?" I asked, walking over to the sofa, where he'd sat down. He didn't look at me: he just sank his head desperately into his hands.

His hair looked bad; he hadn't shaved; I doubted he'd even showered in several days. I could tell by his eyes, he'd been drinking, even if he wasn't drunk.

"I'm in trouble, man."

Shit... It had to be bad, then. Lion's problems were always major, never piddly shit.

"You know it's been a year and a half since I stopped dealing..." he started. Hearing the word *dealing* was all I needed to imagine where this was going.

I grabbed a pair of pants draped over the sofa and put them on.

"Don't tell me you're back up in that shit, Lion!" I shouted.

He rubbed the back of his neck and glowered at me. "What do you want, man? I couldn't turn down the chance to make that kind of cash... Luke's living with me now. The dumbass wanted to do it himself, but he just got out. I wasn't going to let him take the risk of getting snatched again..."

"Oh, so he can't take the risk, but you can? You're a fucking idiot. If you don't watch out, you'll be the one getting pinched!"

"Don't you dare judge me!" he screamed, standing up. "You've got everything!"

I was trying to keep myself from kicking his ass because he was my friend and I knew he had money problems—but wasn't that what the fights and the races were for? Maybe they were illegal, but that wasn't the same as slinging drugs. He could get a ten-year bid for that, or more.

"What's the trouble, then?" I asked.

He looked all around, then pinned me with his green eyes.

"I gotta hand over a package at the Gardens tonight. It was supposed to be on the beach, just a quick handoff, but the call came through, and now I have to go to the hood."

Damn. The Gardens was one of the hardest hoods in LA, and Lion and I were pariahs there after a major squabble. My dad had handled it for us, and we had sworn never to go back.

"Don't even think about asking me to come along…"

"It'll be quick. We'll drop off the shit, and we'll head straight back, bruh."

Fuck! I didn't want trouble. Not now, when I was getting my life back on track. After what had happened with Ronnie and Noah's dad, I'd sworn I wouldn't get into any more bullshit. I wasn't going to drag my girlfriend into that. Ronnie and everything that happened afterward, all that was my fault. None of it would have happened if I hadn't brought Noah into that world.

"I'm not going, Lion," I said, making sure he knew I was serious.

He was surprised for a second, then pissed right afterward.

"It's suicide going there alone, and you know that… At least keep an eye on the ride while I do the drop. You said we were brothers, through thick and thin, and I need you now."

Fuuuuuuuck.

"Drop off a package, that's it?" I asked, already knowing I would regret it.

His face lit up.

"I hand it over and we're out, bruh, I promise," he said, getting up. I remembered when I'd gone to live with him and had to accompany him on runs. We were way younger and more irresponsible then. I didn't want to fuck up again. There was too much at stake. I couldn't go back to that world, not anymore.

"I'll drive," I said, grabbing my keys. I wanted to tell him to fuck off, but Lion had always been there for me when I'd needed him. I'd have liked it if he'd escaped that world, but there was nothing I could do. My father had offered him a job at the company, and Lion had turned him down. His grandfather's garage was his life, and he wouldn't give it up. Turning down my father's offer meant turning down the one chance he had at a better life, without problems.

Noah was arriving home the next day, so I had plenty of time to help him out, get home, shower, and be ready to grab her from the airport.

Neither of us said a word as we got in the car and pulled out of the lot.

"Thanks for this, Nick," Lion said, looking out the window.

"Does Jenna know you're slinging?"

He tensed when I mentioned his girlfriend.

"No, and she's not gonna know," he replied cuttingly. That was a warning, no doubt about it. I wasn't supposed to get mixed up in his business, but there he was forcing me to. Whatever.

As I headed into the Gardens, things I wished I could forget started coming up...Ronnie, his friends, the races, Noah's kidnapping, her piece-of-shit father pointing a gun at her... All that shit had happened close to here, and I'd sworn I'd never come back.

"Take a right," he said when we reached an intersection I knew well.

"You're not taking me to the Midnight, are you?" I asked nervously.

The Midnight was a club where every dealer in the city gathered to do business. Part dive, part dance spot, it was where the worst people in town came to have fun. When we were younger, we used to hang there and get wild, but then things turned ugly. We'd been in there one night with a guy who moved serious weight for a rich clientele. I decided things were too hot, and I turned to go. But you can't just turn your back on that life. They gave me an ass whooping I could still remember perfectly: they broke three of my ribs. After that, I definitely wasn't going back, and I'd never set foot in there again, especially because the thing with my mother and sister happened soon after, and I'd had to go live with Dad again.

"Yeah, but it's cool. I told you, just a minute. I'll hand this shit off, get the money, and we're out."

I stopped by the corner of the bar. From there, I could see people entering and leaving. I had no interest in running into any dickheads from my past. I squeezed the wheel and watched Lion get out and head for the door.

When I thought sometimes about that part of my life, I couldn't understand how I'd fucked up so bad. And yet now, when I had everything I needed, when I knew what it was to love another person more than anything in the world, even more than myself, I found myself back in the same shit.

I waited impatiently for Lion to come out, and when he didn't, I started to feel nervous. Fifteen minutes had passed, and if what he'd said was true, he shouldn't have needed more than five.

I cursed under my breath, hit the button on the key fob, got out, and slammed the door. As I approached the door, the two bouncers eyed me up.

"Where you think you're going?" one asked, getting in front of me.

"Hey, easy, bro, I'm just looking for a friend," I said, counting to ten in my head.

Before he could respond, a guy with facial piercings came out, looked me over, and said, "Let him in."

The goon scowled at me and stepped aside. I rolled up my

shirt sleeves as I passed him, knowing this wasn't going to end well. My suspicions were right: as I followed the guy with the piercings to the back room, I saw Lion on the ground with a black eye and a split lip.

My fists clenched before I could even think about it, and my entire body was poised to strike.

"Look who we have here." The voice uttering those words was one I knew very well. Cruz, Ronnie's friend, the same guy who'd pounded me out that night I'd been stupid enough to walk down the wrong alley in the wrong part of town. When I saw him, memories of everything that had happened with Noah came back to me. I had tried as hard as I could to leave that shit behind, to focus on my future, on Noah, to protect her, to take a different road from the one I had started down as a teenager...but seeing Lion there laid out on the ground, and this asshole surrounded by guys just as bad as him, made all the rage I'd suppressed for months surge back up.

"I knew it would just be a matter of time till you showed your face around here," Cruz said, leaning back on the table behind him. His black hair had grown out and was now pulled into a little ponytail. His arms were covered in tattoos, and from his eyes, I could tell he was high, even if I didn't know on what. "Your friend owes us money. He was smart bringing his rich friend here to bail him out."

I looked away from him and back toward Lion, who was staring at the ground.

"I don't owe you shit, motherfucker. You better go ahead and make some other plan to get your money back because you ain't getting shit from me."

I chose each of my words carefully. I had no idea how I was going to get out of there. Lion was done for. Deep down, despite my anger, I felt bad for him, seeing him still caught up in that world I'd escaped. But at the same time, I was so pissed, I wanted to whoop his ass, too, for being an idiot and for dragging me into his bullshit.

Cruz walked over to me slowly.

"You know...it's too bad Ronnie ended up in the big house, but for me, it worked out perfectly. Everything he had is now mine...so listen closely." He stopped a foot from my face. "I'm not as dumb as he was. Your little friend here owes me three thou. I'm gonna get it back. I'll take it in cash, or I'll take it in blood, you decide. You make things even, and we're good, or I'll fuck him up so bad, his momma won't recognize him."

I clenched my jaw, trying to keep the one thing that mattered in my mind: Noah. I didn't want problems. I wasn't looking for a fight. Jenna popped into my head. If she saw Lion like that, let alone worse, her heart would break.

"I don't have three thousand in cash. I'm not a drug dealer like you."

Cruz cracked up laughing, and his lackeys followed suit.

"Don't worry, pal, we got an ATM around the corner. We can go together. What do you think?"

I took a deep breath to keep myself from knocking him flat and turned toward the door. I knew they would follow me. We needed to get out of there. Even if we did give them the money, we were risking our lives being there. If we had been on neutral ground, it might have been a different question...

Once we were outside, the fresh air cleared my head, and I took a quick glance around to take stock of the situation. There were guys standing on corners in groups, an unhoused person or two, two girls talking with three guys in a car. I needed to bounce.

Lion edged over to me while Cruz and his three friends followed us to the ATM two blocks away.

"You're a fucking idiot," I said, stomping my feet. Even if he was my best friend, he deserved to pay for this.

"They played me," he excused himself, then spit on the ground. "They told me I could sell the blow, and whatever I couldn't move, I could just bring back to them, and now they're saying I've got to pay for whatever I didn't get rid of. They're scum."

"You've got a bigger problem than those assholes, and you need to figure out how to solve it," I said, walking toward the machine.

Cruz hurried over. I was losing my patience, so I turned around and hissed, "Stop fucking around... Give me some distance, or I swear I'll rearrange your face."

Cruz smiled, lifted his hands, and walked backward. He was being chill because he needed that money. I took my card out and punched in my number. I hoped I wouldn't have any problems with the withdrawal. Three thousand dollars: that was what I'd made for the entire four weeks I'd been away from Noah.

"Here—take it. And try not to run into me again," I threatened him, handing over the cash.

Cruz counted it and grinned.

"You never should have left here, Nick. You're a better fit than you think... This goody-two-shoes role you've been playing lately, it don't fit you..."

I turned around, ready to walk away.

"I should have told you," he added, "back when your girl got kidnapped and you sent the cops out, you know I walked right out the front door and got away? How is Noah, by the way?"

That was the last straw. My fist moved so fast that I wasn't even aware it had struck his jaw until I saw him lying there on the ground. He sat up fast, and his boys threw me on the ground close to him. The first blow came right afterward and landed square in my left eye.

"Don't you ever say her name again, motherfucker!" I rolled on top of him, and I pounded his face I don't know how many times.

Just then, I felt a kick in the ribs.

"I'll kill you, you son of a bitch," Cruz said, and before I could react, the three guys were kicking me while I rolled back and forth. The first ankle I could grab, I pulled on with all my strength. Feet and fists rained down on me, blood was flying, but the adrenaline in my veins kept me from feeling a thing. I was blind with rage. Hearing my girlfriend's name in his mouth threw gasoline on the fire.

I climbed on top of the guy I'd pulled down and started hitting him in the stomach. Out of the corner of my eye, I could see Lion taking on two others. We weren't going to last long; it was four against two, and Lion was on his last legs. I could take on two guys with no problems, three even, but four? Even I had my limits.

Someone kneed me in the jaw, and my vision blurred. I fell to the ground facedown and got hit again, this time in the stomach. I couldn't breathe. Every attempt to get oxygen to my lungs failed.

"Don't come 'round here again," I heard. "If you do, you won't walk back out."

15

Noah

MY TRIP HAD COME TO AN END. I HAD SEEN MAGNIFICENT SIGHTS, had swum at the best beaches, had eaten traditional cuisine... Still, when the plane from New York touched down in LA, all I could feel was glee, glee and an anxiety that made me nauseous.

I stood up as soon as we heard the ding that said we could unbuckle our seat belts. My mother seemed to think my anticipation was a bit much, but I was overjoyed that we were in first class and could leave before everyone else. I hurried out the door as soon as it opened and onto the jet bridge that led into the terminal. My mother was driving me crazy, dragging her feet. What the hell was keeping her?

Fortunately, since we'd had a layover in New York, I didn't have to wait and show my passport. We just walked down a long passageway, caught an escalator, and we were outside. It was 7:00 p.m. in Los Angeles, and the first thing I saw was the blinding light of the setting sun, which I struggled for a few seconds to peer through. William was there. But where was Nick?

I looked all over as the hum of the escalator droned on, and finally I had no other option but to walk over to my boyfriend's father. He smiled and opened his arms to hug me, but I could tell from his eyes that something was bothering him. I didn't want to be rude, but I wasn't especially in the mood to hug him either.

"How's my weary world traveler?" he asked during our brief embrace.

"Where's Nicholas?"

He looked down at me for a moment, but before he would answer, he saw my mother. She ran toward him with open arms, and he pulled her in tight. I didn't understand what was happening. She stood back long enough to kiss him on the lips. I turned away to avoid watching.

"Where's Nicholas?" my mother asked, just as I had before.

Will looked back at me and shrugged as though to say, *What did you expect?* "He sent a text saying he couldn't pick you up. He'll be in touch as soon as he can be."

That didn't make sense.

"That's all?" I asked incredulously. My joy deflated like a balloon, and disillusion took its place.

William shook his head, and I turned around as he and Steve took our suitcases. I grabbed my phone and called Nick. It went straight to voice mail. I hung up before he could hear my deafening silence.

Why hadn't he come to pick me up? Was he working? If so, he could have come anyway; he did for my birthday. He'd said he'd been happy to leave everything to come see me...

Had those weeks apart made him stop caring about me as much as he used to?

Jesus, what the hell was I thinking? Of course he cared about me! We'd talked—he was dying to see me, he'd told me so...

I dialed again.

"Nicholas, I'm at the airport and you're not here. What's going on?"

After leaving the message, I slipped my phone back into my jeans pocket. I turned to look at my mother, who couldn't keep her hands off William, and then walked alongside Steve as we left the airport and headed for the car. Steve always knew where Nick was—he always knew where everyone was—that was his job as head of security for the Leister family.

"Do you know what's up, Steve?" I asked, staring straight at him. I knew Nicholas trusted him. Anytime something happened, Nick called him, and he'd even sent Steve before when he couldn't pick me up or he wanted to make sure I got home safe from somewhere.

Steve looked away, and I knew then that something had happened that no one wanted to tell me about. I grabbed his arm and forced him to look at me.

"What the hell's going on?"

"Don't get upset, Noah. Nicholas is okay. He'll be in touch once you get home."

I hadn't even been back a half hour, and I wanted to strangle him. What was he playing at?

———

The trip home seemed eternal, especially because what I wanted most was to go to Nick's apartment. I had no idea what was going on, but I didn't like it one bit. I knew why Steve didn't want to tell me anything. It was getting late, and I was sure Nicholas wanted to me to stay at home that night... All sorts of images flashed through my head. Most of them bad.

It was dark by the time we got home. I wished I could see him there, imagined him there waiting for me, as if all this were just some sick joke. He hadn't answered my calls. It was starting to worry me...or maybe piss me off; I still wasn't sure.

"Noah, please, try to look happy. You're coming back from a European vacation, not from an insane asylum."

I was sure my mother was happy about all this. A part of her wanted to see how many times Nicholas could disappoint me because she wanted me to leave him. She had this idea that there was something that would be the last straw. She was wrong.

I went up to my room without answering. It wasn't just Nicholas who hadn't picked up. I'd tried Lion and Jenna as well. Finally, Nick picked up after letting it ring five times.

"Noah," he said dryly.

"Where are you?"

I listened closely, but all I could hear was his breathing, deep breaths, as if he weren't sure what to tell me. My heart was full of fear...an irrational fear, driven by the fact I had no idea what was going on.

"It's okay, I apologize, it's just that something came up, and I couldn't leave." His voice sounded sad—sad but also steely.

"Is everyone okay? Are you okay? Lion and Jenna wouldn't pick up either," I said, sitting down on the bed. The sound of his voice had calmed me slightly.

"I'm great." I didn't believe that. Something had happened, and he didn't want to tell me what.

"I'm going to your apartment," I said, getting up with determination.

"No."

His voice was so cutting that I froze with my hand on the doorknob.

"Nicholas Leister, you will tell me right now what's happening, or I swear to God I'll pull out every hair on your head one by one."

"I'm sorry, but I'm not in the mood for this," he said, taking a long time to reply. I didn't care for that tone. "Stay home, and wait for me to call you."

He hung up.

I looked at the phone as if it were the thing that had mistreated me. I dialed him again, hitting the screen so hard, I almost cracked it. Straight to voice mail.

Was he talking to someone? Who the hell could it be? Was he not picking up on purpose?

I reached into my nightstand, where I kept the keys to the Audi. But they were gone.

Was this some kind of joke?

I left my room and headed straight for the kitchen, opening the drawer where we kept the spares. None were there. My mother and William were nowhere in sight, and I didn't even want to think about what they might be doing.

Was my car outside? I hadn't even bothered to look. I walked toward the door, but just then Steve emerged from his office holding his phone, with an intimidating look on his face.

"Were you talking to him?" I asked, pointing a finger at him.

"Noah, he asked me not to let you go out. He'll explain everything tomorrow."

I laughed. It sounded strange. I could sense Steve was embarrassed, but I knew he'd do as Nick said.

"It's late. Get some rest, and you'll see him tomorrow."

Bullshit.

"Fine, you're right."

Steve seemed relieved and watched me closely as I turned around and climbed the stairs. He was out of his mind if he thought he would prevent me from leaving my own home. I entered my room, ready to wait as long as I had to. Pacing nervously, I took out my phone again.

There is no justification for what you're doing, and when I see you, you're going to get it.

He answered me right away.

Don't be nasty. I love you. Get some rest and I'll see you soon.

See you soon? For real?

I went to the bathroom to wash up. I felt gross after all those hours in the airplane. I looked at the clock: it was 9:00 p.m., and I couldn't even think about breaking out before eleven. I laughed at that thought: *breaking out*, like I was in jail.

I was going to kill him...

Once I was halfway presentable, admittedly with my hair still wet, I peeked into the hallway. I couldn't hear anyone. But then, you never did hear anyone in that enormous house. My plan was to go to the garage and take my old car. The same one that had broken down a thousand times but that I couldn't stand to think of selling—or junking, since that was more likely. I'd known that heap of trash would end up coming in handy one day.

The garage door was at the back of the house, so I didn't need to go near the front door or Steve's office. I walked downstairs, making as little noise as possible, and grinned when I saw my precious car next to Mom's BMW. There was a motorcycle there, too. I'd never asked whose it was, and honestly, I was tempted to take it, but I didn't know where the keys were, and I was sure Nicholas would kill me if he saw me show up late at night with a motorcycle, especially since I'd never driven one in my life.

I got in and pressed the button on the garage door opener, thanking God one more time that the house was huge and no one heard me leave.

I had nearly an hour's drive ahead of me, so I cranked up the music and opened the windows to try to stay awake. I wished I were in my convertible and not in this car that had a top speed of around forty-five.

I knew I shouldn't take the interstate at that hour. I hadn't even slept in twenty hours, but I didn't care; the need to see Nicholas and the feeling that something wasn't right were stronger than anything else.

The drive took forever, and when I finally reached his building, I felt more nervous than ever. Not just because I was finally seeing him after a month but because I knew he'd get mad at me for going all the way there alone at that time of night.

As I got into the elevator, I realized I didn't have my keys. Shit... Now I was going to have to ring the doorbell at one in the morning. My heart was galloping when I saw the door in front of me. I knocked instead of ringing. I don't know why, but it seemed more reasonable. I did so softly, not dramatically. I was already trying to calm things down before I had even seen him.

No one opened.

I knocked again, and then I saw a faint light under the door. Had he been sleeping? I heard a curse, then an insult. Finally the door opened. There he was.

I don't think anything could have prepared me for what I saw. I had to hold my breath. My hands came straight to my mouth to muffle a scream. He hadn't expected me there, and now I knew why.

"Goddammit, Noah," he said, leaning his forehead on the doorframe. "Can't you just do what I ask of you one fucking time?"

"What happened to you?" I whispered. His entire face was one big bruise, his left eye was greenish and leaking pus, and his lip looked cracked all the way through.

"I told you to stay home!"

Now that I was there, now that I saw him, I understood why he hadn't come to pick me up. He was destroyed; he'd been beaten to a pulp... The terror at the sight of him in that state mingled with my joy at seeing him, but whatever fantasy I'd had of seeing him again after weeks vanished terribly before my eyes.

I looked at his bare chest, with a bandage wrapped around his ribs...

Someone had hurt him. They'd hurt him badly. They'd hurt Nick. My Nick.

"Don't look at me like that, Noah," he said, turning around and bringing his hand to his head.

I didn't know what to say. I was speechless. That was the last thing I needed, the last thing I wanted to see. That wasn't just a beating. For me it was something worse: it brought back memories I wished would be gone forever.

"Don't cry, dammit!" he shouted, turning around again and wiping away the tears on my cheeks.

"I don't understand," I said, and it was true: I didn't know what had happened, why he was hurt. I was shocked. Nothing was the way I had hoped it would be.

Nicholas pulled me close and squeezed me tight. I was scared to touch him, I didn't want to hurt him, but instinctively, I wrapped my arms around him, and I felt his lips on the top of my head.

"I missed you so much," he said and stroked my hair, smelling my shampoo... When he pushed me away a bit, I opened my eyes to look at him. His left eye could barely open, and that blue I fell in love with was almost gone, replaced by pain and suffering... He bent over to kiss me, but I pulled away.

"No," I said, frightened.

I shut my eyes. Memories, memories, so many damned memories... My mom beaten up, my father dead, me bleeding on the ground waiting for her to come home...

I moved away from him and hid my face in my hands.

"Why do you do these things, Nicholas?" I asked in a muffled tone.

I hated to cry, especially in front of people, and especially because of something that could have been avoided. He stood there staring at me. I think he was hurt I had rejected him.

"Can't you just be a normal boyfriend?" I chastised him. My tone was harsh. I was hurting, everything was hurting me—the sight of him, the loss of that dream I'd had of us reuniting.

But when I said that, I could see I'd wounded him, and that made me feel guilty, even if I still refused to take my words back. He must have gone back to fighting for money, or else he'd gotten drunk and mouthed off to the wrong person. Lion was probably involved—Jenna, too. That's why neither of them had picked up when I'd called.

"You shouldn't have come," he said with restraint. So now he could control himself? Now, when it was too late. "I didn't want you to see me like this, but you never fucking listen!"

"You don't get to order me around, and you can give up expecting me to do whatever you want when you won't even give me a fucking explanation. I was worried about you, Nick!"

"Dammit, Noah, I had my reasons!"

"Your reasons are why someone beat the shit out of you!"

His chest was rising and falling as he looked at me. I didn't know what to do. I was furious at him for returning to that world I hated so much, but I also wanted to hold him and never let him go again. I was about to break down, seriously, and I didn't want to do it in front of him. He grabbed me as I turned and headed for the elevator, but I jerked my arm away.

"Don't touch me, Nicholas! Not now! I mean it!"

"Are you serious? We haven't seen each other in a month…"

"I don't care! I don't even recognize you right now. I thought you'd be waiting for me at the airport with a smile because I'm an idiot, a fool who expects a person to do the things they promise me when it's obvious they won't."

"You haven't even let me explain myself!"

"What explanation are you going to give me? That you ran into a wall?"

He glared at me, and I crossed my arms waiting for his so-called explanation. You could hear a pin drop. Nick tried to hug me again.

"Do not touch me," I repeated, dead serious.

And so we stood there, neither of us knowing what to say.

"It's not what you think," he said. "I had to help Lion. He was in trouble."

"What kind of trouble?" As I asked, I saw how raw his knuckles were.

He came close to me again, and when I didn't stop him, he continued. "It was about money. Look, Noah, I didn't want this to happen, I swear to you." He knelt so he could look me directly in the eyes. "I've been waiting for this day ever since you left. I bought food, I cleaned up the apartment, I even bathed the cat. Please, believe me, all I wanted was to see you. You're the one thing I care about."

The fragrance of his body invaded my senses. The warmth of his fingers on my cheeks made the ache in my heart diminish slightly because even if what I was feeling was his fault, he was also the only one who could make it disappear.

I took a deep breath and, hesitantly, held him back.

"Loving you is the most complicated thing I've ever done," I said.

But it was impossible to stay mad at him.

"I'm dying to kiss you," he said, as though asking for permission.

I waited for a few seconds before replying. "Do it, then."

And I could tell he was still smiling a second later, when his lips touched mine.

16

Nick

I'D FUCKED UP. THE FEAR ON HER FACE WHEN SHE'D SEEN ME confirmed it. But I didn't care. She was there with me again, and I was dying to kiss her.

When her soft lips pressed against mine, I felt a prick where mine had been cut. But still, I didn't resist. Noah must have noticed, though, because she stopped.

"Did I hurt you?" she asked, alarmed, her feline eyes, so adorable, roving my face, with their lashes damp from tears that, once again, were my fault.

"No," I replied, distracted, wrapping my hands around her waist and pulling her close again. "This is a dream. I've been wanting to kiss you like this for weeks."

But Noah stopped me before I could resume.

"You winced," she said. "I can tell it hurts."

What? "I didn't wince."

"You did," she said and traced a line from my cheek to my lower lip. I clenched my jaw. Okay, it hurt, but it was nothing compared to the pain of not seeing her for days, not kissing her, not making love to her. "Let me clean up your hands," she said.

She turned, and I was no longer holding her. I wished I could have been quicker, grabbed her, tossed her over my shoulder, and taken her to the bedroom, but one of my ribs had a hairline fracture. I wasn't even supposed to be out of bed...but there I was, like always, not listening to orders. I watched her go to the kitchen. At last, my apartment had life in it. The cat emerged from who knows where and started rubbing himself against Noah's feet.

"Hey, N, how's my pretty boy?" she exclaimed, effusive, bending over to pick the thing up. I sat down on one of the kitchen chairs while she cuddled with the cat and looked around for the first aid kit. When she found it, she sat down and spun the seat of her chair to face me.

"You look fantastic," I said, loving the sight of her blushing.

"I wish I could say the same for you."

I smiled. Parts of my face hurt that I hadn't even known existed.

"Give me your hand," she said gently.

I did so, and as she cleaned my wounds, which were barely bleeding anyway, I realized she was even prettier than before she'd left. Her hair was redder, with blond streaks here and there, and her tanned skin was an almost-bronze color that highlighted her face. Her lips were always swollen after she cried...and after we hooked up, and as she looked at me, I couldn't stop thinking about all I wanted to do to her. To have those lips on my body, those hands on my back...

"Nicholas, I'm talking to you," she said loudly, awakening me from my daydreams.

"Sorry, what did you say?" I asked, trying to express my flared-up desire.

"I said, how's Lion?"

Lion... I didn't even want to hear his fucking name.

"He was in the emergency room for a couple of hours, but he's fine. He's back at home."

Noah was carefully examining my wounds as she cleaned and disinfected them.

"And Jenna?" she asked, bending over to grab some scissors off the counter. As she did so, I got a primo view of her breasts, and I had to take a deep breath to calm myself. Did we really need to talk about that now? I couldn't give less of a shit about Jenna, to tell the truth. Sure, she knew what had happened. I mean, we hadn't told her we were selling drugs—or, to be precise, that her boyfriend was selling drugs. She was taking care of Lion now.

"They're together. I'm sure she's being a pain in the ass," I responded, impatient for her to finish up and look at me. She seemed nervous; I could tell by how carefully she returned everything to the first aid kit.

"I want to know exactly what happened. Tell me who it was, Nick. Who did this to your face?"

"Don't worry about it, okay, Noah? It won't happen again."

"Fine, but I want you to tell me," she replied.

"And I want to make love to you," I said.

Now I had her eyes on me, just as I wished.

"You can't," she responded, standing with a slightly quivering voice.

I tugged her between my open legs. "Oh, I can."

She looked doubtfully at my wounds and my bandaged midsection.

"No, Nicholas, you're hurt. You can't even breathe without your ribs aching, I'm sure of it," she said, stopping my hands with hers as they began to climb her T-shirt.

"Don't worry about me, Freckles. The pleasure will be stronger than the pain, I guarantee it." As I uttered these words, I took off her shirt, leaving her standing before me in her bra. I was getting excited just looking at her.

I could feel her heart pound as I kissed her nipples, and her pulse in her neck, I could even see it; the blood was rushing through her veins, getting her ready for me.

I stroked her back—I had forgotten how soft her skin was, how perfect... Sometimes I couldn't believe my luck. When my hand stopped on the clasp of her bra, she crept away from me.

"Goddammit," I said, not even thinking.

"No, Nicholas, we're not going to do it."

I laughed.

"Stop looking at me like that," she warned, pointing a finger at me that I immediately reached out and grabbed, bringing it to my lips for a kiss. As I nibbled it, I noticed how her body responded. Extending my legs, I trapped her, keeping her right where I wanted her. Now I moved my lips to that special part of her neck that I knew drove her wild. A sigh escaped her as I licked it.

She wrapped her hands around my neck and played with my hair, and in that moment, I knew I had won the battle. I turned my attention to the tops of her breasts as she rubbed my lower back. She shook; her nails dug into my spine. I hissed—I don't know if it was from pain or pure carnal pleasure, and I didn't have time to figure it out, because once more, she escaped me.

"Nicholas, you can't!" she shouted, both aroused and angry.

Dammit! I reached out to touch her, but she resisted, and I could see the determination in her honey-colored eyes.

"You know perfectly well how this is going to end. You can either keep avoiding me and making me chase you, which will only make my aches worse, or you can stop fucking around and get back here."

That must have gotten to her. She looked angry now.

"You want to see how fast I can walk out that door?"

"What I want is to fuck."

Her cheeks turned blood red. I guess she wasn't expecting that answer. Her reaction amused me.

"You're being vulgar, you know that?" she counterattacked.

With a diabolical grin, I said, "I've always been vulgar, Freckles. It's just that I usually control it when I'm around you, even if you make it hard for me."

I was reaching the end of my patience.

Clutching her hands, I stood, leaned down, and kissed her, sliding my tongue into her mouth. My lip hurt, but I didn't care. I'd had worse wounds than that, and nothing was going to stop me from kissing Noah that night. I'd been waiting too long.

A second later, she slackened, then responded with equal enthusiasm, her tongue caressing mine in little circles, then plunging in desperately. When she squeezed my back, I yelped in pain.

She stopped and looked at me with concern.

"Quit," I said before she could utter a word. "In five minutes, I'm going to be making love to you. Don't waste your energy on words."

She obeyed. I could tell she was dying to do it, just as I was. She seemed to hesitate for a moment, but it was evident that there was no turning back. But she didn't go to the bedroom. She took my hand and forced me back on the sofa.

"What are you doing?" I asked, more turned on than I'd ever been.

"We're going to do it my way."

Her feline eyes glimmered with desire.

"The only way you know how to do it is the way I've taught you, Freckles."

She straddled me, tossing her hair back over her shoulder. "I've been to France. I've learned all kind of things."

I scowled. I didn't like that comment one bit.

"Don't be an idiot," she said, pulling off her bra. The sight of her breasts made me lose the thread of my thoughts. "Now, you're going to hold very still."

17

Noah

I DIDN'T WANT TO HURT HIM, BUT I NEEDED IT, TOO. I WANTED to feel his hands, his expert fingers, to be kissed by him all over, in all the places he wasn't supposed to do it. For him to make me his and to forget every other girl he's been with.

"This will be the only time you're ever going to be in control, so enjoy it," he said condescendingly. But he was turned on. I could feel him underneath me, hard as a stone.

"We'll see about that," I said to him, bending over to kiss his jawline. I wanted to try to avoid his lips—I didn't want to hurt him—but it would be hard. I hated being cautious when what I wanted was to make love freely; I wanted him to dominate me with his body, the way I liked, to pick me up, to let our skin touch and give us pleasure, not pain. But at the same time, having total power over him was very exciting, too.

My tongue drifted over his stubble to his right ear. He smelled so good. Like Nick. Like a man.

He took hold of my breasts, and I almost yelped when he squeezed me tight.

I moved my hands down to his stomach. That body was a

work of art, a sculpture! My fingertips felt the muscle beneath his warm skin. I wanted to kiss every inch of him. Stopping at his pants, I smiled, watching him quiver as I nibbled at his neck.

"Don't be mean, Freckles. I won't wait much longer," he warned me, grabbing me around the waist. I stopped him before he did what I knew he would.

"Unless I remember wrong, there was something you wanted me to do," I said, hoping to fluster him, desiring to see him lose control of himself. But he stared at me firmly.

"Not today, Freckles," he said, clearly struggling to get the words out.

I unbuttoned the top button on his pants.

"Why not?"

He completely lost control of his breathing.

I pulled his pants all the way down and started slowly stroking his body. He closed his eyes. I knew he wouldn't last long. We hadn't done it in a month.

"Because if you do, I'm not going to let you leave."

When I heard those words, I stopped, trying to regain control of the situation.

He bent over, and at the same time, a diabolic smile appeared on his face.

"Better do what I say," he told me, and he tugged down my underwear, leaving me completely naked.

His eyes were drilling into every centimeter of me, and I was happy I had gotten over the shame I used to feel at first. There's nothing like trusting a person fully, showing them all your insecurities, seeing that they don't only accept them—they adore them.

"I hope I can drive you as crazy someday as you do me," I said as he started kissing my stomach and his hands rubbed me where I was most sensitive.

"You drive me crazy every time you breathe, Noah."

I pushed him backward softly onto the sofa and put both hands on his shoulders. I sat on his lap, his mouth sought mine eagerly, and he lifted me, guiding me, entering me very gently. I closed my eyes, enjoying him, enjoying having him inside me again...

"Now you're up," he whispered.

Bracing myself against him, I started moving up and down, not rushing, wanting to give my body time to get used to him after a month's absence.

"You're killing me, Noah," he said, grasping my buttocks and making me go faster. I tried to resist—I wanted to take it slow, enjoy it, drag out the pleasure as long as possible—but he wouldn't let me: even battered and bruised, he was so much stronger than I was.

"Jesus, Nicholas," I complained when I was ready to orgasm. "Slow down!"

He leaned forward, and his eyes, so close to mine, made me submit as his hand traveled down to the place where I was already dying from pleasure.

"Like that," he said and leaned in to bite my lip.

My God... It was all just too much, his words, his hand rubbing me, him sliding in and out... My body needed to be free after all those weeks without him, having nightmares, being sad that he'd not come to find me at the airport, afraid when I found him with his face destroyed... I started speeding up myself. He grunted deeply from pleasure, and at the same time, I shouted almost desperately, and after waves of infinite pleasure, we reached orgasm together.

"This is where I need to be, every day."

I looked down and pulled his face up to my mouth. He kissed me; he didn't care at all about the pain. We were together. That was all that mattered.

When I opened my eyes the next morning, I felt a tickle on

my nose. N was licking my face. I smiled, sat up, and realized I was alone in the room with the light coming in through the window at a strange angle... I rubbed my eyes, disoriented, trying to remember where I was, in what country, in what bed, and how I had gotten there.

Nick shirtless, in sweatpants, standing in the doorway was the finest sight I could imagine.

"At last. I was starting to get worried," he said, leaning against the doorframe.

I looked at the window, then him, then the window again. "What time is it?"

"Seven," he said, walking into the room. "In the evening," he added, grinning.

"Are you kidding?"

He sat next to me. "You've slept like fourteen hours."

Jesus...! I couldn't wrap my head around it. Fucking jet lag...

"I need a damn shower."

I got up and went to the bathroom. I looked like hell. I even locked the door because I didn't want Nicholas to get in the shower with me like that. Living with him was going to be tough. In the mornings I wasn't a person yet, and I was afraid he'd fall out of love with me if he saw me looking like a zombie every day. He got up looking like a Greek god, and his groggy face just made him more attractive than normal.

I got under the hot water and let it stream through my hair. The water revived my senses, and I awakened and shook off the feeling of stupor.

When I got out, I could only find a towel to wrap myself in. I stepped out dripping water, looking for my clothes, and that was when I heard the door slam, followed by shouts.

"Where is she?"

Shit! Mom!

I tried to run back into the bathroom so she wouldn't see me naked, but she intercepted me halfway. As we stood across from each other, she looked beside herself, totally unable to process what was happening.

"How dare you?" she shouted. "How dare you disappear for hours like that?"

I was horrified. We'd argued before, lots of times, but I'd never seen her so mad. Nicholas came over and stood in front of me, so I couldn't see her.

"Calm down, Raffaella. Noah didn't do anything wrong."

The muscles in his back were as tense as the strings of a guitar, and the air grew so thick, it was impossible to breathe.

"Get away from her, Nicholas," my mother ordered him, trying and failing to keep calm.

I stepped to one side, and my mother glared at me furiously.

"Get dressed right now, and walk out that door."

I didn't know what to do. I was terrified by seeing her out of control like that for the first time in years.

"Noah's not going anywhere," Nick declared calmly. That was when William, who had just come upstairs, appeared.

"What the hell is going on here?" he shouted, looking first at my mother and then at us. "Who did this to you, Nicholas?" His father looked with horror at the bruises covering his torso.

"Your son is out of control, and I don't want him anywhere near Noah," my mother said. She turned to Nick and hissed, "You're violent, you get in fights, you have lowlife friends, and I'm not going to allow you to get my daughter involved in all that shit! And that's the last word!"

"Mom, stop!" I shouted, before I said something even worse. "I'm sorry I didn't tell you I was leaving, but you can't just burst in here and..."

"I can, and I will, as often as I have to. You're my daughter.

Now grab your things, put on some clothes, and get in the damn car!"

"NO!" I shrieked, feeling like a spoiled brat but unwilling to let anyone tell me what I could and couldn't do. I wasn't a little girl anymore.

"You were kidnapped, Noah!" my mother shouted in response. "You were kidnapped, and I thought something like that had happened again. You nearly gave me a heart attack," she confessed, her eyes full of tears.

"I'm sorry, Mom," I repeated, and I really felt it, but I couldn't lose my nerve, not anymore. "But soon, you won't be able to know where I am at all times. You can't get in this state every time you don't know where I am."

Looking at me coldly, she said, "Get dressed and let's go home," pronouncing each word slowly, not seeming interested in a reply.

I didn't want to go—that was the last thing I wanted—but my mother was on the verge of hysteria. I needed to get her away from Nick, especially because I was on the verge of telling her I was moving in with him.

"Wait for me in the car. I'll be right down," I finally said. Nicholas cursed, standing there next to me. My mother pretended she didn't hear him as she and William walked out into the hall. I heard them shut the door a second later.

"Don't go, Noah. If you go, you're telling her she's right," Nicholas said angrily.

"You saw her. If I don't go, it'll be worse."

He sighed in resignation. "I can't wait for you to move in here."

I was scared of telling my mother what we had in mind.

"It won't be long," I said.

He squeezed me in his arms, and with my cheek on his chest, I couldn't help but think that a part of me was lying to him.

18

Nick

As I watched her go, I felt all the wrath I'd been holding back spilling over like lava from a volcano. I was so tired of all this shit… Raffaella's words kept echoing in my head.

Your son is out of control, and I don't want him anywhere near Noah.

I went to the kitchen and tried to calm down.

You're violent, you get in fights…

I cursed the moment I had decided to help Lion.

I'm not going to allow you to get my daughter involved in all that shit!

I was going to have to change if I wanted things with Noah to actually work. We were about to take a major step, a decisive one for our relationship, to show that we were actually serious. That was one reason I wanted her to come live with me, because no one seemed to take us seriously. Sometimes I felt like the few people who knew the truth were placing bets behind our backs about how long it would take us to break up, trying to guess how much pressure we could take.

I grabbed my phone off the counter.

I had a message from Jenna.

> Lion's OK. We need to talk. You know perfectly well I
> don't believe a damn thing you both told me. I know
> you're with Noah, but I need to see you. Call me when
> you can.

I knew this would happen. I also knew it was easy to lie to
Jenna. I could make up any old bullshit, and she'd buy it—or she
used to, but that might not work this time. Lion was on shaky
ground, and I couldn't just leave him hanging. Jenna needed to
know he was in trouble.

I sent her a message telling her we could meet up in an hour
and got into the shower. I felt good remembering how Noah had
worried about me, taken care of me, suffered when she saw I
was wounded... No one had ever made me feel that way before.
My father used to get pissed off when I showed up with marks
from fighting, and he usually wouldn't say a word to me till I'd
healed. That was probably one of the reasons I got into that kind
of trouble, to piss Dad off and keep him off my back.

I got out of the shower, dressed in jeans and a T-shirt, took
a pain pill, and walked out the door. Noah's old car was parked
outside.

Her mother had made her go with them. I didn't even want to
imagine what they were saying about me... My stomach ached. I
couldn't stand them trying to get in her head like that. My biggest
fear was that Noah would end up giving in to her mother, seeing
me as someone she shouldn't be with.

Another message from Jenna came through.

> I'm almost there.

A few minutes later, I was parking at a Starbucks near the mall, fifteen minutes from my apartment.

When I saw Jenna through the window, sitting on one of the sofas inside, I knew I should be very careful how I said everything to her. When I went inside, I could see the vehemence in her eyes. I sat down in front of her, trying not to wince, but not a single gesture of mine was going to escape her that day.

"Y'all are a couple of fucking idiots, you know that, right?" she said, setting her green tea Frappuccino or whatever that green drink was down on the table.

"I don't know why that surprises you all of a sudden," I replied. I wasn't happy with the situation at all. I didn't want her to go on thinking I was the same Nick as a year ago. I had changed, or so I wanted to believe. Her boyfriend, though, was the same dickhead as always.

"You honestly want me to believe this all happened over a fucking poker game?" she said, leaving me mute for a few seconds. Poker? What the hell was she talking about? "Especially knowing how badly you both play... Nicholas! You have got to stay away from the gangs!"

So Lion had fed her a line of bullshit...great.

"Look, Jenna, I've had a very bad day, okay?" I didn't want to lose my cool then, and I certainly didn't want to take it out on her. "Lion's a big boy. He knows what he's doing. He's worried about money, he's worried about the garage, and he's worried about you." I looked at the ground as I spoke. "He's going to realize sooner or later what's right for him. In the meantime, you need to give him space. It's not easy to just turn your back on that life. You know the races are just around the corner, too, and that's got all of us feeling edgy... Lion will figure it out."

"Races? I thought we were past that this year, Nicholas."

Shit! I shouldn't have said anything, dammit!

"We are, but what I mean is the guys are on edge, so like…
it just happened that we got in a little fight yesterday, and it
turned out worse than we'd thought. It's nothing for you to
worry about, though."

She looked at me leery-eyed, but she seemed to accept my
explanation. Then she looked around, as though realizing someone
or something was out of place.

"Where's Noah?"

"Not with me, as you can see," I said with irritation.

Looking more serious than before, she asked, "What did you
do?"

I laughed bitterly. "So you just take it for granted that I'm the
one who's done something?"

Jenna's expression told me Noah's mother wasn't the only one
who thought I was bad for her. And Jenna usually took my side.

"Did she see your face? If so, she must be a wreck. It seems like
you'll never understand, Nicholas…" She paused for a moment, as
if the sight of me had some kind of effect on her, but not enough
to keep her from gathering her strength to continue: "If you go on
like this, she'll wind up leaving you."

"Shut up."

She didn't seem to like that response, but she went on. "Noah's
my best friend, and over the course of this year, she's told me things
you might not even know. Either way, violence is something she
just can't deal with. Your face, your wounds…you know perfectly
well what kind of memories they call up for her."

"Goddammit, this isn't something I planned, okay?"

"Nicholas, get a damn grip!" she replied, raising her voice.
"Noah is not okay. She has nightmares. Recently my brother shot
me with one of those toy bullets, and it gave me a black eye, and
when Noah saw me, she freaked out, thinking someone had hit
me. She slept in my bed that night. You should have seen how she

was tossing and turning; something must have really gotten to her because she never stays the night with me."

I shook my head. "I've slept with her a million times. She sleeps like a baby. That's all in your head. Noah's fine."

I could feel the blood boiling in my veins. I hadn't gone there to listen to this shit. Nothing was wrong with Noah. My wounds had upset her, I knew that. Dammit, that was why I hadn't gone to get her from the airport; that's why I had *planned* not to see her for several days, to spare her the sight of me in that condition. But Noah didn't have nightmares, that much I knew. Jenna was the one who should be worrying about her boyfriend: Lion was selling drugs, but Jenna couldn't get it through her head that her life and Lion's were totally incompatible.

I got up before I said something I'd regret.

"I may have my problems with Noah, but don't forget about yours and Lion's. If I were you, I'd stop sticking my nose where it doesn't belong and worry about my own relationship."

"My boyfriend is the way he is because of you."

I blew out all the air I'd been holding in. "Fuck you, Jenna," I said and left.

After an hour driving aimlessly, thinking about all Jenna had said, all that Noah's mom had said...I reached the conclusion that I needed to ignore them. I couldn't expect any different from the people around me. I'd created that image of myself, and it wasn't going to be easy to change. It was almost impossible for anyone to take me seriously. But even if Noah still didn't trust me, I knew she thought I could improve. Noah loved me. She was *in love* with me. I knew she didn't think like Jenna or her mother and that she would never say to me the things they had. I'd shown her I could do better.

I parked next to the beach and walked along the shore as the sun lowered over the horizon. There were people out walking their dogs and occasional couples enjoying the solitude. I let the sound of the waves ease my mind, let my fears and insecurities in relation to Noah go back to the place where I kept them well hidden.

A while later, when I thought my emotions were under control, my phone rang. I picked up without even looking, assuming it would be Noah. But I heard silence on the other line, followed a few seconds later by "hello, Nicholas."

It couldn't be. Of all the people.

"What the hell do you want, and why are you calling my cell phone?"

"I'm your mother, and I need to talk to you."

Madison appeared in my mind, and I stopped with my heart in my throat. "Did something happen to my sister?"

"No, no, Maddie's fine," Anabel said.

"Then we don't have anything to talk about," I replied, ready to hang up.

"Wait, Nicholas!"

"What the hell do you want?" I repeated.

After a few seconds, she said, "I want to talk to you. Just for an hour. We can have a coffee. There are lots of things that have never been cleared up, and I can't let you go on living your life hating me the way you do."

"I hate you because you abandoned me. There's nothing more to say." I hung up before I could hear her reaction.

All the rage inside me started surging forth again. My mother was the worst thing that had ever happened to me. I was the way I was because of her. My relationship with Noah would have been totally different if I'd had a decent model to follow. I'd have known how to treat women, how to trust them. Anabel Grason had nothing to say that I needed to hear. But now she supposedly wanted to see me?

The tension of that past month, the insecurity, the fights, the sorrow, the solitude I'd felt without Noah, the knowledge that I'd disappointed her, not being at the airport when she wanted me there, it was all just too much for me. I ran and ran down the beach until I couldn't think anymore.

19

Noah

THE SILENCE WAS AGONIZING ON THE WAY HOME.

When Will parked, I got out of the car and shot upstairs. I didn't want to talk to my mother. In all honesty, I didn't want to talk to anyone. Since I'd gotten back, everything had gone wrong: I didn't see Nick at the airport, I found him all beaten up, we argued, I fought with my mother, and I had to listen firsthand to what she thought of him… I needed to get away from all of them. I needed space.

When I walked into my room, the first thing I saw was a fat envelope on the bed. It was from school. I opened it and felt a knot in my stomach as I looked through the dorm documents. When I was looking into housing months before, I had checked the option for a roommate. That had been my plan, sharing a dorm room on campus, but now everything had changed. I'd decided to live with Nicholas, and I would have to call the school and let them know.

I was scared of the moment when I'd tell my mother. She was going to kill me. And a part of me, the part of me that was still just a little girl, was scared to admit to her that I was going to live with a guy my first year of college.

I couldn't believe it was two weeks until I'd have to do it... I would have liked to pack my bags right then and go, but I'd have to deal with the situation. My mother needed to learn to live without me. Anyway, I was sure William wanted to live alone with her. Since we'd gotten there, all we'd done was cause him problems, me especially.

I grabbed the papers and shoved them into my desk drawer. I put on my pajamas, even though I wasn't tired after sleeping all day, and I got in bed, ready to think about nothing.

It took forever to get to sleep, and when I did, the nightmares came back. I knew I was looking for Nick in my sheets, I knew when I felt him near me, my fears would vanish, but he wasn't there, and he wouldn't be able to protect me...

The sunlight was dazzling...for a moment, I didn't know where I was, but then I managed to situate myself in my dream.

My father was with me.

"Noah, there are times in your life when people will do things you don't like... Think about when Mom doesn't do the things Papa tells her to, then Papa has to punish her, right?" my father said while we were both sitting by the seaside watching the waves crash against the cliff.

I nodded, listening to him, saying yes to whatever he said. That was easy because his questions were almost always rhetorical; you didn't need to think about the answer because the question already implied it.

"The thing is, your mom doesn't know what's good for her. She doesn't understand that I'm the only one who knows that."

My father grabbed me around the waist and set me on his lap.

"You're my girl, Noah. You're my little treasure, and you'll always do what I say, right?"

I nodded, looking into my father's eyes, those eyes that were exactly like mine, the color of honey. Only his were bloodshot from alcohol.

"So, next time I tell you to scram, to leave your mother where she is, what are you going to do?"

"Go to my room," I whispered almost inaudibly.

My father nodded with satisfaction. "Don't ever disobey me, honey... I don't want to do anything I'll have to regret later...not to you. After all, you and I, we're the same, aren't we?"

I nodded and smiled while my father grabbed a string off the ground and started knotting it nimbly.

"This will be our tie, so strong that no one will ever break it."

I looked at the knot, a figure eight. My father had made me tie one many times...

And I never stopped until it was perfect.

The next day, I got up with bags under my eyes. I'd had a horrible night, and it didn't help that breakfast was so uncomfortable. William didn't utter a word, and my mother scowled at me in silence, pretending to read the newspaper. A wicked part of my brain wondered what it would be like to drop the bomb on them that I was going to live with Nicholas right then, but just thinking about it gave me the urge to throw up.

I was happy when my phone started ringing. I'd been waiting for Nicholas to call me. I left the kitchen, ignoring my mother's reproachful expression, and answered.

"Hello?"

"Is this Noah Morgan?" a woman asked on the other line.

"Yeah, who is this?" I replied, taking the stairs two at a time. She was silent until I reached my bedroom door.

"This is Anabel Grason, Nicholas's mother."

I was dumbstruck. Anabel. Half my problems were her fault—my problems and those of the person I loved most. She'd abandoned him, and now he wanted nothing to do with her.

"What do you want?" I asked as I shut the door behind me.

Hesitant, finally sighing, she said, "I need to ask you for a favor. I know Nicholas doesn't want to see me, but I don't care. I need to talk to him, and I need your help. You're his girlfriend, right?"

Her tone was so gentle that I wasn't sure what to do. Unsettled, I sat on the edge of the bed.

"I won't do anything Nick doesn't want. The two of you need to work it out. I'm sorry, Mrs. Grason, but you must understand I'm not exactly a fan of yours, and honestly, I think Nicholas is better off without you."

There it was. I'd said it, and I wasn't going to take it back now... She had abandoned Nick, my Nick, when he was just twelve years old—leaving him with a father who was too busy building his empire—without any explanation, and now she wanted that relationship back? She must have been sick in the head.

"I'm his mother, and there's no way he's better off without me. Things have changed, and I want to see him again."

I wasn't about to give in. I had tried to talk to Nick about that very subject, and he had made it very clear to me that I should stay out of it. Anabel was a big no for him, and I knew him enough to realize he wasn't going to change his mind.

"I'm sorry, Mrs. Grason, but Nicholas has repeatedly said there is no discussing this."

"Then meet me on your own, just the two of us. Nicholas doesn't need to know. Just pick a place."

What? I couldn't do that. Nicholas would kill me. He would feel betrayed if I talked about him to the woman he hated most in the world, the woman who had hurt him more than anyone had... No way.

"You don't understand. He doesn't want to see you, and there's no way I'm going to lie to Nicholas."

I was being firm. I guess all that stress from recent days was rising to the surface. Plus, I needed to defend my boyfriend, keep anyone from harming him, including me.

I heard Anabel take a deep breath. Then she went on.

"Here's the deal," she said, changing her tone to a more strident one. "My six-year-old daughter has a father who spends half his time traveling all over the world. I can't be with her all day, and I know Nicholas wants her to spend some time at his apartment. It's fine with me, but my husband refuses to talk about it. If you do what I ask, if you meet with me and help me find a way to recover my relationship with my son, I'll let Nicholas visit with Madison when my husband is away. But if you don't, I'll do whatever I can to make sure Nicholas doesn't see his sister again."

Damn. Maddie was everything to Nicholas. I couldn't believe that woman would threaten such a thing. Was that the kind of relationship she wanted with her son? One based on deceit and blackmail? I felt my blood boiling with rage. I wanted to hang up on her and let her know very clearly what I thought of her proposal, but it was Maddie we were talking about. If Nicholas had his way, she'd be living with him. He'd talked to lawyers, his father had tried to find a way to let him have her for a few weeks, but it was impossible: if her mother didn't agree, there was nothing to be done... I knew I was treading dangerous ground, but I couldn't let that woman come between Nick and his sister.

"Where do you want to meet?" I asked, hating myself for letting her manipulate me.

I could almost hear her smile on the other line.

"I'll let Nicholas know he can have Maddie next week. We will meet when I bring her. Don't worry, it'll be our secret. No one will have to know."

"I don't want to lie to him, and eventually I'll tell him. I promise you he won't like it. What you're doing, extorting me, is going to have the opposite result of the one you want. Nicholas doesn't forgive easily, and you are the person who's hurt him more than anyone else in his life."

"You haven't heard every side of the story, Noah. Things aren't always the way you believe or the way you've been told."

I didn't want to hear another word from her. "Send me the address of the place you want to meet."

I hung up without waiting for a response and lay down on the bed, looking at the roof and feeling guiltier than I ever had.

Eventually, my mother came to tell me she and Will were going to a charity ball on the other end of town and that they wouldn't be staying at home that night. She said I should invite Jenna over, and I agreed without really thinking about it. Nick was the one I wanted to have sleep over, but a part of me was scared to call him and for him to realize I was hiding something. I spent the rest of the day torn, but when I saw he hadn't called me either, I went back to bed, determined to spend the night alone with my nightmares.

20

Nick

AFTER WHAT RAFFAELLA HAD SAID, PLUS THE CONVERSATION WITH Jenna and the call from my mom, I spent a few days in a fog. What scared me was that they might be right. I wasn't the perfect boyfriend. Till recently, I hadn't even been anyone's boyfriend! When my mother had abandoned me, I'd sworn I was never going to give anyone the power to hurt me again. No way I was going to leave myself open to rejection after that.

But with Noah, everything had changed, and I felt like I was dying inside when I thought something might go wrong, that I might not be good for her, that she would end up leaving me the way my mother had.

Her not calling me didn't exactly help ease my mind. I didn't understand why Noah hadn't wanted me to come see her. My boss told me my father was going to the other end of town, and all it took was one phone call to verify that and to figure out that Raffaella was going with him. That meant Noah was at home alone. I was pissed for a moment, but as night fell, I remembered Jenna's words: *Noah is not okay. She has nightmares.* All I could do to stop thinking about this was show her they weren't real. So I got my keys and left.

It was pitch-black when I stepped out of the car. My father's house was barely visible—no one had thought to turn on the porch light. That irritated me. After turning the key in the lock, I hurried upstairs. For a moment, I thought Noah wasn't there because I didn't see the light under her door. But then I heard her. She was crying. I opened the door, my chest tight with apprehension. It couldn't be. It was dark in her room, and she was twisting in the sheets. I hit the light switch, but it didn't turn on. Goddammit. The power was off.

When I saw Noah up close, her face was streaked with tears, and her fingernails had dug so deep into her palms that one of them was bleeding where the skin had broken. I was at a loss. Ignoring the alarms going off inside me, I sat down next to her.

"Noah, wake up," I said, pushing aside the hair that her tears had made stick to her face.

It was pointless. She was still asleep but stirring, as if hoping to look away from whatever she was dreaming about, whatever had put her in that state of desolation and fear.

I shook her, softly at first, and then insistently. But she didn't seem to want to wake up.

"Noah," I whispered in her ear. "It's Nicholas. Wake up, I'm here."

She made a noise, and I saw her hands ball even tighter into tiny fists. She was really hurting herself.

"Noah!" I shouted now.

Then her eyes opened. She was horrified. The only time I'd ever seen her like that was when those assholes from her school had locked her in a closet. She looked around the bedroom before seeming to locate me, and then she must have realized that everything she had dreamed was just that—a dream, a nightmare, and nothing more. She threw herself into my arms, and I felt her heart racing.

"Easy, Freckles," I said, squeezing her to calm her down. "I'm here. It was just a bad dream."

Noah buried her face in my neck. I panicked when she started to shake and sob. It tore at my very soul. What the hell was going on? I pulled her onto my lap. I needed her to look at me. I needed to understand what was happening.

"Noah, what's up?" I asked, trying to conceal the fear in my voice. "Noah, Noah, stop!" I ordered her because the soft approach was just making her worse. I hadn't seen her cry like that in ages.

I pushed her away slightly and held her face in my hands. For a moment, she looked away, but then I grabbed her chin and forced her to meet my gaze.

"How long have you been having nightmares?" I asked, recognizing that what Jenna had said was true: Noah wasn't okay. I cursed myself for believing that she and I had left our pasts behind us.

"It was just this once," she said amid heaves. "I don't know why…"

I wiped away her tears with my knuckles, knowing she wasn't being honest with me.

"Noah, you can tell me the truth," I said, disappointed that she didn't trust me.

She shook her head, seeming calmer now. "I'm glad you're here," she whispered.

"Really?" I asked. I still didn't understand why she hadn't called me.

"Of course I am… I'm sorry about what my mom said. You know it's not true." She hugged me. I wondered if she was trying to make herself believe her own words. Her mom could think what she wanted. What worried me was knowing Jenna was right, that Noah wasn't okay, and that she didn't trust me enough to be honest about what was going on…

I took her hand and opened it so she could see the wounds in her palms. They dismayed her, but she didn't look surprised in the least. This wasn't the first time, I could tell.

"Is it because of me?" I asked, struggling to maintain my composure, trying to forget all the things that could have made Noah relive the worst moments of her youth... My face was still scarred by the blows I'd gotten right when she was returning from Europe. I was a constant reminder that violence hadn't disappeared from her life, and I had to control myself not to turn around and run out, since it was clear I was doing her more harm than good.

"Of course not," she responded automatically. "Nicholas, don't make more out of this than what it is. I just had a night-mare, and—"

"It wasn't just a nightmare, Noah," I replied, trying to control myself. "You should have seen yourself. It looked like someone was torturing you... Tell me what you were dreaming about, because I know this has happened before."

Her eyes widened with surprise when she heard me say this. She got up and walked a few steps back, finally turning around and saying, "It hasn't happened before."

I got up.

"Bullshit, Noah!" I shouted.

Why would she lie?

"Nick!" she said, turning to face me. The only light piercing the darkness came in faintly through the window. "This has nothing to do with you."

I wanted to believe her. I knew this had to do with what had happened to her when she was a little girl, but I thought it would end when her bastard of a father died. It crushed me to know her demons were still pursuing her. I tried to soothe her, but she observed me with suspicion even as she let me approach.

"Listen," I said, resting my hands on her shoulders. "Just tell me when you're ready." I hated that the moment wasn't now, but I continued. "You know I'm here for you. I hate seeing you hurting, Noah. All I'm asking is what I can do to make you feel better."

Her eyes went moist. Noah had cried more in those past two months than I could have ever imagined... She never used to cry at all... And now I didn't know which was worse.

I pulled her close and held her. She was so small...I couldn't stand knowing something was tormenting her. Turning my cheek until I faced her, she told me, "Nick, stop thinking this is your fault." Her eyes gleamed, her voice was raspy, and all I could think was that there was nothing else like this, and I was part of it, and I would kill for those glassy eyes. "You're the one thing in my life that brings me peace. The one thing that makes me feel safe."

"What are you scared of, though?" I asked. I couldn't help it.

Her expression changed, and the transparency of a moment before was now hidden behind a wall that kept rising between us no matter how many times I tried to knock it down, especially when certain subjects came to the surface.

But I couldn't press her, and I couldn't wait for her to answer, because the sound of something breaking downstairs startled both of us.

"What was that?" Noah asked, her eyes on the door, her face once again looking fearful.

I got between her and the door. It must have been Steve or Prett.

"Who else is in the house?" I asked, making sure I kept my voice calm.

After a few seconds, she responded: "Just us."

I could feel her pressing into my back.

Shit.

21

Noah

HEARING SOMETHING SHATTER DOWNSTAIRS HAD SCARED THE hell out of me, but for a moment, I was happy for the interruption.

What are you scared of?

That question was so complicated, touched on so many issues in my life, that I could answer it any number of ways, and that made it the worst thing anyone could ever ask me, especially Nick. If I started listing all the fears still present in my mind, it would cause a lot of problems. Some stuff was better to leave buried, even if it occasionally rose to the surface and messed up my life.

"Please tell me you put the alarm on, Noah," Nicholas said, walking toward the door and cracking it to listen close as he peered into the darkness.

"We have an alarm?" I asked, feeling like an idiot and actually getting scared.

"Jesus, Noah," he groaned, walking out into the hall and motioning for me to be quiet and stay where I was.

I ignored him, following close behind. For a few seconds, there was silence, apart from our breathing. But then we could hear voices. Men's voices.

Nicholas turned, grabbed my arm, and dragged me back into the bedroom. Terrified, I watched him bring a finger to his lips.

"Give me your phone," he whispered, trying to stay calm, but I could tell it wasn't easy for him.

I nodded, then cursed. "I left the damn thing by the pool!"

How could I be so stupid? I always had my phone on me, and now that I needed it, it was outside in the yard.

"Well, mine's downstairs, on the table by the door."

His brain started clicking. "Listen to me. I want you to stay here."

I shook my head.

"Dammit, Noah, stay here. I'll go to Dad's room where there's a phone and dial nine-one-one!"

"No, stay with me," I begged him in desperation.

I was so fucking scared... I had never been the victim of a robbery or anything like that. It was true that the kidnapping had been bad, but it hadn't made me any stronger when it came to facing situations like this. More like the opposite. I was so scared, my hands were shaking.

"Nicholas, they turned off the power. They probably cut our phone line, too."

Before he could respond, we heard the voices again, this time closer by. Nicholas hushed me with one hand. There was no doubt about it. They were coming upstairs. A glance back at me must have sufficed to let Nick know that whatever he had in mind, he needed to take me with him.

"Stay close behind me, and don't make a sound," he warned me. Then he opened the door and walked out into the dark hallway. I was present, but at the same time, I was inhabiting those memories it was best not to return to, the ones that stoked my fears in the darkness. Nothing good could happen in the dark... or only one thing, but this wasn't the moment to think about it.

"What is that?" I asked, my breathing halting from fear.

"Nothing," he said, walking over to the window. As he opened it and peeked outside, I saw what was sticking out of the top of his jeans.

"What the hell are you doing with a gun, Nicholas?" It took all the self-control I could muster not to shout.

He turned to me with a serious expression. "Noah, I want you to climb out this window," he ordered me, ignoring my question. "There's a tree out there. It has lots of branches; it won't be hard for you."

I felt hot tears rolling down my cheeks again. I shook my head... I couldn't take the risk; I couldn't fall out a window again... I just couldn't.

"Nicholas, I can't," I confessed. Why was fate determined to make me relive things I wanted so desperately to leave behind?

"Why not?" he asked incredulously, as if I were insane, as if I didn't realize the danger we were in. We were trapped in the house, and not just that, whoever was downstairs had cut off the power, which probably meant they'd been planning this for some time. They must have known William was away, just as his service staff did.

Suddenly, a look of comprehension crossed Nick's face.

"Noah, this isn't the same as jumping out a window, babe," he said calmly, his eyes returning constantly to the door. "I climbed this tree a thousand times when I was a kid. You're not going to fall. You're not going to hurt yourself."

I knew what he was saying made sense, but I was paralyzed with fear. Windows, jumping...what that had meant for me in the past was devastating. I put my hands instinctively over my stomach, right where my scar lay.

Seeing me do that, Nicholas looked sad, but he covered it up as best he could. That was a taboo subject; I never talked about it, and neither did he...even if we were going to have to eventually.

"Please, Noah, do it for me," he asked. "I can't let anyone hurt you again."

I tried to put myself in his place. If something happened to me, if the people who had broken into the house saw us, I had no idea what could happen. I was scared for Nicholas. I knew what he was like, and I knew his natural tendency would be to run straight into the line of danger. If he was still there with me, that meant just one thing: I mattered more to him than anything those people might steal or destroy.

"You go first, and I'll follow after," I said, trying to keep my emotions in check. I knew if I went down first, he would probably go after them, and seeing his gun, I was scared of what could happen to him, more scared than I had been of anything else up to then.

By his scowl, I knew I had him. He'd definitely been planning on staying behind.

"Sometimes I could strangle you," he said, but he followed those words with a quick kiss on the lips.

Happily, the house was big enough that no one could hear us whispering.

Nicholas climbed out the window with ease, and I walked over to watch him descend. The branch was around nine feet off the ground. Memories of my accident assailed me. When I'd jumped out that window as a kid, I hadn't even realized what I was doing... I remembered I'd been so scared that all I cared about was getting out of that hellhole of darkness and abuse. My father was the boogeyman, the monster every child is afraid of, but at that moment, I didn't have a mom around to tell me it was just a nightmare. The monster had been real, and I'd had to jump to escape him.

Nick was soon on the lawn motioning for me to hurry behind him. Hearing a noise on the other end of the room, I shivered, went out the window legs first, and grabbed onto the tree trunk. I needed to go down before someone saw me. Nick was ready to catch me if I fell; that dissolved my fears. Soon he was holding me, and I could breathe easily again.

"Come on," he said, pulling me toward the backyard. "Where's your phone?"

We looked all around, scared someone might pop out in the night.

Thank God it was where I left it, on top of a deck chair, but that wasn't all. Thor, the dog we both adored, was lying a yard away next to the pool. It was weird that he hadn't barked—that hadn't occurred to us until now—and now I felt even more scared. Nicholas jogged over to him and put his ear on his chest while I covered my mouth with one hand in dread.

"He's alive," he said, and I walked over and kneeled beside him. The dog was breathing regularly, as though asleep, with no signs of injuries.

"They must have drugged him," Nick said, petting his head.

I bent over and kissed the dog's furry neck.

"Come on, Noah, they might see us," Nick said, and we left Thor behind.

Nick grabbed the phone and dragged me behind the pool house, pushing me into the wall and pressing into me to protect me with his body. That reminded me of my birthday party, and I thought how ironic it was that now we were in that same position, hoping not to be discovered.

He looked down and dialed emergency services, telling them what was happening, that someone had broken into our home and we were hiding. They told him a patrol was on the way and we should stay put. When he hung up, he hugged me and kissed my scalp.

"Are you okay?" he asked. "Don't worry, they won't see us here. Everything will be fine."

I was so nervous, my hands were shaking. The nightmare, knowing Nicholas had heard me, what he'd told me afterward, having to jump out that window... I wanted to roll into a ball on the ground and wait for everything to go back to normal. I needed to escape my bad memories.

"Can I have a kiss?" I asked him instead of responding. I felt the adrenaline coursing through my veins, and I wouldn't calm down until the police got there.

He seemed to think it a strange request, but he bent over anyway and answered my wishes. It was supposed to be quick and sweet, but I wrapped my hand around the back of his head and tried to get him to do it harder. Pushing my back against the wall, he made all of it—what was happening just then, the frustration of the day I'd gotten back from Europe after a month apart, my fight with my mother, my doubts—disappear in an instant. He slowed when he saw the situation was getting out of hand, but he didn't let me go, and I stayed close to him. My hands touched something in the waistline of his pants, and he stepped back until we were completely apart.

In silence, panting, I watched him as he looked at me, took the gun out of the back of his pants, and put it on the ground where it wouldn't bother him. The pistol gleamed in the moonlight, and I was scared.

"You shouldn't have that," I warned him. But before he could respond, we heard the sirens of the police cars. He came back close to me and said, "Please, don't leave my side."

I nodded and took his hand, ready for whatever awaited us.

When we emerged from our hiding place, we saw the police cars. People were milling around the door, and even neighbors were there, scared or just interested in what was going on. Two guys had tried to rob us. They'd been caught red-handed and hadn't managed to get away. The worst part was that they'd been armed, and that reminded me that Nick had been, too.

I didn't say a word while he spoke to the cops and told them everything that had happened and how we'd escaped through the window. They wrote everything down, got the power back on, and told us we should go to the station to give a statement.

"You can take care of that tomorrow, Mr. Leister," the policeman said, looking at me with worry. "Probably you should get some rest for now."

"I hope they rot in jail," Nicholas said, looking at the squad car as it departed our home.

After that, and a few conversations with the neighbors, the last policeman left, and everyone else followed suit. I called my mom to let her know what had happened.

"Tell Nick to stay at the house with you tonight," she said, and while that surprised me, I felt a warm gratitude I hadn't known for some time. "We'll be there as soon as we can."

When I hung up, Nick took me inside, locked the door, and keyed in the code for the alarm I hadn't known existed. I swore then and there, I'd never leave it off.

"Let's go to bed," he said, grabbing my hand and walking upstairs.

In his room, he gave me a clean pajama T-shirt to wear. We changed clothes in silence, totally absorbed in our thoughts.

"If I hadn't decided to come..." he said, and I saw the fear in his face. The images that had plagued my mind must now be plaguing his, I thought. "That's why I want us to live together, so I can always be there when you need me."

Now I saw it clearly: the sense of safety I felt with him, how good I felt when he was there... It was true what he was saying—I needed him. He was the one I trusted, the cure to my nightmares, the one who could scare my demons away.

"I'll tell my mother, Nick, I promise," I said, banishing all doubts from my mind. There was no denying it now: Nick was the guy I needed to be with. A genuine smile crossed his face, and he kissed my lips and hugged me tight. It was weird, being there in his room. We hadn't spent much time together in those four walls because he had moved out almost as soon as we got together, but still, I thought of the first time we'd slept together…how nervous I'd been, how beautiful it had been. He had treated me as if I were made of glass… Now, the way we were with each other was so different… As time passed, everything seemed more intense, as if we needed more and didn't know how to manage our desires…

"Come here," he said.

I did as he asked, got into his bed, and curled up in the sheets, clinging to him and resting my head on his chest. The last thing I remember is that I was dreaming, but of something far more beautiful than before: him.

22

Nick

I WOKE UP WITH NOAH WHISPERING INTO MY EAR.

"Nick...wake up."

I didn't open my eyes, I just grunted, and her tongue started slowly and softly caressing my jaw.

Shit.

"Nick," she repeated several times as her hand crept down my chest and stopped for a moment on the dark hair on my belly.

"I'm beat, Freckles. If you want something, you're going to have to try harder."

It was strange to have Noah trying to get my attention that way. I was usually the one going after her. I liked this role reversal.

"I guess I'll have to look for someone else," she said then, getting my attention and putting me on alert. I felt her pull away, and I opened my eyes and pounced on her so fast, she couldn't have gotten away if she'd wanted to.

She took a deep breath as I slid a hand under her T-shirt and squeezed one of her breasts.

"Freckles, we've hardly slept," I said, my mouth descending to her neck. "What's this early morning sexual harassment about?"

"You're my boyfriend. I'm just trying to make you do your job," she replied, pushing her hips into me and breathing hard against my bare shoulder.

"You can make me do my job as a boyfriend whenever you like, but hold still for a minute," I said, immobilizing her on the bed. She was so small beneath me...! I wanted to kiss her slowly until we forgot everything, even our names. "You do know our parents might be here, right?"

I didn't give a shit about our parents, but I decided to make her wait a little longer before I gave her what she wanted. In response, she wrapped her legs around my waist and squeezed me. "Since when do you care?"

I smiled in the shadows, and right away, her hand was on my pants, trying to get inside them, but I stopped her before I lost control.

"Unless I remember wrong, last time you were the one taking the reins, Freckles. Now you're at it again? Who gave you permission?"

"Permission?" she repeated, her eyebrows raised. "Keep acting smart and you won't get anything at all."

I laughed. "Babe, you won't regret waking me up," I assured her, pulling off the T-shirt, rubbing her body, and maneuvering to where I wanted to be. I kissed her legs and thighs, counting to ten to keep control of myself. Noah stirred, sighing, gripping the sheets, and I knew I was about to make my promises reality. "Look at me," I ordered her.

As we locked eyes, she said, "Oh, God."

"You like that?" I asked, and just then, I heard a noise behind the door.

I cursed, got on top of Noah so she was completely concealed beneath me, and pulled the covers over us.

"What are you doing?" she asked. "I was about to..." Just

then, I covered her mouth with one hand while the door opened with a creak.

"Nicholas?" Raffaella asked.

Dammit!

"Raffaella, I was asleep," I replied, trying to maintain the calm in my voice while Noah lay beneath me, stiff as a board.

"Sorry. I just wanted to thank you for staying here with Noah."

Noah—I could feel her just then, shaking beneath me.

"No worries. I wouldn't have wanted to leave her alone," I said, smiling, caressing her now. I looked down and could just barely glimpse Noah's eyes, so big that I almost cracked up laughing.

"I know," Raffaella said serenely. "Okay, well, I'll let you sleep. Your father and I were hoping we could all have breakfast together in a bit."

"Great," I said, frowning from pain as I felt Noah's teeth sink into my arm. Her mother shut the door, and Noah slapped my shoulder.

"Idiot!" she snarled.

I laughed again and kissed her, sliding my tongue between her lips and savoring her while my fingers toyed with her. A few flicks, and all her anger had subsided.

"You're a douche," she said, closing her eyes, enjoying my attentions.

"A lucky one. Come here." I took off my underwear and pulled her to me without waiting, grunting into the pillow as I felt her. She murmured something unintelligible while I started stroking, not wanting to waste time.

"Please, Nicholas, I need to finish…" she whispered, digging her nails into my back. I'd left her hanging before, but now I caressed her again, wriggling my way between our bodies.

When I heard her gasp, I stopped for a few seconds, trying to stretch the time on so I wouldn't come, too.

I started over, going slowly, waiting for her to recover. Nothing compared to feeling her like this, with no barrier between us, skin against skin. Since Noah had gone on the pill, I was in heaven.

"Just one more," I said, slowing down. "Let's try and finish at the same time."

And we did. Together, we reached that spectacular liberation that left us exhausted for long minutes. We lay still in bed, trying to recover our breath.

"That's what happens when you try to waylay me in the morning," I said.

"I'll try and remember that for next time."

Months had passed since the last time I had breakfast with my father in the kitchen. I think it was shortly after Noah returned from the hospital after the kidnapping. Doing it again was very weird. Raffaella was there, too. We were a happy family, I guess.

I didn't want them to see how little I cared to be there. Plus, Noah didn't like seeing me in a bad mood with her mother there, so I tried to act relaxed. Noah sat next to me. She wasn't so much eating her cereal as playing with it. The radio was on in the background as always, and the way my father and Raffaella were sitting there across from us told me this wasn't just a casual meal together.

"So…" my father started, looking back and forth between Noah and me. "How's everything going? You'll be off to school soon, Noah. Do you have everything ready?"

"Not even close. I still need to get started packing," she said, putting a huge spoonful of cereal into her mouth.

I tensed when I saw she wasn't saying anything about living with me. This was as good a time as any, but she showed no sign that she was ready to pull the trigger.

"Do you know who your roommate will be yet?" her mother

asked, and Noah almost choked. I stretched out a hand and struck her softly a few times on the back.

"Not yet," she said in a raspy voice.

Shit. I wanted out of that kitchen. Now.

Raffaella looked at my father, and they both looked back at us.

"We wanted to talk to you both," he began. "I realize we haven't exactly acted like a family these past few months... We've had our dustups, and we want to try to resolve that so we can all get along a little better."

I wasn't expecting that. As my father and I met eyes, I put my cup of coffee down on the table. I was all ears.

"Are you going to finally accept that we're together?" I asked.

Raffaella stiffened, and my father gave her an almost-threatening look. "We accept that you are young, and you like each other, and..."

"We love each other, Mom, it's not just *like*," Noah said, finally intervening.

Her mother pursed her lips and nodded. "I get it, Noah, I promise, and I know you think I've been ruining your life because I don't accept your relationship, and maybe you're right...but you're very young, and the nearly five years' age difference is a big one, especially when you've just turned eighteen. All I'm asking is for you to take it slow. Nick, I hope you can understand that my daughter still has a lot to learn. She's about to head off to school, and I want her to experiment and have fun and enjoy to the maximum—something I never dreamed I could give her."

I could feel the rage kindling and starting to slowly burn inside me.

"Are you saying she doesn't have fun with me, that I'm not going to allow her to enjoy college?"

"What she's saying is for you not to base everything you do

on each other. You've still got a whole life ahead of you, and we don't want you to take things too fast," Dad said, trying to still the waters. "So, on that note, we wanted to propose a deal. Like a peace treaty. What do you think?"

"I'm not interested in any kind of treaty. Noah's my girlfriend, and there's nothing to negotiate."

My father sucked in a breath, and I could tell he was struggling not to start shouting.

"Then I need you both to do us a favor. And if you do, we promise not to get mixed up in your relationship anymore."

"What type of favor?" I asked, wanting to get to the damned point.

My father seemed to be weighing his words carefully.

"In a month, Leister Enterprises will be celebrating its sixtieth anniversary. We're going to have a charity reception. All kinds of people will be there, and all the money we raise will go to an organization that feeds people in developing countries. It's a vital affair for the company, Nicholas, you know that perfectly. We're undertaking new projects, and we need to give a strong and unified image when we are in front of the press and the other guests."

"I know how important it is. I've helped organize it," I said. "And I don't know what it has to do with my relationship with Noah."

"It's very simple. If you both show up to the party as a couple, you can imagine the articles in the press... Everyone will focus on you and how scandalous your relationship is. No, Nicholas, don't interrupt me," he said when he saw I was about to cut him off. "I'm well aware of what kind of relationship you both have, and however much we dislike it, you're within your rights. You're stepbrother and stepsister, you're not related by blood, but many won't see it that way. I need to present a solid image of our family, and if you show up acting like a couple, lots of the people at the party will be confused and will look down on us. I'm talking about older people, people with lots of money, who simply don't accept that kind of conduct."

"This is ridiculous. No one's going to notice us. My God, no one cares what we do or don't do."

"That would be true if you hadn't spent the past few years being seen with the kinds of girls who end up in magazines. You know perfectly well that the press has always had its eye on you, Nicholas. Just look at how they crowd around you every damned time you decide to show up at some function."

Noah looked at me askance, and I cursed between clenched teeth. Dammit!

"Are you asking me to go to the party alone and act like Noah is my little sister?"

"I'm asking you to take a friend, a female friend, and avoid the spotlight. Noah will go with a date, too. We'll pose like a family for the cameras, we'll have dinner, chitchat, negotiate with some of the big players in attendance, and then everyone can go home and back to their normal lives."

Before I could explode, Noah butted in. "Sounds fine," she said. I glared at her.

"Screw that. You're not going to a major event like that with some dickhead who thinks you're on the market. No way."

Raffaella now opened her mouth again. "Nicholas, this is what I'm talking about when I say you need to calm down. It's just a party. Your father is telling you how important it is. This doesn't mean Noah's going to marry some other guy. For the love of God, if she wants to go alone, that's fine with us, too."

I took a few deep breaths and stood.

"We'll go, we'll pose for the cameras as you wish, but I'll warn you, when they eventually figure out what's going on with us, Dad's going to look like a fucking liar."

We walked out to the backyard. I was so mad that I stared wordlessly at the waves breaking on the cliff below the house, trying to calm down. I felt Noah's arms embracing me from behind and her cheek leaning softly on my shoulder. Putting a hand on top of hers, I felt a little better.

"It's not such a big deal, Nick..." she said. I turned and looked at her sternly.

"For me it is... Noah, I can't stand people thinking you're not mine."

"But I am, you know I am, and it's just a stupid party. We'll be there for a few hours at the most. Don't overthink it."

I shook my head. "It's important, though. This is the last time I give in to something like this." I kissed her. "I want to shout to the whole world that I'm with you. I can't believe you don't feel the same."

She shrugged and smiled. "I don't care what anyone else thinks. You know I'm yours. That should be enough."

I sighed and kissed the tip of her nose. *It should be, but it isn't,* I thought to myself. Things needed to change.

23

Noah

I WAS GOING TO MEET UP WITH JENNA THAT AFTERNOON. I HADN'T seen her in a month, since before I'd gone to Europe, and I had the feeling she was avoiding me. Finally she'd agreed to let me come to her house. As I was waiting by the door, I couldn't help admiring their huge front yard. They didn't have a private gate like the Leisters, but it was a far walk to reach the entrance. They had a bunch of very tall trees and yellow swings and a small pond with frogs and pretty flowers to the right of the house, which gave it a fairy-tale air. Almost all the mansions in that development were incredible, but Jenna's had something special about it, and that was probably thanks to her.

"Come in, Miss Morgan," Lisa, the maid, said. I smiled back at her.

"Is Jenna in her room?" I asked. I could hear video games in the background, so I knew her brothers were home, at least.

"Yes, she's waiting for you," she answered. Then she took off running when she heard something break in another room.

I laughed as I headed toward the stairs, which were next to an elegantly decorated sitting room and a bar with hundreds of bottles of liquor meant to tempt you.

I knocked on Jenna's door and went in, and I found her sitting cross-legged on her zebra-skin rug surrounded by suitcases and piles of clothes. Her hair was pulled back on the top of her head. A smile appeared on her face when she saw me, and she got up to give me a hug.

"I missed you, Blondie," she said as she let me go. It was weird not to see her jumping around or dragging me over to sit on the bed so she could gossip and grill me for the latest details in my life. I could tell something was bothering her, something that kept her from being her usual energetic, entertaining self.

"What are you doing here?" I asked, trying to hide my worry. She looked around, almost clueless.

"Oh, this!" She sat back on the floor and motioned for me to do the same. "I'm deciding what to take to school. Can you believe it's so soon?"

Despite all the times we'd talked about college, our independence, and how we would make sure to come see each other, I was surprised she seemed so excited to go.

"I haven't even started packing my bags..." I said and remembered with apprehension that I still hadn't confronted my mother to tell her I'd be living with Nick. I also needed to tell Jenna, but something told me this wasn't the time.

I spent a few minutes helping her fold T-shirts and looked around, distracted, anxious to find out what was going on with her.

Jenna's room was the complete opposite of mine. While mine was blue and white and tranquil, an invitation to relax, Jenna's had pink walls and black furniture. She had hung up a big mannequin with a bunch of necklaces around its neck; we'd tried to untangle them before, because they were supercool, and we wanted to wear them. But our attempts were in vain—they'd never be more than decorations. On another wall, a black-and-white zebra-print sofa that matched the rug was turned toward the TV across from it. She, too, had a walk-in closet, but just then it was an utter disaster.

In the background, I heard Pharrell Williams playing. I was surprised she wasn't humming along. I looked at her for a few more seconds. Since when did Jenna Tavish spend more than five seconds in silence? I laid the T-shirt I was folding on the ground.

"You can go ahead and tell me what's up with you," I said in a slightly firmer tone than I had used thus far.

"What do you mean? Nothing's up," she responded. But she then got up and turned her back to me, sitting on her immense bed, which was covered in clothes and fashion magazines.

"Jenna, we know each other... You didn't even ask how my trip was. I know something's going on with you. Now spit it out," I said, getting up and going over to her. I didn't like seeing her like that: my friend, my best friend, normally so cheerful and alive, all depressed.

She looked up from a piece of paper she was holding in her hand, and her eyes were damp.

"I had a fight with Lion... I've never seen him like that before. He's never yelled at me that way." A tear streamed down her cheek. I couldn't believe what she was telling me.

Lion was a sweetie pie. He could be an asshole sometimes, the same as Nick, but that didn't change his nature. He treated Jenna like a queen. I couldn't imagine what could have happened to make them argue.

"What was it about?" I asked, afraid it was because of the beating Nick took the other day and the trouble Lion had gotten into...or rather, that they both had gotten into. But I decided not to say anything.

Jenna wrapped her arms around her legs and rested her head on her knees. "I decided not to go to UC Berkeley," she said.

I opened my eyes wide. Jenna had worked so hard to get into the same college as her father. And it wasn't just the family connection—it was Berkeley! One of the best schools in the country.

"What? Why?"

Jenna huffed. "You're looking at me just like Lion did, like I've committed a crime or something." She let her hair down and pulled it back again, the way she always did when she was nervous or angry. "UCLA is a great school. You're going there, Nick goes there..."

"Yeah, but Jenna, Berkeley is a huge deal. Even if you go there, you can still see Lion on the weekends. It's not like the Bay Area is on the moon..."

"I'm not going!" she said desperately. "I don't know what's up with Lion lately, but he's being weird as hell, and there's no way I'm moving to another city unless I know he's okay."

I nodded. I understood her perfectly. "So what exactly did Lion say?"

"He completely lost his shit. He told me I was an idiot for changing schools just because of him. He said there was no way I could put my future at risk because of us..." Her voice cracked, and I could see she was about to lose it. "He threatened to leave me!"

I opened my eyes wide with surprise. What the...?

"He's not going to leave you, Jenna, and you're free to do what you want. He's crazy about you. There's no way he'll stop seeing you over this."

Jenna shook her head, wiping away tears with the back of her hand. "You don't get it—he's changed; he's different. I don't know what it is, but all he talks about is making money. The other day..." She choked back a sob. "You should have seen his face, Noah. I mean, not like Nicholas wasn't worse for wear, too, but they could have killed him, and it was all the fault of..."

Her eyes met mine as she left the phrase hanging.

"The fault of what, Jenna?"

She looked away, stood, grabbed a pile of clothes, and dropped it into one of the open suitcases on the floor, making it seem as if she didn't want to look at me.

"Nothing. I just don't like Lion getting involved in stuff like that. Doing the things he and Nick were into last year..."

"They don't, though, Jenna. They've changed. Nicholas has changed," I said.

She turned to me and laughed, with an incredulous expression. "No they haven't! Nicholas is still wrapped up in the same shit as always."

I stood still, feeling a pressure in my chest that made me unable to breathe for a few seconds.

"What the hell are you talking about?" I asked, angry now, though I didn't know why. I wasn't going to let Jenna take her bad mood out on me, let alone Nick. She was telling me a bunch of lies.

She seemed to regret her words, but that didn't stop her.

"Our boyfriends are fools. They're still up to their necks in shit, and they're just trying to make us believe they've cleaned up their act!"

"They have, Jenna! Nicholas doesn't hang out with those people anymore. He's changed!"

Again she laughed, but this time, it was cruel. I didn't recognize her just then—I didn't know who she was—she was trash-talking my boyfriend for no reason, not even making sense, as if it were his fault Lion couldn't accept her decision about what school to go to.

"You're more naive than I thought, Noah, honestly. You don't know anything."

Now she was trying my patience.

"What do I not know?"

"They're talking about going back to the races," she replied bitterly. "Both of them. Next week. I bet nobody told you that, did they?"

I was speechless.

"Nick will never race again, not after what happened last year," I finally managed to say.

"Well, it's just a matter of time till you see for yourself."

———————

As soon as I could, I left. I didn't want to keep talking to her; I didn't want to keep listening to her. Nicholas wouldn't race again. We'd both promised each other we wouldn't make that mistake. Those races had made Ronnie my enemy, and then he'd almost killed me, not to mention schemed with my father to kidnap me. What had been fun at first had turned terrible and dangerous, and that was why I didn't believe a word Jenna was saying.

When I got home, it was almost dinnertime. I went in, trying not to make noise, and heard my mother in the living room. I didn't want to talk to her, so I crept into the kitchen, grabbed a ready-made salad from the fridge with a Coke Zero, and hurried up the stairs. Right as I was placing everything on the bed, my phone rang.

Another unknown number.

Shit. That could only mean one person. I let it ring, feeling my pulse speed up. I still felt guilty for telling Nicholas's mother that I would meet her to talk about him behind his back, but the social worker had called Nick to tell him she'd decided his sister could stay with him for a few days, and he was elated about it. There was no turning back. Maddie wouldn't arrive till Thursday, there were two days left, but I knew as soon as Anabel set foot in LA, she'd want to see me.

The phone rang again, and again I didn't pick up. Then a text message came through.

YOUR FAULT | **173**

See you at the Hilton at LAX at noon. A.

Shit. Anabel Grason had just sent me a message. I erased it as soon as I read it. I didn't want there to be any proof of what I was about to do. I felt awful, as if I were betraying Nick, and deep down I knew that I was. But apart from wanting his sister to spend a few days with him without a social worker around or the clock ticking down, I wanted to know what that woman had to say, what her angle was, apart from pumping me for details about her son.

I typed a short and simple response.

OK.

I lost my appetite after that, as well as what little dignity I had, at least in regards to that woman.

———

"Come on, Noah, pick one," Nicholas said, exasperated.

"I'll go for beige," I said after thinking it over for a long time.

Nick rolled his eyes.

"If it's beige, we'll just leave it green, the way it is," he said, taking the sample out of my hand.

"Green?" I said with disgust. "You're going to stick a little girl in a green room?"

The woman who was helping us and had waited patiently while we chose a color for Maddie's room decided it was time to interrupt us.

"Green is very stylish, even if you're still on the fence... How far along are you?" she asked, looking at my stomach and smiling.

It took me a few seconds to figure out what she was insinuating.

"What? No, no!" I shook my head.

Nicholas turned serious and stared icily at the employee.

"Oh, I thought..." she said, looking at Nick, then me, then my belly again.

She'd thought I was pregnant and we were choosing the color for our baby's bedroom. Our baby... God, why did I have to think about that? It gave me an uneasy feeling.

"We're choosing a color for my six-year-old sister's bedroom," Nicholas said, putting the samples on the counter. "Do we look like we're about to be parents? My girlfriend's eighteen and I'm twenty-two. Why don't you think before you start drawing stupid conclusions?"

I was shocked. What was that outburst about?

"I...I'm sorry, I didn't..."

I understood how she was feeling. The look Nicholas gave her was the same one he gave me when I was upsetting him.

"It's fine. We'll go with white. You can tell the painters to come out tomorrow," I said, trying to calm things down. Nicholas's blue eyes looked furious, but he didn't say more.

After we paid, there was an uncomfortable silence. I couldn't take it, so I forced him to look at me when we got to the car.

"Are you going to tell me what's up?"

Nicholas looked elsewhere, and that just made things worse. I was scared...scared I wouldn't be good enough for him. Scared I couldn't have kids, shouldn't even think about it, especially now, because if I did, I might break down and fall into a black hole and never be able to crawl out.

"I can't stand people sticking their noses where they don't belong. That's all," he said, and gave me a kiss on the forehead.

I knew he was hiding something. And I knew exactly what he was thinking...but I didn't want to hear about it. Not then.

I hugged him, leaned my cheek into his chest, tried to cheer up. I ignored the fear that threatened to come out at moments like that and got into the car as if he had never uttered those words.

We spent the rest of the afternoon buying furniture for the room. It would all be delivered the next day, which meant we had twenty-four hours to put it together if we wanted the room ready for her on Thursday. Nick was excited; I could see it in his eyes, in his enthusiasm as he picked everything out. Leaving aside the flare-up over my supposed pregnancy, I'd had a good time going to the shops and toy stores with Nick.

We bought a blue single bed for her and a few things to play with. Nick wanted the room to look like mine: more or less neutral and not too cheesy. When we got to his place, I was exhausted, and I flopped down on the bed as soon as I walked in. He lay down over my back, pressing me into the mattress while giving me just enough space to breathe. His mouth looked for my ear, making me shiver.

"Thanks for doing this with me," he whispered, leaving hot kisses on my neck.

With my cheek pressed into the mattress, I couldn't see his face, but the feel of his mouth on my skin was enough.

But despite that, I came out with the words "I was with Jenna yesterday," uncertain how he would react to that mention of my best friend. He stopped, tensed, and I could feel his weight rising off me. I turned around and leaned on my elbows, observing him. His back was turned as he removed his T-shirt and let it fall to the ground.

"Great," he replied.

I frowned as he walked into the bathroom and almost slammed the door shut. I walked in after him without knocking, feeling I didn't need to.

He was leaning on the sink and looked up when he heard me.

"You know...?" I said. "We *were* talking."

"So?"

Why is he talking to me that way?

"You getting on the defensive only confirms to me that what Jenna told me you're up to is the truth."

He turned around. "What is it I'm supposedly going to do, then?"

I hated when he adopted that tone of voice. I wished I hadn't even brought the whole thing up, but if it was true he was thinking about racing again...

I looked at his nude torso, the scabs and scars... That had to stop.

"You can't go on doing this stuff, Nicholas," I said, measuring my words. "Jenna told me Lion was going to start racing again..."

Without even looking at me, he walked around me and back out. "Lion's a big boy. He can do what he wants, no?"

"So you're not going?" I went on, just wanting to put myself at ease.

"No, I'm not going." He turned and stared at me. "And honestly, I couldn't give less of a shit about what Jenna has to say about me or our relationship."

That got to me.

"Jenna's not what matters. It's that you shouldn't have gotten into that fight with Lion! You told me all that was over!"

"It is over! Noah, honestly, I already told you. Lion was in trouble, and I lent him a hand." He exhaled, came over, and hugged me tightly. "I didn't know it would get out of hand like that, but I won't make the same mistake again, okay?"

"No more fights, Nick. No more dangerous situations. You promise?" I asked, arching my body as he started kissing my neck.

"I promise."

24

Nick

WHEN I OPENED MY EYES THAT MORNING, THE FIRST THING I SAW was Noah's face a few inches away. Her head was resting on my shoulder and almost her entire body was on top of mine. I had to struggle not to laugh; it was as if she had tried to climb me and had gotten stranded halfway up.

I brushed a lock of hair out of her face and let my thumb stroke her skin covered in freckles...those freckles that drove me wild, not just on her face, but on her breasts, her thin shoulders, her lower back... I loved being the only person who knew every inch of that body perfectly, where every mark, every curve, every wound was...

I looked at that little tattoo behind her ear, the same one I had on my arm. I had decided to get it because I liked the idea of a simple thing being so strong if you just tied it the right way, but now it meant so much more. Now I liked to think I had gotten it because of her... It was ridiculous, but the idea kept going around and around in my mind, both of us getting that same tattoo because somehow we knew we'd end up finding each other...

My phone rang. I stretched my arm out and grabbed it. It was

Anne, Maddie's social worker. I still couldn't believe my mother had agreed to let me have her for my birthday weekend, but I wasn't going to complain. This year, there would be no parties, no stripteases, nothing out of this world: this year, I would spend the day with the two girls I loved most in the world.

Maddie was excited to be with me. She couldn't be happier. I talked to Anne for a few minutes to find out when the flight would be in and where we would meet, and I hung up with a huge smile on my face. Finally I would be with my sister the way I'd always wanted.

The painters got there soon afterward. I'd wanted them there before seven because I had to leave for the office at eight thirty. When I showed them the room, they said it was small enough that they'd be done in a few hours.

I wasn't happy about leaving my girlfriend asleep in my apartment with those guys, so I woke her up just as they were getting started.

"Noah, get up," I said, patting her on the shoulder.

She grunted and kept sleeping. I got dressed, watching the clock on my bedside. If I didn't want to be late, I needed to leave right then.

"Don't you know what the words *summer vacation* mean?" she said, turning in the sheets and burying her head under my pillow.

Goddammit. I didn't have time for this.

I grabbed my phone. On the third ring, Steve picked up, alert and awake, as always.

"Nicholas."

"I need you to come to my apartment and stay with Noah till the painters are done."

Noah opened her eyes when she heard this. "You're kidding, right?" she said, sitting up and rubbing her eyes like a four-year-old.

No, I wasn't joking one bit.

"I'm on my way now," Steve said.

"I'll wait here," I said and hung up.

Noah crossed her arms, angry, staring at me. "You honestly need a shrink."

I smiled, ignoring her tone, and continued putting on my clothes. I was going to be late, but I didn't care. Better than leaving Noah alone with two strangers.

"I'm just taking care of you," I said, knotting my tie.

"I know how to take care of myself," she replied, getting up and walking past me to the bathroom.

I sighed as I heard the water start to run in the shower. She could get mad if she wanted to, but there were too many crazy people in the world to take those kinds of risks, especially with her. She'd already been kidnapped once. I'd make sure she never was again.

She came out ten minutes later, her hair dripping, wrapped in a towel. "You're still here?"

I smiled. She looked sexy when she was pissed. "Steve's parking, so I'll head out now... Where's my kiss?"

She was to die for. I walked over to her and slipped my tongue in her mouth until her legs trembled.

"I'm going to get you wet," she warned me, taking a step back.

"I always get you wet, so I guess that's fair," I responded with a smile.

"You're gross," she said, but her anger was gone, and her eyes told me lust had replaced it.

We went back to kissing, but just as things were getting hot, the doorbell rang. Noah pulled on my tie, trying to keep me there, but I walked off. I was in a hurry. I couldn't waste more time.

"See ya," I said, turning around.

As I shut the door behind me, I looked back to see her staring at me, letting the towel fall on the wooden floor.

Fuck!

I got to work in the nick of time. My office was at the end of the hall, and I went straight there, not even stopping for a coffee. I knew my father was coming in that day, and God forbid he saw me arrive late... He wasn't above making me the coffee boy for the whole staff.

What I didn't expect was to find him in my office...talking calmly with a girl I'd never seen in my life. She was sitting in my chair and smiling politely at something my father had just said. They both turned when I walked in. My surprise turned to anger when I saw a second desk on the other side of the room by the window...my window.

"Hey, Son," my father said with a friendly smile.

At least he was in a good mood. That was new!

"What's going on?" I asked, looking back and forth between the girl and the desk.

"Nicholas, this is Sophia, Senator Aiken's daughter. She's going to be doing an internship here. I offered it to her."

My eyelids dropped as I looked at the senator's daughter. I had no idea what my father had offered her. My guess was he was just trying to get in good with her father. At any rate, I didn't know why any of this should have to do with me.

"You've been interning here a long time, you're about to graduate, and I told Sophie you'd be happy to help her out, give her a leg up in the field."

Fuck no!

Sophia smiled at me dryly, probably with aversion. Fine. I was happy to know the feeling was mutual. My father, probably bothered by my silence but too polite to mention it, just stared at us before saying, "Well, Sophie, I hope you like it here, and you've got my number if you need anything. Otherwise, Nick will help you out."

"Thank you, Mr. Leister. I'll keep that in mind. And thank you again for this opportunity. I've always wanted to work with Leister Enterprises. I think the steps you're taking to expand the business are crucial. A knowledge of the law is the most important thing when you're moving into new markets. With your son's help, I'm sure we can make something big happen."

So she was an ass-kisser, too. At least she was good at it. My father gave her an approving look, and me an admonishing one, before walking out.

"I can tell you're a politician's daughter," I said. "You're in my chair. Move it."

She smiled and got up slowly. I couldn't help looking her up and down. Black hair, tan skin, brown eyes, long legs. In a pearl-gray tube skirt and a spotless white shirt. A real daddy's girl.

"Don't let my looks deceive you, Nicholas. I'm here to stay."

I ignored the remark, sat in my chair, opened my email, and got to work.

25

Noah

MADDIE WOULD BE THERE SOON, AND WE NEEDED TO FINISH HER room. I had told my mother I'd be staying there during some of the days she was with Nick, and since I didn't want things to go even further south between us, I went home like a good girl once I'd made sure all the junk had been cleared out of Madison's room and there was space for the furniture to be brought in and assembled. Nicholas would be supervising everything, and he wouldn't see me until after I'd spoken with Anabel Grason.

Time passed quickly afterward. I had hoped to be able to better prepare myself, but before I knew it, the morning of Anabel and Maddie's arrival was there. I was nervous; I knew Nicholas was, too. He had sent me a bunch of photos asking me if I liked the room, if his sister would like it, if we should change the furnishings, if it might be better to put the bed under the window instead of in the corner, if the dresser was big enough, if she'd like the remote-control train as much as he did.

I laughed on the other end of the line. "Nick, she's going to love it. Anyway, your sister's coming to see *you*, not her new room."

He paused. "I'm nervous, Freckles. I've never spent more than a day with her. What if she starts to cry all of a sudden because she misses home? She's a little kid, and I'm a grown man. Sometimes I don't know how to deal with that stuff."

I smiled in the mirror in front of me. I loved when he worried like that: Nick, who was always so self-assured, so commanding, so bossy. When he let down his guard and showed me how tender his heart was, all I wanted was to hug him.

"I'll try to be over there most of the time," I said, sitting on my bed and looking up at the beams in the ceiling.

"What? You're going to be here the whole weekend, no?" he replied, changing to a more serious tone.

I bit my tongue. Just then, someone knocked at my door.

"Can we talk for a moment?" my mother asked, coming in and observing me. I nodded, happy for the first time in my life to have my mother interrupt a conversation with Nick.

"My mom wants to talk. I'll call you tomorrow, okay?"

I hung up before I regretted it, setting my phone down on the mattress next to me and watching my mother pace back and forth. She looked distracted and a little upset. We hadn't had the best time lately, either of us. It had been weeks since we'd really talked, and things would certainly get worse when I told her about my plans.

"Are your suitcases almost packed?"

I knew she was feeling me out. I never packed my bags until the day before. I'd inherited the habit from her. We didn't understand why people needed weeks to pick out their clothes, shove them in a suitcase, and zip it, but still, I shook my head, thinking I'd take advantage of this attempted reconciliation to tell her I would be living with Nick.

"Almost. Listen, Mom…" I started to say, but she interrupted me.

"I know you're champing at the bit to get out of here, Noah," she said, grabbing a shirt and folding it, distracted.

I took a deep breath, watching her eyes glaze over. "Mom, I don't..."

"No, Noah, let me tell you something: I know the past few days have been difficult, that we haven't gotten along well since we returned from Europe, and believe me, I get it: you're in love, and you want to spend all your time with Nicholas... I just would have liked for *this*..."—she pointed at the two of us—"to stay intact. You and I have always gotten along well. Even when you were going out with Dan"—I frowned hearing my ex-boyfriend's name, but I let her go on—"you used to come running to my room to tell me how the night had gone and all the romantic stuff he'd said to you, remember?"

I nodded, grinning. I could see where she was going.

"Now that we're getting close to the time you'll leave, I just wanted to tell you I've tried to give you the best things I could. I really wanted you to consider this place your home. I wanted you to live here, surrounded by all these opportunities. Even when you were little, I dreamed of seeing you in a room like this, with more toys and books than I could have ever hoped to give you on my own..."

"Mom, I know I was unbearable when you told me we were coming here, but I understand now why you did it, and you don't need to explain anything, okay? You gave me everything you could, and I know it's hard for you to see me with Nicholas, but I love him."

She closed her eyes when she heard this and forced a smile. "I hope you grow up to be a wonderful writer someday, Noah. I know you will, and that's why I want you to take advantage of every opportunity life gives you. Study, learn, and enjoy college. These are going to be the best years of your life."

"I will," I whispered, and though I smiled, I felt a little guilty that I couldn't bring myself to be sincere with her and tell her about Nick.

The next morning, I got up early. I was nervous and went down to breakfast trying to put out of my mind what I was about to do. Maddie would be there in a few hours, and there was no chance that her mother would back down now. I repeated a thousand times over that I was doing this for him, that this was forgivable, but deep down, in some hidden corner of myself, I also wanted to get to know Anabel and find out what she wanted from Nick and why she'd decided to leave him behind.

I barely ate any breakfast: half a piece of toast and a coffee with milk. Nick informed me that he would be picking up Maddie at the same time I was meeting with his mother, so I had time to come up with something when, inevitably, he asked me where I'd been. While he was distracted taking Maddie to lunch, I would dispatch that clandestine meeting as quickly as possible.

I was well aware of what kind of woman Nick's mother was. She was the typical posh millionaire's wife who liked to blab about all the yachts, horses, and mansions she had all over the world. Since I didn't want to draw anyone's attention, I put on a light-blue high-waisted flounced skirt and a yellow Chanel top I'd had for some time. Jenna had given me some white Miu Miu sandals, very pretty, very expensive, but whatever, they went well with the outfit. This was one of the few times I'd gone out dressed head to toe in name brands, but I didn't want Anabel to intimidate me. Everyone knows a well-dressed woman is a powerful woman.

When I got to the Hilton, a man in elegant clothes walked over to my convertible. I gave him the keys, praying he wouldn't scratch it. My sandals clacked on the sidewalk. The automatic doors opened, and inside, I found an elegant reception hall with little chairs distributed strategically over thin beige and brown rugs. In the back was an enormous split stairway, just as in my house. I had no idea where to go, so I walked to the desk, where two well-dressed girls smiled at me.

"How can we help you, miss?" one of them asked, and I could tell from her eyes that she was admiring my outfit. She must have been asking herself how a girl her same age could have all that I had and be facing her from the other side of the counter. There were times when I was thankful not to be the type of person who cared about fashion and money. I had never wanted this stuff; it had never mattered to me. I was by nature a simple person and in no way saw that girl as less than me.

"I'm supposed to be having lunch with Anabel Grason... I don't know if she's left me a note or something..." I said hesitantly. The girl looked at her computer, nodded, and smiled.

"Mrs. Grason is waiting for you in Andiamo. If you go down that hall, you'll find the door on the right. Enjoy your lunch."

I smiled and tried to maintain my composure as I walked over. Just as I reached the restaurant, my phone buzzed. I looked at the message: it was a photo of Nick and Maddie in McDonald's. I smirked as I saw her gap-toothed smile: her two front teeth had fallen out! I couldn't imagine what Nicholas was saying to the poor girl! Still grinning, I wrote back to say I'd catch up with them soon. Then I put my phone on airplane mode.

I looked around at the cozy, unpretentious dining room, with its elegant chairs the color of milk tea, the white tablecloths on the square tables, the white plates and garnet napkins, the well-tended decorative plants. As soon as I walked in, the scent of freshly made pasta and pesto invaded my senses.

I took a deep breath when I saw Anabel and walked over to her. Her outfit was graceful, as I'd imagined: a beige pantsuit and an attractive black blouse. She was wearing stiletto heels, which made her several inches taller than me. She smiled, and I stretched out my hand before the situation got uncomfortable: I had no idea what the custom was when you were secretly having lunch with your boyfriend's mom, who'd abandoned him ten years ago.

"Hi, Noah," she said warmly.

"Mrs. Grason," I replied with good manners.

She sat down and motioned for me to do the same.

"I'm glad you accepted my invitation." After saying this, she brought a glass of wine up to her lips, leaving a red stain on the rim.

So this was it. I took a deep breath.

Her blue eyes were piercing, just like her son's, and I felt a shiver run up and down my spine.

"You're a very pretty girl, Noah. But I'm sure you know that. If you weren't, my son wouldn't have taken an interest in you, naturally."

I forced a smile. That remark rankled me, as if she were saying Nick's and my relationship was something superficial, empty, but then, her relationships probably all were… All the money she'd invested in trying to look like a thirty-year-old made it obvious that was the kind of person she was.

"We could probably spend hours talking about nothing, Mrs. Grason, but you made me come here for a reason, and I'd just as soon get to the point," I said, trying to be nice, hard as that was. My suspicions were right: I didn't like that woman, and I never would. "You wanted me to do you a favor. Tell me what it's about."

Anabel smiled, maybe even with admiration. I think she liked my being so direct with her.

"I want to have my relationship with my son back, and you're going to help me," she said. She took an envelope out of her designer bag and handed it to me. It was made of high-quality thick marble-ized paper, with Nicholas's name written on the outside in calligraphy. "All I need is for you to make sure Nicholas reads this letter."

I looked at the envelope with distrust. I had no idea how I could convince Nick to read it. Plus, giving it to him would mean admitting I'd seen his mother, and there was no way I was doing that.

"I'm sorry, but I don't know how a simple letter will help you get your son back. You abandoned him." The hatred in my eyes must have been evident to her—the same hatred I felt anytime someone hurt a person I cared about. I just couldn't keep it inside.

"How old are you, Noah?" she asked, shoving the envelope toward me.

"Eighteen."

"Eighteen," she repeated, as though savoring the word, smiling like an angel—the kind of smile appropriate for a child, not a grown woman, and certainly not her. "I'm forty-four... I've been in this world a lot longer than you, I've lived through many more experiences than you, and so before you judge me the way you already have, you should stop and think about the fact that you're just a little girl, and the worst thing that's probably ever happened to you is when they took you away from your home and moved you into a mansion in California."

"You don't know one thing about my life," I said in an icy tone.

The image of my dead father shot through my head, and I felt a sting in my chest.

"I know a lot more than you think. I know things even you don't know, things you'd prefer never to know. And with just a few phone calls, I can make all that come out."

A diabolical smile appeared on her face. She picked up the letter, stood, and walked over beside me. Slowly, nimbly, she slipped it into my bag, which was hanging on the back of my chair.

"Make sure Nicholas reads this," she whispered. "Otherwise,

this whole fantasy you've been living and all this money that's rained down on you from heaven will go up in smoke."

I stood, feeling something like an electric shock.

"Don't get in touch with me again," I said, trying to control myself after that threat of—I didn't know exactly what.

"Don't you worry. I have no intention of doing so. But I repeat: if you don't want your worst nightmares to come true, be sure you do what I've asked."

I turned around and walked out without even ordering anything to eat, ignoring the malice implicit in her words, passing through reception, and emerging outside.

I'd been an idiot, an out-and-out imbecile for meeting with that woman. Nicholas had warned me—he had talked to me about her, about how cruel she was, but I'd been stupid enough to let myself get dragged in, and she'd told me a pack of lies. Because that's what they were, lies, and I wasn't going to think about them for one more minute. I took out the letter, tore it into a million pieces, and scattered them in every trash can I passed.

For me, that meeting had never happened.

26

Nick

NOAH HAD HER PHONE TURNED OFF FOR THE WHOLE AFTERNOON. It was starting to worry me... I tried not to let my nerves get the better of me. Regardless of the situation, that never helped. My sister was with me, Anne had brought her as promised, and I was happy she'd be with me for the next four days. I wasn't going to let anything ruin that time for me, and as for Noah... I tried to tell myself she'd just let her battery run out.

"Nick!" Maddie shouted in that unique voice of hers. We'd gone to Santa Monica, to the pier. I'd always told Maddie about that place, about the beach, the attractions, how the kids could climb into the Ferris wheel and see the ocean from way up in the air... But my little sister, unlike most normal children, had taken off for the aquarium and had her face pressed against the glass looking at the mollusks and sea creatures on display. I walked over to her.

"Mad, be careful, one of those monsters might break the glass and get you!" I warned her before grabbing her around the waist and heading toward the exit. Night was falling, and I wasn't sure what time she usually had dinner or went to bed.

"You cold, midget?" I asked her, then took off my jacket, bent over, and draped it over her shoulders.

A smile appeared on her puffy little lips. "Are you happy I came?" she asked, and her innocent eyes told me the answer mattered more than it should.

I smiled and zipped her up. She looked like a ghost in that garment that was nearly dragging on the ground, but it was better than her getting sick.

"Are *you* happy to be here?" I asked, trying to roll up the hem.

"Of course I am!" she shouted. "You're my favorite brother. Didn't I ever tell you that?"

I laughed. Like she had any other ones to compare me with...!

"No, you never told me that, but you're my favorite sister, too, so it works out perfectly, no?"

She smiled, and it touched my heart.

"You wanna go on the Ferris wheel?" I asked, and she replied with an enthusiastic, earsplitting "*yes!*"

The pier was packed with people and their families, and the breaking waves made you want to never leave. The evening was precious. Just as I was about to take out my phone to call Noah again, I heard her. As I looked into the crowd, I saw her smiling from ear to ear. I was sure I was doing the same.

"Hey, Maddie!" Noah called, dazzling as always, capturing the attention of my sister, who ran off toward her.

"Noah!" she shouted, and I laughed watching them. My joy grew even further as I watched Noah bend down, pick her up, and hug her gently.

Maddie had taken to Noah easier than I had thought. Of course, Noah was a joy to be around, but Mad wasn't easy, I had to admit. I adored her because she was my sister, but she could be curt and a brat: she didn't get along with everyone, she didn't like people invading her personal space unless she really trusted them, and if I were honest, she was a little spoiled, like every six-year-old girl whose parents bought her everything. She was my princess of darkness, I liked to say. But Noah adored her and she adored Noah, so there was nothing to worry about.

When I reached them, Noah gave me a strange look, as though she were relieved to see me or something like that. I smiled and pulled her in for a hug, squeezing Maddie between us.

"Noah, let's all three get on the Ferris wheel!" Maddie kicked her legs back and forth so we'd set her down and took off running toward the rides. Watching her, I wrapped an arm around Noah's shoulders and kissed her head as we followed.

"You okay?" I asked.

"Of course! Your sister's gorgeous," she said, changing the subject.

"Without her two front teeth?" I asked. "It's taken all the self-control I can muster not to make fun of her, Freckles."

Noah laughed but said nothing more. She was acting strange, but I decided to let it go for now. We met Maddie at the head of the line and paid for three tickets. She was talking nonstop, recounting all that she and I had done and how she had taken an airplane to get here and how happy she was to be staying with me. Noah followed her, amused, occasionally turning toward me with a grin.

It was chilly, without a cloud in the sky, and the sunset was gorgeous from where we sat. Noah leaned into me, staring out into the ocean and the last glimmers of light. I draped an arm around her and pulled her in closer. She met my eyes and smiled as only she could.

Maddie fell asleep in the car. That was normal: she'd gotten up early and had had a busy day. As I drove along the interstate, with

Noah driving her own car beside me, I couldn't help but think of my conversation with Lion that morning.

He'd called to tell me the races were next Monday. After Noah's kidnapping, I'd kept my distance from the gang and the streets. I didn't want any of that to affect my life, especially now that it could endanger my girlfriend and my family. But Lion was Lion, and he lived in that world, and unfortunately, I couldn't take him out of it, not unless he was willing to change. It's not that he liked it, but it was quick and easy money, and that's why he had asked me to go with him and race on his team as we'd always done. I'd offered to lend him money, but Lion was too proud to accept it. I'd agreed to drive with him because I knew he needed the cash and because, apart from last year, there'd never been any problems. I'd always loved cars, and racing at night, in the middle of the desert, with all that adrenaline, that speed, the feel of victory...I loved it.

Noah would kill me if she found out. Jenna had already been dropping hints, and though I thought I had convinced her that I wasn't mixed up in Lion's doings, I'd have to do more to get her off my back. Lion swore to me Jenna didn't know when the races were, and anyway, it would be one and done: we'd go there, race, win, and return home. No problems.

The one thing I could do to clear up any of Noah's suspicions was hang out with her on the same Monday as the races. We'd have dinner on the other end of town, as far as possible from the track, and then... I'd stand her up. I'd come up with some excuse why I couldn't help it, and that way I'd know, at least, that she was as far from me as possible, somewhere safe. She'd be furious, but I'd make it up to her when I was back.

Satisfied with my plan, I parked the car, got out, and went to open Noah's door once she was parked, too.

"Everything okay, Freckles?" I asked, caressing her cheek and pushing her hair out of her face. She'd been quiet all evening, and now that my sister was asleep, I could pay more attention to her. I noticed she was dressed up.

"I'm tired, that's all," she said, getting out without even looking at me.

"What did I do this time, Noah?" I asked, mentally analyzing everything I'd said and done since we'd met each other on the pier.

She grinned. That calmed me down slightly.

"Nothing, silly," she said, and I relaxed further when she turned and stood on her tiptoes to kiss me. I wrapped my arms around her waist and pulled her in. Her kiss was soft; mine was hard: my tongue opened her lips and tasted her with delight. She didn't hold back, but she seemed distracted.

I pulled back to look at her. "You're hiding something, and I'm going to find out what it is," I said, half joking.

I opened the back door and smiled like an idiot looking at that gorgeous little girl asleep next to her dreadful stuffed rabbit. I unbuttoned her seat belt and picked her up. Then I went around to the trunk, pulled out her tiny suitcase, and, with Noah at my side, took the elevator up to my apartment.

I didn't want to wake Maddie up, so I took her straight to bed.

"Sleep tight, princess," I said, kissing her cheek.

I closed the door behind me and saw Noah there waiting for me, leaning against the wall next to the bedroom. We needed to talk, and I wanted her to be first.

"You want to take a bath with me?" she proposed with a mischievous smile.

I smirked, took her hand, and led her to the bathroom, opening the tap and watching the tub fill up.

"You look good today...very elegant in that outfit," I observed, pulling carefully on her hair tie. When it fell, her hair spread like silk over her shoulders. "What did you do this morning? Apart from ignoring me, I mean."

YOUR FAULT | 195

She looked at the buttons on my shirt and with trembling fingers started to undo them one by one. I grabbed her hands, stopping her, a little anxious about whatever she was hiding.

"I hung out with my mom," she said. "My battery went dead. That's why I missed your calls."

I nodded and let her continue. When she had taken off my shirt, she leaned forward, and I closed my eyes, feeling her lips on my skin.

Nothing compared to Noah's caresses, the feeling was incredible; they made me feel so good...so at peace with myself. She was my drug, made just for me, able to drive me absolutely wild. I opened my eyes and cupped my hands over hers as they surrounded my neck in turn. I wanted to have her in the bath, relaxed. Maybe that way, I could figure out what the hell was going on.

I took off her top and that skirt that made her skin glimmer. Then I knelt and took off her sandals. Her body was incredible, athletic, not too thick or too thin. I could spend hours just admiring it.

She took off her bra and underwear and slipped into the water. I wanted to tell her it was hot, but she didn't react; she just sank in up to her shoulders. I got in, too, and when she moved forward to make room for me behind her, I wrapped her in my arms. I clenched my teeth. It was burning!

"Jesus, Noah!" I complained in those few seconds till my body got used to it. "Are you not on fire right now?"

"No," she responded distractedly, lifting some soap bubbles and observing them.

I pressed my cheek to her ear and enjoyed just being with her undisturbed and comfortable. But it upset me, not being able to guess what was going on in her head just then.

"Can I ask you a question?" she said, breaking the spell.

"Sure."

"But you have to promise you'll answer me truthfully."

With my hand on her stomach, I began to trace little circles around her belly button. I was curious to know where she'd go with this, so I said yes, even if I wanted to toy with her for a moment beforehand. I let my fingers go a little lower than they should have, and I heard her breathing grow more halting. "Do you think your father loved your mother? Before they got divorced, I mean."

I hadn't expected that, and instead of clearing up my doubts, it left me even more disconcerted.

"I guess he loved her, yeah...but in almost all my memories, they're either fighting or Dad's away working... My mother wasn't an easy woman, but he brought his own share of problems..." I remembered all those times he'd ditched us because he had to work or because he was just too tired. "When I was little, I started thinking fathers usually lived far away and only came home when they were tired or hungry. Of course, when I got older and could go to friends' houses, I realized it wasn't like that, that fathers could be around and it could be lots of fun. One of my classmates' dads used to take him to school and pick him up every day, and they would go out for pancakes and play baseball in the neighborhood park... I was jealous of him. He made me realize fathers could spend time with their kids."

I got lost for a moment in those memories, and it wasn't until Noah turned that I realized I'd been transported to another time. I forced a smile and let her pull my head close and kiss me.

"I shouldn't have asked," she said.

I pulled back so I could look her in the eyes. "You can ask me anything you want, Noah. My life hasn't been a fairy tale, but it's been close to it, if I compare it to what some people have to go through. Not everyone's made to be a parent, and some people really try and fail anyway."

I wasn't going to sit there and cry about how my parents hadn't gotten along. My childhood hadn't been perfect, but it would be ridiculous to piss and moan about it, especially in front of her. Noah felt bad for me, I could see it in her magnificent eyes, even though my life had been a walk in the park compared to hers. Maybe my father had been a selfish asshole when I was a kid, but at least he hadn't tried to kill me. Sometimes my mind would mess with me, making me imagine Noah as a little girl, not much bigger than Maddie, hiding from her dad, forced to jump out a window... How could she even waste a second of her time pitying me?

"You think normal families exist?" she asked me. I knew what she meant: the kind of family you see in movies, with normal parents who go to work and their biggest worry is how to pay the mortgage at the end of the month.

Was that what she'd been thinking about all afternoon? Had she said something to her mother that morning? I was furious at the thought of Raffaella pestering her about how our relationship couldn't be. I sat there thinking about it for a few seconds.

"That's the kind of family you and I are going to be. What do you say? But no worries about the mortgage, obviously."

Noah laughed, but I wanted to show her how serious I could be.

"Now it's my turn to ask the questions," I said. "Where do you want to do it, in the bath or in bed?"

27

Noah

I COULDN'T GET THOSE WORDS NICHOLAS'S MOTHER HAD UTTERED out of my head.

Her threat frightened me, but I didn't want to keep going down a road that I wasn't certain I could travel on my own. I felt guilty for tearing up the letter. I had no right to do it, it wasn't mine, but I didn't want that woman hurting Nick again. What had Nick said that morning when the painters were there? That he wanted to protect me? Well, that's what I was doing for him, too.

Nicholas was my medicine, my distraction, my safe space. I turned around to face him, thankful the tub was big enough to do so, when he asked, "Where do you want to do it, in the bath or in bed?" He had a dark look in his eyes. I could tell he needed me, especially after delving into his past. I needed him, too, because if I kept hammering away at that issue, I'd uncover truths better left buried...at least for now.

I sat in his lap, and our mouths joined soothingly. We needed each other just then. The day had been intense for both of us, even if in completely different ways.

With his hands on my back, he bent over me and venerated my

mouth. My hands climbed his shoulders and touched his rugged cheeks, damp from the water. His fragrance overwhelmed me and warmed me from inside.

"You're so beautiful," he said. His mouth left my lips and followed my jawline, nibbling until he reached my neck. My hands felt his chest, his abs, and he pulled me into his torso, skin to skin, without an inch between us. "You're so warm, so soft," he kept repeating as his tongue tasted my naked wet skin.

I let out a gasp as I felt his hands move up and down my back, and he tipped me backward, resting his mouth on my left breast, tasting me, while I hungered for his caresses. I sat up and pressed into his hips. He sought my mouth with his, and our tongues toyed with each other as if in a dance...

"Look at me," he said, and when I opened my eyes, I saw his were fixed on my face. They were the same blue I was used to, but something was different, something hard to express in words. "I love you, and I'll love you for the rest of my life," he declared, and I felt my heart stop, then race again. He lifted me slowly with his arm around my waist and lowered me on top of him, with a gentleness almost as moving as his words. When he penetrated me, I opened my mouth to let out a cry, but his lips silenced me with a deep kiss.

"Can you feel it? Can you feel the connection? We're made for each other, babe," he whispered in my ear as he moved gently, in a slow rhythm that drove me crazy. His words continued in my head as he pleasured me the way only he knew how. And only he ever would.

I love you, and I'll love you for the rest of my life.

"Promise me," I said as a horrible fear gripped me, body and soul, a fear of losing him, a fear of not having what I was experiencing just then for the rest of my life.

His eyes were shadowed with desire, and they looked at me, confused.

"Promise me you'll love me always, promise me," I almost begged him.

Without answering, he got out of the tub, carrying me, his hands firmly gripping my thighs. I wrapped my arms around him and buried my face in the hollow of his neck, biting my lower lip to keep from screaming as I felt him so deep inside me while he carried me to the bedroom. Both of us were dripping wet. He laid me down on the bed without pulling away.

"What's the point in promising?" he asked as our breathing synced up. I was about to explode, and he knew it; his hands fed every part of my body that needed his touch. "You've got me under your spell... I'm more yours than I am my own. I'll do whatever you ask, whatever you want. I promise, babe."

And with his words and his body glued to mine, I stopped feeling so cold.

The next few days were amazing: sharing all those moments with his sister, moments we could never have experienced at a distance, with the few hours he was normally permitted to see her. For Nick's birthday, we went to Disneyland, and even if it was a place for kids and we spent the day just chasing Maddie around, I loved seeing Mickey and his gang sing Nick "Happy Birthday." A year before, around that time, we had just started going out, and if anyone had told me then I'd be seeing him with a pair of mouse ears on, eating a cake shaped like a Disney princess, I'd have told them they were out of their mind.

The time passed quickly, and soon it was time to take her back to the airport. The stewardess who said she'd look after her until she made it to Vegas was waiting for us next to security. After those days together, the goodbye was harder than we had imagined.

"You okay?" I asked Nick as we went back out to the car. He was holding my hand, squeezing it so tightly, it was almost painful.

"I will be," he said.

I didn't want to press him because I knew Nick didn't like to talk much, especially when it was about his feelings. His sister was his weak point, and knowing she was leaving to stay with parents who barely even had time for her didn't help matters. It wasn't until he'd been driving for ten minutes that he spoke to me again.

"Should I drop you off at home?"

An alarm started going off inside me. Jenna had called me the day before, while Nick was giving Maddie a bath, to tell me she had found out the races would be on Monday. I didn't want to believe her then, but if it was true, then Nick wouldn't want me around. I almost said no, that I'd stay at his place, but I couldn't do that to my mother; she was mad enough as it was. Plus, I needed to finish packing my bags. School would start in five days. I needed to talk to Mom, even if what I really wanted to do was tell her after I'd already moved in with Nick and there was no turning back. It was risky, but it would be easier to ask for forgiveness rather than permission.

"Yeah, home's good," I said, looking out the window, trying to decide what to do about the races. When we got to the house and he parked in the driveway, I assumed he would get out, at least to say hi to his dad, but he didn't even cut the engine. Still stranger, he asked, "Should we have dinner tomorrow?"

Surprised, I said, "What?"

He smiled, but his eyes looked preoccupied.

"You and me...we can go somewhere nice... What do you think?" He reached out and stroked my hair as he proposed it. I hadn't seen that coming. Maybe Jenna was wrong about the races.

"Will you pick me up?"

He looked toward the house. "I don't think I can, I've got

work all day... It would be best if we just meet there. I'll text you the details."

There wasn't a trace of hesitation on his face. Maybe he was being sincere? Jenna could be wrong about all that. I smiled. I hated doubting Nick. He wouldn't lie to me. He wouldn't go to the races, not without telling me, especially after all that had happened.

"Cool, I'll see you there, then," I said, resting a hand on the door.

"Hey!" he said before I got out. "Thanks for being with me these days. It wouldn't have been the same without you."

I touched his cheek, leaned in, and kissed him. As his face pushed into mine, I prayed he wasn't lying to me.

———————

Jenna came by the next afternoon. I'd never seen her so depressed. She and Lion were going through hard times, and it didn't help at all that she was absolutely convinced they'd be racing that night. When I told her Nick would be waiting for me at Cristal, a fancy restaurant downtown, she looked at me with disbelief.

"I know what I'm talking about, Noah. And there's a hundred percent chance that our fucking boyfriends are going to get in trouble tonight."

I sighed and tried to find a pretty dress to wear. I was tired of trying to convince Jenna that Nicholas wouldn't lie to me, least of all make me go to a restaurant if he was planning to bail on me.

"How are you and Lion doing? Is he still mad at you?" I asked, more to change the subject than for any other reason.

Sitting on the sofa by my dressing table, Jenna went pale, making the blood red of her nail polish stand out more.

"If by *mad* you mean our relationship now consists of screaming at each other and then fucking like crazy afterward, then yeah, I guess he's still mad at me."

YOUR FAULT | 203

"Well, that's putting it delicately!" I replied, somewhat surprised by how blunt she was. Jenna wasn't the naive little rich girl people thought. But even if she tried to make light of things, I could tell she was a wreck and much more nervous about that night than she let on. If her theory was correct, Lion would take part in any race he could get into, regardless of the law, regardless of the fact the people who showed up for those events had almost killed us the last time we'd been there, as long as he could make some cash. And we both knew that if Lion kept going down that road, it was likely he would end up in jail, just as his brother had.

"By the way, I saw Luca the other day," she said, getting up from the couch and flipping through my hangers. I looked at her reflection in the mirror.

"What's he like?" I asked warily.

"To be honest, he seemed really nice, but sort of…I don't know, like I got goose bumps when I met him." She stopped to look at a plain white shirt. Her mind was clearly elsewhere and had been for more than a month. "He's handsome, not like Lion, but you can tell their parents must have been good-looking… He's got the same green eyes, but they're mysterious. He seems like he's got secrets, and I guess Lion doesn't want me to know them because when I went over there the other day, he did everything but kick me out."

Her voice quivered as she said this. I hated seeing her sad. The old Jenna was nothing like the one I had in front of me now. Where was that eternal smile, that glimmer in her eyes, the nonsense she loved to spout at all hours of the day? I wanted to give that idiot Lion a piece of my mind.

"Why don't you come to dinner with me and Nick tonight?" I proposed. I knew Nick would be fine with it. Jenna was his friend, and he'd probably help me get her in a better mood.

Jenna shook her head, exasperated. "You honestly still think he's taking you to dinner?"

I took a deep breath. "Nicholas wouldn't lie to me, Jenna, and he wouldn't leave me hanging."

She paused, reflecting on my words. "Fine...but I'm only doing it so you're not by yourself when the idiot doesn't show up the way he told you he would. That way we can go find them together."

I shook my head, but I couldn't help feeling a bit of uncertainty as I heard her.

A few hours later, we were freshly showered and dressed for the night. Jenna had dragged her feet, and I'd had to convince her to find a nice outfit and throw on some makeup. We weren't going to McDonald's, after all. Finally she put on a pair of leather shorts and a white blouse with flats. I chose a snug black dress and a pair of white platform heels. I let my hair down and put on lipstick, too.

Jenna rolled her eyes at me, but she didn't say anything. Just then, I got a message from Nick.

> The reservation's under my name. Grab a couple of drinks and wait for me inside.

I showed the message to Jenna, but she ignored me as we left my room.

It took us nearly an hour to get to the restaurant. There was a reservation for three under Nick's name, just as he had promised. The place was pleasant, with little French-style tables and soft romantic lighting. It was funny, being there with Jenna, with all those candles around, but it was also hard to imagine being there with Nick. That place was too cheesy for him. Jenna started cracking jokes while the couples around us stared at us, clearly irritated.

"Noah, take my hand, maybe they'll think it's our anniversary and they'll rain confetti on us from those lamps overhead," she said with a ridiculous flirty expression. I laughed, and we drank a glass of white wine—at these fancy places, they never asked for an ID—as we waited for Nick to appear.

Forty minutes in, the jokes weren't funny anymore, and I had a bad feeling in the pit of my stomach.

The sound of my phone vibrating pulled me out of a trance, and I scowled as I read the message that had come through:

> Hey Freckles, sorry, I can't come tonight. We're up to our ears in work, and if I don't finish the reports I've been asked for, I can kiss my internship goodbye. Please don't get mad, I'll make it up to you... you and Jenna have dinner and enjoy yourselves.

I could feel a fire burning inside me, something I'd been trying to suppress the entire time we'd been waiting. I couldn't believe he'd been so stupid to think this strategy would work.

I looked up at Jenna, who seemed to feel sorry for me, despite everything.

"Where the hell are those damn races?"

28

Nick

As soon as I hit *send*, I knew there was trouble in store. That was right when we were leaving my apartment. I wasn't happy about any of this, but I could feel the adrenaline flooding my nervous system, and a part of me had missed that. I mean, things were great now, but the fights, the races, all the crazy shit I used to do had been an escape valve for me, and it wasn't easy just to give all that up. I told myself I was doing this for Lion, but I was doing it for myself, too. I wanted to do it; I even needed to. All the memories my mother had stirred up, my little sister saying bye to me at the airport, the feeling that Noah was hiding things from me, and my inability to help with her nightmares had all kept me in a state of constant nervous tension, and it didn't help knowing that everyone was trying to keep us apart.

Time and again, I told myself she was safe with Jenna, far from all this shit, that neither I nor anyone else would put her in danger. I didn't want her there that night... There were times when I just needed to be alone, and this was one of them.

I put on my helmet and got on my motorbike. Lion and Luca were going to drive the cars to our destination. This year, the races were in the city, not the desert. The course wouldn't be long, but the stakes were incredibly high. If we won, we'd walk away with a big pile of cash, and Lion needed it.

The music was blasting as I maneuvered my bike between the people. Lots of them clapped and whistled when they saw me arrive, and I was psyched when I pulled up to join my gang. I couldn't deny it—I had missed this.

"Look who's here!" Mike, Lion's cousin, said, walking over.

We bumped fists as I got off the bike and laid my helmet on the seat.

"What's up, bro?" I asked, looking around. I hadn't seen those people in a long time, and soon they were surrounding me, cracking jokes at my expense, drinking like fish, with their stereos turned up so loud, my ears ached.

Lion showed up a few minutes later, and everyone cheered when they saw him pull up in the Lamborghini I'd rented for the occasion. That reminded me of last year, when my little blond demon had raced and had annihilated Ronnie, surprising all of us and almost giving me a heart attack. Noah could drive, and watching her had pissed me off and turned me on in equal measure.

As everybody around me danced and acted stupid waiting for the stragglers to show up, I took out a cigarette and leaned against my bike. I needed to know that Noah was all right and had made it home.

She hadn't answered my message. That didn't give me a good feeling. She was probably mad, but she was with Jenna, so it wasn't like I had left her hanging at the restaurant...right?

I couldn't call her because of the noise all around me, so I baited the hook with another message.

How was dinner? You back home yet?

I took another hit of my smoke and saw her reply:

In bed in my pajamas.

I sighed with relief. At least that was out of the way. With Noah at home, I could relax and concentrate on what I had to do that night: race, win, and kiss that world goodbye forever.

Lion waved to me, and we walked over to talk to Clark, the guy who had designed the course. We stood in a circle while he showed everyone who was racing where we would start and finish. There would be four contestants. This was a major race—you had to pay five thousand dollars just to get in—but the winner would take a huge chunk of that, plus a cut of the bets.

"As long as no problems come up, you'll be back in ten minutes. We've blocked traffic off, but if the five-o show up, that's out of my hands," Clark said, looking around at us. The other two guys I knew—they were good, and one of them was from Cruz's gang, formerly Ronnie's.

I'd seen him earlier at a corner surrounded by his guys, all of them as high as he was. I hated them, and I also wanted my revenge for the other night, wanted to make them pay, not with blood but with their money, which was the only thing they really valued.

"See you back here in ten," Clark said.

I turned to Lion and his brother. "I don't think we'll have a tough time, but I don't want any bullshit. If things get ugly, we're out, understood?"

Luca was planning on riding with Lion in the passenger seat. I wanted to go alone; I hated racing with someone beside me: it distracted me, and I felt I didn't have total control of the car. They nodded, and we turned around to head for our cars.

Just then, a flash of something caught my eye. My body under-stood it before my eyes focused on the red Audi that had just pulled up. My heart stopped, and when I saw those long legs step out of the vehicle, my nerves, which I had managed to keep a tight rein on, exploded.

"No fucking way!" Lion exclaimed behind me.

I felt my feet racing over, my breaths turning to heaves, getting out of my control as I saw Noah standing there surrounded by all those assholes. My steps grew longer, trying to shorten the distance between us, wanting to make it to her side before anyone else did. Her eyes locked with mine. She crossed her arms. There was hatred in her face. It was all I could do not to stuff her back in her car and peel out with her, but before I could think my plan through, her arm shot out and smacked me hard across the face.

"You goddamned liar!" she shouted over the music and the people yelling.

I took a few deep breaths to calm down. It was pointless.

"Get in the car," I ordered her between clenched teeth.

"Fuck that, Nicholas!" she replied, her arms cocked to shove me backward. I stopped her, grabbing her wrists. "Don't you dare! Don't you fucking dare give me orders!"

I pushed her against the Audi and squeezed against her, immobilizing her.

"I repeat: get in that car, and go back where you came from. You've got three seconds, hear me? I don't care how mad you are, goddammit, you shouldn't be here. Do I have to remind you what happened last time?"

Her eyes were burning, boring holes into mine. It was all I could do not to throttle her. It didn't matter if I was there. No one was going to hurt me. There was nothing there I couldn't deal with. But Noah? The fear that someone might see her... I turned instinctively to where Cruz was standing with his friends. He still hadn't recognized her.

"Hell no, you don't have to remind me! I was there,

remember?" She was trying to wriggle away from me. I looked down at her dress... Was she trying to be conspicuous?

"Stop, dammit!" I ordered her, interlacing the fingers of one hand with hers while the other grabbed her chin and forced her to look at me. "This isn't a joke, Noah. I need you to go."

"There's no way I'm going unless you leave with me." With that, she jerked her face to one side.

I leaned my arms on both sides of her, pressing her into the car to shield her from the people gathering around us. I looked down at her, sniffed her, to try to calm myself down more than anything else. But instead of touching me, her hands hung dead at her sides.

"You shouldn't be here," I whispered in her ear. We both knew I was making her tremble.

"Neither should you."

I noticed then that she was wearing makeup, that her short dress revealed her bare legs provocatively. She'd done that for me, and I'd left her in the lurch to enter a drag race.

"I'm sorry, Freckles," I said, grabbing her around the waist. The fabric of her dress was so thin, it was as if I were embracing her skin. That, and her anger, which was also sexy in its own way, made me want to kiss her desperately and seek her forgiveness.

I bent over to try, but she looked away.

"I can't have you lying to me," she said.

"I won't do it again."

"I don't believe you."

Those words hurt, but I didn't want to let her see that.

"This is the last race I'll ever drive in, Noah. Ask Lion: I said the same thing to him this morning. It's over, Noah... This is my last goodbye, and I'm only doing it because Lion needs me."

"You can't keep doing this stuff for him, Nicholas." Her voice was worried, not angry. "I know you love him like a brother, but

I talked to Jenna, and he's not the same as before. You supporting him here is only going to make things worse."

She was right. I kept moving ahead in life while he was digging his own grave. Either he would climb up out of the mud, or he would sink down in misery like Cruz or like his own brother, Luca.

I reached out and pulled Noah to me. I would never make her worry about me again. Those days were over.

"I'll do everything I can to get Lion to leave this behind with me," I said, and I was overwhelmed with happiness when Noah reached up and touched my cheek. That caress meant she'd forgiven me.

I stroked her spine and kissed the side of her face, rubbing my nose next to her ear.

"Go home, please. I'll be there as soon as this is over."

Noah didn't say anything. But I took that as a sign of agreement.

I turned around and saw the three other drivers talking with Clark.

"I gotta go."

She nodded. I kissed her on the lips and waited to go over to where the rest of the guys were standing until I saw her with Jenna next to her Audi and the two of them seemed ready to go.

"Good luck, everyone. See you on the other side," I said to Lion. That was my go-to line before racing.

He smiled, but I saw something else on his face that gave me a weird feeling just before he turned and got into his car.

I walked to where the Lamborghini was parked, got in, and started the engine. Lion got in the car Luca had driven over in and pulled up to the starting line. A girl in a bikini top and tiny shorts was standing in the middle of the cars with two flags held high. The city shone brightly behind her, waiting for us to rip through its streets. Fast, no mistakes…that was the only way we could be sure of avoiding trouble.

Just then, right as the countdown started and my hands were gripping the wheel, the passenger door opened, and Noah got in beside me.

"What the fuck are you doing?"

The starting gun echoed, and the flags fell. The race was on.

29

Noah

WHEN JENNA TOLD ME HOW THE RACES WERE GOING TO GO, I WAS scared, and when I saw Nick's car on the starting line, ready to take off, I ran toward it, forgetting the consequences, and got inside. Nick looked at me, first with surprise, then with fury. Terrified, I looked at his feet and reminded him what we were there to do:

"Step on the gas, Nick!"

With lightning reflexes, he tore off and caught up to the other cars before I even knew it, destroying their initial advantage.

"I'm going to kill you! Do you hear me?" he shouted. We were almost into the city, and I knew I needed to be quiet and let him concentrate.

For a split second, he looked over at me and shouted, "Put on your damn seat belt!"

After flinching, I did as he said.

I was going to pay for this, big-time, I knew, but I needed to be there with him. This race wasn't like last year's. It didn't matter how many times I told him not to do it; Nicholas made his own decisions and sometimes left me out. Well, this was my decision: If he was racing, I would, too. If he put himself in danger, so would

I, and I couldn't care less what he had to say about it. I'd deal with the consequences later.

"I told you to go," he screamed, punching the steering wheel. He was livid, but I was, too, and I wasn't about to back down. This wasn't the way to do things, and I wanted him to know that if he was still in that world, I would be, too, and if me being there helped him leave it behind, then it was worth the risk.

"Yeah, but I chose not to," I said, staring at the road. His jaw clenched, the veins popped out in his neck, and I was so scared, I shrank back in my seat.

When we reached the first curve, my feet moved as if I were stepping on the pedals. I was enjoying myself so much, my body was pure adrenaline. I wished I were in Nick's seat, gripping the wheel and showing him how damned good I was. Even if things had gone to hell last time, I had won; there was no denying that.

Nick was good, but at that moment, all I could see was a guy who hadn't stopped to think about how much what he was doing could hurt us. No matter what happened, Nick kept turning back to the dark side, and when he did, he dragged me down with him. He had supposedly quit racing and doing all those things that reminded me of my father, but there we were, and I hated myself for doing something that could have destroyed my family—and loving it.

My brain disconnected from those problems and focused solely on the cars in front of us. In front, not behind. We were losing.

"You need to speed up, Nicholas."

The vein in his neck swelled even more. I bit my lip; I was so nervous.

"I can't believe I'm going a hundred with you in the car."

This is a competition, goddammit, not a walk in the park!

"Well, this car can do two hundred, so step on it, or we're going to lose."

"Shut up!" he shouted.

I closed my mouth and left him to his own devices. My hands were quivering. By the time he hit 120, he had nearly caught up to the others. Lion was in the lead, the other two just in front of us. Either we took them on the next curve, or we'd never be in the lead. I prayed for Nicholas to get it right. If we lost, he'd kill me; he'd claim it had all been my fault.

But then things changed suddenly, and I watched with horror as we pulled ahead of one guy only to see other cars on the road. They must not have cut off the traffic in that section, so suddenly we found ourselves in the middle of a bunch of regular drivers. I didn't like this at all; I didn't want someone getting hurt... This wasn't supposed to happen.

"Shit!" Nick hissed, hitting a curve and trying to dodge two cars that were going forty. With spectacular control, he veered past the car in third place. I couldn't help but cheer.

Lion was the one person in front of us, and even though second place also got a portion of the purse, the competitive side of me wanted to win. Nicholas aced the next curve—I had to give him credit—and I had to press my hand into the dashboard to keep from getting jostled. We were hot on Lion's tail, close but not close enough... I shouted when Nick pulled into oncoming traffic to pass a truck that deafened us with its honking. Not even I would have risked that, but it did help us get ahead. If we could shoot past him at the next intersection, we'd win.

"Come on, Nick! You've got to pass him!" I shouted.

He looked at me, fuming, and just then, with only a few feet to go until we reached Lion and his brother, the needle on the speedometer dropped from 140 to 75.

"What are you doing?" I shrieked, incredulous, turning to him and watching with horror as Lion put distance between us.

"I'm teaching you a lesson," he responded, gunning it again, but it didn't matter—Lion had just crossed the finish line.

Indignant, I took a deep breath. "I can't believe it... We could have won!"

"That money's for Lion. We just needed to take first and second. The order didn't matter," he said as we crossed in turn.

He screeched to a halt, and I prepared myself for whatever he had to say to me, but then flashing lights caught his attention, and he turned to look out the back windshield just as the sirens started echoing. His expression transformed completely.

"No fucking way!" he said, hitting the gas again, speeding up quickly, breaking every traffic law known to man before pulling onto the next exit. Honking horns and shouting pedestrians made it impossible to hear. Only then did I start to realize what was happening.

Nick's phone rang.

"Pick it up," he ordered me, his eyes on the road. "It's in my left front pocket."

I bent over and reached inside, pulling it out.

"Put it on hands-free." He grunted.

I did, and an unknown voice resounded inside the car.

"Dude, the cops are here. They've got us. This is bad!"

"What the fuck, Clark? You told me this was all taken care of!"

"I know, I don't know what happened. Somebody must have snitched! You need to get off the road ASAP!"

"Where's my bike?"

There was nothing but racket on the other line. Apparently the cops had shown up at the empty lot where the race started. We were in a better spot than the rest of them, but I was so scared, I couldn't think straight. All I saw was danger, and I told myself Nicholas was stupid for going there. He should have listened to me; we should have left—both of us.

"Toni took it to the spot. You know what to do. If you hurry, I don't think they'll catch you."

Nicholas grabbed the phone, which was lying on my leg, hung up, and smashed it against the dash.

"Nicholas…" I said, terrified. "They can't catch us." If they did, the consequences would be terrible. I might get kicked out of school, and he already had a record—things could be even worse for him. Maybe even his father would struggle to get him out of it if they wound up arresting him this time.

"They're not going to catch us," he said softly. He stepped on the gas and pulled onto a road I'd never been down. He seemed to know where he was going, and I just sat there praying for a way out. The patrol cars were onto us, I knew that because I could hear the sirens, but they were too far away to catch the license plate.

We kept going. Then Nick turned down a side street, and soon we reached a long line of warehouses and garages. Then, finally, we found ourselves on a muddy driveway that led to a building with the number 120 on the outside. A rolling door automatically went up, and he pulled inside, next to the motorcycle I'd seen in our garage.

"Get out," he said, and I was too scared to disobey.

I saw a bunch of crates and old furniture inside. It must have been a storage space of the Leisters' that Nick used on occasions like this.

He quickly grabbed a canvas sheet off a table and covered the car, lifting a cloud of dust that nearly blinded me and made me cough as I walked away. I felt him behind me. He grabbed my waist, turned me around, and pushed me into the car.

"Now you better do everything I say, Noah. I'm dead serious," he said, rage oozing from his every pore. "If it weren't for your bullshit trauma, I'd leave you here so you'd finally learn to keep out of my goddamned business."

I blinked several times, surprised by his harsh words, wanting to cry. Even if he was right, he was the one who'd gotten us into this situation. He had been the one who'd decided to go back to that world. I swallowed my pride and nodded because I knew the most important thing just then was that we not get caught.

He pulled me over to his motorcycle. There was only one helmet. He pushed it down onto my head. As I briefly met eyes with him, I had no idea how to interpret what was going on in his mind. He got onto the bike, and I climbed on behind him, bending over and wrapping my arms around him before we took off into the cool night.

———

With every minute we spent on the road, my anger grew. I couldn't believe I was sitting on a motorcycle, running from the police, putting up with his tantrums when he had been the one who'd done all this. I felt my hands tense on his firm stomach, and his body answered back, maybe in spite of him. He took one hand off the handlebars and grabbed mine.

What is this supposed to mean?

Ten minutes later, he rounded a corner and stopped at a gas station.

"Don't move," he ordered me without looking back, hopping down and going inside to pay.

I didn't miss my chance. I got off, threw the helmet to the ground, and ran off, not wanting to even look at him.

"Noah!" he shouted. I heard him coming up behind me, and when I looked back and saw him, I ran even faster. I didn't want to see him. I didn't want him to touch me, to shout at me. All I wanted was to be as far away from him as possible.

That night, it was he who had crossed the line, not me.

I ran until I reached the back of a building under construction. I pulled on the door to the fence and snuck inside. Nicholas couldn't squeeze in if he tried, so I stopped, and when I heard him outside, I looked through the grating and saw his eyes looking out of control.

"Come out."

"No."

He grabbed the fence and started shaking it. He was angrier than he'd been in the entire year we'd been going out.

"You think I can't climb right over this fucking fence?" he challenged me. It was obvious he'd already thought about it.

"And what are you going to do once you get over it, Nicholas?" I asked, raising my voice and feeling my body tremble from the cold. The adrenaline was draining, and Nicholas's words were resounding in my skull.

He stopped for a moment. I guess he didn't know.

I rubbed my arms with my hands. I was freezing, I wanted to go home, and I didn't want him to take me there.

"Fuck, Noah!" he shouted, finally exploding. "I told you to leave! You never do what I say! They could have caught us today, we could be in a fucking cell right now, and I'd be going crazy thinking about what might happen to you!"

"Did it ever occur to you that you're not the only one who gets to call the shots in this relationship? That I worry about you, too, and that I'm tired of you lying to me and leaving me out of things?"

"I know how to take care of myself. You have no fucking idea!"

I opened my eyes wide. I couldn't believe what I was hearing.

"I don't know how to take care of myself?" I roared, walking close to the fence. "What the fuck do you know about taking care of anyone? I've taken care of myself and my mother since I was five years old! All you've done is get drunk, take drugs, and fuck around with criminals even though everything in your life was served to you on a silver platter!"

Nicholas stepped back, obviously surprised by what I was

shouting, but I couldn't control it. I had been afraid for him that night, afraid for both of us, because he had risked it all, every single thing we had, everything I had never even dared to dream I could have.

"I'm trying to protect you! But you won't let me," he responded, evidently hurt.

I brought my hands to my head. "Maybe you're the one I need to protect myself from," I whispered, in tears, shocked to be expressing aloud things I had kept to myself for months. "You keep saying you're going to change, that you're going to stop doing all this, but then you don't, Nicholas!"

He looked at me, like he was unable to believe what I was saying.

"At least I try! I left it all for you, I tried to be better, but you put yourself in danger on purpose. You don't trust me, you don't tell me things, and you think I don't know?"

"Are you talking about my 'bullshit trauma'?"

He sighed and closed his eyes, and when he looked at me again, I knew we had crossed a line. "I didn't mean to say that."

I laughed mirthlessly. "But you think it." I turned around and walked off.

"Noah, come out of there, please," he begged as my fears piled in my chest and tears welled in my eyes and I could do nothing to stop them.

"Fuck!" I sat on the ground and wrapped my hands around my knees, burying my head there so he wouldn't see me cry.

"Noah!" he shouted desperately, and I heard the fence shake as he kicked it. "Come out!"

I lifted my head and looked at him. He appeared frantic, but so was I, because I had so much inside me that I hadn't said, and I wasn't sure he'd love me the same if I let it all out. Everything he did just made me retreat deeper inside myself.

"I don't want to be near you right now!" I shouted with all my might. "You're hurting me!"

Pain distorted his features, and his arms jerked on the fence as he tried to climb it. I stood up. This was madness.

"And you hurt me, goddammit!" Unable to get over the fence, he kicked it again. "I've given everything I have for you, absolutely everything, I opened up to you...and now you say I'm hurting you?"

I wasn't going to explain things to him. If he couldn't see the damage he'd caused, then there was no point in it.

"Just go!" I hissed, grabbing a brick and throwing it as hard as I could toward the fence. But it hit the ground before it reached it. "If we can't make this work, Nicholas, then you should go."

He turned around and cursed, and after a few moments, he turned back to face me.

"Look, I'm sorry, okay? I really am. I was an asshole, but I freaked out when I saw you at the race. I was so mad, I still am, but I also know that if I hadn't gone there, we wouldn't be in this situation right now."

"What do you think it felt like for me to see you there, Nicholas?"

"I know, okay, I get it... But, please, I can't stand this distance between us. I need you to come out."

I took a deep breath and wiped away my tears. "We haven't solved anything. You know that, don't you?" I said in a near whisper.

He stood there looking at me, and his expression was enough to make my feet decide for me. I walked toward him and came out through the cracked gate. He pulled me in, wrapped his arms around me, squeezed me as if it hurt him physically not to have me next to him. I breathed in the scent of his body, and my heartbeats slowed instantly. How could he be my sickness and my cure at the same time?

"You stood me up," I reproached him. I couldn't shake off that disappointment.

"I wanted you to be as far from me as possible."

"You told me once we weren't made to be apart from each other."

"And we aren't. I was a jerk. It's not worth it. It's not worth racing if the outcome is me losing you."

I was going to answer, but just then, we felt a vibration. Nick took out his phone, and I waited while he picked up.

"Easy, Lion," he said, then swore to himself. "Yeah, yeah, I can get her out, don't worry. Give me twenty minutes, and I'll be there."

I felt a jab of fear when Nick put his phone in his back pocket and looked at me.

"They arrested Jenna."

30

Nick

When we got to the North Hollywood Community Police Station, Luca and Lion were leaning on their car. Luca was smoking, and Lion was running his hands over his head. When he saw me, his eyes seemed to light up, but that didn't detract from the sorrow on his face.

"What happened?" Noah asked, taking off her oversize helmet and walking over to him. I came up behind her, took it out of her hands, and hung it on my forearm. "How'd they catch her?"

"The cops showed up at the lot. Somebody had to have snitched," Lion said. "I find out who did it, I swear I'll kill them!"

"Easy," I said, trying to think of what to do. I could call Dad, but if he found out what we were up to that night, who knew what his reaction would be. As I thought this, I looked at Noah and wondered what her mother's feelings about it would be, too.

"Where's Jenna? Do they have her locked up already?" Noah asked, obviously getting ready to go inside and try to bail her out herself.

I grabbed her tight. "Don't even think about it, Noah. I don't want you to step one toe inside there. Wait here with Lion while I make a couple of calls."

Despite their gruff expressions, they both decided to listen to me for once. A name popped into my head, and I looked for it in my contacts. This was the last person in the world I'd have turned to ordinarily, but in these circumstances... The phone rang for what seemed like hours until I finally got an answer.

"What the hell are you doing calling me at this hour in the morning, Leister?" I heard a groggy voice reply on the other line.

I took a deep breath, swallowing my pride. "I need your help, Sophia."

A half hour later, we were still waiting for my new coworker to show up. I'd turned to her because I knew she had contacts nearby. Her father lived in a nearby development, and she was handling a lot of our pro bono work, so she knew her way around cases involving minors. If I remembered right, she had helped get a kid out of jail for a possession charge and even had the arrest expunged from his record. Sophia Aiken might be a pain in my ass, but she knew what she was doing.

A white SUV pulled around the corner. It had to be her. I told Noah and my friends to get in the car and let me handle it. I didn't know what kind of mood she'd be in, and I preferred to deal with her on my own. From what little Lion could tell me, it had all happened fast: Jenna didn't even have time to get in the car; they chased her down while she was running away. She wasn't the only one arrested, but for now, I couldn't deal with the others. They'd known the risks they'd been running, and my friend was my top priority.

Luckily someone had taken care of Noah's car, and Clark assured me they'd have it back at Dad's house by the next day. The last thing I needed was the cops getting Noah's tag number and her having to deal with them. I walked away from Lion's car toward Sophia.

"You owe me a big one. You won't live long enough to repay this," she said, getting out of her car dressed impeccably, but with her hair pulled back clumsily in a ponytail.

"Thanks for coming," I said, trying not to back talk her. She seemed to be enjoying herself with that smug grin of hers.

"Did you just thank me?" she asked, perversely amused. "I almost think I'd like to hear that again."

"If you get my friend out, you will."

I guessed my face said it all, and she looked over to the car where Lion, Luca, and Noah were waiting nervously.

"I don't know what kind of shit you're into, Leister, but you're getting more intriguing by the day."

It took all the patience I had not to tell her to go fuck herself. "Can you get her out or not?"

"What's her name?"

I hesitated briefly. "Jenna Tavish."

"Tavish? Like Tavish Oil Corporation?"

I nodded nervously.

"You're kidding, right?" She was angry, but I could tell she was going to do it. "You're calling me, an intern, to get the daughter of a petroleum bigwig out of jail?"

"We need discretion. We don't want anyone to find out. Anyway, she didn't do anything. She was just in the wrong place at the wrong time." I was praying for all this to work out.

Sophia started chuckling as she looked through her purse. "If I had a dollar for every time some delinquent said that…"

"My girlfriend's no delinquent, you hear me?" Lion shouted. I didn't even realize he'd come up behind me.

Putting a hand on his shoulder, I said, "Easy, Lion. Sophia's here to help, right, Soph?"

With a condescending smile aimed first at me, then at Lion, she told me she would help us. "But don't call me *Soph* again, otherwise we're going to have problems."

I laughed at the seriousness in her tone.

Sophia ordered us to stay outside while she started making calls. After what felt like an eternity, she went inside, and we all waited for her to work her magic.

I stuck my head in the car window to talk to Noah. She looked tired and had dirt and grime on her from the construction site.

"You okay, Freckles?" I asked. Luca was passed out next to her, seemingly indifferent to all that was happening.

Noah nodded without even looking at me, but before I could try to get her attention, I heard the door to the station open, and there was Jenna, only slightly worse for wear, with her hair undone and a small scratch on her right cheek.

Noah opened the car door and took off toward her.

Sophia came out behind her grinning, looking satisfied, her eyes pinned to mine. I smiled, watching her get back in her car and return to where she'd come from. Maybe she wasn't as big a pain in the ass as I'd thought.

My peace of mind didn't last long: the dry crack of a slap cut the silence of the night. When I turned, I saw Lion with his hand on his cheek, looking at Jenna cluelessly.

Shit!

"I don't want to see you again, you hear me?" she shouted, tears coursing down her cheeks.

Noah looked over at me, as if asking for help, but I was as clueless as she was, and we were both waiting to see how Lion would react.

"Jenna, I'm sorry. Listen..."

"No!" she roared, stepping back. "Don't you dare ask me for forgiveness! You swore to me this was over. I've been putting up with your shit all summer and waiting for you to change, for you to just do the right thing for once! And now I'm over it!"

I walked over, not knowing what to do. I understood Jenna, but I saw Lion's side of it, too.

Lion looked lost, desperate, and he reached out to touch her. He looked stunned when she jerked away. "Jenna, I'm just trying to give you all you deserve... I've been saving up, you know..."

That was the straw that broke the camel's back. Jenna stepped forward again and shoved him as hard as she could, sobbing now. "I don't give a shit about money! You're the one I'm in love with! Do you not get that? You, not your stupid money!"

Lion grabbed her by the wrists to stop her from pounding on his chest.

"You let them arrest me... The old you would never have left me alone. I was everything to you..."

"You still are, Jenna, I love you," he said, trying to get her to look at him.

Jenna shook her head, then looked up, and we knew something bad was coming next.

"You have no idea what it is to love someone." She tugged her hands free from Lion's grip and walked away from him. "I'm not going to let you drag me down with you."

"Jenna..." Lion sounded broken. This was going to crush him.

"I want to go home," Jenna said to Noah, who walked over and hugged her as I approached Lion.

"Dude," I said to Lion, "I'll get them both home. You just try and chill, okay?"

Lion seemed almost not to see me as Noah helped Jenna into the back seat.

"Take the bike," I said, tossing the keys to Luca, who had woken up and gotten out of the car in the meantime and was watching the scene without emotion. He caught them in midair.

"And take care of your brother," I added before getting into the driver's seat.

I'd have liked to stay with Lion, but I knew the best thing I could do just then was get the girls to safety and pray they'd see things differently the next day. Noah said she wanted to stay at Jenna's house, and when I kissed her goodbye, she felt cold and distant. I'd gotten a clear warning about what could happen if we weren't careful. Noah was surely thinking the same thing.

I was afraid my friend and I had crossed a line, one we hadn't even known existed before that night.

I spent the next two days with Lion. He looked like hell, drunk and in need of a shower, as he lay around on his sofa at home. His apartment stank like weed and grime and looked like a dump. Luca couldn't have been happier, though, and with his brother down in the dumps, he had the run of the place. His four years in the pen had done nothing to correct his bad habits, and I was worried about the influence he might have on Lion.

"You need to wash up, bro, you stink," I told Lion, bagging up all the trash lying on the sofa and the end table. I was getting pissed. It wasn't my job to clean up their shit, but I did it because I knew he needed help.

"Leave me alone, dude. I just want to drink and forget about all this."

I dropped the bag, furious. "Lion, it's been two fucking days, okay? I'm not telling you to just get over it, but at least get off the fucking couch."

"Jenna's all fucked up, and it's my fault. I wasn't good enough for her. Fucking rich people, man. How's a guy from the hood like me supposed to make a girl like her happy?"

"You gotta be a fool to hook up with an oilman's daughter..."

Great, now Luca was giving his two cents. Lion tossed an empty beer can at his head.

I had to do something about that relationship. Lion had his problems, but he needed Jenna; she made him whole.

"If you think Jenna's laid out on her bed crying over you, you're wrong," I said, washing my hands. Lion sat up then and looked over at me. "She's on the beach with Noah. This is supposed to be their last day out with their old classmates before they take off for college."

"She's out with those dickheads from that fancy-ass school?"

I raised my eyebrows.

"Don't look at me like that. You're different, the rest of those people blow," he said, getting up and going to the bathroom. "Give me five minutes."

I dropped the bag on the floor and smiled at Luca. At least I'd gotten Lion up off the sofa. As for calling me a rich dickhead, well...I'd get him back for that.

Honestly, I wasn't that crazy about Noah being on the beach with the people from her graduating class either. I'd promised to leave her alone, but what was going on between Jenna and Lion gave me an excuse to go make sure everything was okay...that we were okay, to be more precise. We hadn't seen each other again since our fight, and I wasn't sure where things stood with us. I needed to see her and talk to her.

They'd started the day at the home of one of Noah's friends, Elena something-or-other, who had a place right on the beach... not like that was special for those kids, of course.

I parked outside, noticing there were a lot of cars here for what Noah had told me would be a small gathering. When we went inside, there were more than a hundred people there, almost everyone in a bathing suit. The music was blasting in all the rooms. Lion looked so out of place among those people that I walked him to the back of the house.

There, overlooking the shore, I saw two bonfires and big groups seated around them roasting marshmallows and drinking straight from the bottle.

"I thought she'd be crying, but look," Lion said, pointing at two girls walking along the shore with their arms around each other, holding what looked like a bottle of tequila.

Jenna and Noah. Great.

We walked over. When they saw us, they turned to stone for a second. Then they burst out laughing.

"Look who we have here, Noah, Dickhead One and Dickhead Two," Jenna said, bringing the bottle to her lips and frowning. They were both wearing swimsuits and tiny shorts.

Lion walked over to her cautiously. "Hey, Jenna, can we talk?" he asked her, clearly nervous.

Jenna looked at him like an insect under a microscope. "Sorry, Dickhead Two, but I'm not in the mood," she said, stumbling.

"So that means I'm Dickhead One?" I asked.

Noah shrugged. "Sometimes," she said, but she didn't stop me from putting an arm around her waist.

"Can I at least take you home, Jenna? You're drunk," Lion said, holding her up when she nearly tripped.

"Let me go," she shouted, jerking away and falling on her butt in the sand.

Noah twisted free from my grasp. "Leave her alone, Lion."

I watched the scene attentively. I knew Lion almost better than I knew myself, and I wasn't surprised to see him trying to get Jenna back. I would have done the same—in a way, I *was* doing the same.

He leaned down and grabbed her by the shoulder.

"Let go of me, you Neanderthal!" she screamed, dropping the bottle on the sand but not managing to break free of him.

"You can call me all the big names you want, but you're coming with me."

Noah turned to me, flushed. "Do something!" she said, and I held her back when I thought she might go over there.

"She called him a Neanderthal. I can't get involved after that. A guy's gotta have his pride, right?"

Noah grimaced and I laughed, hoisting her over my shoulder and walking to the less crowded of the two bonfires.

"You need to let them talk it out, Freckles. Otherwise, nothing will ever get solved."

Noah was shivering from the cold and drunk enough to forget how angry she was. When I sat her down on top of me, she curled up in my arms and let the fire warm her.

"I'm tanked," she said.

"You don't say! I'd have never guessed."

"I'm still pissed at you, though."

I rubbed her back softly. "I imagined... Anything I can do about it?"

"You can keep touching me like that," she answered, making me shiver. I leaned back and took off my sweatshirt, carefully guided her arms inside it, then zipped her up. She leaned her head on my shoulder, and I felt her breathing on my neck.

"Tomorrow, it'll be a year..." she said sadly, and her lip trembled.

"A year since what?" I asked. But she closed her eyes and fell asleep.

I got up and carried her to the car. She'd had enough partying for one day. I had no idea where Lion was, but I couldn't keep being his babysitter. He knew what he was doing. I put the car in drive and headed home. I hated to think of the hangover Noah would have the next day. It was normal for her to be drinking, but I never liked seeing her like that.

Despite myself, I decided to stay at Dad's. In a few days, Noah and I would be living together at my apartment. Already, I was counting the days.

31

Noah

It wasn't going to be a good day. I knew as soon as I opened my eyes that morning. Not just because of the hangover, the headache, the profound desire to vomit, but also because it had now been a year since my father had died, and it was my fault.

I got out of bed, feeling my stomach screaming at me for all the alcohol I'd drunk the night before, and staggered my way to the bathroom to shower. I didn't even know how I'd gotten to my room. I'd drunk so much tequila, I felt like it was coursing through my veins. I remembered seeing Nick...and Lion.

I needed to call Jenna and find out how the night had ended, but not today... Today I wasn't going to talk to anyone. I was going to shut myself in my room with my inner demons and cry for a father who had never loved me, cry for a person who had tried to kill me and for a little girl who could never make her father care about her.

I knew I was an idiot for thinking about him still, but his words and the guilt that lived within me since his death would never go away. My nightmares were part of my existence when I went to bed, and sometimes, they even chased me throughout the day.

I'd loved him. Did that make me a monster? Was I a monster for loving the man who had hit my mother and hurt her every single day? Was I crazy because I went on thinking that if I'd just acted differently, my father would still be alive?

I closed my eyes, let the water fall over me, passed a sponge over my body. I felt dirty inside... I hated those thoughts. There were times when it was like another person was inside me, forcing me to be a masochist, to act in a way that did not honor me or my deceased father. He didn't deserve my tears. He didn't deserve the grief I felt for him...

It didn't matter how many times he'd taken me to the park or fishing... It didn't matter that he'd taught me to drive when I couldn't even reach the pedals. It didn't matter that I'd used to love watching him race and win.

He had been my father, and my little girl's mind, my twisted little girl's mind, had forced me to look away every time he mistreated my mother. I didn't understand my thoughts or how I'd acted. I tried to analyze myself from another perspective, but none of it made any sense.

During the months I'd spent in the foster home, I had missed my mother, of course, but I had missed him, too... I had missed how he treated me better than he did her. In a horrible way, I had liked being different, knowing my father wouldn't hurt me, that he loved me the most, that I was special to him... Of course, everything fell apart in the end, because he did wind up hurting me...and badly.

The memories, the conversations, came back to me, and there was nothing I could do to change that.

"You suck!" one of the girls at the foster home shouted. There were five of us girls and one little boy in that horrible house with fake parents who didn't love us and didn't take care of us.

"You took away my doll!" I shouted, trying to make myself heard over the sobs of the blond girl next to us. "And when you act bad, you get punished. Didn't anyone ever teach you that?"

"Don't hit her again!" The brown-haired girl with the pretty braids went on pointing at me with her dirty finger and hugging her four-year-old sister, whose cheek was red where I'd hit her.

The other two girls, who were seven and six, got behind Alexia, the dark-haired girl with the braids. I hated how they liked her and not me. All I'd done was take back what was mine—she had stolen my doll; I had a right to hit her, didn't I?

That was how it went when a person was bad.

"You're nasty, Noah. No one likes you," Alexia said. She was almost as tall as I was, we were the oldest girls in the house, but she had a cruel face that I couldn't imitate. Maybe I had hit her, but all I really wanted was for us to be friends. I had tried to tell her that when I was done playing, she could have my doll, that we should share it, but she had taken it away, torn it out of my hands. "No one talk to her," she ordered the others. "From now on, you can stay all alone because meanies like you don't deserve for anyone to like them. You're nasty and you're ugly, too!"

I felt the tears roll down my face, even though I knew I wasn't supposed to cry. My father had made that very clear. Only weak people cried. My mother was weak because she cried; I wasn't.

"Nasty! Nasty! Nasty! Nasty! Nasty!"

They chanted along with her, even the little one who had been crying started smiling and joined in. I grabbed my doll and ran off.

I got out of the shower trying to erase those memories. I looked at myself in the mirror and saw my tattoo. I traced its outline with my finger. It was small, but it meant so much. I took a deep breath to calm down. I didn't want all this to get the best of me. I had done that before; I couldn't do it again.

Just then, someone knocked at the bathroom door.

"Noah, it's Nick," he said.

I closed my eyes and counted to three in my head, then walked to the door and let him in. I didn't know he had stayed over the night before. I turned around, still wrapped in a towel, and grabbed the lotion off the counter. I didn't want company. I needed to be alone that day.

"You all right?" he asked, coming closer slowly, as if trying to feel me out.

"My head hurts," I said, walking past him into my room. I knew he would follow me. I just hoped he could figure out this wasn't the day. Sometimes we could pick up on each other's moods. Hopefully he was able to now.

I walked into the closet and put on a T-shirt, the same one I'd had on the day I moved in there. It was one of the few things that hadn't made it into my suitcases for when I moved. That T-shirt and a pair of tights I was about to slip on.

I felt him behind me just as I took the towel off my head and my damp hair fell over my shoulders. He turned me around, grabbing me by one arm, so I would look him in the eye.

"Are you okay?" he asked, pushing my hair aside.

"I'm just tired, and I have a hangover," I said. He looked the opposite of how I felt. In his Levi's and his white Calvin Klein T-shirt, with his bedhead hair, he was like a runway model.

"I'll make you some breakfast before I go," he said, kissing me on the cheek. "I wish I could stay here all afternoon with you, maybe watch a movie or something, but I need to work."

I sighed with relief. I didn't want him to see me in that state. I wasn't in the mood for companionship. I'd just end up scaring him.

"Don't worry. I'm just going to sleep all day."

YOUR FAULT | 237

I stepped forward and kissed him on the lips, softly, patiently. Our fight on the day of the race was still in my head, the way we'd shouted at each other and he'd reproached me for not trusting him... But what if you didn't even understand the way you felt? How could I explain to Nick what was going on? I just sensed that something wasn't right, and I was dying to seek comfort in his arms, but I couldn't... I was scared of telling him certain things, and I didn't want him to be disappointed or to judge me.

He left, looking worried, and I tried to force a smile to relax him. I don't know if it worked.

It had been a long time since I'd vegged out like that in front of the TV, eating chocolate and watching *Friends*. Some scientific study or other had said eating chocolate flooded your brain with endorphins, but it wasn't working for me; it was just making me gain weight.

That day was a dark one, and however much I had wished at first that Nick would just leave for work, now I missed him, and I really needed him to come give me a hug.

I was surprised to see the chaos in the kitchen when I went downstairs for a soda and more chocolate. Mom was in a pretty dress and sandals, even makeup, and Will soon walked in afterward in a dress shirt and work slacks. I knew something was up.

"Are you having someone over for dinner?"

My mother, who was giving instructions to Prett, turned and looked me up and down with a dissatisfied face. "Senator Aiken and his daughter are coming over tonight."

Senator?

"Just because or for some special reason? Were you not going to tell me?" My mother normally warned me about things like this. Did this mean I wasn't invited?

"He's an old friend of Will's, and they want to start doing business together. Since you didn't feel good, I assumed you'd want to stay up in your room," she said, taking off the apron she had tied around her waist.

Perfect.

"Yeah, if you don't mind, I'd rather skip dinner than hang out with some old dude and his daughter, thanks," I said, a little grumpier than I had intended. I was in an awful mood.

My mother gave me a harsh look. I tried to ignore it as best I could.

"I'll have Prett bring you something."

"Don't worry about it. I'm not hungry." I turned around and went back to my room. Hesitant, I grabbed the phone to call Nick. I knew he was working the next day and wouldn't be coming over, but I also knew one phone call was enough to get whatever I needed from him.

"Hey, Freckles," he greeted me, sounding cheerful.

"Hey. What are you up to?" I asked, feeling him out.

He pulled his phone away from his ear to talk to someone. I heard a girl laughing and then Nick grumbling something about a horrible song.

My body immediately tensed. "Where are you?" I asked, a little cooler than usual, intrigued to know who he was with.

"Right now, I'm walking through the front door." Just then, I heard a door open slowly.

"Where?"

"What do you mean, where? The same place as you—Dad's house."

He was here?

I went downstairs to receive him, almost shaking. I had wanted to see him so badly... It was almost as if a messenger had heard my call and sent him to me. I didn't stop to think what his words signified or about the feminine voice I'd heard over the phone. I'd imagined I'd come out and throw myself in his arms, but instead I found him with her, the girl who had gotten Jenna out of jail.

I stopped in the doorframe.

She was well-dressed, with a tight pencil skirt that hung to her knees and a pale pink name-brand blouse. In her Manolo Blahnik heels—what else would you expect?—she was almost as tall as Nick.

Who the hell was she?

Nick's eyes settled on me, at first surprised, then affectionate. The air blowing through the door whistled through my hair, pulled back on the top of my head. I stepped away to let them through.

"Noah, this is Sophia Aiken, my fellow intern," Nick said, kissing me gently on the cheek.

With a curious smile on her fleshy lips, Sophia extended a hand with a manicure as perfect as my mother's.

"It's a pleasure, Noah," she said.

I nodded, intimidated, feeling completely out of place.

Before I had time to respond, my mother appeared like the perfect hostess she was and greeted the new arrivals, looking over at me as she did so, probably surprised that her sloppy-looking daughter had come down to open the door.

What the hell was actually going on?

"Your father's not here yet, Sophia. If you want to have a drink in the living room, Nick will get you something."

She nodded and followed my mother inside.

Now that the initial shock had passed, all I felt was anger and an overwhelming urge to cry.

"Why didn't you tell me you were coming?"

Nick seemed as confused as I was, and he looked away from my eyes and down at my T-shirt and tights.

My God…had I just opened the door for a senator's daughter looking like that?

"I thought your mom told you... They called me this afternoon and told me to invite Sophia over for dinner. Apparently, her dad wants to meet me or something like that. I just assumed you knew. The other day, with all the stuff with Jenna, I didn't have the chance to introduce you."

"No one told me you were coming. If I'd known, I wouldn't have said I wasn't coming down for dinner." I heard my mother talking to Sophia in the living room. "I can't go in there like this... I'll just go to bed, and we can talk when this is over."

I tried to walk off, but he came around in front of me.

"What's up with you? Just go upstairs, change clothes, and come down for dinner... I only agreed to this stupid dinner because I assumed you were going to be here. I don't know what kind of BS they're cooking up, but I'm not in the mood to sit there and blab about nothing."

"Not my problem, Nicholas," I said, trying to remain calm. "Plus, I think it's weird you never mentioned her to me. You sure do seem friendly with her."

With a scowl, he looked in the direction of her and my mother and then back at me.

"Are you fucking jealous?" he asked, rolling his eyes.

I slapped his arm without even thinking about it. "How can you say that?"

He laughed loudly enough to worsen my bad mood.

"For the love of God! She's an unbearable snot-nosed brat who's trying to get a job at my dad's firm because she doesn't want to work for her own dad. I can't believe you're jealous of her."

"I'm not jealous, idiot!" I murmured, walking past him toward my room.

"If you don't come back down, I'll go find you and drag you back myself," he threatened me playfully. "You know I want you here."

If looks could kill, Nicholas would be six feet underground by now.

_____

I looked at myself in the mirror, frustrated. I wasn't going to get dressed up for that stupid dinner. Forget that.

I took off my T-shirt with the holes in it and threw it on the floor while I looked around for something so I wouldn't have to unpack the bags strewn all over the walk-in closet. I ended up deciding on some tight black jeans, simple, the kind you'd wear for a casual night out, and a white T-shirt that said *I ♡ Canada*.

I grinned. I was sure the senator would love it.

I let my hair down and pulled it back into a ponytail, washed my face, and put on lip liner. That was as fancy as I was going to get that night. Sophie could doll herself up all she wanted; I was pretty in anything…or that's what my grandmother told me, anyway.

When I went downstairs, still in a shit mood, I heard an unfamiliar man's voice. Five people—William, my mother, Nick, Sophia, and her father—were standing around the bar in the living room chitchatting while Will poured drinks. They looked like something out of a magazine: tall, distinguished, elegant. Looking at my shoes, I felt like an intruder.

My mother saw me, and her eyes widened as she noticed my T-shirt, but before she could send me back upstairs, Will noticed me and welcomed me with a smile.

"Noah, come on in. I want to introduce you to an old friend from school. Riston, this is my stepdaughter, Noah; Noah, this is my friend Riston."

Unlike his daughter, Riston was as American as they come: blond, with light-colored eyes like my mother, as tall as Nick, and broad-shouldered. All he had in common with Sophia was the slight almond shape of his eyes and a little dimple in his chin... I had always thought that was supercute on a girl, but now that I saw she had one, I hated it.

I smiled and shook hands with him. I could feel Nick next to me, but not warm and protecting as usual. Instead, it felt like there was a barrier between us.

Soon we walked to the dining room, where Prett had set a table even more lavish than on Christmas. But then, the Leisters had never celebrated the holidays until my mother and I showed up and turned their world upside down. I still remembered how funny it had been, seeing Will and Nick in their Santa hats, and Nick frowning when I forced him to go get a huge Christmas tree and hang up wreaths. No fool, he'd also been sure to put up mistletoe in every corner.

To my irritation, since I'd joined at the last minute, I was seated next to the senator, with Sophia and Nick across from me... side by side.

Why the hell was I so jealous? Was it really so hard for me to keep from comparing myself to her?

They spent the whole dinner talking about some project or other Sophia was especially excited about. She talked about laws, numbers, and statistics as passionately as I'd have talked about the Brontës or Thomas Hardy. I was dismayed to see Nick was interested, too. I could see it in his eyes. And still worse, I couldn't even follow the conversation... All those numbers made me dizzy, and I felt like a total idiot. William kept praising her and talking to the two of them like they were a team. Everyone seemed dazzled by them, like they were a new toy, and that gave me a very unpleasant feeling in my stomach.

Late in the meal, Senator Riston looked over at me. "So, Noah, how's school?"

His question made an intense heat well inside me and rise to my cheeks.

Was it that obvious I had no idea what they were talking about? Was it so obvious that I wasn't a real adult like his daughter and that he had to take pity on me at the end of a conversation, the way you asked a child about the goings-on at daycare?

"I graduated in June, so yeah, I'm just waiting to start my freshman year," I said, grabbing the one glass filled with soda at the table.

I met Nick's gaze across the table, and I felt the sting of awkwardness, of not truly belonging. I couldn't help him with his projects; I didn't even know what they were. Nick didn't talk to me about work. He knew I couldn't contribute in that department... Sophia bent over to whisper something in his ear, and Nick smiled.

What the hell were they talking about?

I barely heard the senator as he went on talking. "...Anyway, you'll love dorm life. That's one of the best things about college..."

I looked over at him and calmly said, "Actually, I'm going to be living with Nicholas." I didn't feel light-headed until silence overtook the table, interrupted by the clang of my mother's silverware as she dropped it unexpectedly.

Nick's eyes were like saucers as he gazed back and forth between our parents and me.

The senator was unsure what to say... I guess someone had forgotten to tell him we were going out.

Sophia, on the other hand, took it with aplomb, and that pissed me off even worse. If she knew we were going out, why hadn't she stayed away from him? I felt bad about what I'd said when I looked at Mom. She was going to kill me that night, that much was certain.

32

Nick

I LOOKED OVER AT NOAH AFTER SOPHIA TOLD ME WE MADE A good couple, but that was the last thing I'd expected Noah to let slip.

I stiffened all over. No sooner than she'd uttered those words about living with me did Noah slide her chair backward and stand. "If you all will excuse me, I don't feel especially well. I think I should probably go to bed." Her face was white as a ghost. Without waiting for a response, she walked out. Her mother seemed to want to go after her, but my father took her hand and whispered something to her. Raffaella glowered at me, and I felt sick to my stomach.

At the same time, I was happy Noah had finally decided to tell her mother something I'd been hoping she'd say all summer, even if this hadn't been the best way to do it. I needed to talk to her. I knew something wasn't right; that was why I'd agreed to come to that stupid dinner, to have an excuse to see her and to spend another night at home. I hated it there, but I loved having breakfast with Noah and getting a kiss from her before I went to work. And I wanted to find out what was bothering her aside from her jealousy toward Sophia—which was ridiculous and had no basis in reality.

I started to get up, but my father's eyes told me it was better to stay where I was. Sophia could tell what was going on and brought up another subject before the situation got too uncomfortable. A moment later, though, I heard the front door slam.

Shit!

I got up, no longer caring what anyone thought, and walked out to the porch, where I saw Noah pulling out in her convertible, speeding down the driveway, and turning away.

What was she doing?

I went back inside to grab my keys from the table by the door. Raffaella emerged from out of nowhere and gave me the nastiest look she could muster.

"I asked you to take things slow," she said. I thought I lost whatever credit I might ever have had with her in that moment.

"Raffaella..."

"I asked for one thing, and your father and I promised not to get involved in your relationship as long as you were discreet. I guess that deal's off now."

What is that supposed to mean? I wondered as she stepped closer to me.

"Go bring her back... This isn't a good day for her to be by herself."

Something lit up in my brain when she said that.

"What do you mean?"

Impassively, she said, "It's been a year since the kidnapping...a year since her father died."

I had no idea where she might have gone. Like an idiot, I kept trying to think of places at the same time as I reproached myself for being so blind. She had even brought it up the day before, when she was drunk, but goddammit! In that state I hadn't realized... How could I have forgotten the date? I still remembered the terror in her eyes as the pistol was pointed at her head. I still remembered how my heart had almost leapt out of my chest when I'd heard the shot... The shot that I thought, for a second, had actually hit Noah. That nightmare had been dead and buried in the back of my mind; I hadn't wanted to dig it up.

But obviously Noah had forgotten nothing. Deny them as she might, the nightmares were still there, and I was sure she'd kept sleeping with the lights on when she wasn't with me. Her father was dead now. He was gone; no one could hurt her anymore. Why couldn't she just say goodbye to those bad memories once and for all?

After thinking things over, I thought I knew where I could find her.

With an anxious feeling, I drove toward the cemetery. When I got there and saw Noah's car parked on the gravel lot by the gate, I breathed a sigh of relief and hurried out. I'd never been to that place. My grandmother was in a private mausoleum on the other end of town. It had cost a small fortune to bury her there, but looking around, it suddenly seemed worth it.

I noticed how cool the night was as I walked in and thought about how Noah had left without even throwing on a coat. I'd nearly laughed when I first saw her at the table in her T-shirt, and I think I'd loved her a little more then, if that was possible, seeing her looking so beautiful, so simple. She didn't have to do anything fancy to be gorgeous. I saw that more and more every day.

I walked between the gravestones, looking for the last name Morgan. Many of them were run-down, and only a few had flowers or any sign that someone remembered the people buried there.

Then I saw her. She was sitting on the grass in front of a stone. From where I stood, I couldn't read the inscription. I watched her for a moment before walking over. She was hugging her legs. She wiped away her tears with the back of her hand when she caught sight of me rushing over.

She stood up, looking vulnerable and lost. I thought I saw guilt in her eyes.

"What are you doing here?" I couldn't help but ask her. I couldn't understand why she'd visit the grave of a man who'd nearly killed her. I slipped off my jacket and laid it over her shoulders as she shivered.

"You shouldn't have followed me," she said, looking down.

"I couldn't help it. Especially not when my girlfriend decided to drop a bomb in the middle of dinner and take off running right afterward."

That made her look a little guilty, but only for a second.

"I was like a fifth wheel at that dinner. You seemed to be enjoying yourself, though."

I wasn't going to let that slide. I got that she was jealous of Sophie, but that had nothing to do with me or with us living together, which was way bigger, way more important, than all that.

"Why did you come here, Noah?" I asked her again, trying as hard as I could to comprehend. "Tell me why you're crying over the death of a man who tried to kill you. Explain it to me because I'm going crazy trying to understand."

She looked over at the stone, anxious. "Let's just go," she said, grabbing my hand. "I want to leave. Take me home, or take me to your place—I don't care," she said, pulling my arm.

Her reaction surprised me. She seemed to be hiding something. Instinctively, I looked over at her father's grave.

The stone was new and very clean, and on top of it was a vase with orange and yellow flowers, which made it stand out from the unkempt tombs around it. The inscription, in elegant letters, read:

JASON NOAH MORGAN
(1977–2015)

Underneath was an engraving of a figure eight knot on the immaculate marble.

33

Noah

NICHOLAS SHOULDN'T HAVE SEEN THAT.

I felt my heart pounding faster and faster till it reached a fever pitch. When he finally looked me in the eye, I could see he was completely lost. And frightened. I didn't like seeing him that way.

"It's not what you think," I said, taking a step back. This was what I'd been running from since the beginning, the thing I didn't want him to know...

"Then explain it to me, Noah... Honestly, I'm trying to understand. I don't think I've ever tried so hard to do anything, but you're not making it easy for me."

I felt ashamed because this was something so private, something that should matter to only me...and I didn't want anyone judging me for it. Least of all him.

"What do you want me to say, Nick?" I shouted, trying to keep the tears gathering behind my eyelids from streaming down my face. "He was my father..."

"He tried to kill you," he replied, confused. "He beat your mother, Noah. I don't get it. What's there to miss?"

His expression made my heart crack. He wanted to put himself in my place, but it was painfully clear he couldn't, and that was what divided us just then and what I feared might permanently tear us apart.

"You'll never get it, Nicholas, because even I can't control what I feel. I don't miss him. It's something else… I feel guilty for things ending up the way they did. In his heart, he…he did love me once."

"You can't look at it that way, Noah," he said softly but firmly. "None of that was your fault. The problem is you're just too fucking good! You're incapable of blaming him because he was your father, and I get that, right? But you aren't to blame for what happened… He was the one who signed his own death sentence the moment he put a pistol to your head…the moment he laid his hands on you that night, ten years ago."

I shook my head. I had no idea how to explain myself, how to explain what I felt inside. Everything was so contradictory… He had hurt me… But what about all the times he'd held me, the nights he'd taken me with him to the track and we'd driven at top speed…when he'd taught me to fish…when he'd taught me to tie a figure eight…?

Nicholas closed his eyes and pressed his forehead to mine. "You're still scared of him, aren't you?" he said, then looked at me. "Even though he's dead, you're still scared of him. You still believe you owe him something, you feel guilty, and that makes you come here. That's why you bring him those flowers he doesn't deserve."

My lip started trembling… Of course I was scared of him… I was scared of him more than I was of anyone. Fear was almost everything he meant to me.

I didn't realize my hand had risen to touch my tattoo until Nick grabbed it and pulled it away.

"Why'd you get it?"

I took a deep breath, trying to calm down, but it was pointless. I knew why I'd gotten it, of course, but could I tell Nick? I saw my reflection in his pupils. And yet there was some essential part of me that was totally absent from that reflection.

"When you're tied too tightly to someone...it hurts when you break free, but it's either that or you're trapped forever. And I'm one of those who's trapped forever."

Nicholas looked baffled. I think that was the first time I had ever seen him at a loss for words.

I hugged him. I didn't want him to feel like that, especially not because of me. It wasn't right for him to have to worry about this.

"I think you need help, Noah," he said.

I pulled away. "What do you mean?"

He paused, cautious, then continued speaking. "I think you need to talk to an outsider, someone impartial...someone who can help you try to understand how you're feeling. Someone who can help with your nightmares—"

"You do help me," I cut him off.

He shook his head, suddenly sad. "I don't, though... I don't know how to do it. I don't know how to get you to understand that there's nothing for you to be afraid of."

"When I'm with you, I feel safe. You help me, Nick. I don't need anyone else."

He brought his hands to his head, as if trying to decide what to say next.

"Do it for me," he said. "I need to see you happy if I'm going to be happy. I need you not to be afraid of the darkness, of your dead father, and I especially need you to stop thinking that you should love him or defend him because, Noah, your father was an abuser, and no one can change that, not you or anybody else, understand?"

I shook my head slowly... I felt lost... I didn't know how to tell him that the first time I'd ever admitted those feelings aloud, the thing I feared most was happening: he was judging me.

"I'm not crazy," I said, pushing him away.

"Of course you're not, babe, but you've been through things most people can't imagine, and I don't think you know how to deal with it... I just want you to be happy, okay, Noah? I'll always be by your side, but I can't fight off your demons. You have to do that on your own."

"By seeing a shrink?"

"A psychologist, not a shrink," he corrected me gently. "I went to one, you know? When I was a kid... After my mom left, I started to have insomnia, I wasn't eating or sleeping...I was so sad, and I just couldn't get over it on my own. Sometimes, talking to a person you don't know helps you see things from a different perspective... Do it for me, Freckles. I need you to try, at least."

He seemed so worried about me...and I knew, deep down, that he was right. I couldn't go on like that. I was scared to be in the dark, scared of those nightmares following me every night...

"Please."

I looked at him for a moment, and all at once, I felt thankful that I had him there. I knew without him, I'd never dare make that decision.

"It's fine. I'll go."

He had edged over to me by then, and I felt the sigh of relief blowing from his lips as he bent over to kiss me.

———

I didn't want to go back home. My mother would be enraged, and the last thing I wanted to do was face off with her.

"I fucked up, right?" I said, rubbing my face as we went back in his car.

His fingers grazed the nape of my neck as he looked straight ahead on the freeway. "That's one way of looking at it, probably, but at least you said it."

I looked over at him, thinking about how real it was now: we were going to live together; the deal was done, and soon. If I wanted, I could grab my things then and there, walk out the door, and start a new life with him.

Nick parked close to the door. The senator and his daughter must have gone because the only cars there were Will's and my mother's. Mine was back at the cemetery... Nick hadn't wanted me to go back alone and said he'd send Steve to pick it up the next day.

Not wanting to get out, with a knot of anxiety in my chest, I leaned my arm into the door and my head into the side window. What a horrible day it had been.

"Come here," Nick said, pulling me over until I was on his lap with my feet in the passenger seat. He squeezed me tight, and I rested my cheek against his neck.

"Everything's going to be fine, babe."

I closed my eyes and let his words soothe me.

"As for Sophia...I know I shouldn't have acted that way, but she's the girl who got Jenna out of jail, and you never even mentioned you worked with her..."

"There's nothing to worry about, Noah. I have no feelings whatsoever for Sophia or for anyone except you... How could I even think of hurting you?"

I nestled my face closer and kissed his collarbone. He smelled so good...and I felt so safe in his arms...in those strong arms that protected me and that cradled me softly, as though afraid I would break.

"Stay with me tonight," I whispered, knowing that meant he'd have to confront his father in the morning.

"Of course," he said, and I felt a huge weight lift off me.

34

Nick

In the morning, I left home early, carrying Noah's two enormous suitcases. I didn't have time to fight with our parents before going to work, and I didn't want them spoiling the happiness of knowing that we had finally started the move and that Noah and I would be together at last.

I went straight to the break room as soon as I got in. I'd had no time for breakfast and was dying of hunger. As I finished my second cup of coffee and was wiping my mouth with my napkin, Sophia walked in.

I was conscious of the fact I'd left her hanging the night before. But it wasn't my fault, and anyway, she'd been there with her dad. I nodded to her and tried to walk past her to the office, but she stood in my way with a defiant expression.

"You know what's fun? When someone invites you over and you're not remotely in the mood, and then they ditch you along with your dad, your boss, and his wife..."

I had to bite my lip not to laugh. Honestly, it was funny when she put it like that. And I kind of enjoyed seeing her so pissed. I sat down at the table, crossed my arms, and said, "Tell me how you really feel, Aiken."

"I mean, they just sat there the whole time, talking bullshit about what a good lawyer you'll be, how bright your future is, how you've turned into such a responsible son."

"What the hell?"

Her brows rose as she walked past me to the coffee machine. I turned, consternated and wanting to hear more.

"Apparently my father thinks it would be just wonderful if the two of us would work together in the future. And when he says *work*, I think you know what he means."

It felt like it was getting hotter in that room.

"What kind of bullshit is this? My dad, calling me a mature and responsible son? I don't know what you took before dinner, but I'm sure you heard him wrong. My father can't stand me."

Sophia blew on her coffee with her bright red lips and took a deliberately slow sip. "My father just loves trying to find boyfriends for me, and William Leister's son, well, I guess he thinks you'd be a real catch. But it wasn't just him—your stepmother was in on it, too. To hear her tell it, she thinks you're the bee's knees, but my feeling is she doesn't like you hooking up with her daughter one damned bit...let alone living with her."

I clenched my fists. I couldn't believe what I was hearing. That woman would be the death of me. How the hell could she dare insinuate that Sophia could be attractive to me, especially compared to her daughter? What kind of mother tries to get her daughter's boyfriend to hook up with someone else?

I squeezed my Styrofoam cup into a ball and tried to control my rage before it took over. Not only were they trying to scheme behind our backs, they'd shown they had no respect for us whatsoever.

With a relaxed expression, Sophia said, "Nick, it's obvious you love her." She rested a hand on my forearm. "But let me tell you from experience: trying to keep a relationship going when it's you against the world…it doesn't usually work out."

With that, she walked off.

I rubbed my face, trying to calm down and at the same time to ignore, once again, all the things that threatened Noah's and my relationship. Since the night before, when I'd grasped how much the death of Noah's father had affected her, a hard-to-ignore fear had taken over me. One thing was to fight hair, tooth, and nail against people determined to make us give up our relationship; another was to take on Noah and her ghosts. Now that I understood that no one but us would be sure our love survived, I couldn't help but think that maybe we weren't giving everything we should. I could take on anything, I could keep struggling to the end, and I would never stop, I loved that girl so desperately that just the thought of her drove me wild, but what if Noah let the others get to her? What if that wall between us, the one I kept hoping would finally crumble, instead grew higher and higher until I could no longer reach her at all?

One thing was clear, just one: no one but Noah could push me away from her. No one.

———————

Late in the afternoon, my boss appeared in the doorway. Sophia was putting her things in her purse, and I was turning off my laptop.

"I've got good news for the two of you," he said with a smile.

"I'm dying to hear," I said sarcastically. It was well known that Jenkins and I couldn't stand each other. He'd be in what was by rights *my* job until I had enough experience to take over, and he knew I had my eye on it.

Sophia gave him a peculiar smile. She loved him, and she was absolutely dedicated to doing her job perfectly and rising through the ranks.

"Two people have dropped out of the Rogers case, and they've asked us to send two replacements from here tomorrow. If I remember right, Nicholas, you wanted to work that case, but you dropped it when you decided to leave San Fran. Well, the legwork's basically done. It's now a matter of taking it in front of the judge and helping out with the defense. It'll be quick and easy, and this is the kind of case that can teach you two a lot."

"Amazing. When do we need to be there?" Sophia looked so excited, I wouldn't have been surprised to see her turning somersaults.

"I got you both tickets to leave tomorrow morning."

Shit!

"So soon? You couldn't give us a little more time to prepare? We've got lives, you know."

Jenkins ignored my tone and continued to talk calmly. "Hard as it may be for you to accept this, Nicholas, the world doesn't revolve around you. The trial starts tomorrow afternoon, and you need to be there ASAP. If you don't like it, I'm sure your father would be overjoyed to hear your complaints."

I stood up slowly and rested my fists on the table. "I'd recommend you not bring my father up at moments like this, J, unless you're in the mood for a curb stomping."

He grimaced. I knew I was abusing my position there as the boss's son, but it was that or actually come to blows with him, and I preferred a little workplace friction to the real problems that could cause.

"Someday, reality's going to hit you like a ton of bricks, Nicholas, and I sure hope I'm there to see it happen." Before I could answer, he turned to Sophia. "Airport. Five a.m. Don't fuck up because if you do, you'll be out on the street!"

He walked off while I sat there thinking about how I'd like to knock his lights out.

Sophia walked so close to me that I had trouble focusing on her words. But the end of the phrase was "... I'll be the one having to pay for it, understand? So control yourself, because I'm not about to lose my job over something you did!"

I ignored her deliberately and walked out, slamming the door.

How was I going to go home and tell Noah I had to go to San Francisco with the same girl she was jealous of and that our parents wanted to hook me up with?

35

Noah

MY MOTHER'S SILENCE WASN'T A GOOD SIGN. IT FELT LIKE THE calm before the storm, and that worried me. I went on packing my bags, getting the last few things, while Jenna sat there counting off all the bad things that were going to happen to me if I went to live with Nick. That was when I realized I would have to start ignoring all her thoughts about our relationship.

Jenna was in anti-romance mode. Since she had split with Lion, she had gone from crying like a baby to adopting a hard-core feminist attitude, and all she could talk about was how women didn't need men by their sides to go on with their lives, and in today's world, you were supposed to enjoy your life without being tied down. For several days now, *fuck Lion!* had been her favorite phrase.

"I was so excited to think that you and me were going to be at the same school, going out at night and pledging at the same sorority and doing all the stuff freshmen do," she said, helping me box up a couple of things.

"I'm still going to college, Jenna. I'm just going to sleep at my boyfriend's place instead of in a dorm."

Jenna rolled her eyes. "Like Nicholas would ever let you go out partying till dawn."

"Nick's not my father. I can go wherever I want," I replied sharply.

"You say that now, but once you settle in, you'll turn into one of those friends you never see because they spend all their time with their boyfriends."

I laughed shrilly. "Like you until just a few weeks ago?"

Lifting a book, she looked over at me. "Breaking up with Lion is the best thing that could have ever happened to me," she said, and I could tell she was trying to convince herself more than me with that remark. "I do what I want now. I don't have to fight with anyone, except for my stupid little brothers. I don't have to feel guilty for being the person I am. I got a sweet dorm setup. We shelled out for the private kitchen… Speaking of, you know what I bought myself today?" She hitched up her long tight skirt just slightly. "See these sandals?"

I nodded. I could tell she needed to brag.

"Know what they cost me?"

"No. I don't want to know either," I said, folding a blanket to put it away.

"Try six hundred bucks. That's right! I dropped some cash on these sandals, and I probably won't even wear them after a few weeks because it'll be cold and rainy, and I won't want to get my toesies wet…"

"Smart," I said, playing along unenthusiastically.

"It is smart because you know what I've learned watching my ex-boyfriend work like a dog just to keep the garage open and pay his rent? I learned money doesn't grow on trees, I learned a lot of people have it hard, but I also realized, if they were me, they'd do the same damned thing. So why am I going to be the idiot who doesn't take advantage of being born into money? I've got everything I want, right? I can buy what I want, choose what school I want to go to, plus, you know my dad just bought a private plane? You heard that right, so if you ever want to go anywhere, just let me know... I'm a millionaire, and for now, money is all I care about..."

Her voice cracked at the end of that phrase, but she dried the lone tear that rolled down her cheek, pointed the book she was holding on to at me, and said coldly, "I'm absolutely fine."

Like me, but unlike many others, Jenna didn't like to show her feelings. If one of us cried, that meant we were really doing badly, and I could tell she must have been feeding herself a pack of lies if she now found herself crying in front of me.

"I know you don't want to talk about it, Jenn, but this is temporary. Lion loves you more than anything, and you know—"

"Don't go down that road, Noah," she cut me off. "We're done, and I'm not getting back on the merry-go-round. We're from different worlds, so drop it. All I want to hear about right now is how drunk you and I are going to get every Friday and how many hot guys we're going to meet."

I didn't want to remind her that I was taken, so I let it go. She needed to feel she had a fellow party girl at her side, so I'd let her think that. In moderation, of course.

She left soon afterward, and I called Nick. We hadn't talked since the night before, and I needed to know what time he was coming to pick me up the next day. I had more things to take over, and I needed his strength and the space in his Land Rover.

It went straight to voice mail, and I left a message saying I needed him to come over the next day and he should call when he had the chance.

Just as I was about to undress, shower, and go to bed to spend one last night at that house, my mother appeared. From her face, I could tell an argument was coming.

"I was hoping you'd come talk to me and tell me that what you said over dinner was just a very tasteless joke."

"It's not a joke, Mom," I said, crossing my arms.

She looked at all the suitcases and boxes scattered across the floor.

"I've done all I can not to get mixed up in your relationship with Nicholas. I was even willing to accept it. But you've crossed a line without thinking once of me or William, and that's something I'm not willing to tolerate."

I didn't like how she was talking to me. She acted like she was talking to a stranger. I realized she was angry, but with that attitude, all her words did were frustrate me further. What gave her the right to tell me how to live?

I was over it.

"This isn't something I have to talk to you about. It's my life, and you need to learn to let me make my own mistakes and my own choices."

"It'll be your life when you can live independently and you have a good enough job to support yourself, understand?"

That was a low blow, and she knew it. Especially when she was talking about money that wasn't even hers.

"You're the one who brought me here!" I shouted, seeing where the conversation was going. "I'm finally happy, I've found someone who loves me, and you're not even capable of being happy for me!"

"I'm not going to let you go live with your stepbrother when you're just eighteen years old!"

"I'm an adult! When are you going to figure that out?"

"Look," she said after breathing hard several times, "I'm not going to play this game. I don't want to argue with you, and I don't have to, but I will make one thing clear: if you go live with Nicholas, you can forget about college."

I stared at her, unable to believe what I was hearing. "What?" There wasn't a shadow of doubt in her eyes.

"I won't pay for your school, and I won't give you money so you can—"

"William's the one who pays for all this!" I shouted, enraged. She was acting like a total stranger. What the hell was all this about?

"I've talked it over with William. You're my daughter, and he'll respect whatever I decide to do with you. If I tell him not to send you one cent, then that's what he'll do."

"You've lost your mind," I said, taking in the significance of what she was saying.

"You think you can just have everything you want, but it's not like that. You get an inch, and you take a mile. Well, that's over. I'm not giving in anymore."

"I'll get a scholarship. I'm going to live with Nicholas. You can keep your husband and your money. I don't give a shit."

She shook her head, looking down at me like I was five years old, and I felt a fire burning inside me. This was getting serious.

"You won't get a scholarship. Legally, you're the daughter of a millionaire. So stop talking nonsense and acting like a brat."

"I can't believe you're doing this." I felt a pain in my chest.

She seemed to hesitate for a moment when my lip started to tremble. "Believe it or not, I just want the best for you."

I laughed. "You're a selfish bitch!" I shouted. "All you ever talk about is how you do everything for me, but you forced me to leave my country so you could marry a stranger, you promised me a bright future, and now that I've finally got all that I want, now that I'm finally happy, you're ready to take away everything, and you're threatening to come between me and the one thing I asked you for, the one thing I've cared about since we got here a year ago."

"You can have everything you want; my only condition is you go live in a dorm. It's not like you'll never see Nicholas again. Anyway, I'm sure it wasn't your idea to move in with him."

"So what if it wasn't! I've made my decision!" I walked to the other end of the room. "If you make me do this, I'll never forgive you."

She seemed not to hear my words. She just crossed her arms and looked at me, utterly convinced that she was right.

"College or Nicholas. You decide."

I didn't even need two seconds.

"Nicholas."

A half hour later, my car was loaded up. I couldn't believe my mother had tried to extort me, especially using my relationship with Nicholas. She had gone into her room after the argument and hadn't come back out. I didn't think she even realized how serious I was. But I was mad. I couldn't care less about leaving the Leister house, and I'd be perfectly happy never to return. There was only one Leister I cared about, and to hell with my mother trying to come between us.

I'd find a solution: I'd get the money, even if I had to work nights.

I called Nick from my car, still sitting in the garage. I'd been trying to get a hold of him ever since my mother had fled to her bedroom. Finally he picked up.

"I'm sorry, Freckles. I thought I'd be back by now, but it didn't happen."

Perplexed, I asked, "What do you mean? Where are you?"

"I had to fly to San Francisco this morning. They've put us on a super-important case. I thought I'd be able to get back tonight, but it looks like I'm stuck here for a few days."

My heart ached. He was gone... He wouldn't be there to give me a hug and tell me everything would be okay. That pain gave way to something harder to bear, and everything I'd been suppressing burst out all at once.

"You're in San Francisco, and you didn't even call to tell me?"

"I thought I'd be back today! It didn't seem like such a big deal. Why are you shouting at me?"

I was seeing red. "What if I went to some other city without telling you? What would you have done?"

I knew I was taking everything that had just happened out on him, but I couldn't help it just then; I needed it. I'd left everything to go stay with him, and he wasn't even going to be there to greet me and help me with my bags. He wasn't there. He wasn't there, and that was all that mattered to me!

"Okay, goddammit, I get it, but they didn't give us any advance warning!"

"Us?" I asked, a knot forming in my throat.

Nicholas went silent for a few seconds.

"You're with her, aren't you?"

"She's my fellow intern, that's all."

Uncontrollable jealousy clouded my reasoning. "So that's why you didn't tell me... You knew how pissed I'd be!"

I heard him curse on the other end of the line. "Could you calm down? You're acting like a child."

"Screw you," I said and hung up.

I tossed my cell in the seat next to me and punched the steering wheel, feeling like a fool. Was this what was going to happen from now on? He'd go to San Francisco with Sophie, and I'd stay in his apartment, broke and not going to school?

Fuck! Everything had gotten so complicated so fast, and the fear of missing out on college made me cry. I hadn't hesitated an instant to choose Nicholas, but my mother was right about one

266 | MERCEDES RON

thing: he was almost five years older than me... He'd be working soon, he'd inherit his father's business, but what about me?

I had nothing, and I didn't want Nicholas paying my way through life. If I stayed in that apartment, I'd miss out on so much. I wouldn't have my independence. I was sure Nick would help me if I asked, but how could I face myself every morning knowing my boyfriend was paying for my home and my studies?

I'd always been independent, and if my mother hadn't married Will, I'd have just applied for a scholarship somewhere... But now, I was the stepdaughter of a rich big shot, and no one was going to give me a cent. College wasn't cheap. Even if I worked like a dog, I was going to end up in debt up to my neck.

As my anger faded, giving way to anxiety, I realized that however much I wanted to live with Nick, however much I wanted to remain always by his side, wake up next to him and all those other things, I couldn't until I was truly independent. My mother was right: even if I was technically an adult, if I didn't have money to start my own life, she would always have the last word.

From an outsider perspective, it was crazy to go live with him. His mortgage was seven thousand a month! I'd thought that was crazy when he'd told me. I couldn't even pay a fourth of that; the mere thought of it nauseated me...

My phone rang and rang. I looked at it. Endless missed calls, some from Nick, some from my mom.

But the answer was obvious: Nick would have to wait...at least for now.

I got out of the car and went up to my room. I dug through my top drawer until I found my admission letter and the information about registering for the dorms. I was supposed to confirm my reservation a week ago. I felt like I couldn't breathe. What the hell would I do now? I sat on the bed feeling my heart pounding as fear overtook me.

Calm down. There's got to be a solution.

Just then, I heard the front door open. Will had come home early from work, and my mother was probably about to tell him that I'd chosen living with Nick over studying. I took a deep breath. If they were going to come between the two of us, the least they could do was find me somewhere to live. Resolutely, I dried my tears and walked out of my room, ready to put my life in order.

I felt strange when I got up the next morning. The day before, I'd been happy, knowing I was going to live with my boyfriend; now my stomach was in knots as I thought about having to share my home with a stranger. After I'd talked to my mother and Will, he had made some phone calls and had finally found me a spot. My own studio was out of the question at that point, but they did get me into one of the better residences, with a private room and a shared kitchen. Will had seemed satisfied, so I'd assumed it was the best he could do.

I got up and turned on my phone. Nick had stopped calling at 1:00 a.m., a long time after I'd turned off my phone. It may have been childish, but I blamed him for not being there with me... I couldn't help it; I was consumed by jealousy plus anxious about my mother and school.

I waited for Will to leave before coming out for breakfast. I didn't want to see him or my mother. While I was finishing my coffee, I got a call from Nick. I decided it was finally time to answer.

"Hello?" I said nervously, chewing on a fingernail.

After a pause, he asked, "Do you think it's reasonable to go the entire night without responding to me?"

Well, I knew it wasn't going to be a pleasant conversation, but I wasn't in the mood to have him pissed at me. Not that day.

"Neither of us is reasonable, so I don't know how to answer your question."

"I didn't call you to argue, Noah, so you can count me out of that game. I just wanted to tell you I'll be home in a week. The situation here is really different from what they told us at first."

"Five days?" I asked, knowing how whiny my voice sounded.

"I know. I won't even be there when you start school. I'm sorry, okay? I didn't plan to have you move on your own, and I definitely didn't think you'd be having to stay at the apartment without me, but there's nothing I can do."

I took a deep breath. I had to tell him. I had to confess that I wouldn't be going to live with him. But I was afraid of how he'd react. He might call my mom and start screaming at her; he was capable of anything. I knew it was going to be a kick in the teeth for him, and for that reason, I decided to play along and wait to tell him in person. Our conversation ended with a bit of tension on both sides, and when we hung up, I felt deeply sad.

Two hours later, Jenna and her father came to get me. I was too angry at my mother to ask her to help me move, so when Jenna offered, I accepted with gratitude. I had only seen Mr. Tavish twice before—he spent most of his time traveling the globe—but I knew he adored Jenna, and that's why he'd canceled all his meetings to take his little girl off to college. He didn't seem upset about having to pick me up and take my things along with Jenna's. We needed to squeeze in, but I managed to fit into his car and fasten my seat belt to take off for what was going to be my new dorm.

I had been to the campus before. Nick studied there, and he'd invited me to frat parties or just to come see him. I'd taken my books sometimes and studied for hours in the huge library, marveling at the millions of volumes lined up in order along its shelves. I knew it would be one of my favorite places in the world, but the rest of the university was amazing, too, with its redbrick buildings and its huge green spaces. It wasn't easy to get into—it was one of the most prestigious universities in America—and I was proud that I'd managed it on my merits alone, without having to ask Will to lend a hand. Once there, I couldn't help but feel sad that my mother wasn't sharing the experience with me. She should have been the one bringing me there, not Jenna's father. I'd also have liked Nick to be there to give me a tour so I could feel that same excitement I saw in all the new students all around us. Jenna was hyper, but I saw sorrow in her eyes, too.

Where were our boyfriends?

36

Nick

I WAS SITTING IN THE VESTIBULE OF THE HOTEL. THE SIGNAL WAS bad in my room, so I'd had to come down to reception, where a bunch of strangers were hanging out. It was late, and I took my phone out for the fourth time to see if Noah had sent me a good night message. I didn't like how the previous day's conversation had ended, and even if she had a day left until classes started, I'd wanted to wish her good luck. I knew she was probably trying to sleep—she might even be in the middle of one of her nightmares. I was happy to be the one person who could make them go away, but that also made me hate knowing she was sleeping alone.

I was relieved she'd agreed to go to a psychologist and had been reading about childhood trauma and how to overcome it on the Internet. She had a list of the best psychologists in the city and had already set up consultations with five of them. I wanted Noah to go back to being herself, without fear restraining her, able to be happy. And if I had to pay a fortune to make that happen, then so be it.

I thought about what she'd suffered at the hands of her father, and a chill ran up my spine while my hand closed into a fist. I had to take several breaths to calm down. Just then, Sophia appeared with her Mac, wearing a pair of plastic black-framed glasses that cracked me up. They looked horrible on her.

"What's up, Leister?"

"Aiken," I said, looking back at my screen.

She sat down next to me on the big white sofa. After two days, I had to admit she wasn't the person I'd assumed at first. She might look superficial and stiff, but she wasn't in the least. She was even funny when she tried to be. Since she was surrounded by men—she was the only woman in a team of five working the case—she did everything she could to fade into the background. She didn't want to be treated any differently.

"You're not in the mood to go out for some fast food, are you?" she asked after typing a few things on her laptop and shutting it suddenly.

With a raised eyebrow, I asked, "Fast food? You?" I tucked away my phone. Still no news from Noah. "I assumed you didn't know what that was."

With a frown, she stuffed her Mac into her bag and got up. In place of her usual heels, she was wearing a simple pair of white sandals.

"I could kill for a Big Mac, with or without you. I just brought it up because I can't stand hotel food, but it's your call. You coming or no?"

I hesitated for a moment, but she was right: the food sucked.

"Okay, but FYI, I'm not great company today," I said, getting up and walking toward the door. With Sophia next to me, I could see how short she actually was without her heels.

She laughed. "Today or any day, Leister. I don't think I've seen you relax once since I met you. Maybe you should get checked out."

I ignored the comment as we walked out into the lot.

"What do you think you're doing?" I asked as she took her keys from her pocket.

"I'm the one who rented the car, Nicholas," she said.

"Sorry, babe, I drive," I said, snatching them before she could react.

I was surprised she didn't argue, instead shrugging and going around to the passenger side.

I let her choose the music, which meant we were listening to trash from the eighties the whole way from the hotel. The weather was nice, even if it was cooler in San Fran than what we were used to in LA. Lots of people hated the steep streets there, but I thought they made the city special, the hills and the colorful houses, so varied and pleasant to look at.

I wanted to bring Noah there. I wanted her to see so many places... Since we'd been going out, I'd only been able to take her to the Bahamas, and that was a vacation to forget.

I put that out of my mind, parking the car at a restaurant I'd found before, when I'd had to spend a week there.

"This isn't McDonald's," Sophia said, unbuckling her seat belt.

"I don't eat at McDonald's," I said, turning off the car and laughing when I saw her scowl. "Come on, Soph, these are the best burgers in the city. If not, I wouldn't have brought you here."

She frowned in disbelief and slapped me on the arm. "I told you before, don't call me *Soph*." She got out. I did, too.

"Sorry, Soph."

I cracked up when I saw her face after that, but then I decided to drop it. A waiter greeted us and sat us on the other end of the restaurant. I didn't like that; I thought he thought we were a couple and wanted our privacy, but since I couldn't actually read minds, I decided not to argue.

She made another comment about her beloved Big Mac, but

she ended up having to swallow her words because, as I'd told her, the burgers there were to die for.

"So you guys are going to move in together," she asked after a few minutes of chitchat and shoptalk. This was the first time Noah had come up. "To spite her parents?"

"Her mother, you mean," I said. "It seems everyone's forgotten that she's an adult and can make her own decisions."

Sophia nodded, but she didn't seem convinced. "She's a little girl, Nick," she said, taking a sip of her drink.

"Maturity isn't some fucking number. It's all about your experiences and what you've learned from them."

"No one's saying otherwise, but you can't forget, she's about to start school. She's going to want to do things, like any girl her age, and unless I'm mistaken, you're a typical controlling boyfriend."

I rested my elbows on the table and my chin in my hands. "I take care of what's mine, that's all."

She didn't seem to like those words. "That's a pretty chauvinistic way of looking at things. You don't own her, Nick."

"Is it time for Feminism 101, Soph?"

"As a woman trying to make my way in a company whose leadership is a hundred percent male, I could teach you a few things about that, but that's not what I'm saying. Your problem is trust: if you were really sure she was in love with you, you wouldn't be trying everything in your power to get her to move in with you despite your family's wishes. I just think it's a dumb move on your part."

"She needs me and I need her. There's not some secret justification there. You just don't know what you're talking about."

Sophia shook her head and stared at me. "I know one thing. There's no way in hell I'd want to be your girlfriend."

"Every girl wants to be my girlfriend," I said. She started laughing, and I grinned. It was obvious I wasn't close to the ideal boyfriend, but hey, I tried.

That gave me an idea.

"So you'll see just what a good boyfriend I am," I said, taking my phone out and going onto the net. "What do you think about blue roses? Pretty, right?"

Sophia rolled her eyes as I scrolled through floral arrangements. "Precious," she said, taking a sip of her drink.

I hit *buy*, entered the address, and typed out a little note for the card, grinning as I put away my phone.

"A dozen blue roses?" she asked.

"Two dozen. The same message twice, so it sinks in."

"What's the message, that you're a smug asshole?"

I ignored her. "That I love her more than anyone else."

After dinner, we went back to the hotel. Despite my misgivings, despite the fact she'd never let me live it down if I ever told her so aloud, Sophia wasn't bad company. Lion had his shit, and Jenna was Noah's best friend, and that meant I had no one on the outside I could talk freely with. Not that I was a big talker in general, but I liked chatting with Sophia and knowing people with normal lives existed. From what I heard, her parents were still together, her older brother was a successful architect, and her father was a respected politician in the Democratic Party, a guy who might wind up on the presidential ballot. Who knew where things would go?

It was nice avoiding all the drama from my regular life, and I could relax in her company, look at things from another perspective. Things weren't so bad, really... With Noah living with me, everything would be easier. She would sleep better, and if she did what I asked, one of those psychologists she'd contacted would help her deal with her problems with her dead dad. Things would get better. I couldn't wait to get home and show her all we could achieve, convince her we were a perfect team, capable of surviving anything.

37

Noah

MY FIRST DAY AT SCHOOL WAS BETTER THAN I COULD HAVE HOPED. The feeling of being in college got into my veins. It wasn't something I could ignore. Wherever I looked, there were young people laughing, taking furniture out of their cars to carry it upstairs, parents saying goodbyes, flyers about parties, parties, and more parties.

My class schedule wasn't bad; I was studying things that interested me and not all the BS we had to learn in high school about Newton's laws or the Declaration of Independence. I wanted books, literature; I wanted to write, read. I was finally surrounded by people who loved the same stuff as me, and the professors, some of them more intimidating than others, only fired our enthusiasm.

I had to admit, I even enjoyed being alone a little bit. I didn't want to talk to anyone—anyone I knew, that is: not with my mother, not with Jenna, not even with Nicholas, though in each case, the reasons were different. Sometimes leaving everything behind and starting from zero made you see that there were lots of doors open to you.

I'd hardly seen Jenna since she had dropped me off at the dorm. We didn't share any classes. She wanted to study medicine.

I didn't see her as a doctor at all, but apparently it had been her dream since she was a little girl. We'd texted each other, and she'd told me she was busy looking for a roommate; I guessed living alone wasn't all it was cracked up to be. I didn't think she'd have much trouble; for many, meeting new people was what college was all about.

When class was over, and I'd gotten to know my teachers and some people from the dorm had invited me out for dinner, I decided to go to Nick's place to be sure N had enough food and to pick up the things I'd dropped off there. I'd been trying to put that task off because I knew it would make me sad, but I also wanted to get it done with before Nick was back. I knew we'd have a fight over it, and I wanted to be sure everything was set up in my place before I had to confront him. Plus, that would help me resist the temptation to say to hell with it all and move in with him.

It didn't take long, but by the time I was done piling all my things by the door, it was late, and I didn't feel like going back to the dorm. I knew I was cheating, that I'd resolved to be alone and that I shouldn't keep trying to hold on to something I couldn't have—at least for now—but I crawled into Nick's bed, onto his side, and hugged his pillow, breathing in that scent no other person had, which made my body react instantly.

My phone buzzed as a message came through.

Guess you've decided to ignore my calls. We'll talk when
I get back. Sleep well, Freckles.

I sighed. Things were weird. It was my fault, for the most part. Stomach quaking, I almost called him to tell him why I hadn't wanted to talk to him. But I hoped he'd think I was asleep and that was why I hadn't responded. I put my cell phone under the pillow and closed my eyes, hoping to get some rest.

In the morning, the doorbell woke me. A little disoriented, I looked around, trying to figure out where I was. It rang again, and I jumped up, wrapping myself in a sheet, almost tripping on my way to the door.

When I opened it, I saw two huge bouquets of roses.

"Are you Noah Morgan?" asked the man whose face I couldn't see behind the flowers.

"Uh, yes," I managed to say.

"These are for you," he said, stepping forward. I let him come in, unable to believe my eyes. He left the bouquets on the table in the living room and took a booklet of invoices out of his back pocket.

"Sign here please," he said amiably.

I did so, and when he left, I stared at the roses on the verge of tears. There was a note, which only made it worse, and I needed all my strength to choke back the sobs.

We both know this sappy shit's not my thing, Freckles, but I love you with all my heart and I know that when I get back, we'll be starting something new, something special. Living with you is something I've wanted ever since we started going out, and a year later, I've finally got the thing I wished for. I hope your first day was wonderful, and I'm sorry I wasn't there with you to watch you bewitch all your new professors. See you in a few days. I love you,

Nick

I picked up the phone and called him.

"Hey, babe," he said in a cheerful tone.

278 | MERCEDES RON

I sat on the armrest of the sofa, unable to take my eyes off those beautiful flowers, sky blue, just like Nick's eyes. I hadn't even known there were roses that color.

"You're crazy," I said with a trembling voice.

I heard noise on the other line, traffic.

"Crazy about you. Do you like them?"

"I love them. They're gorgeous," I said, wishing I could jump into his arms and hide from everything.

"How was your first day of school?"

I told him quickly what I'd done, skipping the dorm and my roommate. I'd never been good at hiding things, and I wanted to end the conversation before he found me out.

"I need to go, or I'll be late to class," I said, chewing the inside of my cheek.

"I can tell something's up with you. I don't know if it's Sophia or if it's me having to leave right when you moved in, but whatever it is, I'll make it up to you, okay?"

I said a quick goodbye and put my phone on the table. I felt horrible, horrible, because I was lying to him and I would be responsible for disappointing him when he got back and realized we wouldn't live together.

Hating myself for it, I dressed quickly, put out food and water for N for the next few days, and carried my last few things out of the apartment. When I turned off the light, I knew there would be hell to pay when he came back and I wasn't there.

I had three days to come up with a plan.

———

I spent the next two days going to class and hanging out with new friends. I'd only talked to my mother once, and that was because she'd threatened to drive down there if I didn't pick up. Nothing was resolved, things were just as uncomfortable between us as ever, and I didn't see that changing, at least not until I'd found it in myself to forgive her for extorting me.

I was sitting in the cafeteria talking to Jenna. She'd already found a roommate, Amber, who worked at an IT company in town while taking classes at the same time. She must have been doing all right for herself, if she could afford campus housing on her own.

"When's Nick back?" Jenna asked as I finished my salad.

"Tomorrow night," I murmured. I didn't want to talk about that.

She seemed to find it funny, almost as if she took pleasure in knowing what a difficult spot I was in. "Does he know you're living with a stranger in a campus apartment yet?"

With a nasty look, I replied, "He'll find out when he gets here and I tell him. Now I don't feel like talking about Nick. Tell me again what the plan for tonight is. I still don't really know what's up."

Jenna gave me a sarcastic look, but she couldn't hold it for long. She got excited.

"These frat guys told me there are parties all over to celebrate the new year. Apparently Phi Delta, the medical fraternity, throws one that's totally off the hook. I can't wait to be there surrounded by handsome doctors, people who understand the future is medicine and not physics or literature... No offense."

I frowned at her, and she laughed, picked up her books, and stood.

"See you in a couple of hours. Pull out all the stops when you get dressed." She winked and walked off, shaking her hips in that way that drove all the guys wild. Single Jenna was something new, something I just couldn't get used to. Since I'd known Jenna, she'd been with Lion, but I guess she must have gotten around before then.

———————————

Unlike most of the parties I'd been to recently—all held at rich kids' beach houses—here, I could finally hang out with people from different backgrounds, different origins, different classes. That was the good thing about it being a public university. I'd never felt totally comfortable surrounded by all those millionaires; being rich was new to me, and anyway, as much as my mother insisted that was my reality, she'd just made clear that it didn't have to be and that she could cut off William's money at the drop of a hat. Here I felt I could finally fit in. I quickly found Jenna, who was with Amber drinking beer in a corner of the kitchen. I couldn't believe it when I saw her with a Budweiser in her hand—Jenna, who always preferred Grey Goose or Cristal. I wanted to snap a photo to make fun of her afterward, but she looked so at ease that I decided to play nice.

"Noah," she said when she saw me come in. I walked over and she hugged me so tightly, she almost strangled me.

It was the first time I'd met Amber, and she seemed as wild as Jenna, almost—just a tad more reserved. She smiled and moved her head to the rhythm of the music while making seductive comments to a boy next to her.

I drank a few beers quickly, and randomly I found myself surrounded by fifty drunk students jumping around a room that had been cleared of all furnishings. The music was blasting, and I could barely hear anything else. Jenna was bumping and grinding against me, and Amber had walked off with the muscular guy she'd been talking to earlier.

"I need to chill for a bit, Jenna!" I shouted as people started to shriek along to a popular song. "I'm going to go to the kitchen!"

She nodded, but really she was ignoring me and immediately joined another group there.

It was hot as hell. I rolled up my sleeves and wiped down my forehead. When I got to the kitchen, they were pouring out a round of shots.

"Hey, new girl," a guy shouted at me from some distance away. "A toast to the hot chicks!"

Every guy in the circle brought a shot glass to his lips, knocked it back, laughed, and shouted. I thought it was funny, but I didn't stick around, going instead to the back of the kitchen and leaning against the table. I took out my phone to check the time, and the guy who'd been shouting came over.

"Here," he said, passing me a shot glass and filling it with amber liquid. "You look thirsty."

"I don't think tequila's the best thing for thirst, but thanks," I said, accepting it and drinking. It burned my throat, and I frowned in disgust. The boy giggled and, as I watched out of the corner of my eye, leaned in next to me, trying to look aloof.

"What's your name?" he asked, grabbing a glass and filling it with water.

"Noah," I said, feeling my head start to spin. I shouldn't have had that shot—the beers were already enough for me.

"I'm Charlie," he said. "We're in the same lit class. I don't know if you remember me. I'm the guy who usually falls asleep in the back."

Funny, I actually did seem to remember seeing him.

"What brings you here?" he asked. "You're not going to find many Shakespeare experts around here. That said, tell me the truth: The science guys are way hotter than the humanities guys, don't you think?"

I smiled. When he said that, any doubts that he might be straight vanished, and that helped me relax.

"I'm here with my friend who's premed," I said with a shrug.

Charlie seemed to enjoy talking to me, and talk he could: he didn't stop for the next ten minutes, with comments about everything from our teachers to our classmates. I was happy to have a friend my age there. I hated being alone, but aside

282 | MERCEDES RON

from him and Jenna, the most I'd said to anyone was a hello or goodbye.

He made a kind of cringey joke about one of our teachers that had me in stitches. A second afterward, he looked over at the door. A guy had just walked in. Almost instantly, he had his eyes on us.

"Great. See that guy?"

I nodded, noticing his unfriendly expression.

"Don't pay attention to anything he says."

I wanted to ask why, but it was impossible, the guy was already on top of us.

"Are you a fucking idiot?"

"As I said..." Charlie murmured then, looking at his companion with a smile: "Behave, there's a lady present."

"I'm tired of playing babysitter with you. What are you drinking?"

I looked back and forth between the two of them. I'd have preferred to leave just then, but I was stuck there. Charlie was blond, more or less my height, and thin, whereas his companion was a good foot taller than us, with the same blond hair and moss-green eyes. It seemed like this was the last place he wanted to be, surrounded by teenagers, something he clearly wasn't.

"It's water, dumbass." The other boy didn't believe him and tore the glass from his hand, bringing it up to his nose to sniff it.

Charlie looked smug and amused.

"If you'd stop growling like a rabid dog, I'd introduce you to my new friend. This is Michael, my brother. Michael, this is Noah."

Michael didn't seem to care about me in the least. Actually, I'd say he sneered at me, as if I wasn't worthy to hang out with his brother or something like that.

Just then, my phone rang. I excused myself and walked outside to hear better. My heart stopped when I saw fifteen missed calls from Nicholas, including one just now. I waited for his name to reappear on the screen, then picked up.

"Noah, where are you?"

38

Nick

I GRABBED MY KEYS, LEFT THE APARTMENT, AND SLAMMED MY door on the way out. Nothing. There was nothing of hers there: no suitcases, no clothes, not even the little things she usually left behind when she spent the night. I was getting heated, not just because of her absence, but also because she'd ignored all my calls. It had been three hours since I'd last heard from her, and I sure as hell wasn't going to call her mom to make sure she was okay. Something told me I'd better leave her out because if my suspicions were right...

"What party?" I shouted into the phone, waiting for her to tell me exactly where she was.

"Can you just calm down?" she answered, and I heard her walking away from the deafening music.

Calm down? "I'll calm down when I see you and you tell me what the hell's actually going on," I said as I got in the car and started it up.

"I don't think I want to tell you where I am."

I froze. Was this a fucking joke?

"Noah, tell me where you are," I asked, feigning calm.

The music was barely audible now, and I could hear her breathing.

"I already did. I'm at a party."

"Give me an address, a street."

She sighed and a second later told me where I could find her.

I had a bad feeling about all that, but I still hoped when I showed up, she would calm my fears. I'd come home early, ready to give her a surprise, take her out to dinner, make up for those days we hadn't been together. But instead, I'd found the house empty apart from the flowers I'd sent, which were wilting on the table.

I arrived quickly, turning a corner to find her standing there. She was leaning on her car with her arms crossed over her chest. She sat up when she saw me and looked at me nervously. I parked in front of her and got out.

I took a deep breath, trying to calm down. Now that I saw her and knew she was safe and sound, I could relax a little bit.

I tried not to let her know I'd been longing to see her again ever since the moment I left. Instead, I just walked over, observing her coolly. She said nothing, but I could tell my silence was bothering her.

"Let's go," I said, turning on my heel before I'd even touched her. "I'm in the mood for a hot chocolate."

"Wait, what?" she asked.

I opened the passenger door, waiting for her to come over.

"I guess you've got a lot to tell me, and I'm not going to do it outside while you're freezing your half-drunk ass off."

I was trying to control myself, trying with all my might not to give in to the temptation to explode, but seeing her there tipsy, incredibly attractive, and alone angered me far more than I was willing to admit.

Noah stumbled over. I closed the door once she got in and

walked around to the driver's side. I cranked up the heat, tore off, and looked for a twenty-four-hour coffee shop. I'd made up that thing about the hot chocolate just to get her off the street. She was shivering; I don't know if it was the cold or the fact she was hiding something from me, but either way, I was now seeing all those ignored calls in a different light.

"Nicholas…I want to go home," she said when she noticed I'd skipped our exit.

"I thought you liked hot chocolate," I said, turning right onto a side street.

I could tell she was staring at me.

"Stop acting like nothing's up," she said. "I can tell you're pissed. So drop the act."

"What would I have to be pissed off about? The fact that you've barely picked up the phone since I went to San Francisco? We both know you love to drive me crazy, so I just hope this isn't some weird way of punishing me for leaving."

She writhed in her seat, uncomfortable, but I tried not to show my irritation as I kept driving.

The road was almost empty… That was to be expected after 2:00 a.m. If anyone had asked me earlier what I thought I'd be doing at that time, it would have been anything but this, and I sure as hell wouldn't have guessed I'd have Noah in the car trying to get as far away from me as her seat would permit.

I parked in front of a run-down diner. Even before I'd stopped the car, Noah was getting out and walking toward the front door. I couldn't help comparing her with Sophia. Noah was as strong-willed as I was, and knowing I was the one in the right this time, she couldn't control herself. I walked in behind her and sat down at the place she'd chosen: a small corner table that looked out toward the interstate.

She stared down at the table. She didn't seem in the mood to talk. When the waitress came over, I ordered a hot chocolate for me and a coffee for her. I was trying to calm the waters because it was weird not to be covering her in kisses after four days apart, but my suppressed anger and whatever she was hiding from me stood between us like an uncrossable sea. When she made no sign that she was about to speak, I decided to go first. No more games.

"Where's your stuff?"

She looked up at me with those honey-colored eyes. She'd put on makeup, and her mile-long eyelashes were casting a strange shadow over her high cheekbones. Her pink lips opened hesitantly, but before she could answer, the waitress returned with our order.

Noah cupped the warm coffee in her hands. I waited.

"Are you going to answer?" I finally said.

She took a few more seconds, then said, barely audible, "I got in a fight with my mother."

I leaned back and waited for her to continue. She looked back up at me, and I could tell it took everything she had in her not to cry. I tensed, but I didn't try to push her.

"I'm not going to come live with you, Nick," she said finally.

I waited for an explanation, and when it didn't come, I asked, "Noah, what are you trying to tell me?"

"My mother told me I had to choose between her paying for my school or me going to live with you, and I…"

"You didn't choose me." I finished the sentence for her.

"I tried, okay? I told my mother I didn't care, I said I *was* going to go live with you, but I can't, Nicholas…"

I shook my head. I'd had enough of this shit. "At least we know what your priorities are."

I got up, and Noah did the same. I threw a twenty on the table, turned around, and walked out.

"Nicholas, wait!" I did, but only because I knew I couldn't

leave her there. "What did you want me to do? I don't have money like you. I can't pay for my school. I don't have a scholarship…"

This was ridiculous. I turned around.

"Don't give me that shit, Noah!" I shouted. There was no one out there, nothing else to hear except the cars roaring down the interstate and the blasting wind. "You know perfectly well this has nothing to do with your mother. She wouldn't come between you and your studies… The problem is you're incapable of facing up to her. There are lots of other options. But no, you walked out without even talking to me!"

She shook her head. "I know her, Nicholas. She's decided she won't stop until you and I break up, and I won't let her win, but I'm also not going to destroy my future over a rushed decision. Living together can wait!"

"I don't want to wait!" I shouted, losing control. "I want you to be with me, Noah. Not with your mother, not with my father, not with some friend. I want us to finally be a real adult couple that makes decisions together without our parents getting in the middle of it. I want you with me. I want you in my bed every night, every morning… If you're with me, I want you to be with me and no one else."

Her eyes widened. "That's why you want me at your apartment?" she asked incredulously, now shouting as loudly as I was. "To watch over me? What the hell kind of relationship is that, Nicholas?"

I brought my hands to my head. This was the last thing I'd expected. Finally, things were going right, finally we would be together without anyone coming between us, and now everything was just like before, but worse. Noah wouldn't even be at my dad's house anymore; she'd be on campus, surrounded by a bunch of assholes, where campus rape was a fact of life.

"If you won't trust me, there's no point in us being together," she declared. Her voice broke on this last word. I walked toward her and held her by the shoulders.

"This isn't about you," I said, hating the part of myself I was revealing, cursing my weakness. "When you're not with me, I think of the worst things. I can't control my imagination. It's something that's just inside me, and I didn't realize it until recently. It happens to me because I love you. The last person I loved as much as you I hate now, I always will, and I have this problem—I can't help thinking of what she did to me."

I couldn't believe I'd finally said that.

"Nicholas, I'm not your mother. I'm not going anywhere."

The image of my mother leaving invaded my mind. I had never trusted another woman again since. I'd sworn to myself that I would never let anyone in, that I would never again fall in love, that I didn't even believe in love, not after seeing the relationship between my parents. But now I had Noah... I couldn't avoid fearing she'd treat me the same. She was mine. I couldn't lose her. I couldn't stand it.

"You left my home," I whispered, kissing her.

She didn't move. I guess she was waiting for me to say or do something. I took my hands off her shoulders and stood back.

"I don't know how we're going to solve this."

39

Noah

WE DROVE TO HIS APARTMENT IN COMPLETE SILENCE. NICHOLAS
didn't even look at me. Once we arrived, I tried to keep calm as I
followed him inside. I felt guilty for everything, even if it had been
my mother's fault... I couldn't help but feel that Nick was growing
apart from me. My problems and my mother were coming between
us, and I didn't know what to do about it. I tried to make rational
decisions, thinking about what would be best for both of us, but
nothing turned out the way I wished.

Even in the apartment, he wouldn't speak to me. I'd have
rather heard him shout at me than that because I realized he was
thinking about things I didn't even want to imagine. He crossed
the living room and walked into his bedroom. I stopped, indeci-
sive. Did I want to go on arguing with him? Maybe I should have
asked him to drop me off at the dorm, but I didn't want to rub
it in his face that I'd moved somewhere else. Without him. And I
couldn't stand the thought of going back there without resolving
this. I didn't want my mother to get away with pulling us apart.

I heard nothing from the other side of the door, so after a few
minutes, I gathered my courage and cracked it.

Nick was there sitting at the foot of the bed. He had taken off his T-shirt and was resting his forearms on his knees. He had a cigarette in his right hand. He looked up from the floor, meeting my eyes when he heard me walk in.

I observed him; he did the same to me. We were just a few feet apart, but to me, it felt like an abyss. I was so scared, so alone, that I couldn't keep myself from walking over between his legs and lifting his face to look him in the eyes.

"Don't let this pull us apart." That was all I could think to say. I hadn't understood how bad things were with us until I heard Nick's words a half hour before.

Nick looked down to my stomach and took another drag off his cigarette. With one hand, I grabbed his wrist; with the other, I took the cigarette away. He looked at me perplexed as I crushed it in the ashtray right beside him. Then I straddled his lap and cupped his face in my hand.

"I need you to leave me alone, Noah," he said in a voice so soft, I thought I'd heard him wrong. I wrapped my hands around the back of his neck, tried to toy with his hair, but he reached up and stopped me. "Don't play with me. Not right now."

His words were hard, cold, and that coldness only grew worse as he got up from the bed and walked past me. I stood.

"I hurt you when I left, and you're scared I'll leave you for good. I get it, but you can't just ignore me like this. You can't!"

Shooting fire from his eyes, he said, "I'm ignoring you because I'm trying to keep control of myself!"

I was startled, hearing him scream at me like that. But then he took a deep breath and spoke again in a normal tone.

"I can help you with your tuition."

I closed my eyes. I knew he'd say that, but I couldn't accept it. "You know I can't let you do that."

"I'm offering you a solution that will make us both happy.

Why do you not understand that your decisions affect both of us, not just you?" he said, his voice rising again.

"Because I wouldn't be happy, Nicholas!" I had hoped to keep calm, but I couldn't. "If living with you means going to war with my mother and your father plus depending on you for money, I'll end up hating it. Can't you see that?"

"Of course I can't! Not when the alternative is you being surrounded by a bunch of people who aren't me! That's the thing I have trouble imagining!"

"I've never given you reason to be jealous, and jealousy's your real problem right now."

"Don't give me that. You're no different."

I wanted to try to explain to him that jealousy was all right, but only to a point.

"I've got more reason to be jealous than you do. You've been with more women than I can count. I've given you everything. You know I'm yours in every sense of the word. And even still you don't trust me."

"You knew what you were doing when you decided to go out with me. I can't change my past."

The distance between the two of us was killing me. Of course, I'd known what I was getting into with him, but I hadn't chosen it; it had just happened. I had fallen crazily in love with him, but that didn't mean that the things he did or had done would affect me any less.

"A relationship with no trust is a dead-end street, you know that."

His eyes darkened. "I don't need to trust anyone. I need you by my side."

Despite his anger, I knew what he was trying to say. "I'm here now, right?"

He shook his head. "You're halfway here and halfway

somewhere else. It's always halfway with you, Noah." He turned to walk out of the room.

"Nicholas, I said I'm right here!" I felt my eyes go damp.

I didn't know what he wanted from me. I'd given him everything I had, everything I knew how to give.

"No you aren't!" he shouted.

"This is all I can do."

"Well, maybe that's not enough."

A horrible fear seeped through me. There it was, the thing I had always feared: not being good enough for him.

"It's not fair, you being the one crying," he said a few seconds later.

"I'm crying because I can't give you everything you want, and you're going to wind up getting sick of me," I confessed, stifling a sob in my throat.

I couldn't stand seeing that I'd disappointed him. I wanted to go because if I didn't, I'd break down, and I didn't want to do that in front of him.

"I should go," I said, wiping off my cheek with one hand and looking away.

I heard Nicholas draw a few deep breaths. Then he crossed the room and kissed me so intensely, I had to hold on to his arms to keep from falling.

"I could never get tired of you—not in a million years." With that, he quickly pushed me down on the bed and got on top of me.

He kissed me again, and despite his gentle words, I could tell something was different about him. The way he touched me, the way he kissed me and took off my clothes were more like a struggle he was engaged in with himself than an act of love between the two of us. I'd hurt him when I left, and there were consequences for that. His kisses intensified, and soon his mouth was roving my neck and my breasts, finally arriving at my thighs.

"Nick..." I whispered.

Nicholas didn't hear me; he was lost in my body, lost in kissing every inch of skin within reach.

"Shh...I don't want to talk anymore, Noah." He hushed me, taking off my panties and climbing between my legs. "We've already said all there is to say."

When his lips met mine, I decided to forget everything.

———

I couldn't sleep.

Nick was next to me breathing slowly, deep in dreams, squeezing me against him tightly. With his arms around me like that, I could barely move. I watched him sleep and felt a knot gather in my throat.

The night before had been so intense, both physically and emotionally, that I'd ended it destroyed. I went to the bathroom to wash my face and try to become a normal person again. When I looked in the mirror, I saw something that shocked me.

"I can't believe it," I said, furious.

I left the bathroom and walked over to him, enraged. He was awake and was observing me imperturbably from the bed.

"Why did you do this?" I asked.

Ignoring my question, he got up, put on a pair of sweatpants, and walked to the bathroom in silence.

"Is this how things are now?" I said, turning to see him gripping the side of the sink and letting his head hang. "You're punishing me now?"

He looked up. "Oh, by kissing you, I'm punishing you?"

I shook my head. I wasn't going to let him turn the tables like that. "You know I hate that, Nick. I don't want to be marked. And you did it knowing I hate it. That just makes it worse. You're an idiot."

"And you're a spoiled little baby. You need to understand everything can't be the way you want."

I laughed sarcastically. "Please! You've never heard the word *no* in your life. That's why you're punishing me, because I'm the first and only person ever to do it."

Nicholas came close to me cautiously. "For me, you are the first and only one."

But we both knew that wasn't true.

"I'm sorry, okay?" he went on. "I got carried away in the moment, but can you please stop acting like I did something wrong? They're just kisses...kisses from me."

I sighed in frustration. I didn't want to fight with him. I'd had enough the night before.

"What if it was you? Would you like it?" I asked.

"Are you kidding?" He forced a smile. "I love your lips. There's nothing I'd like better than a mark that would remind me you had kissed me somewhere."

I wasn't convinced. "You'd let me leave a mark on you. How so?" I dared him.

He looked at me, trying to guess what I was getting at. "Are you talking about something nasty, Freckles?"

His response was funny. But I wasn't about to tell him. Among other things, because I wasn't going to take no for an answer. Grinning, I pushed him out of the bathroom.

"Lie down on the bed," I ordered him.

He looked doubtful, but he did what I asked. I opened a drawer on the nightstand and sat on his stomach.

"What are you up to?" he asked with a dark glimmer in his eyes.

"None of what's probably passing through that perverted mind of yours."

After saying this, I brought a marker to my lips and took the cap off with my teeth. His eyes opened wide.

"No fucking way," he said, reaching up and grabbing my wrists.

"Oh yes fucking way, and you're going to remain totally still while I do it," I replied, jerking away from him.

He rolled over me and pinned me against the mattress.

"Put that back where it was unless you want problems," he warned me, but I could see in his eyes that he thought it was funny.

I kept hold of the permanent marker, though, and I intended to use it.

"Just tell yourself it's something I'm going to do to you. Me alone and nobody else. I've never drawn on anyone's body before. That will make it sweet, special."

He lifted his head and observed me with curiosity and interest.

"You call that sweet and special?" he asked.

"Anything I do with your body is sweet and special," I said with a smile.

"You've been hanging around me too much, that's clear." He rolled back, sitting me on top of him, right where I wanted to be.

"Be good," he warned me, resting his hands on my bare thighs.

This was fun, and even if it wasn't my intention, it was helping me to leave aside that emotional burden that had weighed down on me those past few hours. I bent over him and started tracing out a drawing on his chest. A heart on his pecs, a happy face on his shoulder, an *I love you* over his heart. This supposed punishment soon turned into a love letter composed on his skin...one I had written to him. He stared at my face the whole time while his fingers traced circles on my skin and I worked to make that decoration on his sculpted body as beautiful as possible. I wanted to show him how much I loved him, I wanted him to understand that he was the only one for me.

That ink was covering our pain, drawing a new bond between us.

With a smile, I grabbed his wrist and wrote one last message on it: *You're mine.*

Forever.

40

Nick

I DIDN'T TAKE MY EYES OFF HER ONCE AS SHE DID WHATEVER SHE wished to my body. That was any man's dream, but it never occurred to me that whatever she wished would mean drawing a bunch of dumb shit all over me. Still, observing her the whole time, as I was allowed to then, was priceless. She was concentrating so hard on what she was doing that she had no idea how incredibly beautiful she was to me in that moment.

Her cheeks were slightly flushed and her eyes swollen from crying the night before. I knew I shouldn't be such an asshole, but I loved the way her lips looked after she'd cried... It made me want to kiss her till the end of time. I took advantage of her being distracted by her task to soak in her every gesture and to stroke her thighs and knees.

At some point, my hand strayed too far into forbidden ground, and she gave me a sharp look to make me stop.

"Keep still," she ordered me with an amused smile, then looked down at my wrist. I let her sketch out one last thing.

"I'm done," she said, putting the cap on the marker and coming down to kiss me on the lips. Staying still that long with her half naked on top of me had been torture.

Holding her waist, I rolled over until I was on top of her.

"Now what am I supposed to do?" I asked, leaning on my forearms to keep from crushing her. Her hand climbed to my face and stroked my hair.

"Leave and show my masterpiece to the world," she answered with mischievous glee on her face. I pushed my thighs into her, feeling her so fragile beneath me, so small, so perfect… I felt the urge to cry when I realized these moments weren't going to come as often as I wished now. I had to let her go, had to let her live on campus surrounded by a bunch of dickheads who would be fighting to get her attention. Neither those kisses nor anything she could tell me were enough to make me believe no one would ever steal her from me.

Losing her…just the thought of it hurt me inside, scared me. The feeling weighing on my chest was terrifying, like two giants sitting on my heart. Ever since my mother had left, I had kept that feeling stuffed away, closing myself off from everyone else. I'd told myself I would never feel that again…but now I was so vulnerable, so exposed with that beautiful girl who could have crushed my heart to dust if she'd wanted to.

I looked down at what she'd written on my wrist, and a warm, gentle tingle ran over my body. I was hers… She had written that on my very skin, and I realized nothing would make me happier than belonging to her, body and soul.

I knew she'd seen the darkness in me, my weakness, my irrational desire to clutch her close, to keep her within reach at all times. I couldn't help it—I couldn't help my feelings or the way my love for her kept growing with every second.

"I'm going to let you go…for now…" I said when I saw her blink with surprise. "But you know, Freckles, this can't last. When I want something…I get it, and I don't care who I have to get through to do it."

She half closed her eyes as she shifted beneath me. "So what if you have to get through me?"

Her question distracted me for a moment.

"You're in my heart, babe. I think I've already gone through you."

She smiled, and I sat up in bed, getting ready to dress.

"You're not going to shower?" she asked as I pulled a T-shirt over my head.

"Are you hinting at something? Do I smell bad?" I said, grinning and looking down as I tied my shoes.

Noah was still wearing one of my T-shirts, and her hair was sticking out in every direction. We were always late, and I didn't understand why she didn't take the opportunity to get dressed when I was doing the same. Instead, she was sitting there on my bed giving me a goofy stare.

"I figured you'd want to run and wash off my Monet," she said.

I smiled and stood in front of her at the foot of the bed. Her foot was lolling on the white sheet, perfect like every part of her.

"I'm happy to wear this artwork of yours, Freckles; it bears your signature. It'll stick around until it fades away." I stretched out a hand and grabbed her foot, pressing it into my chest and massaging her ankle. "Honestly," I went on, lifting my shirt and pointing to one of my obliques, "I think this elephant right here gives me a sort of interesting macho air."

She stared at my bare skin, and I smirked, pulling on her ankle until she was almost falling off the bed and her shirt had slid up to reveal the bottoms of her breasts. Her firm flat stomach was there for me to see, along with that lace underwear that could give me a heart attack.

"You see something you like?" I asked, bending over and kissing her belly button tenderly.

She closed her eyes for a moment. How could she smell so fucking good?

"You," she responded simply.

But there was no time for that. I grinned and let her wrap her legs around my back. I needed to get her out of that room. I walked down the hall and into the kitchen, smiling as I deposited her on the counter. She frowned as she felt the cold marble on her skin. I left her there and started taking food out of the fridge to make breakfast. I could tell she was watching my every move.

I made a fruit salad, juiced some oranges, and whipped the eggs before scrambling them.

"Can I help you?" she asked, but I refused.

"Let me make you breakfast one last time," I responded with an unavoidable slight scowl. She shrugged and said nothing.

When everything was ready on the island in the kitchen, I grabbed her again and sat her in my lap. She wrapped her arm around my neck and played with my hair, and I fed her, lost in thought. As she ate, she, too, seemed distracted, her mind probably racing.

I knew that however much the two of us tried to put on a happy face, what had happened the night before was still there with us, inhabiting the apartment like a ghost. Nervously, I pushed her head back and kissed her, savoring the delicious taste of freshly squeezed oranges on her lips.

She was surprised by this sudden fit of passion, but evidently it pleased her. Her tongue wrapped around mine as I jerked her into me.

When I pulled away, my forehead was still touching hers, and our eyes locked. That shade of honey in her irises made me melt, and I felt the irrational urge to shut her up in my bedroom and never let her go.

"I love you, Noah... Don't you ever forget that."

Her eyes shone with unbelievable brightness while her fingers stroked my cheeks and lower lip. She seemed to be lost in thought. She started to lower her hand, but I stopped her and brought it to my lips. I kissed every knuckle carefully and then let her finish eating.

She was pensive before; now she seemed barely aware of my presence.

"What time does class start?" I asked, unable to bear the silence.

"Twelve thirty."

"I'll drive you there."

After dropping Noah off, I met up with Lion, and we got in my car, heading out for a beer.

"I'm thinking of selling the garage," he said.

"What?"

The garage was the most important thing Lion had. It was his business, his family's business. Lion kept his eyes focused on the road, moving his feet nervously.

"I need to make things right with you know who."

I rolled my eyes. "I don't see how you're going to make things right if you can't even say her name."

"I'm still pissed at her," he confessed, sighing. "But her father called me last night."

I looked over at him incredulously. "What did he say?"

"Old man Tavish has always treated me well. He never looked down on me like all those other rich people, you know...he's straight up."

Greg Tavish was a good man, and he'd done an impeccable job of raising his daughter. Jenna was the person she was because she'd never wanted for anything. Even I had envied her when we were little kids.

"So anyway...we were talking. At first he just wanted to know how come Jenna didn't talk about me anymore at home, and then he said she'd been crying nonstop for two nights straight."

I could tell he didn't like knowing that Jenna was sad, but realizing that being apart hurt her, too, and that he wasn't the only one in pain, was clearly a relief to him.

"He told me he'd give me a job at his company. I'd be starting at the bottom, of course. To rise up, there'll be tests to take, lots of work, but with time, he said I could make it. That guy's a machine, Nick. You should have heard him... He's so self-assured, so smart... It's no surprise Jenna adores him. Who wouldn't want a dad like that?"

I stared at the car in front of me.

"You don't have anything to say?" Lion asked.

My mind had strayed into dark territories. I couldn't help comparing my father to Greg—couldn't help thinking about how Jenna's parents accepted her relationship with Lion, a guy from the streets, nice enough, sure, but still, someone who had no money and had never graduated. Jenna's father had never cared, while there I was fighting tooth and nail to get my own family to accept me.

"I think it's the best thing that could have ever happened to you, bro," I said, smiling.

For the first time in years, he looked secure. My best friend's green eyes reflected utter calm.

41

Noah

I DIDN'T SEE NICK FOR THE NEXT THREE DAYS. WE WERE IN contact, we talked at night, and he sent me messages while I was in class that made me blush, but we never found an opening to hang out.

I did go out with Jenna, though. Not to the clubs, not to dance, just to a couple of bars near campus. You had to go before happy hour hit, otherwise they were all packed. One day, Jenna brought Amber, her roommate, to Ray's, one of the popular spots. We had a good table and were watching a group of guys shooting pool a few feet away, very obviously trying to get our attention. Three hot girls with no guys around—that was enough for them to come over and talk.

Amber told us repeatedly how hot she found one of them, a skinny redhead. He looked kind of raggedy but also sweet. In just five seconds, she had a whole movie going in her head.

"I think we'll call our firstborn Fred, you know, like from the Harry Potter books. I've always been a fan. Our children will probably inherit his red hair..."

"Why don't you go over there and tell him you already know

the name of your first child? I'm sure that'll be enough to make him fall in love with you," Jenna encouraged her. She was sloshed already and seemed disgusted every time someone of the opposite sex looked over at us.

"Hey, Noah," Amber said, ignoring Jenna, "one of those guys won't take his eyes off you." I looked back, hoping it was Nick.

But what I found was a totally different pair of eyes. He was the furthest thing from Nick, but Amber was right: he wouldn't take his eyes off me. He was tall and blond and wielded his pool cue like an extension of his own body. Something about him seemed weirdly familiar. But I looked away from him to concentrate on my friends.

"Maybe he's from one of my classes, but I don't know, honestly," I said with a shrug.

Jenna looked over at him, uninterested in being subtle. "I've seen that dude. I think he was coming out of the biology building. He's no freshman, I'll tell you that. He might even be a professor... Maybe he can teach you a thing or two...!"

I knew what she was insinuating. To hell with that.

He was bent over the table, his hair in his face, concentrated on the game, his eye on the ball, and that allowed me to look at him closer. No, he wasn't a teacher; he was too young for that, although he definitely wasn't a freshman either. I racked my brain trying to figure out who he was, but it was impossible. A few minutes later, we'd changed the subject and were talking about other nonsense.

"Hey, can you get me another drink?" Jenna asked Amber.

While she went to the bar, I decided to wait for the bathroom. To get there, I had to walk past the pool table. I had forgotten about the guy there already, and so, when he got in front of me, making me stop in my tracks, I was surprised.

"Hey," he said simply, with a curious expression.

"Hi," I responded, looking at his face and remembering right then where I'd seen him: at that party I'd gone to with Jenna the night Nick had come back from San Francisco and taken me home with him.

"Sorry, I didn't mean to startle you, I just... You were with my brother at a party a few days ago, right?"

"Yeah, we've got a class together," I said.

He nodded. I didn't remember his name, but I did remember his bad attitude when he'd confronted us.

"I'd love to ask you a favor. My brother is an expert in disappearing acts, and I haven't seen a sign of life from him in a while. If you run into him in class, can you tell him to call me? It's important."

I said yes. He pulled out his wallet, looking for something.

"I know it's a lot to ask, but I don't know anyone he hangs out with... If you see him acting weird or he looks like something's wrong, could you call me at this number?"

I grabbed his card. "Of course, don't worry," I said, seeing genuine worry on his face. "Nothing's wrong with him, is it?"

Charlie was too cool to lose as a friend. Thanks to him, I'd laughed more in those past few days than I had in ages. He seemed to always be in a good mood. I loved that. And he was capable of laughing at everyone, even himself, without the least trace of cruelty.

His brother smiled tight-lipped, hinting that he preferred not to talk about it. "Nothing you need to worry about."

His response struck me as curt, but his voice was so sincere and friendly that I couldn't help but smile back as he turned to his game.

I looked down, read the card, and shivered.

MICHAEL O'NEIL
PSYCHOLOGIST
(323) 634-7721

I went back to my dorm soon after. I was tired, and I kept thinking about what Charlie's brother had said. Getting a psychologist: that was on my list of things to do. Nick had asked me to do it, for him, and I'd agreed, but I hated having to open up to a stranger and tell him all my fears and secrets. It wasn't easy for me to talk about my problems, especially with someone I didn't even know. Still, my nightmares hadn't gone away, I was still scared of the dark, and I knew I couldn't keep putting it off forever. But what if they analyzed me, judged me, told me I was crazy? My mother had tried to take me to see a therapist before, I'd even gone when I was little, but all I did was cry so much in the office that she'd finally let it go, buying me nightlights for my room and calling it a day. The nightmares, though, those were new, something that had only come about after my father's death.

I got into bed and looked at the card again. Was this a sign? This Michael seemed like a good guy, and more importantly, he wasn't too old. I felt better about that because our therapy sessions could be more like simple conversations between friends. I wanted to talk with Charlie first, though, plus I wanted to ask why his brother was worried about him, even if I wasn't sure I was ready for us to share our problems with each other.

I knew if I ended up opening up to him, I'd just look for some excuse why his brother wouldn't be a good therapist for me, so finally I decided to call Michael directly and ask his thoughts. I did so the next day, after my morning classes, when I had a bit of free time. I told him my problem in a rough outline, without going into details. He told me he'd been working for the university as a campus psychologist for two years now. He encouraged me to stop by his office. I didn't know what to tell him about Charlie. He hadn't been to class, but I knew he wasn't much of a morning person.

I was jittery but also relieved that I had taken that step, small as it might have been. Now I just had to go and see how it was, if I felt comfortable talking with him about my issues.

I spent the rest of the morning in a café close to the English department. I was nauseated, just shy of frantic, as I ordered a coffee and took out one of my required books. It wasn't the most pleasant place, so I picked one of the more isolated tables.

After a while, I got a strange feeling. I looked up, and there he was: Nick, with a to-go cup of coffee in his hand and his Mac under his arm. It was as if my body were capable of sensing him. Worse, I wasn't the only one who had noticed. There were five girls at the table next to me who had been chatting the whole time but who now lowered their voices to whispers as they gawked at him. And they were far from the only ones, as I could tell with my full view of the café. Nick wove his way between the tables and sat down with a group of guys who gave him the usual friendly claps on the back.

"Jesus, he's incredible! Just seeing him is giving me the shivers," one of the girls next to me said, making me immediately tense.

"That's my future husband," another said, "so you can go ahead and take your eyes off him." Everyone laughed. It had never occurred to me that, obviously, Nick wasn't invisible. In fact he was the very opposite, especially in those pants that hung off his hips, that shirt that clung to his body, showing off his muscular arms...and to top it off, he was wearing his glasses, those glasses I found so incredibly sexy, the ones I'd thought he only ever wore at the apartment, when he was with me.

I wanted to run over to him and shout that he was mine, but I couldn't give up the opportunity to observe him and see how he acted when I wasn't around.

He looked like he couldn't care less about the guys with him. They went on making a racket while he focused on whatever was on his computer screen. Two girls went to sit at the same table and looked at him provocatively. One of them said something, and he smiled. I felt an intense heat gathering inside me.

"There's got to be something wrong with him," the girl next to me said.

"There's something wrong with him, all right: he'll fuck anything that moves. I'd never want to be his girlfriend. Anyway, I couldn't be around a guy like that. I'd freeze up and act like a complete idiot every time I laid eyes on him. I'm being serious."

As if he had heard them, Nick looked up from his computer, and his eyes connected with mine across the distance. I thought about playing dumb, but I wanted him to see me, wanted him to know I was on his territory, at his school, where everyone knew him and talked about him.

A smile crossed his lips. I held him in my stare.

"He's looking at us," one of the girls next to me said, and they all started laughing like idiots.

Nick got up, grabbed his things, and walked over, never taking his eyes off me. I looked back down at my book, waiting to see what he would do. I clearly heard the chair next to me being pulled out, and then he sat down.

"Hi," he said, and without waiting for a response, he pulled my chair around so we were face-to-face, my knees almost touching his.

The girls next to us watched us, speechless.

I had butterflies in my stomach. I couldn't help it. His presence made my hormones go into overdrive, the same as happened to every woman in his presence.

"Hey," I said, a bit rigidly. I was used to women looking at him. But I'd never heard what they said about him, had never been on the other side. When he was with me, I knew girls looked at him, but I was free from the torment of listening to them. Now I realized there was a whole line of women waiting anxiously for me to screw up so they could take my place.

I'd never want to be his girlfriend. He'll fuck anything that moves.

I looked back at my book, too nervous knowing that everyone was watching us. I hated hearing what they'd said; they seemed to trivialize him, make him into something superficial, like he was just handsome and nothing else. Nick was far more than a pretty face.

"Well, this is what I'd call a warm welcome," Nick joked.

My brow furrowed. "I didn't know you had class today. I assumed you wouldn't be here. You could have told me."

I was starting to get pissed hearing those girls, who wouldn't stop whispering and giggling.

"It wasn't my plan, but I had to turn something in. Now that we don't live together, I've got lots of free time." I looked in his eyes, and they hinted at all I was missing by not living under the same roof.

"I didn't know you had so many fans around here," I said, changing the subject. I didn't want to get into an argument about my living situation again.

Nick looked at the girls at the next table over. Even that got under my skin.

"You jealous?" he asked.

I didn't want to respond. Instead, I bent over the table and grabbed his shirt, pulling him in close.

"I feel like there are too many people here who have no idea who I am," I admitted, while his eyes roved my face and a seductive smile appeared on his lips.

"Nothing wrong with you claiming what's yours, my love."

Those words were enough for me. Our lips came together in an exquisite kiss. The silence at the next table over was enough to make me grin. I'd meant to just give him a quick one, but Nick had other plans in mind. He pulled me over onto his lap, opened my lips with his tongue, and explored my mouth.

My back was turned to the rest of the people in the café. People must have known what we were doing, but they couldn't exactly see. Nick bit my lower lip, sucked, and nibbled, as though placing a seal on our love. He was enjoying himself, and pleasure was darkening his eyes.

"I love me some PDA," he confessed, tracing little circles on my lower back with his finger, making me shiver.

Then I felt something strange. I made him move his arm so I could look. He had a bandage on his wrist.

"What happened?" I asked, scared.

He hesitated for a few seconds. That only made it worse. "Nothing. Don't worry about it."

I imagined him getting in another fight, and I looked him over for more signs of damage, but he didn't have a scratch on him. Nor were there any bruises on his knuckles.

"Why do you have that bandage, then, Nicholas?" I asked.

He leaned back, with a hard-to-interpret expression on his face. "Don't freak out or anything, okay?"

Lifting his wrist, I asked him again what had happened, with an alarm sounding faintly inside me.

"Take a look," he said.

I lifted the bandage and saw a tattoo, the skin around it slightly swollen. "What the...?"

Nick pulled the bandage off the rest of the way and laid it on the table. "I think it's time for it to breathe, no?"

There, on his smooth skin, in black, in my handwriting, was the thing I had scrawled down there three days before: *You're mine.*

"Tell me that's not a real tattoo," I said.

"You honestly think I was just going to let that fade away?" he asked, looking at it proudly.

"You're crazy, Nicholas Leister!" I shouted, feeling all kinds of contrary emotions. A tattoo, that was forever, a mark on his skin that would mean he'd always remember me...two words declaring he was mine.

"You were already a part of me long before I got this tattoo. This is simply a reminder of something I always have inside me, Freckles. No need for you to overthink it."

I got scared. I realized how much that meant, and despite his gentle words, a pressure in my chest made it hard for me to breathe.

"I gotta go," I said, starting to stand, but he reached up and held me there, narrowing his eyes, looking serious.

"You're freaking out. That wasn't my intention." He definitely didn't like where this was going.

I shook my head. I felt like I couldn't breathe, and I needed to be outside. I could feel everyone in the place watching my every move.

"A tattoo, Nicholas...that's for life," I said with a knot in my throat. "You're going to regret getting it. I know you are. What if one day it turns into a bad memory, a ghost that's chasing you down? You'll regret it, and you'll hate me because it will remind you of me even when you don't want it to—"

His lips silenced me with a quick kiss. It felt tender, but I could feel the tension in his body.

"Sometimes I don't know what to do with you, Noah. I really don't."

He picked up his laptop and walked back to where he'd been before.

Shit... Had I hurt his feelings?

———————————

I couldn't sleep that night. Nick's hurt, bitter expression was the reason. I felt guilty for how I'd acted, for reacting that way. And I understood then that I needed to talk to someone about it. I needed someone to help me—to help me be what Nick expected of me.

The next morning, I had my first session with Michael O'Neil.

"Tell me about yourself, Noah. Why do you think you need my help?"

His office wasn't the way I'd imagined it. There wasn't a couch to lie down on or a bunch of weird objects or anything like that. It was just a normal office with a desk in the corner, two black couches, a coffee table, some puffy white cushions. The curtains were open on the big windows, letting a warm light in. Michael offered me tea and cookies, and I felt like a five-year-old girl.

I told him more or less what my childhood had been like, my relationship with my father, the problems with Mom. I hadn't intended to reveal all my secrets in the first session, but Michael was good at getting information out of me without my even realizing it. I told him about falling out the window, my trauma related to the darkness; I told him that just over a year ago, I'd had to leave home and move to LA. I told him about Nick. After all, that was why I was there.

"You mentioned you have a boyfriend," he said, taking a break from his notes.

I squirmed a little on the sofa.

"Tell me about that relationship."

The session flew by long before I'd finished.

"Look, Noah," he said, "this first session has been good to get to know you, but we haven't managed to dive into much... I'd like to have you come in twice a week. The nyctophobia—fear of the dark—is what's bothering you the most; with therapy, we can get through that. You'd be surprised how many people have the same problem. It's nothing to be ashamed of."

I wanted to tell him I wasn't ashamed, I just hated that feeling I got when the lights went out. I wasn't sure if I'd gotten anything out of that hour, but I felt comfortable, and that was what mattered.

Michael got up and walked me to the door.

"It's been a pleasure meeting you, Noah, and I'm looking forward to helping you."

I smiled back at him. His way of talking, so calm, his way of looking at me, all of it transmitted serenity. He must have been pretty good at his job.

42

Nick

I LOOKED AT THE BUILDINGS IN FRONT OF ME. SOMETIMES, BEING up that high was intoxicating; at other times, it made me feel superior, looking down on people without them knowing it, seeing the traffic, the last rays of the sun... I'd never had a problem with heights. Distance, though...that was something I hated. I'd been thinking for a long time, trying to figure out why so often it was so hard to get the things you wanted. Lots of people could criticize me for wondering about that, since I didn't lack for anything, but that wasn't true: one thing, or one person, had caught me in her spell, and I didn't know how to get her to stay by my side no matter what happened.

I hadn't expected her to make that face when she saw the tattoo. I didn't think she'd be overjoyed about it, necessarily, but I sure as hell never imagined it could scare her. Fear never entered into my thoughts or plans—getting frightened was a feeling I didn't really know.

Noah had to live with fear. She'd told me that, and there was nothing I could do about it. If I was around, my presence calmed her demons, and she could sleep without having nightmares, but that didn't mean she was all right. And I didn't want her demons to become mine, too, because every person has limits. I certainly did, even if they were being redefined by that person I couldn't get enough of.

I wanted to know all of her, and when I thought I finally had, she would surprise me with something I didn't know how to take. And that sent me straight back to square one.

What if one day it turns into a bad memory, a ghost that's chasing you down? You'll regret it, and you'll hate me because it will remind you of me even when you don't want it to...

How could she say that to me? Was there any doubt still about the way I felt about her? Was it not obvious that my whole world revolved around her?

I looked at the contract I had received that morning. We had won the Rogers case. I, a novice, had saved what everyone swore was a lost cause. Jenkins had sent Sophie and me out there to lose so he could show we weren't ready for the big time... He'd defended his post with everything he had, but this time, the strategy had backfired.

And there, in my hands, I had a piece of paper with the words I'd always wanted to read on it...a two-year contract as an associate attorney at a firm that had nothing to do with my father, in New York, with my apartment paid for and a salary of 215,000 a year, negotiable after the trial period. It was a one-of-a-kind opportunity and would enable me to start out on my own, thanks to my own merits, without Dad helping me out.

And there I saw it again...that pretty face: the face I'd kill and die for. Noah.

I picked the contract up and slid it into a drawer. There was nothing more to think about.

43

Noah

SILENCE.

That was what there was between Nicholas and me. I had never seen that coming. I was sitting on my bed staring at my phone, thinking about what I could do or say to justify how I'd acted the other day. I missed him, and I was scared I'd tried his patience too much.

Trying to make the best of a bad situation, I started a message to him... but then I erased it, thinking it was better to call, even if that took more courage. I waited anxiously until I heard him pick up.

"Hello?"

A woman's voice.

My heart started pounding, and I could hear the blood rushing in my ears.

"Is Nicholas there?"

My voice must have given my feelings away. I was blind with rage, and only my desire to know what was going on kept me from hanging up when I heard Sophia answer.

She said yes, and soon I heard his breathing on the other line.

"Noah."

Noah. No *Freckles* anymore, I guessed.

I felt so far from him in that instant that my heart ached.

"What are you doing with her?"

I hadn't intended to ask that; it slipped out.

"I work with her."

Taking a deep breath, I tried to find a way to connect with him, but after four days apart, with silence on both ends—something that had never happened before—I was lost. I didn't know what was going on.

The tattoo.

I had talked about it with Michael. I was going to his office almost every day, and we talked about anything and everything. I had never felt able to open up to a stranger like that, but he had helped me, and it had been his idea for me to wait and see how things turned out with Nick. He told me it was never good to pressure people, that I should wait for the anger to subside instead of letting it speak for me.

Well, there we were: talking. But it wasn't exactly the conversation, the reception, that I'd hoped for.

"Nick..."

"Noah..."

We were both talking at the same time, and we both stopped to hear what the other had to say. It would have been funny on another occasion, but not then, not when he felt a million miles away.

"I want to see you," I said, seeing he wouldn't take the initiative.

I could hear him on the other line walking away from the noise around him. I guessed he was shutting himself up in some empty office.

"Sorry I haven't called," he said. "The company anniversary is coming up, and I've been busy with that..."

"I'm going to a psychologist," I blurted out. I don't know why I didn't lay the groundwork before saying that. Maybe I needed to tell him that despite my attitude, I was willing to change, to improve, for him.

"What? Since when? Why didn't you tell me?"

"I'm telling you now."

"You can't just go to any psychologist, Noah. What was the point of all that looking around, making those lists, if you were just going to up and do it without me...?"

"Nicholas, what does it matter? He's helping me. He's young, he's on the university staff, I feel more like I'm talking to a friend than to a doctor."

"A friend?" His tone froze in a matter of seconds.

"His name's Michael O'Neil, he's the brother of one of my classmates, and he says—"

"The school psychologists are just a bunch of underpaid chumps, and they have no idea what they're doing. How old is this guy?"

Incredible.

"What does it matter how old he is?"

"It does matter, believe me. What the hell does a guy who just graduated know about what's going on with you?"

"He's twenty-seven. Anyway, he's helping me... That should be the only thing that matters to you."

"You're what matters to me, and being sure that you get what's best for you, and I promise you, a staff psychologist won't even know where to start when you tell him what's going on with you."

"What are you trying to insinuate?"

"I'm insinuating that I want you to stop seeing that dumbass and—"

I couldn't listen anymore. I hung up and tried to take a few deep breaths to calm down. How the hell had this conversation turned into another damned fight?

I grabbed by leather jacket, put on my boots, and walked out to the living room, where my roommate was watching television. Our place was cozy, with two bedrooms, a shared bathroom, and a living room with a studio kitchen. I couldn't complain—William hadn't slacked too much on the accommodations. My roommate's name was Briar, and after a few weeks living with her, I could say honestly she was a bit of a bimbo. She didn't dress especially provocatively or anything like that; it was just that there was something about her that made any guy with eyes want to get her in the sack, and she was generally happy to oblige. She had dark red hair, almost scarlet, and her eyes were green and exotic. Her parents were famous Hollywood directors, and she knew she'd end up working with them sooner rather than later.

There were no surprises there—if I had that face, I'd have become an actress, too—but Briar had a *to hell with everything* attitude that I found unsettling. She was chatty with me, nice, too, but there was something about her I couldn't quite get a handle on.

"Lovers' spat?" she asked indifferently while she inspected her nails one by one and painted them the same bloodred color as before.

I went to the fridge and took out a can of Coke. Not that I needed caffeine—it would probably give me the jitters—and I wasn't even thirsty, but it was a reflex. I just couldn't stay still. That last conversation had cut me to the core.

"I don't want to talk about it," I responded a little nastily. Briar shot an angry stare at me, and I felt immediately guilty.

We weren't friends or anything, but she'd been too nice to me for me to treat her that way. So I sighed and told her my story with Nick. Honestly, I needed more friends anyway because Jenna had been doing her own thing ever since we started school, and she lived on the opposite end of campus. I didn't tell her about my psychologist, of course, but I did mention the tattoo and my reaction to it.

"Damn, a tattoo. You've really hooked him, right?" she said, sitting on one of the stools around the kitchen table. I spun my can of Coke in my hand, trying to decide how much to tell her.

"What we've got is different from anything I've ever felt for any other guy. It's intense, you know...? One word from him can send me rocketing up to heaven or bury me six feet underground."

Briar was listening attentively. "I've only felt anything like that with one other person, and he turned out to be a manipulator who was just playing with me..." Her words were sincere, and as she uttered them, she pulled off a silver cuff she always wore on her right wrist. "I know what you're saying about intensity."

Opening my eyes wide, I looked at the two scars on her wrist. In her eyes, I saw many of the things I saw in myself when I looked into the mirror. She smiled.

"It's not such a big deal. It's funny the way people look at you when you tell them you tried to kill yourself," she said, putting the cuff back on. "It's a sign of weakness, fine, but whatever, it happened and I'm still here, talking to you, no remorse whatsoever. Sometimes life is shit. We all handle it the best way we can."

Marks on the skin...infinite memories of moments you wish you'd never live again.

"I like your tattoo," she said, and I realized I was touching it. I did that sometimes without realizing it.

"There are times when I ask myself what was going through my mind when I got it."

Briar smiled, pulled up her shirt, and showed me her ribs. In black ink, in beautiful calligraphy, I saw a message that touched my heart: *Keep Breathing.*

I grasped intuitively the meaning behind those words.

"Now's the part where we hug and swear we'll be friends forever," she said, lowering her shirt and laughing blithely.

I could tell I wasn't the first person she'd told about all that. We didn't know each other well, and the way she talked about her past made it clear she wasn't seeking sympathy from anyone. She had no problem revealing her demons, but I saw that was a way of keeping people from knowing her too well. I knew she was hiding many things and that her life had been anything but a bed of roses.

"You in the mood to go out?" I asked, without even thinking about it.

With surprise, she replied, "Well, Morgan, that's not the usual reaction when people hear my story about attempting suicide." That was a thing of hers, for some reason, calling me by my last name. I had yet to hear her utter the word *Noah*. "Usually people just look away or change the subject, but I guess you want to buy me a drink?"

I shrugged. "I'm not like other people. Anyway, I didn't say I'd buy you a drink."

Briar laughed and got down off the stool. "I like you... Let's go out, then."

I smiled and went to my room to get ready.

She had made me see I wasn't the only person with problems or the only girl in the world who had been hurt. Talking with her had made me feel way better than I could have imagined.

"Which of those dudes would you pick up for a roll in the hay?"

We were at a club close to campus. Briar was like a passport for getting a VIP booth. One look always got us past the doorman without even needing to stand in line.

"I've got a boyfriend, remember?" I responded, taking a sip of my drink through a straw.

We'd been drinking for free, thanks to the server, ever since we got there.

Briar waved me off. "Fuck boyfriends. We're speaking hypothetically."

I saw a group of guys at the next booth over staring at us. No surprises there: we were two girls alone at a club, and Briar wasn't shy about looking back at them...

"Cut it out. You're going to make them come over here," I said when she winked at one of the two or three best-looking ones.

"Damn straight," she said with a radiant smile. Her teeth were white and perfectly straight. It was obvious she came from a family with money, but she was nothing like the people I'd met in high school. Or like anyone I'd ever met at all, for that matter.

I didn't want them to come over because they'd be impossible to ignore while Briar was there flirting. Plus, the one who came over to sit with us had brought along a friend.

"Hey, precious," the blond guy said, the one Briar had been eyeing dreamily.

The other one, darker-haired, reminded me of Nick. That wasn't good, and I felt immediately uncomfortable.

After ten minutes of chitchat with no depth whatsoever, Briar dove in and started making out with the blond guy while I was stuck repeating to the other one that I had a boyfriend and wanted to be left alone.

"Your boyfriend's not here, and I know you like me. Admit it, you're getting nervous," he said, scooting in closer.

I pursed my lips. "I'm not going to say it again," I warned him, angrier than I probably should have been. "I don't want anything with you, nothing whatsoever. I wouldn't give you the time of day, got it? Now beat it."

He reached for my knee, and I swatted him away, standing.

"Are you deaf as well as stupid?" I shouted over the loud music.

"Why don't you do like your friend instead of being so uptight?"

Briar had now separated from the blond and was giving me a suggestive look. "Morgan, no one's going to know."

That was ridiculous.

"I'm leaving."

I walked out of the VIP area in a rage, furious I'd ever set foot in that trashy club. Unsurprisingly, Briar didn't follow me. She had already made it clear to me that we were both free to do as we wished.

Once outside, I stopped to catch my breath. I was drunker than I'd thought at first. Just sitting there and drinking had been a bad idea. Now the whole world was spinning.

I unlocked my phone and opened a ride-sharing app. When I did, I saw several missed calls from Nick. He had pissed me off with his reaction to my finding a psychologist, and I'd decided not to pick up, but now, all at once, I was tired of being angry with him. I sent him the address of the club with a message.

I'm here. Can you pick me up?

He responded right away.

Be there in five.

Soon afterward, I saw his Range Rover parking next to the sidewalk, and I didn't really know what to do. I wasn't sure where we were at just then or how I was supposed to act. It was weird the way we'd just left everything hanging lately. I decided to stand there and wait for him to get out.

As he crossed the street in my direction, someone started shouting my name. It was the guy from the bar.

"You're not going to come back in? I was just joking before," he said, reaching me before Nicholas did. As I turned to Nick, he wrapped one arm around my waist and with the other pushed the guy away.

"Go." His voice was as frozen as the weather that night. I shivered. The guy looked up at Nick.

"Who are you?"

"The guy who's about to split your face open if you don't get away from my girlfriend."

I felt worried, seeing how angry he was.

The dark-haired kid stepped back reluctantly. "She didn't say shit about you when she was flirting with me back inside."

My eyes opened wide...the jerk.

Nick let go of my waist and stepped forward. "You've got one second to get out of my sight, and if you don't, you're going to have problems, get it?"

This was spinning out of control. I grabbed Nick's hand. "Come on, let's go. Please," I said softly.

I didn't want them to fight. I just wanted to get out of there.

The idiot from the bar seemed to understand this could turn out badly for him; there was no question about who would go down if the two of them were to fight. The door to the bar opened, and the music from inside echoed out into the street. Briar emerged, holding hands with the idiot's blond friend.

"What's going on?" she asked, coming over. Nick turned on his heel. His entire body went tense, and I knew this wasn't going to turn out well.

44

Nick

I LOCKED EYES WITH THE GIRL WHO HAD JUST COME FROM THE BAR. Briar Palvin.

I couldn't believe it.

The guy she was hanging off let her go and walked over to his friend. I was pissed enough to take on four guys if I had to. But seeing Briar there threw me off. I saw surprise in her face just as I looked away to concentrate on the other two assholes.

"What? You're going to do something, dumbass?"

I clenched my fist, ready to shut his mouth for him. They thought I'd back down because there were two of them... Big mistake. The only thing that kept me from leaving them both on the ground bleeding was the girl who was squeezing my arm just then.

"Nicholas, please," Noah insisted.

The blond guy stepped forward, right into my personal space.

"If you're smart, you'll back off," I said, controlling my tone.

"Or else what?" The other one came up beside him. I could easily have flattened them both, but that wasn't what I wanted. It wasn't the time nor the place, especially not with Noah around.

I looked over at Briar and saw she had walked away and was coming back with the gorilla who watched over the door. The big guy sneered at us as he came to a stop.

"Get out of here if you don't want me to call the cops. I'm talking to all three of you."

I guess the guys got scared because they backed down, so I escaped the need to bruise my knuckles and get into an even worse fight with Noah.

But I had a bigger problem now. I knew it when I saw Briar walk over to Noah and wrap an arm around her. I tried as hard as I could to come up with something to say to that girl with the fire-red hair. Her eyes were utterly indifferent to me.

"Aren't you going to introduce us, Morgan?" she asked in that angelic voice that she used whenever it was convenient for her.

Nervous, Noah looked at me and bit her lip. I'd have liked to tell her to stop, not to hurt herself, but then she said something, and every single alarm in my body went off.

"Nick, this is my new roommate, Briar. Briar, this is my boyfriend, Nicholas."

I stood there for a few seconds before I managed to reach out and shake the hand she presented to me.

I couldn't believe this was happening. Briar Palvin was the last girl I'd ever have chosen to live with Noah. She had known the very worst parts of me. And when I said the worst, I meant the worst.

"It's a pleasure. Nicholas...?" she said, waiting for a response.

"Leister," I grunted through pursed lips.

As if she didn't know... I couldn't understand why she was pretending not to recognize me, but it was too late for explanations. Anyway, the last thing I wanted was to give Noah more reasons to doubt our relationship. Briar Pelvin was a part of my past, and that's where she was going to stay.

"We're on our way," I said, pulling Noah off toward my car.

"Wait," Noah said, wriggling away. "Are you okay to drive, Briar?" she asked, worried.

I wanted to pick Noah up and stuff her in the trunk. She was always worried about things that weren't her business. Briar knew perfectly well whether she was in any condition to drive, and if she wasn't, she could figure out a way to get home safe and sound on her own. I knew her games.

"Yeah, don't worry about it. Go patch things up with your boyfriend," she said, pretending to whisper, though I could hear her perfectly.

Noah smiled at her, as if they'd been friends all their lives, and I got in and hit the ignition, trying not to listen.

As Noah turned around to get in the passenger seat, I met Briar's gaze. Her feline green eyes revealed more than I had expected, and I knew when I saw her smile that I had to get Noah away from her as soon as possible.

It was silent as a grave while I drove. It had been a long time since Noah had seen me angry, looking for a fight. I'd promised her that was over, but it was hard to leave behind that part of myself. I'd never been a good little boy, and when I saw that idiot getting close to her...

I cut the motor and turned to look at her. She was shifting nervously in her seat.

I pushed a lock of hair out of her eyes. She didn't move, but her skin got goose bumps as my fingers paused on her earlobe. She looked at me, first at my eyes, then at my wrist. There was something strange in her expression. I took a deep breath.

"I got the tattoo because I wanted to, Noah. I like those words, and I like them even more coming from you. Plus, you're the one who wrote them there."

"Can I see?" she asked.

I stretched out my arm, and she carefully grabbed my wrist

and turned it over, exposing it. Then she traced the words she had written with her fingertip.

I shivered.

"I like it," she said finally, looking back at me.

Why was it so complicated to love her? If she would just let go, we would be perfect for each other. If she weren't so scared, I'd love her without any ifs, ands, or buts.

I pulled her toward me, but she pressed a hand against my chest, stopping me. She looked down and froze.

"Nicholas, no. We always do the same thing," she said.

"What same thing?" I asked.

She looked away from my eyes and toward the streetlights in front of us.

"You can't act the way you did over the phone and then come here like nothing's happened and give me three or four kisses and then it's all forgotten... I'm going to a psychologist for you, I'm doing therapy, I'm telling my entire life to a perfect stranger for you, and what is it you're worried about? That he's young, and that, according to you, I'm too fucked up for him to be able to help me... The fact is you're jealous."

"It's not jealousy, Noah. I want you to be okay. I want the best psychologist for you, not just the first one who comes along."

"You want to control everything, Nicholas, but there are things you can't control. It's my decision who I want to tell everything to and who I choose to trust. All you seem to be able to think about is how my psychologist is a man. But there are men everywhere! You can't just keep me trapped in a bubble! You wouldn't be acting like this if it were a woman treating me."

"I just want the best for you! For you to fucking get better for once!"

Her eyes opened wide, surprised and incredulous. Then I saw the pain in them a second later.

Shit.

"To fucking get better," she repeated, her voice cracking on this last syllable. I didn't even have time to stop her from getting out of the car and slamming the door.

Getting out as quickly as I could, I caught her as she dialed a number on her phone.

"Who are you calling?" I asked.

When she turned and looked at me with tears in her eyes, I said, "Noah, I wasn't saying there's something wrong with you," trying to assuage her.

"Get away from me," she said, holding an arm out to fend me off as she brought the phone to her ear. "I'm not sick, Nicholas. I can't believe you said that to me."

Goddammit!

She stepped back, I stepped forward, and she repeated the words, "I said, get away from me!"

I cursed between clenched teeth as I heard her tell someone where we were.

"Noah, listen," I pleaded as she put her phone away.

With fire in her eyes, she said, "Nicholas, this isn't easy for me! I'm doing everything I can to try to be normal, to get our relationship to work, but you aren't trying to understand me. All you do is throw stuff in my face; you don't trust me, and I'm over it!"

Those words were like stakes being driven into my heart one by one.

"Noah, that's not what I intended," I replied, trying to get her to calm down. "I don't think you're sick. I never thought that. All I want is for you to get better, not to be afraid, to stop running from me—that's it."

"No, Nick, what you want is for me to get better according to your definition of what that means," she said, hugging her bare arms. "This is nuts... You're the one who needs help! You're seeing threats where there aren't any!"

I charged over, not caring that she was backing up or that her eyes were telling me to stay where I was. I grabbed her arms and crouched to look closely at her.

"You're doing it again... You're looking for any excuse you can find to distance yourself from me. Why?"

She shook her head. "I think we need some time," she said, looking at the ground.

"You can't be serious."

A tear balanced on the edge of one of her eyelids, as though unwilling to fall.

"I think we both need time to look at things with a different perspective. We need to miss each other, Nick...because right now I don't even recognize you. We don't recognize each other. All I see is jealousy everywhere, and that's not good."

"Don't do this. Don't pull away from me." I grabbed the sides of her face, came close, tried to touch her lips with mine.

"It's just a few days, Nick. Give me time to assimilate every-thing that's happened. I didn't just leave home; I left my second home—your home—too... I've started talking about my past. I'm stirring up old memories. It hurts, and I'm worried there's not enough of me for you."

I pulled her in, hugging her tightly.

"You're all I need, my love. Please don't pull away from me." I pushed her head back and kissed her as gently as I could, full of tenderness, but also full of passion. She quivered and pulled away.

"We've both got problems we need to take care of, Nicholas. Screaming in each other's faces isn't doing anything. You need to learn to trust me, and I need to stop running from the things I feel. I love you too much, Nick. I love you so much, it hurts."

I couldn't breathe, but I couldn't turn around and leave, not without her, not as I watched her swallowing her own tears.

"That's exactly why there's no point in us being apart. We're not made for that, you and I, remember?" I said, wiping away a tear that had escaped from her beautiful eyes.

"I need to think... I need to know what it is I want, what I'm missing, because right now, all I ever do is think about you, and even if a part of me knows that I need you, there's another part of me that's disappearing. Nicholas, without you, there is no Noah, and that's not right. I can't depend on you in that way because I'll wind up losing myself... Don't you see that?"

What I saw was a gorgeous girl destroyed, and it was my fault because I didn't know how to make her happy. Why not, though? What was I doing wrong? What had happened to those days when Noah had smiled at me a hundred times a day? Where was that shimmer that used to overtake her as soon as we locked eyes?

Was she right? Was I changing her?

A sudden glare lit her up from behind. Noah looked back, and as I saw her face, I could tell she was about to fall apart.

I took a deep breath and tried to set my feelings aside.

"I'll give you a week, Noah," I said, looking straight at her to try to convince her of the seriousness of my words. "I'll give you a week to miss me through your every pore, seven days for you to realize where you belong is with me and no one else."

She stood still, and I bent over to kiss those sensual lips, that precious mouth, that mouth that belonged to me, and I hugged her close, sharing my warmth with her, my desire, my pain at letting her go.

We were panting when I pulled away.

"Seven days, Noah."

I watched her get into the car. When I saw a flash of red

behind the windshield, I realized it was Briar who had come to get her.

The fear of them talking made me instantly repent about letting her go.

45

Noah

I LOOKED CLOSELY AT THE CUP IN MY HANDS. THE STEAM TWISTED upward and warmed my face. It was starting to get cold—summer was behind us, and as I watched clouds form over my hot chocolate, I struggled to grasp what Michael was trying to get me to see. Talking to him was helping me, or so I thought, but every word that came out of my mouth made me more and more confused about my relationship with Nicholas.

"I've always been scared of the dark," I told him. "I've always had the feeling I was underwater, sinking, unable to keep myself afloat. When I met Nick, that was the first time I could breathe, could make it back to the surface. How can that be a bad thing? Is it really possible there's something wrong with it?"

Michael got up and walked over to the sofa where I was sitting, observing me closely.

"You have to learn to swim on your own, Noah. Nicholas can't always be your life preserver. Either you learn to swim, or the least thing that comes along might make you drown."

Six days had passed, six long days in which we hadn't spoken a word to each other. At first, Nick had tried to get in touch. I'd been very close to forgetting about the need for distance and begging him to come see me at my dorm, to hold me in his arms...

"You're doing a great job, Noah, you're listening to me, you're learning to survive without him, and only then, when you learn to walk alone, will you be able to do it with someone else."

I took a deep breath. We always ended up talking about Nick, when what I wanted was for him to help me with my fears, my nightmares...

I stood, setting the hot chocolate down on the table and walking to the window. It was almost nighttime outside. I saw a group of students leaving their evening classes.

"I just want to be...normal," I confessed, not wanting to turn around or see his reaction to my words.

But just then, he grabbed my arm and turned me around, and his eyes were searching for mine.

"Noah, you are normal. You've just been in situations that are far from normal, okay? You're mixing up your fears and insecurities with your love life with Nicholas, and that's why I'm trying to make you see that this relationship isn't the right one for you."

He let me go, and I sat on the sofa.

"I don't want to talk about Nick anymore."

Michael sighed and sat back in front of me to look down for a few seconds at his notes. "Let's talk about how the past couple of nights have been. Did you try turning your lights off?"

I nodded. I hadn't gotten much out of it, though. My nightmares were still there, and I still felt incapable of turning off my lights for a whole night and sleeping in the dark.

"Your fear is directly related to what happened with your father. You yourself told me that before he attacked you, you used to shut the door to your room and sit there in the dark, and you felt safe. In a way, your father flipped all that around. That's why it affects you so much. The very thing that protected you has become your worst nightmare."

I hated remembering that night, hated feeling his hands on my skin again, his fingers pulling at my ankle and immobilizing me against the mattress. I closed my eyes and clenched my fists over my knees.

"The person who was meant to protect you betrayed you, an adult, someone who knew what they were doing. You were a defenseless little girl. You were alone, Noah, no one helped you, and you did what you had to do to escape. You were brave. You didn't hesitate. You fought for yourself when no one else could."

I opened my eyes, thinking of my mother. Of how she'd tried to fight back, but nothing good came of it. She only managed to make things worse. Watching her, I learned that sometimes it was better to stay quiet, to just let him shout at us... My father always told me he was doing it for her sake, but I was different—he'd never laid his hands on me because I was a good girl.

"He loved me. He didn't ever want to hurt me..."

On the morning of the seventh day, I woke with a strange feeling in my stomach. That was the last day we were supposed to be apart, and I didn't know if I was ready. All the cells in my body wanted to see him, but that separation was also helping me reconsider many things. I decided to go to his office to see whether we'd been apart long enough.

I got nervous as I set foot inside Leister Enterprises. As I stepped out of the elevator, a middle-aged woman pointed me to Nick's office. I had never been there, and I felt as small as an ant. Everything was gleaming, including the glass walls. In the middle, past reception was an enormous vestibule with white sofas on a dark black carpet. Gray, black, and white...why didn't that surprise me?

Then I saw him.

His office had glass walls. He wasn't alone. I felt uncomfortable as I saw Sophia sitting on his table. Her cheekbones rose as she laughed and chatted, making broad movements with her hands. Nick looked impatient, but at the same time entertained, and was clearly trying to keep himself from laughing as she spoke.

I walked over to the door, and he saw me. As he got up, Sophia turned, and the smile vanished from her face as he greeted me, opening up with the simple word "Noah."

I didn't really know what to say. All my insecurities, that dreadful jealousy, took back over. I couldn't help it. She was perfect...perfect for him.

"Hello, Noah. Nice to see you again," she said, grinning.

I tried to smile back.

"Would you mind giving us the office for a minute, Soph?" Nick asked.

Soph.

She nodded and walked out.

As we walked over to his desk, Nick grabbed a piece of paper and stuffed it into a drawer. Then he hit a button, and the walls started to darken. In fifteen seconds, I could no longer see anything outside those four walls.

Then his hands were on me, the heat of his body engulfed me, and he pulled back on my ponytail and pressed his lips into mine. It wasn't a deep kiss, and soon he had pushed me back a few inches to let his eyes rove my body, my face, my trembling hands.

"I missed you, Freckles," he said with a hard-to-decipher expression on his face.

I felt like I was drowning, and suddenly, all I wanted was to get out of there and to hear Michael again telling me I was strong enough to fight against anything, that I needed to confront my fears, that I was strong, that I was smart, that no one and nothing could knock me down... All I'd needed was to see him and her together, and my self-esteem had collapsed through the floor.

"What's that piece of paper you just put in the drawer?" I asked, to distract myself more than for any other reason. I watched him turn suddenly tense.

"Nothing, just work stuff," he said. "Noah, please tell me this stupid break is over because I'm about to lose my mind. You haven't answered my calls, you've been ignoring my messages..."

"I needed time to think," I said, and my voice sounded hard and distant.

Frowning, Nick asked, "Noah, what's going on?"

"I need more time."

He had been caressing me, but then he stopped, and as he did, I felt very small beside him. He looked down at me and said, "No."

"Nicholas, I..."

"I haven't seen you for seven days, I've given you time to think, even though I don't know what the hell it is you're supposed to have been thinking about..."

He walked toward the window behind his desk. Before he could say more, the door opened behind me, and Sophia walked in.

All she needed was one look to realize things weren't going well.

Nicholas walked toward her, turned back to me, said, "Wait here," and walked out.

Sophia and I looked at each other in an uncomfortable silence. As she walked over to her desk and pulled out her chair, she said, "Sit down if you want. Can I make you a coffee or something?"

I said no and remained nailed to the spot.

"Noah...I think I know why you're here... You need to realize, it's a once-in-a-lifetime opportunity. I'd give anything for that job.

It's not like New York is on the other side of the world, lots of people have long-distance relationships, and it would just be—"

"Wait, what?"

My heart started galloping, and I was afraid it would burst out of my chest.

"What did you say?" I asked, walking toward her.

She repeated the same words that had just emerged from her mouth, and they echoed in my head like some bizarre chant.

Opportunity. New York. Long-distance relationship...

Sophia looked at Nick's desk and then at me, and her eyes opened wide as her cheeks flushed scarlet.

"I...I thought that Nick..."

"What opportunity are you talking about?"

Sophia shook her head. "You'll have to ask him, Noah. I shouldn't have said anything. I just thought...I thought he'd told you, especially since they're putting so much pressure on him to decide."

"Nicholas hasn't told me anything, but since you've started, you might as well finish. What the hell is going on?"

I knew I was on the verge of exploding, and I preferred not to do it in front of her. I needed to leave, but I couldn't do it without finding out what she was talking about.

"A major law firm in New York has offered him a position for two years. Winning the Rogers case brought a lot of attention to us from important people. I'd like to say it was all me, but we couldn't have done it without Nick."

I didn't even know they'd won the case or that Nicholas was interested in working in New York. I sure as hell didn't know anything about him going away for two years...

I needed to go. I needed to go before Nicholas came back.

"Tell Nicholas...tell him I had to go, that I wasn't feeling well..."

Before I could walk out, Sophia grabbed my arm and looked

at me through those chestnut-brown eyes surrounded by long lashes. Her heels made her taller than me, and I didn't like that. I didn't like it at all.

"I know you don't want him to go…but you need to support him now, Noah."

In a rage, I jerked away from her, saying, "Don't you dare tell me what I should or shouldn't do with my boyfriend."

In two minutes, I had ridden the elevator downstairs and walked out.

Two years? He was thinking of going away and leaving me here for two years? Why did she know this and I didn't?

You need to support him now, Noah.

Why didn't Nick trust me? Why couldn't we tell each other everything without being scared of what the other thought?

I sped out of the parking lot, blinking to try and keep my tears from blurring my view of the road.

46

Nick

I NEEDED TEN OR SO MINUTES TO GET JENKINS OFF MY BACK. THE asshole couldn't shut up about how stupid it would be for me to reject the offer from New York. I had to take it, he said. It would take my career to the next level, blah, blah, blah. Obviously it would be a dream come true for him because he'd have me off the scene and wouldn't have any more obstacles blocking his rise in Dad's company. That would be like killing two birds with one stone. He kept me busy with his scheming long enough that when I returned to the office, only Sophie was there.

"How long ago did she leave?" I asked, stopping in the doorway.

"Five minutes ago. But Nick..." Something in her tone made me freeze and look at her. "I told her about New York, and I don't think she took it very well."

"You did what?"

I could tell she was nervous.

"I thought that's why you guys had been fighting. I'm sorry, I know I screwed up, but I didn't mean to..."

Fuck!

I stormed out of my office, headed for the parking lot, and when I got in my car, I took off for the university.

I couldn't believe she'd spilled the beans, especially when that issue was over and done with. I didn't know how to get people to understand that I wasn't interested, that I was going nowhere. Sophia had been a huge pain when I told her there was no way I'd go. I wasn't crazy, I knew it was a huge opportunity I was rejecting, but I wasn't about to leave Noah, not even if they'd offered me a job at the White House. Jenkins had been on my ass ever since he'd heard about it, and I'd wasted ten minutes listening to him call me an idiot while I repeated that I wasn't going anywhere. And now I had to confront Noah at a moment when our relationship was a straight-up catastrophe. The whole thing was getting out of hand.

I called to tell her I was going to her dorm. I wanted to explain what was going on to her, but as usual, she ignored every one of my calls. Fifteen minutes later, I was parking in front of her dorm, and as I got out, I started asking myself how I could explain things without ending up with her chewing me out about the same things she'd already thrown in my face before. The last thing I wanted was to make her ask me for even more time apart and for that time apart to turn into an eternity.

Damn Sophia and her damned mouth.

I knocked three times and waited for the door to open. When it did, it wasn't Noah.

Shit.

"Leister," Briar said in her cloying voice. All she was wearing was a thin gown. Her red hair was pulled back in a bun, and on her face was that smile that brought back so many bad memories.

"Is Noah here?" I asked, looking past her.

"She's in her room," she said, stepping aside to let me in.

Well, that had been easy. I ignored her and walked to Noah's room, but when I opened the door, it was empty.

I turned to see Briar staring at me with a diabolical grin, sitting on the kitchen counter with her nightgown pulled up over her thighs.

"Oops...I forgot, actually she's not here. Sorry. My memory sucks."

I ignored her as I headed for the door, until I saw she'd put a padlock on the inside and had locked it behind my back. Trying to control myself, I closed my eyes and summoned all the common sense I could muster.

"Open the fucking door."

"I see you've got the same mouth as always." She slid off the counter and opened the fridge. "You in the mood for a beer?" she asked, looking me over from head to toe. "Or maybe something else... You're not much of a beer guy anymore, are you?"

Getting into an argument with her just then was the last thing I wanted. Goddammit. I had tried not to think about the fact Noah was living with her, but I knew something like this would happen sooner or later. I had just hoped today wasn't the day.

"Briar, I'm not going to play games with you. Not now, not ever. Open the door."

Leaning against the counter, she pulled the key out from her cleavage. "You want it?" she whispered sexily. "Come get it."

I strode over in three steps as her wild green eyes observed me, amused. But I knew what was behind them. Briar hated me. She had her reasons to.

"Give me the key, Bri," I ordered her. "Don't play with me. You know you'll end up losing."

My words made the smile vanish from her lips.

"I thought I'd never see you again."

I closed my eyes, trying to still my resentment. "Me neither... And I sure as hell didn't think you'd be living with my girlfriend... Briar, you can't tell her anything. Are you listening to me?"

I saw a look of bitterness cross her face, and for a moment, I was speechless.

"You worried I might say something that will open her eyes, Nick?" she asked innocently. Briar could put on a thousand different acts, wear a thousand different faces. But I had seen them all.

If Noah ever found out...just the thought of it terrified me.

She grimaced. "You don't know how to love anyone. Least of all that girl. You don't deserve her."

God knew I didn't deserve her. I didn't need this, not now. I didn't want to dig up old memories, feel the same old guilt from before. I'd left all that behind. I let it go when I went to live with my father, a year before I met Noah, and Briar wasn't supposed to be here. She'd left, and she'd sworn she'd never return. Why in the hell was she back?

"Maybe you're right, but I'll stay with her until she tells me to go."

Unable to believe what she was hearing, Briar reached up and stroked one of my cheeks with her finger.

"You do love her," she said, as if that were impossible. "So now you're supposed to be different?"

Her hand reached my hair, but I grabbed it and forced her to step back.

"I'm not the same person you met three years ago. I've changed."

Her full lips smiled. "Nick, you were born a son of a bitch, and you'll die a son of a bitch."

I jerked her toward me, losing control for a second, and with my free hand forced her to drop the key. Once I grabbed it, I tried to relax, taking deep breaths.

"I know it's pointless to tell you this now, but I'm sorry for what I did to you... I really am sorry for what happened."

"You feeling bad may do something for you, Nick, but it doesn't do shit for me. Now get out of here."

I did so, but just before, I wrote a note and left it on Noah's pillow. I'd made a decision.

47

Noah

I WENT STRAIGHT FROM LEISTER ENTERPRISES TO CHARLIE'S. I didn't want to see anyone who would try to convince me not to be angry at Nicholas; I didn't want Jenna telling me that she understood where I was coming from but that Nick had a right to accept a job lots of people would kill for.

I wanted to be selfish. I needed to be selfish when it was about Nick. Two years apart...? It had only been a week, and we were almost going crazy.

I'd never been to Charlie's home, but I had dropped him off before, so I knew the address. When I rang the doorbell, I heard a noise behind the door before he opened in a state I'd seen him in more than a few times: drunk as a skunk.

"Noah," he said, slurring my name slightly. His eyes were bright red, and he stank of alcohol.

"Hey...you mind if I come in?"

Drowning my fears and insecurities in alcohol was the last thing I needed to do. But one drink never hurt anybody.

Charlie smiled and invited me in. We spent the day in his room sharing secrets over a bottle of tequila. I told him what was going on with Nick, and he confessed that his boyfriend had left him. He was an alcoholic, he told me, and I felt immediately guilty: getting drunk with him was clearly a bad idea, then, but in my defense, he'd already been well on his way before he'd opened the door for me.

"If my brother saw me like this, he'd kill me," he said. "He thinks his bullshit therapy can help me, but actually he's the one who needs to be in therapy... He can be a real asshole, you know? You have no idea what it was like growing up with him when my mother died..."

It saddened me to see he really wasn't the happy, carefree kid he appeared to be. I didn't know about his past, and it made me realize everyone had secrets they didn't want to reveal.

Since alcohol wasn't going to solve anything, I said we should eat something and watch a flick. We put on *Shrek* and cracked up, and I forgot all about Nick for a few hours.

It had been a long time since I'd had a friend I could share simple moments like this one with. Jenna was too out there; all she ever wanted to do was party or shop, and only a few times had we ever just sat on the couch and hung out.

It was almost nighttime when the door opened and Michael came in looking pissed. I didn't expect to see him there, but I realized then that it was his apartment, too. Charlie lived with his brother because he barely had enough money for school.

I don't know why I felt uncomfortable—maybe because I was used to seeing him in his office, maybe because he knew almost all my secrets, fears, and insecurities. He looked across the room and spotted me. Lines appeared in his forehead, and I sat up straight, almost as though I expected him to chew me out. We'd stopped drinking hours before. Charlie had even taken a cold shower and looked relaxed, so I prayed Michael wouldn't guess at what we'd been up to.

Noting the tension in the air, Charlie said, "Hey, Brother, what's up? You feel like watching something with us?"

Michael started unpacking a supermarket bag at the counter. "Have you eaten?" That was his only response. He hadn't even said hi to me. Feeling strange, I got up, ready to go.

"I should leave, I think," I said, picking up my purse.

Michael stared at me for a moment before saying, "I brought food for dinner. You can stay if you want. In the meantime, you can tell me why you decided to skip your appointment today. I was waiting until seven for you."

Shit! I'd completely forgotten... That was why he was acting so weird, because I'd left him hanging.

Charlie glanced at me out of the corner of his eye and said he needed to go clean his room.

Some timing.

I walked over to the marble counter where he was laying out his groceries. "I'm really sorry, I totally forgot."

"Don't worry, we'll catch up in the next session. You like mushroom risotto?"

He seemed so relaxed, so different from when he'd come through the door. All the anger in that look he'd given me before was gone. I nodded, dropping my purse in the chair and deciding it would be better to stay than to risk offending him after I'd already left him hanging.

I put on an apron and helped him with the mushrooms and the sauce. Charlie knew nothing about cooking, and when he came out, he basically just bothered us trying to stick his fingers in the sauce to taste it.

We sat at the coffee table and talked about nonsense while we ate. It was nice to see Michael so relaxed; it was also strange seeing him outside of work. He seemed younger, and he had a flair for cooking: the risotto was incredible. We exchanged recipes. He knew what he was talking about.

I had a smile on my face as I returned home that night. I'd felt relaxed, good, in a way I hadn't for a very long time. With Nick, everything was so intense, just one look from him electrified me, one touch of his lips made my stomach quake.

I had needed to get away from that intensity, spend at least a few hours on my own, not letting someone else's shadow fall over me and tell me what to think or how to feel. I'd needed to forget all that, turn off the phone, let myself go—stop feeling so much.

And I'd managed to do that, to catch my breath, to just be Noah, not someone else's Noah, but my Noah. But as soon as I entered the apartment and went to my room, I found Nick's note. I picked it up, nervous, and read:

I'll give you more time. If that's what you need, if that's what you need to realize I love you and you alone, then I'll do it. I don't know what to do to make you believe me, make you see that I want to take care of you and protect you forever. I'm not going anywhere, Noah, my life and my future are with you, my happiness depends on you alone. Stop being afraid: I'll always be your light in the darkness, my love.

My heart skipped a beat when I read those words, and I felt even guiltier for what I was doing to him. Nick was ready to give up a job that was second to none for me...

I grabbed a bottle of water, went to the living room, and flopped down on the sofa. This was a huge mess, no doubt about it. I was scared that if Nick stayed, he would hold it against me in the future that he'd passed on that opportunity. Sophia's words kept echoing in my head: *You need to support him now, Noah.* Why was she getting involved? Why was she talking as if he mattered to her? Why had Nick told her about everything and not me?

I hated Sophia, I truly did. I knew I didn't have any real reason to, but my jealousy had taken over. I was jealous because she seemed perfect for him and then I looked at myself and saw the polar opposite.

I don't know how long I stayed there sitting on the sofa before I fell asleep. When the light coming through the windows woke me, I realized I wasn't alone. A pair of eyes stared at me as I sat up warily. Briar was there with a cup of coffee in her hands.

"Good morning," she said, a strange smile on her face.

"I guess I nodded off," I said.

"You've got mail," she said, handing me a white envelope.

I read it quickly and realized I'd totally forgotten what it was about. It was an invitation to the sixtieth anniversary of Leister Enterprises.

"Shit!"

Briar grabbed the letter out of my hands and read it. "Is this the gala they've been talking about in the media for like a month?"

I didn't know what she was talking about, but I nodded anyway. It was the stupid party where Nick and I were supposed to act like a stepbrother and a stepsister who loved and respected each other as family. This was the absolute worst time to go to an event like this, especially given that we were fighting.

"Goddammit, why does it have to be now!" I exclaimed, getting up to pour myself a coffee.

There was a strange gleam in Briar's eye.

"It says here you can take a date. Unless I'm mistaken, you're not talking to your boyfriend right now, are you?"

I mean, sort of... It was more complicated than that. Anyway, I'd forgotten about the plus-one. Nick had told me we'd go together, so I just assumed I was going to have to deal with the stupid party beside my boyfriend I was pissed at, a mother and stepfather I barely spoke to, and people I'd never seen in my life.

"I don't really know where we're at right now, but no, I'm

not going with him…" I rested my head in my hands and closed my eyes. The party was that weekend, and something told me my problems with Nick wouldn't be solved by then.

"I could go with you if you want…" Briar said a few seconds later. I looked up at her. "I mean it, I don't care, plus I could probably meet some influential people at an event like that… You know, in life, it's all about contacts. We'd be doing each other a favor: I'll stick with you so you don't get bored, and you'll give me the chance to hook up with some big-name agent."

I thought it over. It didn't sound like a bad idea. It was better to go with her than to show up alone, at any rate.

"You really don't mind? It's going to be boring as shit, and I'll have to play the role of perfect daughter, shaking everyone's hands and taking a bunch of dumb photos."

She smiled, showing me her perfect white teeth, looking like an angel fallen from heaven… Briar threw me off completely. I had no idea what to make of her.

"I don't mind at all. You'd be doing me a favor."

After saying this, she turned on her heel and entered her bedroom.

I just had two more days before I would see Nick at the Leister gala. I had no idea how we'd act around each other. I was surprised to see he really was giving me distance, but I wondered if there was some reason behind it that I didn't know.

Two more days, Noah. Two more days, and then you'll see him, and everything will go back to the way it was before.

I kept repeating that to myself over and over and trying to distract myself by buying my dress and accessories for the gala. The dress code for women was a long gown and heels. I called

Jenna, and we went to the mall, where we walked around, talked, and window-shopped.

"I was thinking about going, too, but Lion's been calling me every day for a week. He won't stop saying he needs to see me, he wants to take me to dinner, he wants to talk, to see how I am... What now, Noah? I miss him so much, it hurts, but I'm scared... I'm scared he'll hurt me again. I'm scared of things going back to how they were."

Listening to her, I couldn't help but compare her situation with my own. Nick and I hadn't broken up—I couldn't even imagine that happening—but still, that time apart seemed to mark a before and after in our relationship.

"You have to go, Jenna. At the very least, Lion deserves for you to hear him out. You've been split up for more than a month. It's time to put your cards on the table. I know you keep saying you're better off without him, but we both know that isn't true."

She started chewing one of her nails compulsively, and I grinned.

They were made for each other. I don't know how they could fail to realize that.

I tried at least twenty dresses. My mother had told me to put everything on my emergency credit card. I had originally planned on borrowing something to wear, but I didn't want to have to worry about it.

I went to Chanel, Versace, Prada... It was hard for me to stomach those prices. For a moment, I thought of buying a brand-name dress at half price from a consignment shop, then keeping the rest of what it would have cost for myself, to pay for my food and other necessities, but I discarded the idea. Mom would look at her statement and would figure out what I'd done.

We wound up at Dior, which was one of Jenna's favorites. The prices were complete madness, but I let her drag me along and pretended I wasn't buying it for me, almost as if I were doing an errand for someone else.

The worst thing that can happen to you in a place like that is that you fall in love with something. And I did. It was there, in the middle of the shop, displayed on a mannequin. My eyes traveled over to it as soon as I walked in.

"Jesus, Noah... That's the one. That's your dress," Jenna said next to me, almost as stupefied as I was.

The fabric was pearl gray. I touched the soft silk with my fingers. It was gorgeous—I couldn't help but admire it.

"You have to try it on," Jenna said, and a second later, a salesperson was all over me like I was a Hollywood star. We were taken to a side room where they helped me try it on. The upper part of the dress was a kind of corset studded with tiny diamonds against a silver background. The skirt hung almost to the floor, showing off my curves like water dripping over my skin. There was a slit up one side that rose almost to my hip. It was absolutely perfect.

When I emerged from the dressing room, Jenna was gobsmacked.

"It's fucking incredible."

I looked down and grabbed the ticket hanging from one side. When I saw the price, I nearly choked.

"It's seventeen thousand dollars, Jenna."

She showed no surprise whatsoever.

"What did you expect? This isn't the Gap. You need to be able to hang with everyone else there. Trust me, this will be far from the most expensive gown there. Plus, you look like a dream, Noah. I mean it; I feel like I'm about to cry."

I rolled my eyes and looked at myself in the mirror.

It really was beautiful. That pearl gray was a perfect contrast to my tanned skin and my hair. Plus, it was a special occasion. I'd be wearing it in front of the cameras... I'd be wearing it, more importantly, in front of Nick.

Yeah, I definitely wanted to see Nick's face when I showed up looking like that. If this gala was going to be our reunion after two weeks with barely a word...then like Jenna said, it needed to be spectacular.

48

Nick

THE GALA WAS A DAY AWAY, AND NOAH AND I STILL HADN'T SPOKEN. I was worried. Worried about her, about us. I felt a pressure in my chest that kept me from working. That morning, my father had come by the office, had given me the invitations for the next day, and had reminded me of what he and his wife had asked of Noah and me a month or so before. I hated the thought of seeing her after all those days without touching or holding her, knowing we'd have to pretend there was nothing between us. It was like a terrible joke. My bad mood was palpable, evident to anyone who came close to me; I'd had so many arguments with the staff, I'd have definitely been fired if Leister hadn't been my last name.

"I've reserved three cars for tomorrow. One will take Ella and me, another will be for Noah and her friend, and the last one will be for you and Sophie."

I looked up immediately from the document I was skimming. "What did you say?"

My father glared at me in a way that revealed to me I wasn't the only one who'd gotten up on the wrong side of the bed.

"Aiken asked me to, Nicholas, and I'm not in the mood to

argue about it. He won't be coming. Sophia will take his place, and he asked me to let her join our family."

"Does she even know?" I asked, getting up and slamming the office door shut. "Sophia told me she wasn't going to the gala. She said she was heading to Aspen tomorrow morning."

Dad took off his glasses and pinched the bridge of his nose.

"That was then. Riston's had something important come up in Washington. He's got to go, so Sophia will have to substitute for him. Riston asked me to handle the details, and naturally I couldn't say no."

I shook my head. I could already imagine the problems this would bring. "I'll ride in the same car with her. But I'm not going to be her date."

My father observed me with indulgence. What I'd said was absurd. It didn't matter what the invitations said: if we showed up in the same car, people would think we were together...and the same went for Noah and whoever she was with.

"You're causing problems for me and my girlfriend," I reproached my father between clenched teeth. He sighed on his way to the door.

"Your relationship with Noah is already causing you problems, Son... If she can't put up with you taking a friend to a party, it sounds to me like you've got some thinking to do."

I ignored his words and let him go. I couldn't let Noah come to the gala and see me with Sophia without prior warning. I had to tell her first. The last thing I'd gotten from her was a text with the word *thanks*. I'd promised her space, but if I didn't take care of this issue with Sophia, a lack of space would be the least of my worries. I got up, grabbed my keys, and went straight to her dorm.

Luckily, I got there just as she was pulling in. She parked next to me and looked over with surprise when she saw me get out. I waited to see how she'd react.

She came over cautiously, stopped, and looked me up and down, on edge. "I'm glad to see you're still here and not in New York."

She turned around and climbed the steps to the front door to her building. Was she still fucking mad? I cursed and followed behind her, ready to put this subject behind me once and for all.

I looked at her dress, and especially her curves in it, as she struggled to open the door. I'd never seen her wearing it: yellow, with little flowers all over.

Finally she got the door open... I'd have helped her, but I was too busy watching her from behind.

When she went inside, she turned with pouty lips. "Stop looking at my ass, Nicholas."

I laughed and closed the door behind me, looking around her place to make sure there wasn't anything there that might hint at Briar's presence, but I didn't see anything.

"Sorry. I just like your dress," I said, looking at her intensely. Actually I hated it: I hated the way it clung to her breasts and danced over her knees, tempting me. Noah gave me a condescending look and dropped her bag on the kitchen counter.

I walked over, waiting for her to say something else. She looked nervous. I didn't expect that. She walked to the refrigerator and took out two beers.

"You want one?" she asked. Her cheeks were flushed because she was uncomfortable or maybe because I was devouring her with my eyes.

"Definitely," I said, reaching out and stroking her fingers as she passed me the bottle.

I knew when I touched her that way, it made her shiver, but I pretended not to notice. I was there to calm things down, to explain the New York situation, even if the only thing I could think about was slipping my hands under that dress and making her shake all over.

I put the lip of the bottle on the counter's edge, struck it. The cap popped off, and I brought it up to my lips. Noah looked down at her own beer, seeming lost for a moment. I grinned, took another sip, and stepped closer to her.

"Here, Freckles," I said, handing her my bottle and opening the one she was holding the same way.

She hesitated before bringing the bottle to her lips and letting the cold liquid drip down her throat. I watched the contractions in her neck as she swallowed. I took a deep breath, trying not to grab her. Something told me it wasn't the moment, at least not if I wanted a pleasant response. I could control my body, but I couldn't control my eyes.

She walked to the sofa, seeming unsure of what to do next, and started sorting through her magazines, just to keep her hands busy, while I leaned on the counter. Finally she turned, dropped what she was doing, and threw her hair back, frustrated.

"Stop looking at me!"

I smiled. "You're not leaving me any choice, babe. I can't touch you, I can't look at you... being your boyfriend is becoming a torture."

She crossed her arms with an irritated, uncertain expression. "Why are you here, Nicholas?"

I was just a few feet from her, but she felt miles away, and I hated that. I missed her... I knew I had promised her space; I just wanted to tell her about the thing with Sophia in person...and before that, I wanted to make sure we were okay. Or as okay as we could be.

"I know I told you I'd give you some space, but I wanted to see you, even if it was just for half an hour."

I didn't think I'd ever seen her at such a loss. She came over, but when I walked forward to meet her, she stepped back again.

"Why didn't you tell me?" she finally said in a bitter voice.

It wasn't hard to imagine she'd ask that. I knew what had made her angriest about New York was hearing about it from someone else.

"Because I was never planning on going anywhere. At least not without you."

She bit her lip. I wanted to reach out and caress her, but I didn't know if it was a good idea...especially at that moment.

"Then you would do it... If I went with you, you'd do it."

She wasn't asking, and to be honest, I hadn't thought about it.

"I'm fine where I am, Noah. I like where I work, and I like the way my future looks." I wasn't elated about inheriting my father's business because before that, I'd have to work for him for who knew how many years, but that was an insignificant detail compared to what it meant to be on the Leister company's team.

I looked into Noah's eyes and tried to decipher what was happening in her head.

"You're not even going to ask me?"

I frowned. "You want to go to New York with me?"

"No."

"Then...?" I replied, sighing with frustration and looking at the ceiling.

"I don't want to go, obviously, because I just started college here. It's barely been a year since I left Canada... But...if it's really that important to you, Nicholas, then...I guess I'd be willing to do it for you."

I looked down at her again. "You'd do that for me?" I asked, trying to see whether something in her face indicated she wasn't telling the truth. But I could tell she was being sincere.

"Nicholas...I love you," she whispered. "It doesn't matter that we're not doing well right now. If you asked me, and it was important to you, I'd say yes. I'd go anywhere with you, you know that..."

A wave of infinite love crested in the center of my chest right where I had felt that gaping absence during the two weeks we'd been apart. Christ, that distance had ached!

Coming close to her, I wrapped a hand around her waist, almost pinching one of her ribs, and all I wanted her to know was how I would do everything, give everything, to be with her and make her happy.

She held her breath. I think I could even hear her heart beating faster.

"Thank you," I whispered.

I brushed her hair aside, touching her neck. I wanted to smell her aroma, recall that essence unique to her and her alone.

I rubbed the tip of my nose on her chin and neck, inhaling and closing my eyes.

Her breathing sped up in time with mine. She grabbed my arm, and her whole body trembled.

"I miss you," I said into her ear. "I'm so happy you want to go with me, but I can't accept that job. Not yet. I want to stay here, and I know you do, too, and that's exactly what we're going to do, okay?"

I didn't wait for her to respond before kissing her on the throat. She moaned. Softly, I ran the tip of my tongue from her clavicle to her earlobe and bit down gently. Our bodies reacted in time with each other. I pulled away to observe her. Her excitement, her longing, were so evident that I had to stop myself from taking her on the spot.

"Have you had enough time?" I asked.

"I...I don't know."

I didn't like that answer. Maybe I needed to remind her of how much she'd missed me.

"I'm not going to do anything you don't want to do, my love," I whispered, grabbing her around the waist. "I'll just take it slow, and you can tell me to stop anytime."

She said nothing, and I lifted her on the counter, delicately opening her legs and nestling between them.

I smiled, hoping to ease her mind because my gut told me she was nervous. I knew a lot had happened between us and that I hadn't dealt with it well, especially over the past month. That's why I had wanted to take those two weeks to understand her, to try to figure out what I was doing wrong.

I touched her face, rubbed those freckles that drove me mad, traced the line of her jaw, her thick lips... Noah's breathing was speeding up; I could see that under the fabric of her dress. Normally I would have stripped her bare, taken her to the bedroom, touched all the places her clothing kept concealed.

But I wasn't going to keep making the same mistakes. I was going to take it slow and be sure she was comfortable the whole time.

"I want to kiss you."

She looked back at me in silence, but her eyes seemed to tell me she wouldn't refuse, that she wanted it as badly as I did.

"I'm going to kiss you."

I brought our lips together, full of longing, and enjoyed the feeling of pressure, that unique connection that made everything negative in the past few days disappear. I bit her lower lip, licked it, bit it again. No man could resist the draw of her lips, and that included me. I grabbed the back of her neck and pulled her in tighter, then leaned her back, holding her up with my other arm. I pulled back, then came in for more, this time twisting my tongue around hers. She didn't hold back. The taste of her made me lose what little self-control I had left.

Unable to keep my hands from roving her body, I felt Noah sit back up and pull me hungrily toward her in a passionate embrace that could only lead to one thing. I reached down, pulled her dress over her thighs, rolled it up around her hips, then bent down to kiss her legs. My hot kisses didn't leave a mark—I'd learned that lesson by now. But Noah grabbed my head and brought me back up for another kiss. In her intensity, I could sense that she wanted me.

I carefully lifted her off the counter, holding her beneath her legs and walking with her to her room. I shut the door and went straight to her bed. Her hands were stroking my hair and neck. I got on top of her and pulled at her dress until it came off over her head.

"I hate that damn dress," I said, throwing it to the other side of the bed.

"It's new," she said, pulling me close and planting her lips on my neck. She bit and sucked, and I grunted in response.

"It's horrible."

She laughed. "Liar."

Finally, I could see her body, that body that seemed designed for me, that body that I alone had touched, caressed, kissed.

"I could spend hours just looking at you, Noah. You're precious in every sense of the word."

Instead of replying, she observed me as I took off my shirt and fell on her nude torso. She was wearing a lace bra, but it was so thin, it might as well have been nothing. My lips grazed the thin fabric, and I felt her growing stiff.

"Nick..."

She could barely say my name, and that made me want to keep going.

Carefully, slowly, I kissed her stomach. My fingers caressed her flanks; they descended to her hips and lifted her legs until she wrapped them around my back. My hips began rocking over hers.

A wave of pleasure washed over both of us. It had been too long.

Then Noah pushed me onto my back and straddled me. Her blond hair spilled over her shoulders, and she flicked it back to look me in the eyes. I could see two halves of her struggling with each other, and I stopped, resting my hands on her thighs and waiting until she finally spoke.

"I...I don't think it's a good idea for us to keep going. I feel like if we keep going...then everything we've tried to accomplish these past two weeks will go to waste."

The person who was talking seemed not to be her but that damned psychologist who was treating her. He was the one who'd been encouraging her to stay away from me for weeks. When I saw how her body reacted to my caresses, saw in her eyes how she wanted to continue, I knew my assumption was correct.

I sat up with her over me and brought my face close to hers. "You want to stop?" I asked, hoping she would say no.

I could tell she was deliberating. Her hand rose to stroke my chin slowly, and she kissed me. "I don't. But it's better, at least for now."

I took a deep breath, trying to calm down. We were both panting. I nodded, kissing her on the nose. "You want me to go?"

Something like fear crossed her face. "No, stay."

I had the sense that wasn't the only thing she wanted. But I smiled and helped her get out of bed.

"You hungry?"

We ordered sushi and had it sitting on the rug in the common room. There was a horrible movie on TV, and as soon as we'd turned it on, we stopped paying attention to it.

I was leaning against the sofa, with Noah in front of me with her legs crossed and a sarcastic smile on her face.

"I don't believe you," she said, shrugging.

My brows lifted, and I stood, stretching out a hand to her. "Come on. I'll show you."

She got up, and I waited for her to move the furniture around a bit to make some space. Then I walked over to her stereo and looked for the easy-listening station.

The first song to come on was "Young at Heart" by Frank Sinatra.

Perfect.

"Come here, you little doubter."

She watched me, amused but uncertain, while I stepped close to her, wrapped one arm behind her back, and clasped her fingers with the other. I took a moment to prepare, then started moving. I took her along with me, just as I'd been taught, just as I had done ten or more years ago.

We went slowly at first, but once Noah let herself go, I was able to really move with her.

"I can't believe I'm dancing with you in my living room to Frank Sinatra, of all people. What have you been smoking, Nick?"

I smiled, pushed her away, brought her back in, spinning her so her back pressed into my torso. I cradled her in my arms and slowed down... Her head rested on my shoulder as I squeezed her, kissed her on the head, then spun her around again to face me.

I felt the way I had in the early days of our relationship. I didn't know how to explain it, but Noah was smiling, relaxed, and I reflected her mood. My irritation was gone, and all I wanted was to remember that moment forever: her in my arms, swaying with me as if all our problems had vanished after those days of absence...

"I love you," I said, feeling every letter of those three words coming from my heart.

Instead of responding, she squeezed my hand tighter, kissed my chest, and we continued until the song was done. We went on that way for a long time, not so much dancing as simply holding each other to the rhythm of the music. As she started to slacken in my arms, I realized she was falling asleep. Leaning down to wrap one arm around her knees, I picked her up.

"What are you doing...?" she asked, her eyes barely open.

"Let's keep dancing... I'm good at it."

I smiled as I opened her bedroom door, then backed into it to shut it. "You're great at it. Especially when I'm holding you up."

I laid her in bed, and she struggled to open her eyes again as I took off my T-shirt and jeans.

"You're staying," she said, and a sweet smile crossed her lips.

"I'm staying," I responded, sliding between her sheets. She came close to me and rested her head on my chest. "Now sleep, my love."

49

Noah

IT WAS AS IF I WERE FLOATING AMONG WHITE CLOUDS AT NIGHT-
fall. I felt the sun's heat on my body and the warm sensation of
resting so deeply that my mind was struggling to bring me back to
reality. I felt so good, inside and out; that cold from the past few
days had vanished, and when I finally managed to pry my eyes
open, I understood why: two azure lights, stunning and sensual,
were staring at me. I wanted him to close them; so much intensity
without warning was too much for my already-raging hormones.
His hand, resting on my back, started tracing little circles.

"How long have you been awake?"

He smiled. "Since you started snoring an hour or so ago."

Irked, I grabbed the pillow and tossed it at his head. The blow
didn't have much of an effect; I still wasn't totally awake.

I rolled over, grunting, and turned my back to him. He didn't
wait a second to edge over to me and pull me into him. He wove his
fingers into mine and stretched our arms out in front of my eyes.

"I miss having you in my bed."

I missed it, too. My God, that was what I missed the most.
Who could have imagined all the things that could happen

between two people who love each other in a bed. I didn't just mean sex; I meant something more—how the mattress becomes a place for confessions, for midnight caresses, for trust, a place where you can put all your worries and hang-ups aside, at least when you are truly in love. There's something magical about sleeping with someone and sharing your dreams. We hadn't really done anything the night before, but I was certain that my body and mind had been calmed by the mere knowledge that he was there.

When his hand turned, I saw his tattoo. I loved seeing those words on his skin. I loved them because I had written them, I was the one who made him do crazy things like that because we were in love…crazily in love.

The night before, when we'd been dancing and I could feel his heartbeat by my ear…it was so special that I was scared for it to end. I didn't want it to end, and that's why I'd held on until I couldn't keep my eyes open or my body standing. The Nick of the night before was the same Nick I'd fallen in love with, the same Nick I loved to the point of insanity. That had been one of those moments when I understood we really were perfect for each other. I wanted to believe we could leave the past behind and that if we kept struggling, we could make it. That was what I wanted more than anything in the world, and I was willing to do whatever it took.

But why, then, couldn't I stop thinking about the way we'd fought before? And was this intimate moment between the two of us that morning the calm before the storm?

Nick turned me around and climbed on top of me. "You're awful quiet… I wasn't being serious about you snoring. You know you don't snore."

I smiled and pushed aside a lock of hair that had fallen into his eyes. "I liked dancing with you last night."

He smiled—that smile I loved so much but saw so little of. "I told you I was a hell of a dancer."

I rolled my eyes. "Nicholas Egotistical Leister, that must be your full name," I said, turning away when he tried to kiss me. In response, he squeezed my ribs, tickling me until I started laughing.

"I don't have a middle name. Middle names are for losers."

"I've got a middle name, asshole."

He started giggling and turned his face away.

"Noah Carrie Morgan! Oh my God, I forgot! Your mother must have been drunk when she picked that! You're not going to use your telepathic powers on me, are you?"

I shoved him hard, but he didn't move an inch. I'd read that stupid Stephen King book, too, and no, my mother hadn't chosen that name because she thought I'd be some screwed-up girl everyone hated; it just happened to be my grandmother's name.

"Dickhead!" I groaned, laughing, then going slack over the mattress.

He sat up then and looked down at me. "I love you, Freckles, along with each and every one of your names."

He kissed my cheek and let me go. I got up. I needed to shower. I grabbed my things while Nick got dressed next to me, observing me from the corner of his eyes. All of a sudden, he was being strangely quiet. Before I could make it to the bathroom, he stopped me, grabbed my hand, and sat down with me on the edge of the bed, looking up at me.

"I need to tell you something...and I don't want you to get mad."

I looked at him with suspicion.

"I'm not going to the gala alone tomorrow."

That was the last thing I expected him to say.

"What is that supposed to mean?"

I knew my tone of voice had changed dramatically, and I felt the room temperature drop several degrees in that moment.

"I'm supposed to go with Sophia."

And there it was: we were right back at square one.

"I came over yesterday to tell you in person. I don't want you to get mad. We're going there as coworkers. That's it."

"Why didn't you tell me before, then?" I asked, now angry.

"Because we were so happy together, and I missed you so much…"

I didn't want him to go with her… The last thing I needed just then was to feel that things were slipping out of my grasp. But maybe this was the moment, the one Michael had said a thousand times would come, when I needed to finally start acting with my head instead of with my heart…

"Fine. Do what you've got to do, and we'll talk it over afterward."

I turned around to go to the bathroom, but Nick stopped me again.

"Tomorrow, when this is all over, we'll go far away from here. We'll take a weekend together. We'll go and fix things between us. You know I would never even set eyes on a girl who wasn't you."

I laughed bitterly. "Remember those words the next time you freak out and get jealous over someone."

He nodded. I think he accepted my words. Cupping my face, he looked me in the eyes with the purest sincerity.

"I love you, and there's no one I even think about apart from you."

I closed my eyes and let him kiss me, and when he left, I went to the bathroom.

I tried to shut out all those negative thoughts that kept cropping up and tormenting me, those thoughts I had been working on for two weeks, the things I'd been struggling to look away from, trying to change to feel better about myself, more secure, braver. I couldn't go back to the starting gate—I wouldn't. So I tried to banish my demons and trust Nick.

One thing was true, though: I was going to look so fucking hot that my idiot boyfriend wouldn't be able to take his eyes off me.

———————

Later that morning, before the gala, I hung out with Briar and Jenna, who couldn't stop blabbing and laughing. It was way more fun than I could have hoped. Jenna had invited the woman who did her mother's hair over (and hers whenever she had a big event), and in expectation of her arrival, we'd turned my dorm into a regular beauty parlor.

We gave ourselves mani-pedis and a no-holds-barred waxing, and I took a bath with Himalayan salt and rosewater so my skin would smell delightful. I moisturized with an almond oil my mother had bought ages ago. I'd worn it once, and Nick had said it made him want to lick me all over.

I smiled, looking at myself in the mirror in my underwear. I'd chosen the most provocative bra and panties I could find. I swore to myself that the night to come would be unforgettable and that Nick would never look at another girl until the end of his days.

"Is this the dress?" Briar asked, taking it down from its hanger in the closet.

I nodded, taking a look at my phone. Mom had sent a text saying a car would come pick us up and take us to the estate where the event was being held. I was getting nervous. I wasn't sure what to do or how to act when I got there, but I tried to put my fears aside when Jenna's hairdresser showed up. Briar said she'd take care of her own hair—she was used to being dragged onto the red carpet by her parents and knew exactly how she liked it.

I put on a satin robe, sat down, and let Becka get to it. That extravagant-looking woman put curls in my hair and surrounded them with an intricate crown of braids. It hurt when she was twisting it, but I put up with it because I knew the result would be incredible. An hour and a half later, I was looking at myself in the mirror and smiling.

"I love it," I declared, turning and checking myself from all angles. Jenna picked up the dress and handed it to me. I put it on carefully, admiring the delightful rustle of the silk against my skin.

"You're going to cause a stir," she said, passing me my clutch, which was just big enough for my phone and my lipstick.

I hugged her.

"Jenn, try and work things out with Lion. He loves you. Don't forget that," I said. She nodded, and I went to grab Briar. She was wearing an attractive beige gown that left little to the imagination. Her hair was pulled up on one side, with a cascade of curly locks hanging down on the other. She looked fantastic.

We said a quick goodbye to Jenna and walked toward the rented car that was waiting for us outside. I was surprised to find not a chauffeur, but Steve, dressed to the nines. As he saw us descending the stairway, he smiled and passed me a rectangular box.

"It's from Nick," he said. There was something strange, almost unfriendly, about the way he said it. I looked at the box and the accompanying envelope.

Briar gave me a strange look as I laid them both in the seat without opening either. "You don't want to know what he got you?"

I shook my head, focusing on the road. I needed to keep a cool head. When the night was over, we could talk about whatever we wanted. I'd wait to open my heart till then.

The estate was outside of town, and my nerves only grew more strained over the course of the long drive. When we got there, I was surprised to see the trees flanking the road all covered in white lights. A row of limousines was waiting to drop all the passengers off at the door. When our car came to a stop, a man in a suit opened our door. I had to try to keep a lid on my insecurities. When he helped me out, at least thirty pairs of eyes focused on me.

"Good evening, ladies," the man in the suit said, and he touched a button on his earpiece, whispering something I couldn't hear.

My mother had told me not to stop for any photos until I found her and William. I turned to Briar as the man in the suit motioned for me to follow him.

"I can't miss this," she said, observing the photo-call with calculating interest.

"You sure you don't mind staying by yourself?"

She rolled her eyes and turned her back to me. Her elegant legs marched off toward the group of people gathered in front of the camera, and I knew there was no need to worry about her.

I was led past a huddle of reporters interviewing numerous guests. I felt overwhelmed until my eyes met my mother's... We hadn't seen each other since the night I'd left home a month back, and even if enough time had passed to put our problems aside, when I saw her, I knew we still had a lot to talk about.

"You look lovely, Noah," she exclaimed when she saw me, bending down for a quick hug.

She looked like a movie star: Her hair was in curls and pulled back with a bejeweled silver hairpin. Her dress was burgundy and made her look much younger than her true age. I'd always been amazed by how well-preserved she was because she wasn't a strict dieter or anything of the sort.

"Thanks. You, too," I responded, looking toward the corner where William was speaking with reporters from the *Los Angeles Times*.

Standing apart from the crowd, but still easily seen, I watched the cars arrive and the elegantly dressed guests getting out. My mother was projecting her voice to talk to various acquaintances as they passed. It was a madhouse, and it was already starting to stress me out. I couldn't remember all the people I was getting introduced to, and we still had to wait for William to stop talking to the stupid reporters so we could finally take our goddamned family photos.

A wave of excitement shot through the photographers, and I looked over to see a car that had just stopped next to the carpet. There he was, and my God, who could have seen him without going gaga: Nicholas got out of his limo, his face serious, professional, despite the catcalls from the photographers. He buttoned his blazer and reached out a hand to the girl who was riding with him. Sophia Aiken was dressed in a spectacular black gown, tight, incredibly sensual. As I observed them from a distance, I had to suppress the urge to vomit.

I turned away just as William started walking away from the reporters to greet me. He was beaming. I guessed this was his night... I'd been thinking so much about myself that I'd forgotten how important this all was for him.

"Thanks for doing this, Noah. You look great," he said with a smile.

I nodded, ignoring my mounting irritation. I saw Nick say something to Sophie, break away from her, and walk toward us.

When our eyes met, I felt a thousand butterflies take off in my stomach. His eyes widened as he saw my dress. Lord...Nick in a tuxedo.

Before I could do something crazy, I turned around and looked at the amazing gardens, the lights, the journalists... Wasn't that one a well-known newscaster? And that guy over there, didn't he just get hired for the new Spielberg movie?

I felt Nick's warmth a few minutes later. My whole body shook when his jacket brushed my lower back. Will and my mother were right there in front of me. Their eyes turned toward the recent arrival.

"Hey, Son," Will said distractedly just before a woman came over to say something to him. My mother smiled nervously and turned to listen to the woman's instructions about the photos.

I looked back at the gardens. Nick said nothing, but his finger traced a line from my shoulder to my wrist in a way that was both subtle and incredibly tempting.

I turned, thinking I would warn him with my eyes that the best thing he could do was leave me in peace—no touching, no alluring stares, no kisses or anything like it. But whatever warnings I thought I'd issue got stuck in my throat when I saw him there, so close, right in front of me, and more imposing than ever.

His mouth said nothing, but his eyes said everything. I felt as if he were stripping me nude as they traveled over my body, their gaze palpable, as if he were stroking me with his hands. I could already feel his lips kissing me, moist and delightful, on every inch of my bare body.

God, stop it, don't think about that right now.

He bent over to kiss me on the cheek.

I closed my eyes and breathed in his familiar scent, which was mixed subtly with the aroma of tobacco. Had he been smoking? Was he as nervous as I was?

"You look gorgeous," he whispered in my ear before standing up straight and acting like nothing had happened.

He walked past me to the journalists while I stayed there stunned, watching him. They peppered him with questions, and he responded while I observed from a distance. The way he moved, the way he talked smoothly with all those people dying to know about the youngest Leister, the self-assurance in his every movement...

He stepped back to type something on his phone. Just then, I felt mine vibrate.

By then, Nick had put his away and returned to answering questions, and his father had approached him. The cameras were trained on the two men. I looked down at my screen:

I'm going to take off that dress so slowly I'll make it the longest and most erotic night of your life.

An inopportune heat made my body glow from my toes to my cheeks. I looked to both sides, hoping no one had noticed the effect his words, his mere presence, had on me.

Finally, they let us into the salon, where the waiters were serving glasses of champagne on elegant glass trays. There was glass and crystal everywhere, and candles...yes, hundreds of candles and soft white lights that invited you to settle in, talk, spend an unbelievable evening.

Now that people were mingling, Nick came over to meet me.

"Did you like my present?" he asked as we walked off, leaving the journalists behind us.

I needed some distance from him. We had promised we'd work things out once everything was over, and I wanted that night to end as quickly as possible.

"No presents, Nick. I want to get this night over with and forget that you came here with another woman."

He sighed and brought a hand up, evidently meaning to caress me, but then he realized he couldn't. He closed it into a fist and brought it down by his side. I looked away, frustrated—by the situation, by everything.

"I could fuck all this up, Noah. I could do it. All I want right now is to bury my hands in your hair and kiss you until I'm breathless... Just say the word, and I'll do it."

I bit my lip. I knew he was telling the truth. If I asked him to, if I told him how much I was suffering that night, nothing would make him happier than to ruin the whole event on my behalf.

But Will had asked us to behave, and I wasn't going to turn our parents against us even more.

"I'm good," I assured him, even as I dreamed of him wrapping his arms around me just then. I missed him. I missed our moments, touching each other, our kisses. I missed the Nick and Noah moments; two weeks had been too many, and the night before hadn't sufficed for us to get everything out and fix our problems once and for all.

I realized my mother was watching us from a few feet away. People were noticing us, damn it. Every eye was on Nick.

"You need to go. People are looking at us, and the last thing I want is for us to have done all this for no reason."

Nick looked to either side, then back at me.

"It's just a couple of hours. Then I promise I'll devote myself to you, body and soul... until everything is back to the way it was before."

His words hung in the air between us for a few infinite seconds.

Until everything is back to the way it was before.

50

Nick

WITH CLENCHED TEETH, I WALKED AWAY. IF IT HAD BEEN UP TO me, I'd have told her to hop in a car with me, and we'd have left. I didn't want to be there. I didn't give a shit that dad had asked me to be. All I cared about then was having Noah back, and hanging out with Sophie wasn't going to help me do that.

As soon as I'd seen Noah, I'd known that night was going to be torture. Everyone was watching her, no one was capable of ignoring her when she was there looking so beautiful that it almost hurt your eyes. She shone all over: her skin, her hair, her eyes, her face, and her body in that dress that fit her like a second skin. Her waist was so narrow in her corset, I wondered how she could breathe, but it was worth it to be able to see her like that.

My fingers were itching, I wanted to touch her so badly, kiss her, savor her, love her for hours. I missed her so badly, and I didn't know what the hell I was thinking wasting time with this farce.

I crossed the room, stopping to grab a drink from one of the waiters and pouring it down my throat in one gulp.

I knew it had been idiotic to go there with Sophie, and that was the last thing I planned on doing for Dad. No more favors, no more putting stupid games ahead of my relationship.

Before I reached the dining room, where they would serve the dinners, give speeches, and close the night off with a performance from one of the finest orchestras in the country, I was surprised to run into a pair of bright green eyes. I stopped for a moment, then walked cautiously over to where she was standing, next to a small table in one corner of the hall.

"What are you doing here?" I asked Briar, restraining myself to keep from cursing.

She grinned, but I could see the poisonous rancor behind that pleasant expression.

"Morgan brought me. Are you honestly walking around here with another woman right in front of her nose?" Instead of looking at me, she looked past me over my shoulder. I turned back and saw Sophia talking with people from the company. A lot of them were friends with her father, people she knew fairly well and could be comfortable with. Sophia told me outright she didn't want any problems with Noah. She had insisted on coming alone, but I couldn't permit that, not after the senator had explicitly asked my father to have me bring her.

We both knew there was nothing there, just a good friendship between two coworkers. She'd screwed up by telling Noah about New York, but the way she'd apologized was so sincere and so heartfelt that I could tell she wanted nothing more from me than to be good colleagues.

"She works in my office. What do you care, anyway, Briar? Why are you even here? We both know this is the last place you'd want to be."

That remark wiped her cheesy smile off her face.

"The world is the same as it's always been, but I'm not as naive as I used to be. The other day you told me you'd changed.

Well, I have, too. I don't let people treat me like a fool anymore. So don't think for one minute I'm afraid of being here."

I refrained from speaking. I wasn't about to get into it with her again. If she was there, I guessed what she was saying was true. I looked around at the rich and famous there walking, talking, drinking, boasting of their supposed accomplishments, each jockeying to look better than the other, then back at Briar, at the hatred concealed by that facade of hardness she always wore.

I wanted to respond to her, but something…or rather, someone, caught my attention. I looked over at the main door, and my entire world shook.

Anabel Grason had just arrived.

My mother was here.

What the fuck was she doing here?

I clenched my fists and walked to the other end of the room. I couldn't believe she had the gall to show up there. And why? Why the hell had she even wanted to? I felt a pressure in my heart and the urge to vomit.

Turning around, seeing everything in red, I bumped into my father, who appeared out of nowhere to stop me before I could do anything stupid. He took a quick glance around and grabbed me by the arm, pushing me toward one of the windows. The sun had gone down, and the light poured in from the lamps in the garden and, intermittently, from the moon, which was hidden now and again by the quickly gathering clouds.

"Nicholas, take it easy."

His expression was serious, his eyes stern. He wanted to get my attention, but the only thing I could see was that woman I hated more than anything else.

"What the hell is she doing here?!" I almost shouted, and my father pushed me even farther from the other guests.

"I don't know, but I'll take care of it. Listen to me, Nicholas, you need to stay calm, okay? You can't start a scene right now."

For a moment, I felt hypnotized as I looked into his eyes, a darker blue than mine. I had my mother's eyes; everyone had always said that. He patted me on the cheek.

"I'll talk to her. You don't have to do anything."

I nodded, letting my father take control of the situation. I didn't want to see her; I didn't want to talk to her. All I wanted was for her to be as far away from us as possible. And yet it was obvious to all that she was there to convey a message—she'd already tried to contact me before. And whatever she had to say, I was sure it wasn't good.

My father tried to transmit calm to me. But I could tell even he didn't feel it. He turned his back and vanished into the invitees.

I looked for Noah. She was talking to a small group of people and seemed to be having fun. She wasn't aware of the danger she was in, but before I could do something—take her hand, hug her, stuff her in a car and take off—another girl appeared in my peripheral vision.

"You should hear how everyone on the team is talking about you, Nick. Word's gotten around about your accomplishments. People are already speculating about when you're going to take the baton from your father." Sophie smiled, but I could barely nod in reply. "Are you all right?"

All right? I was in hell.

I looked all over for Briar again. I couldn't see her anywhere, and every part of me grew suddenly anxious. There were too many potential problems in one place.

Before I could respond to Sophia, people started sitting down for dinner. Trying to keep cool, I put my hand on Sophia's waist, guiding her to our place at the table.

I was grateful for the dim lighting in the dining room. I

was so out of sorts that the last thing I needed were spotlights shining down on me. My family's table was in the center of the room, close to the stage where the orchestra would play, where the speeches would be given, and where they would hold a charity auction for an organization the company had been supporting as long as I could remember. When I got there, I saw Noah seated next to her mother. Briar had disappeared. There was pain in Noah's eyes as she looked away to keep from seeing me with Sophia.

Dammit.

Sophia greeted her politely, along with the rest of the people at the table, and before I could sit, I heard the voice of the one person I knew I'd be glad to see that night, and I turned around swiftly.

"Where's my grandson? There he is—an old man's pride and joy!"

I grinned as I saw my grandfather Andrew slowly approaching the table. People were so distracted talking and looking for their seats that no one noticed the arrival of the one man there I didn't have a single objection to.

Andrew Leister was eighty-three years old. He was the one who had built this empire. His sparse white hair had once been black like mine and my father's. He had a lot in common with my father, but he lacked his coldness. My grandfather was the closest thing to a father I'd ever had.

All the unpleasant memories my mother had brought to the surface vanished, replaced by those moments when all I'd cared about was riding horseback on my grandfather's farm, fishing in his lake, and finding the nastiest frog I could to hide in Dad's closet to surprise him.

Grandad.

I shook his hand, and he pulled me in to squeeze me in his arms.

"When were you thinking you'd come see me, you little devil?"

I laughed, then stood back to admire him. "Montana's far away, old man."

He grunted as he looked me up and down. "I remember times when we couldn't keep you away from the place. Now all you care about is surfing and your stupid beaches." He breathed hard, making his way into a chair. "Imagine: you have grandchildren, and they turn into typical bloody Americans on you."

I laughed aloud, happy that no one but Noah, who couldn't take her eyes off us, had heard that remark. My grandfather had emigrated from England when he was twenty years old to start his company in this country. However much time he'd spent here, he'd never stopped reminding me that his roots weren't here and I should never dare take him for anything but an Englishman.

Dad appeared then and looked at his father with a blend of affection and impatience.

"Dad," my father said, shaking his hand. My grandfather didn't hug him the way he had me, but he did narrow his eyes with interest.

"Where's that new wife of yours you have yet to introduce me to?"

My father rolled his eyes just as Raffaella appeared next to him. The past year had been so intense that we hadn't had time to travel to see my grandfather, and now that he was here, I realized how much I missed him.

Noah stood and looked at me. I could see how uncomfortable she was when my father called her over to introduce her. The whole thing should have been different: I should have been the one introducing her then, and I should have been able to tell him she was the love of my life.

My grandfather smiled, a bit distracted, then noticed Sophia.

"You're not going to introduce me to your girlfriend, Nicholas?"

Sophia's smile, polite when she had been looking on, vanished, and she looked over to Noah. I rushed to correct his impression.

"Sophia's not my girlfriend, Grandad. She's my fellow intern. She's Senator Aiken's daughter."

He nodded. "I see. That's just as well. I don't want my grandson involved in politics, especially not in your father's kind of politics."

Sophia seemed paralyzed until I burst out laughing. Noah must have warmed up to my grandfather in that moment. But by then, it was time for us all to sit down.

My father's friend Robert Layton, a member of the board, was the one who gave the introductory speech. Everyone lifted their glass of champagne to celebrate sixty years of hard work. Just afterward, dinner was served. I looked all over the room, trying to locate my mother among the tables, but it was impossible.

Raffaella seemed out of sorts. She hardly touched her food, and she looked tense every time she took a sip of her champagne. Noah, in the meanwhile, talked cheerfully with Grandad, who seemed to have a good impression of her. Now and again, she turned to Briar, who had showed up a bit late with glassy eyes and pink cheeks. The alcohol she'd drunk was leaving visible marks on her, and that only made me more anxious.

When we were done with dessert, my mother's elegant, svelte figure made an appearance. I grew tense as I watched her stop beside Noah.

Everyone fell silent, and Noah stiffened like a corpse when she heard my mother's voice behind her.

"Good evening, Mr. and Mrs. Leister and the rest of you. Congratulations on the anniversary."

51

Noah

MY HEART STOPPED WHEN I HEARD THAT VOICE. FOR A MOMENT, I thought I was imagining it, but a quick look at Nicholas sufficed to confirm that what I'd heard was real.

Anabel Grason was there.

I turned in time to see her stop next to me, and I felt every ounce of air in my lungs vanish.

"I'm so happy to see all of you, especially you, Andrew. You must be very proud to be the founder of such an empire."

Nick's grandfather, who had just been talking to me about English literature and what a disaster America was, now smiled, stiff but friendly, his thin wrinkled lips slightly pursed.

"Very nice to see you, Bel. It's been years."

My eyes were struggling to decide whom to look at: Nicholas, who appeared to be on the verge of committing murder, or my mother, who suddenly captured all my attention. She was as pale as the white linen napkins on the table, and her posture was as tense as a violin string.

Before Anabel could tell some cold lie, William scooted his seat back and took the reins, his eyes fixed on his ex-wife.

"We should talk. In private would be best."

Anabel turned to him, her tight body squeezed into a bloodred dress, and with a studied smile, she said, "I'm sure Raffaella would like to be present as well."

My mother looked up at her in a way that was plainly threatening. "I would recommend you leave. This is neither the time nor the place."

What the hell was going on?

I was scared, scared that the suspicions I'd felt ever since I had lunch with that woman would turn out to be real.

Nick and I met eyes across the table just as someone grabbed the microphone to announce that it was time to take to the dance floor.

The music started blaring and everyone stood, smiling, unaware of the family crisis unfolding right in front of their noses, ready to dance and enjoy the party.

I knew I needed to get Nick away from her. In fact, I couldn't think of anything else. Turning around, I walked over and grabbed his hand. He looked lost as I tugged him out onto the dance floor. I had no idea what our tablemates had thought seeing us leave together; I had no idea if it was obvious that our way of looking at each other was anything but fraternal; all I cared about just then was making sure Nick was okay.

I tried to get him to notice me, but he was still focused on the other end of the room. When I looked over there, I saw William disappear through a doorway with my mother and his ex-wife.

"What do you think they have to talk about?" I asked, a knot in my throat.

Nick looked down, as if he'd only realized in that moment that I was with him. "I have no idea, and I don't want to know either."

I tried to imagine the state he must be in. I'd seen him like this before, and I knew he would explode sooner or later.

I touched his cheek, forcing him to look at me, thinking that agreeing to meet that woman months ago was probably the worst mistake I could have ever committed. Just the sight of Nicholas reminded me that his mother's presence brought him incomparable pain.

If he found out I'd been with her...

"Nicholas, I need to tell you something," I said, my voice trembling slightly. I didn't know how he'd react, but with his mother in the next room over and clearly prepared to make a spectacle, it was likely she would mention the time we met, and if Nick found out from her lips...he'd probably never forgive me.

"What?" he asked.

I took a deep breath, trying to find the right words, but then, someone interrupted us. It was Sophia, and her face was filled with worry.

"Nicholas, I think you should go see your parents."

We pulled away from each other, each looking at her before glancing back at the door.

"I'll go," I said, wanting to keep things calm.

Nicholas grabbed my arm. "No," he said resolutely.

"Nicholas, she doesn't matter to me. There's no reason for you to confront her."

He looked like he was about to lose it.

I turned to Sophia. "Don't let him go near that door."

Before Nick could react, I took off across the room.

As soon as I approached the door, I could hear the shouting. For a moment, I was unsure whether to enter, but when I remembered my mother's face, how tense she'd seemed... I knew she needed me. Nick's mother could be a monster.

I carefully opened the door, and the three of them—William, Anabel, and my mother—turned to look at me, all of them red in the face from arguing. Anabel was next to the window and

clearly enjoying herself. William looked faint. And my mother...
my mother was sitting on a sofa as if she wished to vanish and
never reappear again.

"Oh, lovely! Come on, Noah, I think you should hear what I
have to say."

Hearing this, my mother's attitude changed, and she got up to
stand between the two of us. "Don't you dare involve my daughter
in this! Don't you dare!"

William came over and tried to put his arm over her shoulders,
but then, something I'd thought would be impossible occurred: my
mother shook him off violently and slapped him across the face. I
froze. Everything happened so quickly that I couldn't hear the door
opening behind me. But I did feel a pair of hands on my shoulders.

"Don't you touch me again!" My mother turned her back to
William and walked toward me. "Noah, we need to go, now."

Nicholas walked around in front of me and stood between us.
"What the hell is going on here?"

Now it was Anabel's turn to speak up. She walked away from
the window, clearly happy with the scene she was causing and
the sight of my mother smacking the only man she'd ever loved.
"What's going on is I've come to claim what's mine."

William laughed bitterly, quickly getting a hold of himself,
looking more furious than I'd ever seen him.

"All you want is fucking money. You're getting a divorce from
that imbecile you call a husband, and so here you come telling lies
to try and ruin something you could never do anything about: the
fact I love that woman more than you could ever imagine."

My mother turned around, tears pouring from her eyes, and
stood still, her fingers trembling, her eyes focused on her husband.

"Every day I ask myself how you could deceive me for years
with a little girl who only wanted one thing: for someone to save
her from a hell she went looking for herself."

My breath was racing. What was she getting at?

She went on: "Now you like to pretend you're the best father in the world, and you throw it in my face that I left Nicholas behind, but you gave me no option! You traded us for her, and you had the balls to try and throw me out on the street."

William burst out laughing. "I tried to divorce you long before I met Raffaella. Nicholas wasn't even six years old then. I told you I didn't love you anymore, I told you I'd take care of your every need, but you wouldn't accept that. You wanted to perpetuate that farce of a marriage and go on living under my roof, and I agreed for the sake of our son."

Nicholas was listening to each of his parents' words, almost as if his life depended on it. It seemed he was hearing the answers he'd never had, as if he were finally understanding why everything had turned out the way it had and why he'd had to grow up without a mother.

"What are you talking about?" I asked, looking at my mother, not understanding a thing. Pulling away from Nick, I looked at William. At the drop of a hat, I'd found myself wrapped up in something I hadn't even imagined could exist: two families bound together in unimaginable ways and with terrible consequences.

"You and Raffaella have known each other for years?" Nick asked, not seeming to believe it.

Anabel turned and looked at him with surprise. Then she looked at me. "You didn't give him the letter, did you?"

My heart was pounding. Nick looked me in the eyes. The poor thing had no idea.

I shook my head, but the words caught in my throat. "I…"

"Noah and I had a very interesting meeting a few months back. It's incredible what a person can do for money and for the sake of morbid curiosity, isn't that right, Noah?"

Anabel looked almost insane. Nick stared at me incredulously.

"That's a lie!" I shouted at that devil of a woman. "Nicholas, it's not what you think! I agreed to meet her because she told me otherwise, she'd stop letting you see Maddie. That's the only reason!"

"You saw her behind my back! You never told me?"

Nicholas's eyes pierced my heart. I'd never seen such pain in them before. I knew I'd betrayed him by meeting with her, but it hadn't been curiosity or money that had motivated me. I did it for him. All that woman wanted was to come between us, and her mere presence so upset him that he couldn't listen to what I was telling him.

"Nicholas, listen..."

He wouldn't let me complete the sentence. He stepped back, gave everyone a hateful look, and walked out, slamming the door.

I turned back to that demon woman. "The only reason you came here is to cause more harm than you already have!"

Anabel looked unfazed by all that was happening around her. She was calm, relaxed even. She seemed to be in her element. Her face hardened when she heard the door slam, and she turned back to William with determination. "I've come to inform my daughter's father that the girl is his and that he must take responsibility for her."

For a moment, I wasn't sure what I was hearing. I looked at her, then at William, as he brought his hands to his head, and finally at my mother, who was a wreck, almost paralyzed after striking the one person who would never have hurt her.

And then, it all made sense.

William stepped forward between the two women. "You know what, Anabel? You're a fucking liar, and I don't believe a single word of what you're saying."

Anabel opened her bag and took out some papers, showing them to him as if they were printed on gold leaf while I remained still, watching the soap opera unfold before me.

"It's a DNA test. I always had my suspicions, but I never wanted to find out because I was afraid Robert would leave me. But he's turned out to be exactly like you, and now he wants to take everything away from me. Well, that's not going to happen. Madison is your daughter, and you're going to have to provide for her care."

My mother continued standing there in silence. Tears rolled down her cheeks.

William tore the pages from her hand, looked them over for a moment, and then glared at her.

"Lies. This is just a bunch of fucking lies. I never took any DNA test. I never submitted to this, so you can get out of my sight before I call security and have you kicked out."

Anabel smiled smugly. "The results are correct. You think it was hard to find someone to go into your house and get a DNA sample? You didn't think it was odd when you got that call about a break-in and nothing was stolen apart from a hairbrush?"

Oh God...the thieves who broke in last summer... I couldn't believe it; it had to be a lie. This was madness. Anabel had hired them; she must have paid their bail to get them out. I'm sure it was easy for them to hide the hairbrush from the police.

William was speechless. Anybody would be after a revelation like that.

Anabel turned to me with spite. "Look at you, judging me. How dare you."

I walked straight up to her. "You know what I think? You don't deserve to be a mother."

Anabel chuckled and looked over at my mother. "Funny you should tell me that, when your mother was the one who left you alone at home with a man who nearly killed you while she was fucking my husband in a five-star hotel."

My mother stepped in front of me and shouted, "Get out!"

Anabel giggled again and continued, with pity, "I left my son with his father because I thought it was best for him. Never in my life would I have left him with an abuser."

My mother covered her mouth with her hand and began to sob uncontrollably. Anabel walked out. I turned to my mother, waiting for her to deny what that woman had just told me.

"Mom...?" I hadn't realized my voice would crack until the word came out.

"Noah, I..."

Could the words of that witch possibly be true? Could my mother and Will really have met long before they'd married? When my father had almost killed me, had it really been because my mother was with another man?

"You said...you said you were working..." I responded, tears streaming down my cheeks, blinding me to everything in the rest of the room.

My mother tried to come near me, but I stepped back, keeping a distance.

"Noah, I never thought that could happen. You have to believe me. I always...I always felt so guilty for what happened, but..."

"How could you?" I shouted, wiping my tears away violently. "How could you leave me alone with him?"

William walked up beside her. I hated him with all my strength just then. I hated him so much, I thought I'd never be capable of forgiving him. "Noah, calm down. None of us wanted that to happen. None of us could ever have imagined that..."

I covered my face with my hands, unable to believe what they were saying. The fog that had settled on my life was finally lifting, and it revealed things were far, far worse than they'd seemed.

"I never thought I would say this, but Anabel Grason is right: you are worse than her, and I will never forgive you. You've ruined my life. You've ruined me."

I didn't let them respond. I just turned around and headed for the door, ready to escape. I slammed it behind me, wiped away my tears again, probably smearing my makeup all over... and I realized I had no way of getting home, no one to pick me up. I didn't want to call Steve.

A bundle of nerves, I took my phone out of my clutch and saw four missed calls from Briar.

I didn't even know if I would be able to get outside, let alone explain to her what had happened, but I tried to calm myself because there was no point in continuing to dwell on what I'd just found out. My mother would get the prize for the worst mother of all time. Fine. I just needed to go, needed to hold the one person who could console me just then, the person who had walked out looking at me with the same hatred he'd felt for his mother.

My heart in my throat, I called Nick. His phone was off—that was unusual. He always complained that I never picked up the phone. I realized then that he wasn't just angry: he saw my meeting with his mother as a betrayal.

I couldn't believe how complicated things had become in such a short time. I couldn't believe what my mother had done, the way she'd lied to me for years, about leaving me alone, about her relationship with William, about everything. And now it turned out Madison was Will's daughter. How would Nick take that?

I was so stressed that I felt grateful when I saw Briar come through the door. She found me there, froze, then ran over to hug me. "Morgan?"

I collapsed onto a sofa, and she sat down beside me.

"I'm so sorry, Noah..." Briar said, wrapping an arm around me.

"I can't believe what happened," I started saying, but I couldn't choose the right words. I couldn't even tell her what was going on because she had no idea about me or my family's history.

"I wanted to warn you, I really did...but he's like that. He was that way with me, and he will be with you... Nicholas is incapable of loving anyone."

My thoughts froze, and I looked up until my eyes met hers. I knitted my brows. I didn't understand. Briar reached up and wiped off the tears still rolling down my cheeks.

"I hoped you hadn't seen it, but...it's obvious you have."

I grabbed her hand to pull it away and scrutinized her face, trying to understand what she was saying.

"What are you talking about?" I asked as a horrible new fear rose in the center of my chest.

"I wanted to tell you...but then I saw how much you loved him, so I decided not to say anything. But then I saw him leave with her, and Morgan, I can't let him do the same thing to you that he did to me. He doesn't have the right to cheat on you right in front of everybody's nose like that."

I shook my head. My hands were starting to tremble.

"He's a son of a bitch, Morgan. He always has been. He told me to keep quiet, to not tell you anything, and I agreed to because I thought he really was in love with you, but after seeing him make out with her, I can't go on lying..."

I could almost hear my heart cracking. If what she was saying was true...

"He left with Sophia?" My voice broke as I uttered her name, and Briar gave me a pitying look, as if trying to understand how I could be so lost.

She must not have known I'd just had two bombs dropped on me: I was mourning Nick, but I was mourning my mother, too...

I stood, and Briar did the same.

"You slept with him, too?"

She remained silent for several seconds. That was all I needed to know the truth.

52

Nick

I WALKED OUT IN A RAGE, DISORIENTED BY THE MUSIC, THE PEOPLE, the candles, and the waiters. My mind had been so far from that farce that the sight of people happy, dancing and drinking, was utterly surreal.

Noah had seen my mother. Noah had met her. Goddammit. How could she?

The mere thought that she had even listened to what that woman had to say drove me insane. I had been very clear about my feelings about my mother: we didn't talk about her, we didn't mention her, we didn't see her, nothing, period.

And now I found out my father had been having an affair with Raffaella since I was a child. I had to reexamine everything because there was a difference between my mother up and leaving me and doing it because her husband was cheating on her. I'd always believed it was the opposite, that she'd left because she wanted to hurt my father. Now everything appeared differently.

My life, ever since the day I was born, had been a lie, and neither of my parents had been capable of putting their fucking issues aside for my sake.

All at once, Sophia appeared in front of me, her face full of worry, and I asked myself what it must be like not to feel the least worry apart from climbing the ladder at work. Sophia was utterly free. She had been so easy to talk to, about whatever, just to pass the time.

"Nicholas, are you okay?"

I stared at her closely, at her tan skin, her black hair, her dark eyes. What would Noah feel like if I betrayed her that way? How would she feel if I stabbed her in the back?

Sophia said something else, but I couldn't even hear her. Consumed by sudden rage, an infinite hatred for everyone that I could no longer even control—maybe even a hatred for Noah because the light at the end of the tunnel had vanished, and she was doing what she pleased, not even caring about what I had done or said or wished for—furious at her, at my mother, I acted without thinking, not even realizing what I was doing until my lips were pressed into those of the girl in front of me. I felt strange; for a few seconds, I was waiting for that vertiginous feeling I always got when I kissed Noah; but there was nothing, just skin touching skin, and that made me even angrier.

I pulled Sophia close, ran a hand through her hair, slipped my tongue into her mouth, looked for that flavor that obsessed me, that made me melt inside. Nothing. Goddammit. I felt nothing. Just then, she must have realized what we were doing, because she pushed me.

"What are you doing?"

I looked at her, analyzed her, wanting to see a person who wasn't there.

Shit.

Sophia was speechless.

I smacked my forehead and drank the entire contents of the glass sitting next to me. The alcohol burned my throat, but I was used to that burning, at least.

"I need to go."

I called Steve and told him to meet me out front. I begged Sophia to go—that was best—and tried to erase every proof of what I'd just done. She was shocked and angry, but she did as I said, grabbing her purse, following me outside, and getting into one of the cars waiting there. When I walked out, a gust of cold air hit my face. I looked up. The sky was dark, threatening.

I walked down the steps without even bothering to smile at the photographers, passing in front of the valets and the other staff, trying to find Steve, who was waiting for me farther off. I reached his vehicle, opened the back door, and got inside, waiting to disappear.

"What happened, Nicholas?" he asked, his eyes on the road as we left the property.

Steve had been with me as long as I could remember. He had picked me up from school, taken me to games, had been there when my parents weren't. I had a special place in my heart for him, and for a moment, I wanted to open up to him and tell him how I was feeling.

With my mind in a million places, I needed some time to see the box in the seat next to me and the note I'd asked Steve to give Noah that night. I put both in my jacket and looked out the window. I'd left Noah alone with my monster of a mother and our parents, I'd walked off without letting her explain herself, and then I'd kissed Sophia in front of everyone there. I felt sick to my stomach and grabbed my phone. I'd turned it off a while ago, as soon as I'd left the main hall, and when the screen glowed, I saw I'd missed a call from Noah twenty minutes before. I'd been a dickhead... I dialed and waited for her to pick up, but she didn't. Her phone was turned off this time. All at once, I felt a profound unease.

"Steve, let's go back to the party... I've got to get Noah out of that hellhole."

We were back in no time. As far as I could tell, the ceremony had continued according to plan, and at that very instant, my father was on the stage delivering that speech he'd been planning for so long. I looked around the room, trying to find her, in vain… I didn't see Raffaella anywhere either. I didn't even want to think of what reason my mother might have had for starting a scandal there or why she had lied, saying Noah had met her for money. I knew Noah didn't have a greedy bone in her body.

With every minute that passed, I felt guiltier for leaving. If what Noah had said was true, the only reason she'd met with my mother was to let me have Maddie. I had been such a jerk, an absolute first-rate asshole!

Increasingly anxious, I walked into the crowd just as everyone lifted their champagne flutes in a collective toast. Right away, the music, which had been silenced for the speech, boomed from the speakers, and the sound of conversations rose again. That was when I saw a red blur appear in my field of vision: Briar. I hurried over to her.

"I'm looking for Noah. Have you seen her?"

Briar laughed and looked at me with contempt.

"So now you're looking for her? You're the worst!" she exclaimed, shaking her head. "For a minute, I believed you, you know? I really thought you had changed… There was even a little part of me that had stopped hating you with all my soul, that was happy for you because, whatever problems you have, you'd finally learned what it meant to really love someone."

Her green eyes told me I wasn't likely to get any further with her. She continued. "You know what? Your father was right the last time I saw him. He told me you were incapable of love, that you harbored a hatred so profound that there would never be room for anything else, and certainly not for a nineteen-year-old girl with a baby on the way."

I clenched my teeth.

"Now I realize he was right…because Noah loved you for real, Nicholas, but you couldn't love her back… You couldn't love me, you couldn't forgive your parents, and you certainly won't be able to love her because you know she's better than you in every way."

"Briar, where is Noah?"

I couldn't believe this was blowing up in my face again. Briar had no idea what I had been through and how every single day, I'd regretted what my father had forced her to do.

Briar was one of many girls I'd hooked up with, and she was never supposed to be anything else. I just assumed the whole thing was a fling. Briar was no saint—she'd been with half the guys on campus before me—but at some point, I found out she'd actually been in love with me. When she realized she was pregnant, she came and told me at home, and my dad found out. To avoid a scandal, he forced her to get an abortion, and there was nothing I could do about it. Briar had problems: since childhood, her environment had been toxic, just like mine. Her parents had never cared about her or given her the things she needed. What happened between us caused her to have a nervous breakdown, and they checked her into the same clinic I'd been in once. I tried to get in contact with her; I tried a million times to ask her for forgiveness when I'd escaped from my own hell, but it was impossible. She had tried to kill herself when she was younger, and the doctors had refused to let me get close to her in case she tried it again.

"I'm sorry for all this, Briar… I never wanted to hurt you. I don't want to hurt you now—not you, not Noah. So, please, tell me where she is."

She grinned vilely and looked me directly in the eyes. "She knows you're cheating on her with Sophia, and she knows about us, too… She's gone, Nicholas. She left more than an hour ago."

An irrational fear invaded my body and left me petrified, my heart about to jump out of my chest. "Jesus! What have you done?"

53

Noah

I DIDN'T REMEMBER RESERVING A CAR. I DIDN'T REMEMBER HOW I got in it. All I could focus on was trying to breathe in and out. I was having a panic attack, one so horrible that my chest was aching, and it felt like someone was tearing out my heart.

I couldn't stop thinking about all that had happened over the past hour. It was like I was trapped in a horror film. Finding out my mother had lied to me my entire life about virtually everything had shattered me inside, but when Briar told me Nicholas had cheated on me, had let me live with someone he had been sleeping with for months, someone he forced to have an abortion... I couldn't take it anymore.

Was this really Nicholas we were talking about? How could he have done this to me? How could he have lied to me, laughed in my face, pretending they didn't know each other? How had they both been able to keep up that farce? And why?

I had never felt anything so hard, so horrible, never before that day had I felt like everyone in my life was betraying me because it *was* everyone, every single person I loved, who had betrayed me that

night: my mother, Nick, even Briar... I'd thought we were friends...
I'd thought...

With trembling hands, I took out my phone. I needed Jenna
with me, by my side, because I had no idea how to resolve this. I
couldn't imagine how I could recover from this blow.

"Are you all right?" the driver asked, looking at me in the
rearview mirror.

All right? I was dying.

Jenna didn't pick up. Then I saw Nick's photo on the screen. I
looked at it with unending pain, a pain far sharper than any I had
ever felt before. Seeing his image, seeing that photo of the two of
us together, smiling at the camera, my pain turned into an irrational hatred that lodged in my soul, a hatred for him and for any
and everyone who had ever hurt me.

I had suffered enough. I didn't deserve this. I just didn't. All I
had done, all I had been through to get to where I was, and then
this... It was like my entire world was falling apart.

"This is your destination," the driver announced just as a
thunderclap crossed the sky, making me tremble.

I paid on the app and got out.

Since Jenna hadn't responded, there was only one person
left to turn to. I went to the entrance of the building and pressed
button number eighteen.

I didn't get the person I expected, but in those circumstances, either of them would have worked. Michael came
down and opened up, and he seemed shocked when he saw me.
I was an absolute wreck; I could barely even breathe. I didn't
care that I'd only known him for a few weeks: he had helped
me, and more importantly, he knew me better than anyone—I
had opened up to him in a way I'd done with almost no one
else.

Seeing him through the mist of my tears, I stepped forward

and collapsed into his chest. He hugged me tight, and just then, I felt my heart fall out of my chest and shatter.

———————

Three hours later, I opened my eyes in a completely unfamiliar room. My head was aching so badly, it was hard for me to focus on anything but the pain, and it wasn't just my head, there was something else, something I didn't understand… Then the truth hit me again, cold as ice.

I felt the tears stream down my cheeks once more, but in silence, as if I didn't want to make things worse, as if I wanted to keep the drama at bay. But why bother? Everything that had happened was horrible, from beginning to end. Everyone had warned me, everyone I knew had told me this could come to pass, and there I was, in a bottomless pit because I hadn't been capable of seeing it or accepting it in time.

I lay back on the cushions and looked around for something to distract me. I saw two lit candles on the nightstand. I considered getting up, but before I could, the door opened, and there, with a steaming mug in his hands, was Michael. It was strange to see him in pajama pants and a gray T-shirt, and it was even stranger to realize I was in his bed, in his sheets, after crying for hours while he held me.

"Hey!" he said, walking in and sitting beside me. "I made you a cup of hot tea with honey and lemon. After all that crying, your throat must be killing you."

I nodded, grabbing the cup and bringing it to my lips. I was so crushed, so lost, that I didn't know what to do or say. My legs shifted under the sheets, and I realized I was no longer in my dress. I was wearing a large white cotton T-shirt.

Michael seemed to be considering what to say, and just looking at him allowed me to see he was even tenser than I was. I looked down at the steam rising from the rim of my tea as I felt Michael's fingers delicately wiping away my tears.

"He doesn't deserve you shedding a single tear for him, Noah. Not one."

I knew what he was saying was true, but I wasn't crying for just Nick or just me: I was crying for us, for Nick and Noah... because there wouldn't be a *we* anymore, right? I would never be able to forgive him. Or would I?

I looked at the raindrops striking the window. It had been a long time since I'd seen a storm like that... The last time had been in Toronto, before my whole life turned upside down, before I fell in love, before everything.

"Anyway, I guess it had to happen..." I said softly, more to myself than to Michael.

It seemed as if that phrase remained there, lingering in the air.

"It's not the first time either. It's almost like I'm not capable of making men love me... My father didn't. Neither did my first boyfriend, Dan. He cheated on me with my best friend. Now history's repeating itself... I'm asking myself if that's why I've been running away from everything with Nick, if there was a part of me that knew this had to happen and wanted to protect me from that pain..."

Michael took the cup from my hand and, without my managing to stop him, kissed me on the lips, pressing me into the pillows I was resting on. I blinked several times, perplexed, then pulled away with a face full of rage. Rage, and...something more.

"You're an idiot if you don't think you deserve to be loved, if you think the bad things that have happened in your life are your fault..." He stroked my hair. "I haven't done my job with you, Noah. I really haven't accomplished anything..."

Again, he pressed his lips into mine, and I felt so lost, I let him do it. My mind seemed to disconnect from my body, just as I had wished it would do since I took that car there. Michael's hands were all over me, and maybe just as a reflex, mine started doing the same.

It was different, the way he touched me; his kisses were different, too. I couldn't say whether I liked them because I wasn't really there. I didn't even know what was happening; my heart and my soul were crushed, blinded, waiting for someone to send a light into that bottomless pit and show me the way out.

───────────

When I woke up, it was five in the morning. My brain seemed to be functioning again, and I realized what I had done. It felt like someone had struck me with a mallet in the middle of my chest, hard and precise, and I had to drag myself from the bed to the bathroom to vomit.

I felt sick, truly sick, as if a virus were inside me, eating whatever life was still left in me. I looked down at my body. I was still in that white T-shirt, but my underwear had disappeared. Flashes of what had happened started to reappear in my mind, and I could do nothing to stop them. His hands, his mouth, his naked body on top of mine...

Oh my God.

I retched and brought myself up to my knees in front of the toilet to vomit again for minutes straight. It seemed like an eternity. Then I rested my face on the edge of the sink and started crying again. I didn't even know how many tears I had spilled since the night before, nor did I understand how I had any left. I wanted to burn that shirt, shower in boiling water, scrub my body with steel wool... With all my strength, I wanted to cleanse myself inside and out and ball up in bed waiting for time to pass before I raised my head again.

Like a robot, I started picking up my things, trying not to make noise. I didn't want to put my party dress back on, but I also didn't want to walk out of there naked. I ended up taking a sweatshirt Michael had left on a chair. I'd burn the dress and that damned sweatshirt later; I'd throw everything I'd worn in the fire, burn all the memories and all the things he had touched, because—for God's sake—I'd let him touch me, let him do even more...

When I turned on my phone to book a ride, I saw dozens of missed calls on my screen. Most were from Nicholas; he'd called me every five minutes for the past six hours... Jenna had called, too. So had my mom.

I rolled my eyes and ignored all of them, reserved a car, and left Michael's apartment without making a sound.

It was raining buckets, and soon enough, I was soaked, but since I felt dirty, I let the water wash over me, and it actually made me feel better. For a few minutes, I tried to forget everything and concentrate on the plunking of the waterdrops against my face.

The car honked, waking me from my daydream, and I rushed over and got in the back seat. I'd have just as soon caught a plane to Canada, to somewhere with no memories of my boyfriend, where I wouldn't run into any of his exes, but before then, I had to go to my dorm.

It didn't take long to get there—Michael lived on campus, too—and when I looked out the window and saw who was waiting for me on the front stairs, I nearly fainted.

No. I couldn't see him. Shit... I needed to get out of there.

But Nicholas had already seen me, and before I could tell the driver to take me somewhere, anywhere else, Nick had already opened the door and pulled me out of the car.

"Noah, please, I've been looking for you like a madman all night. I thought something had happened to you. I thought..." He looked so desperate, and I was such a disaster, that for a moment, I almost let him hug me, I almost let him hold me in his arms, I nearly begged him to get me out of there, to take me away, just so

I wouldn't have to feel anymore what I felt in those moments. But then I remembered the reasons I was in this state, it all hit me, and even more intensely because I had him in front of me right then. He was with me, and I could see and not just think about all I had lost.

I shook and thrashed so hard and so fast that for a few seconds, Nicholas couldn't grab hold of me, but when he did, near the door of the dorm, he grabbed both sides of my face and forced me to look into his eyes.

"Listen to me, Noah, please, you have to listen to me."

He looked so desperate... The rain had died down, but we were both soaked and freezing.

"Noah, this was all a big, stupid misunderstanding. I've been looking all over for you because I knew what you were thinking, and I was dying inside knowing that you thought I had cheated on you..."

I blinked, not grasping what he was saying.

"I've been a dickhead, okay? I know I have. I was an idiot, leaving you alone last night with our parents, and if you want to hate me for kissing Sophia, fine, but—"

His words pierced my soul, and I tried to jerk away from his grasp. He'd just admitted that he'd deceived me, that it was true, that he'd kissed her.

"Let me go!" I shouted, but that only made him grip me tighter.

"Goddammit, Noah, I'd never cheat on you!"

He shook me, and I looked up from the damp, muddy ground, ready to listen to him.

"It was just a stupid kiss, one stupid kiss I gave her, out of anger, because I was mad at you, and okay, you're right, I was an asshole, because I knew you were jealous of Sophie, and I took advantage of that to get revenge on you. But it wasn't you I wanted revenge on, Noah. I just let the Nicholas from years ago carry me away, that person you helped me to leave behind; and I swear to you, I'll never let him come back. That was the worst mistake I've made in my life. And you know why? Because now that I've kissed another woman, I've realized how fucking in love with you I am, and I'm never going to kiss anyone and feel the things I feel when I kiss you; if I'm not with you, I feel nothing. If I'm not with you, it's like I don't even have a soul..."

I started analyzing everything he was telling me, and at the same time, my pain was replaced by a terrible fear.

"You haven't been sleeping with her?" I asked in a hoarse voice.

Nicholas stood back and let the water fall over him for a second.

"I hate you asking me that, but I'm going to be straight with you because everything has gotten so fucked up so fast that you deserve an answer." He looked straight at me, as though he wanted to emphasize the sincerity of his words. "Never, I insist, never have I cheated on you with anybody. It never once passed through my head, and it never will, Noah."

I felt such relief, it was like medicine to all the wounded corners of my mind and heart.

"But...Briar told me..." I started to say.

"Noah, what happened with Briar and me was shit, and I should have told you about it, but things were so rocky between us, our relationship was on the edge of a cliff, and I didn't want to make things worse by telling you I got your roommate pregnant when we were younger, let alone that my father forced her into getting an abortion to avoid a scandal. I was scared you wouldn't understand. Everything happened so fast that it got out of hand, and Briar ended up having to pay the price."

Nicholas's father had been the one to force her to get an abortion? Briar had told me it had been Nick.

"You're not sleeping with her?"

Nicholas cursed and stared at me again. "I'm not sleeping with anyone but you, Noah. I can tell you don't fully trust me yet, and I get that, I really do. But we can work it out. Together, we can get past it."

My head started spinning 'round and 'round... Nicholas wasn't cheating on me?

I felt so lost, I didn't realize the tears were running down my cheeks again until Nicholas pulled me tightly into his chest.

For a moment, I didn't hug him back because my mind needed to pass from hating the love of my life to loving him madly in less than a second.

"What am I going to do with you, Noah?" he asked me, stroking my wet hair and back.

I was so cold, so shocked, that when Nick asked me if he could come inside, I just nodded and let him lead me.

When we walked through the living room and I saw it looking just as it had when I left it less than ten hours before, I started to panic. There were glasses from when the girls had been drinking as they helped me get ready; there was clothing thrown on the sofa, shoes on the floor, makeup... It was so trashed that I walked away from Nick and started ordering it compulsively.

"Noah, what are you doing?"

"I just need to tidy up...clean up in here a little. I need—" Nick's hands stopped me and turned me around.

"Noah, take it easy, okay?" He looked me all over, and I was so scared, so terrified he'd find out what had happened that I felt nauseous. "You're shaking. I'm freezing, too. Let's take a hot shower, okay? We can talk about the rest of this tomorrow..."

I started shaking my head. Guilt was eating me up inside. More than anything in the world, I wanted to take off my clothes and get under the shower, but I couldn't do that in front of Nicholas; I couldn't even look him in the face.

He'd just told me he hadn't cheated on me with anyone, that it had never even passed through his head. He had kissed Sophia, sure, but what did a kiss matter after thinking he'd slept with her? Nothing.

"Nicholas, I..."

I saw the worry in his eyes, and it was just then that he realized the state I was in and what I was wearing.

"Where have you been all this time, Noah?" He didn't seem to be reproaching me; he was just observing me with curiosity. "Jenna was calling you at the same time I was. I even talked to your friend from school... Where were you?"

I shook my head again and closed my eyes, as if that could save me from what was about to happen.

"I...I..." I couldn't pronounce the next words.

Before Nicholas could draw his own conclusions, my phone began to ring, one of those stupid ringtones that only worsened the incredibly surreal feeling of the entire situation.

Nicholas took it from my hands to see who it was.

"Why is he calling you?" His voice was cold. I looked up to see his expression.

He was so tense that without realizing it, I took a step back.

"Why is he calling you, Noah?"

"Nicholas, I..."

One gaze was enough for him to understand what had happened.

"Tell me what I'm thinking isn't true." His voice was so strangled with fear that I would have done anything to escape, anything to disappear from that place, from the world, to simply stop existing. "Please tell me that's not his shirt you're wearing, that what's passing through my head right now is just my imagination... Say it, Noah!" he screamed and grabbed my arms, pulling me out of my state of paralysis, and the tears began to fall again, dripping on the floor, down, down into that dark pit my demons had dragged me to, filled with my mistrust, all my problems.

"I'm sorry," I said so softly, I wasn't even sure he'd heard me. But he had, and he let me go as if my skin had burned him, as if all at once, he wasn't even capable of touching me.

"No...you didn't... It's a lie." He started pacing around the room, his hands on his head, throwing his hair in disarray, then turned again and grabbed my face in his hands.

"Please, Noah, don't punish me for this. I already told you I was sorry. Don't mess with my head. Tell me it's a lie, just tell me that, please." His voice cracked with this last word, and I realized we were both ruined. If I had thought before that I knew what pain was, seeing him in pain because of what I'd done was only that much worse. It hurts when someone breaks your heart, but that's nothing compared to breaking the heart of the person you love with all your soul.

"Nicholas... I've been an idiot... I thought...I thought... I'm sorry, Nick. I'm sorry," I said, stifled by tears, and stroked his cheek. Or tried to. He didn't let me. He stiffened, grabbed my hands, avoided me, glared at me.

"You slept with him?" His voice was so wounded that I was glad for the tears to cloud my eyes so I couldn't see the agony on his face. "Answer me, damn it!"

Those words cut me like a knife. I was disgusted with myself... I thought I was going to vomit again, right then and there. Never in my life had I felt so dirty... He could see it, he could see it in my face—I wasn't the same person. I never would be.

Without a word, he turned and left the apartment.

I stood there for a few seconds, looking into the void he'd left around me, and that brief lapse of time was enough for me to decide that I couldn't lose him, that I couldn't let things end here. What had happened with Michael had been a huge mistake, and

Nicholas would forgive me, he had to, because he loved me and I loved him. I refused to accept that our relationship could end after finding out everything I believed was wrong, after finding out he did love me... I had to make him see that it had been a mistake, that we could get over it. I knew that would be the most arduous battle of my life, but I was going to win it. I had to win it.

I ran out of the apartment and down the steps as quickly as I could. I watched him walking down the street and shouted his name. He stopped and turned to look at me. Soon I'd reached him, but I had to stop a few feet away. The Nicholas in front of me wasn't the Nicholas I knew—he was shattered, and knowing he was shattered made me fall apart, too.

The rain fell, soaking us, freezing us, but it didn't matter; nothing did, not anymore. I knew everything was about to change. I knew my world was about to crumble apart.

"There's no turning back now. I can't even look you in the eye."

Desolate tears ran down his face.

How could I have done this to him? His words sank into my soul like knives tearing me open from the inside.

"I don't even know what to say," I said, trying to control the panic that threatened to shatter me. He couldn't leave me. He couldn't, could he?

He looked full of hatred, contempt... It was a look I'd never thought I'd see from him.

"We're done," he whispered, his voice cracking but firm.

And with those two words, my world sank into darkness, shadows, solitude...a prison designed expressly for me. But I deserved it. This time, I deserved it.

EPILOGUE

Noah

THE NOISE OF THE MACHINES AND THE INTENSE, UNPLEASANT HOSPItal odor made the waiting room intolerable. I'd never liked those places, and if I'd had a choice, I'd have been anywhere but there.

I went out to the hall, sat in a chair, and hugged my knees. That had been my preferred position those past few days, and just like when I got under the covers, I closed my eyes and let my mind wander through places I wished I'd never return to. I could still hear Jenna's voice on the other line, asking for answers I wasn't ready to give, and then William in a rage, telling me his son had been arrested for assault.

I'd gotten to the scene quickly, and that image of Nicholas would stick in my mind for years, I thought. The ambulance had taken Michael away with bruises all over his face and body. Nicholas had broken two of his ribs. I could still see his split lip, the blood on his knuckles, the police driving him away in a squad car. Michael had defended himself as best he could, but there was little he could do against a Nick who had completely lost his mind. I had pushed him to it. Once again, it had been my fault.

I remember Jenna came up behind me, and just then, my legs gave out. She and Lion caught me before I fell, drove me to her house, and took care of me all night, not asking any questions. Lion went to the police station and called William. In the meanwhile, Jenna had sat in bed with me and hugged me while the very last tears I had left poured out. I hadn't cried again since that night. I was now so destroyed that nothing, not even tears, could help with the pain.

And here I was now, visiting the man who had promised to help me but who was responsible for my destruction.

I sighed, and my phone buzzed on top of the plastic chair where I'd set it down. It was Will.

"He just got out, Noah," he said, and I stood. "I had to pull a lot of strings, but in the end, O'Neil decided not to press charges... I guess you were right. You talking to him helped."

A sense of relief filled me. "He's out?" I asked, unable to believe it.

William sighed on the other end of the line, and I could imagine him, his face weary and full of worry, but finally able to admit his son wouldn't go to jail over his stepdaughter.

"Yeah. Despite everything."

I'd never have forgiven myself if Nicholas had wound up in prison. It was hard enough getting up in the morning and going to the hospital. But more guilt weighing on my shoulders—that I couldn't have taken.

Jenna walked down the hall with two coffees and a bag of something.

"I brought you some food, and I'm not going to take no for an answer, hear me? You're going to eat, and you're going to do it now."

Not paying her much attention, I grabbed the coffee from her and took a sip. It was hot, but it didn't warm my body. I was always cold now, frozen inside and out. It didn't matter how many blankets I had over me, something was missing—the most important thing of all.

"Nick's out," I whispered.

Jenna's eyes widened, and she took a deep breath, just as I had done when I found out.

"Fuck…thank God!"

I nodded and looked away.

"Noah," Jenna began, wanting to console me, but I didn't want to listen to her, didn't want to talk, didn't want anyone trying to ease my mind. All I wanted was to isolate myself in my misery. "Things will get better, okay? Michael's fine, he's recovering without any problems, and Nick is out of jail. William will probably get the arrest expunged. Cheer up, please."

I looked at her hand. On her ring finger was a pretty ring, silver with a little diamond. That was my doing, too, in a way, because the night everything had gone to hell, Lion had asked Jenna to marry him, and she'd run off to find me and deal with what had happened.

I was out of it, but not so much that I couldn't see the glimmer in her eyes when she looked at Lion or her eyes settled on her engagement ring. I was happy for her, truly, but her happiness also tore my heart.

I'd never have that, especially after all that had happened. Knowing I'd lost Nick, I was aware of how stupid I'd been. My fear of being hurt had kept me from being loved, because Nick *had* loved me with all his heart, but I had pushed him away over and over until finally I'd dragged him into the darkness that surrounded me almost every hour of the day.

That was what hurt the most. I was used to pain. I feared it, I tried to avoid it as best I could, but when it came, I knew what to do. What was unbearable was knowing he was in pain.

All the times he'd told me he loved me, all the times we'd argued over stupid shit, all the stolen kisses, the caresses, the love he felt for me alone...all that had turned into his worst nightmare.

Jenna took me home that night. I hadn't seen Briar since the gala. At some point, she'd cleared her things out of the dorm. *Just as well*, I thought. Briar was a part of Nick's past I never should have known about because it had nothing to do with me anyway. I understood now that the past ought to remain in the past because when we let it come back, it can devour our present.

I took off my shoes while Jenna messed around in the kitchen, repeating that I had to eat. But I couldn't; the knot in my stomach was so big, there was no room for anything else. I got into bed, leaned my head back, and heard paper crumpling. I felt a jab of pain as I saw that it was the letter Nick had written me.

Fingers trembling, I read it again.

I'll give you more time. If that's what you need, if that's what you need to realize I love you and you alone, then I'll do it. I don't know what to do to make you believe me, make you see that I want to take care of you and protect you forever. I'm not going anywhere, Noah, my life and my future are with you, my happiness depends on you alone. Stop being afraid: I'll always be your light in the darkness, my love.

I closed my eyes.

I'm not going anywhere.
My life and my future are with you.
My happiness depends on you alone...

I brought the letter to my heart and squeezed it.

I'll always be your light in the darkness, my love.

I hugged myself, knowing those words now meant nothing. Nicholas had made it clear he never wanted to see me again. He hadn't let me go see him in jail. He had refused to take my calls.

For him, I no longer existed.

READ AHEAD FOR A SNEAK PEEK AT THE FINAL
BOOK IN THE CULPABLE SERIES, *OUR FAULT*

PROLOGUE

IF NICK AND I HAD BROKEN UP MORE THAN A YEAR AGO, WHY WAS I crying as if it had only really happened now? At one point, I had to pull off the road, cut the motor, and hug the wheel so I could sob without worrying about crashing into anyone.

I cried for what we had been; I cried for what we could have been; I cried for his sick mother and his baby sister... I cried for him, for disappointing him, for breaking his heart, for getting him to love me and then showing him love didn't exist, at least not without pain, and that pain had now scarred him for life.

I cried for Noah, the Noah I had been when I was with him. That Noah full of life, the Noah who, despite her inner demons, had known how to love with all her heart. I had loved him more than anybody, and that was something to grieve for, too. When you meet the person you want to spend the rest of your life with, there's no going back. Lots of people never learn what that feels like; they think they have, but they're wrong. I knew that Nick was the love of my life, the man I wanted to be the father of my children, the man I wanted by my side through good and bad, in sickness and in health, till death do us part.

Nick was *the one*, he was my other half, and now I'd have to learn to live without him.

1

Noah

THE NOISE AT THE AIRPORT WAS DEAFENING. PEOPLE WERE COMING and going frantically, dragging their suitcases, their carts, their children. I looked at the screen overhead, trying to find my destination and the exact time of my departure. I didn't like traveling on my own—I never cared much for flying at all—but there weren't many options. I was alone now; it was just me and no one else.

I looked at my watch and back at the screen. I had time to spare. I could drink a coffee in the terminal and read a while. That would probably calm me down. I walked through the metal detectors. I hated that, hated getting patted down, and it always happened, because I always had something that set of the alarm. Maybe it was that heart of iron I'd been told I carried in my chest.

I dropped my backpack on the conveyor belt, took off my watch and bracelets, took off the necklace with the pendant that I always wore—even if I should have taken it off a long time ago—and set it all down next to my cellphone and the spare change I had in my pocket.

"Your shoes, too, Miss," the young TSA worker said in a weary tone. I got it—the job was the very definition of dull; it probably gave you brain damage, doing and saying the same things over and over, all day, every day. I put my white Chucks on the tray and was glad I'd chosen plain socks instead of little kiddy ones with some embarrassing design. As my things moved forward on the belt, I passed through the scanner and, of course, it started beeping.

"Step to the side, please, hold out your arms and spread your legs," the person ordered, and I sighed. Did I have something metal on me, a sharp object, some kind of…?

"I don't have anything on me," I said, letting the officer pat me down. "This always happens, I don't know why. Maybe it's a filling."

The guy grinned, but that only made me wish he'd take his hands off me sooner.

When he finally let me go, I grabbed my things and went straight to the duty-free shop. Hello? Giant Toblerones? Sign me up. That was the one pleasant thing about going to the airport. I bought two, stored them both in my hand luggage, and went to find my departure gate. LAX was huge, but luckily, I didn't have to go far. Walking over arrows meant to point me in the right direction, I passed by signs that said *Goodbye* in dozens of languages before I reached where I was going. The gate was empty, so I grabbed a chair near the window, took out my book, and started in on my Toblerone.

Things went fine until the letter I'd stuffed between the pages fell into my lap, reviving memories I'd sworn were dead and buried. I felt something hollow in the pit of my stomach as a stream of images rose up in my mind, and what had been a relaxing day took a nosedive.

Acknowledgments

First of all, I'd like to thank all the people who enthusiastically requested this second part. At first, *My Fault* was going to be just one book, but after almost a year of writer's block, starting stories and leaving them unfinished, I knew I had to write the sequel. Nick and Noah's story wasn't over, and once I got started, I couldn't stop.

Second, I want to thank my editors, Rosa and Aina. Thanks for helping me turn this book into what it is now. It wasn't easy to write *Your Fault* in the Wattpad style, uploading chapters every week without being able to work on the novel the way I needed to, or at least the way I was used to. You've managed to make it perfect, and the characters are still true to themselves. I love this new version!

To the design team, thanks so much for making the covers so amazing: you got the perfect Nick, and I thought that was impossible. You've outdone yourselves. I love it!

Thanks to my agent, Nuria: you know that without you, I'd be lost in the literary world, which I wandered into almost without realizing it.

422 | MERCEDES RON

Thanks to my cousin Bar, for reading each and every revision over and over, for always telling me what you think, and for being careful not to hurt my feelings. Your advice has helped make this story what it is. I don't know what I'd do without your help. I wish you were closer and I could share with you what we both love so much: reading.

To my family, thanks for your enthusiasm, your support, and your eagerness to read this. I love you so much!

Garri, you're the big brother I never had. Thank you for being who you are and for coming into my family and never leaving. I haven't got the words to tell you how much I appreciate you.

Ali, thanks for being that friend who's always there, for always thinking of me, and for believing in all my hopes and dreams. We're so different, but I don't know what I'd do without you.

To my fans, thank you. I still can't believe the way you fell in love with my characters. Thank you for all the love you give me on social media. Thanks for your patience and for giving me a family I'm dying to meet someday. I love you all!

And finally, thanks to everyone who bought *My Fault* as soon as it came out. When my editor told me it had almost sold out after four days, I nearly had a heart attack. Thank you, thank you, thank you!

About the Author

Mercedes Ron always dreamed of writing. She began by publishing her first stories on Wattpad, where more than fifty million readers were hooked on her books, and made the leap to bookstores in 2017 with Montena's imprint, launching the Culpables saga, a publishing phenomenon that has been translated into more than ten languages and will have its own movie adaptation by Amazon Prime. Her success was followed by the sagas Enfrentados (*Ivory* and *Ebony*) and Dímelo (*Tell Me Softly*, *Tell Me Secretly*, *Tell Me with Kisses*), which consolidated the author as a benchmark in youth romantic literature with more than a million copies sold.